An excerpt from *Under the Same Roof* by Niobia Bryant

The man was pure temptation.

Even as a foe.

"Ms. Winters."

He is trouble. So much damn trouble.

Alisha cleared her throat and wished it was just as easy to rid herself of her desire. "I have nothing to say," she said, stepping back to close the door.

His hand pressed against it, stopping her retreat.

Wow. He's strong.

She could visualize the muscles of his arm tensing with the move—just as they would if he lifted her body up against his body. To hold. Tightly. As he pressed his face to her neck and kissed her with his delicious mouth as she—

"If you have nothing to hide, why be so abrupt?" Tremaine asked.

She yanked the door open and he stumbled inside, bringing him so very close.

Too close.

D1115621

An excerpt from *Keeping a Little Secret* by Cynthia St. Aubin

When it came to Tiffany Winters, he didn't have a soft spot.

He had a blind spot.

Preston pushed himself up on his palms and gazed down at her, not having the faintest idea what to say or do next.

Tiffany swept a lock of hair away from his forehead, her heavy-lidded eyes fixed on his.

"We'll figure it out, Preston. It's not like I have suitors lining up at the door. And a few months from now, I suspect the dating pool is going to get *very* shallow."

The thought of her as she would look six or even seven months pregnant was having quite the opposite effect on him. Her athletic frame filling out with new curves, glowing like a goddess.

NIOBIA BRYANT

&

USA TODAY BESTSELLING AUTHOR

CYNTHIA ST. AUBIN

UNDER THE SAME ROOF
&
KEEPING A LITTLE SECRET

HARLEQUIN
DESIRE

If you purchased this book without a cover you should be aware that this book is stolen property. It was reported as "unsold and destroyed" to the publisher, and neither the author nor the publisher has received any payment for this "stripped book."

Special thanks and acknowledgment are given to Niobia Bryant and Cynthia St. Aubin for their contributions to the Texas Cattleman's Club: Diamonds & Dating Apps miniseries.

⊞ HARLEQUIN®
DESIRE™

Recycling programs for this product may not exist in your area.

ISBN-13: 978-1-335-45787-5

Under the Same Roof & Keeping a Little Secret

Copyright © 2023 by Harlequin Enterprises ULC

Under the Same Roof
Copyright © 2023 by Harlequin Enterprises ULC

Keeping a Little Secret
Copyright © 2023 by Harlequin Enterprises ULC

All rights reserved. No part of this book may be used or reproduced in any manner whatsoever without written permission except in the case of brief quotations embodied in critical articles and reviews.

This is a work of fiction. Names, characters, places and incidents are either the product of the author's imagination or are used fictitiously. Any resemblance to actual persons, living or dead, businesses, companies, events or locales is entirely coincidental.

For questions and comments about the quality of this book, please contact us at CustomerService@Harlequin.com.

Harlequin Enterprises ULC
22 Adelaide St. West, 41st Floor
Toronto, Ontario M5H 4E3, Canada
www.Harlequin.com

Printed in U.S.A.

CONTENTS

Niobia Bryant is the award-winning and nationally bestselling author of more than fifty romance and mainstream commercial fiction works. Twice she has won the RT Reviewers' Choice Best Book Award for African American/Multicultural Romance. Her books have appeared in *Ebony*, *Essence*, the *New York Post*, the *Star-Ledger*, the *Dallas Morning News* and many other national publications. One of her bestselling books was adapted to film.

Books by Niobia Bryant

Harlequin Desire

Cress Brothers

One Night with Cinderella
The Rebel Heir
An Offer from Mr. Wrong
The Pregnancy Proposal

Texas Cattleman's Club: Diamonds & Dating Apps

Under the Same Roof

Visit the Author Profile page
at Harlequin.com for more titles.

You can also find Niobia Bryant on Facebook,
along with other Harlequin Desire authors,
at Facebook.com/HarlequinDesireAuthors!

Dear Reader,

Writing a book for the Texas Cattleman's Club: Diamonds & Dating Apps was challenging but fun. I wanted to deliver everything: love, conflict, chemistry and steamy sex, plus the extra tension of a jewelry heist and a century-old family feud! And in the end, I loved it! Just an amazing experience...and I hope that is reflected in the story of Alisha and Tremaine.

He's a handsome private investigator instantly drawn to the same woman he was hired to prove complicit in a crime. She's as intelligent as she is beautiful, but the sexy professor/antique dealer loses all semblance of good sense whenever the PI is near—which is always, since she's invited him to live at her estate while he's in town trying to prove *her* family members are jewel thieves!

Think of all the yummy tropes: working together/ at odds, opposites attract, in bed with the enemy. Add lots of chemistry, funny quips and small-town charm with touches of Christmas. And of course, love and a happy ending. That's *Under the Same Roof*.

I hope you enjoy this "Sexy, Funny & Oh So Real" romance. Savor it. Share it. And review it. (Hint!) :-)

Best,

N.

UNDER THE SAME ROOF

Niobia Bryant

As always, this one is dedicated to the wonderful thing called love.

One

The doorbell rang.

Alisha Winters paused in crossing the hardwood floor of her spacious home to eye the double front doors. She wasn't expecting any visitors, but being from a large family with four siblings, a random pop-up was not impossible. She skipped checking the app on her phone that was linked to the new security system she'd recently installed in the original Winters family estate she'd inherited from their grandmother Gloria. As she moved to the side windows that flanked the doorway, the four heart-shaped lockets of her vintage charm bracelet hit against each other.

A tall and well-built man with skin the color of smooth chocolate, low-cut ebony hair and a hint of a beard stood on the stone porch beneath the metal canopy. "My, my," she whispered, her heart pounding a bit harder as she took in his chiseled profile and the way his dark jeans and leather jacket emphasized his lean and muscled frame.

He was a stranger. A sexy one.

When he turned to look over and caught sight of her, his eyes widened a bit in surprise.

Alisha gasped in awareness.

His profile had been only a hint at his good looks. His features were sharp and defined with strong, high cheeks, a straight jaw and an aquiline nose, but his eyes were deep, intense and bright, surrounded by lush lashes. And his mouth was...

So suckable.

She took a brief lick of her own.

The man—this seeming warrior among men—gave her a brief wave and a smile.

She sighed, feeling suddenly breathless.

It was the first time in years that a man had affected her so swiftly. And deeply.

Alisha stepped away from the window and gripped one of the refurbished antique colonial door handles in forged black iron. She smoothed back her naturally curly black hair with her free hand before opening the door. The fall wind breezed inside, carrying with it a whiff of his warm and spicy cologne.

He just keeps getting better and better.

"Hello, Alisha," he said, his voice deep and delicious as he extended his hand.

She wanted to take it and see if he felt as good as he looked, but she paused before doing so. "Do we know each other?" she asked, after realizing that he'd addressed her by name.

At that moment, she set aside her awareness of him and accepted that he was a stranger to whom she was going to let into her home. She stiffened her back and clutched the door pull tighter, wondering if she was going to have to mar his perfect face with a black eye and busted lip. She was more than capable of doing just that.

His eyes widened as if he'd read her thoughts or seen some emotion cross her face. He held up both his hands. "I'm Tremaine Knowles of Knowles Threat Solutions," he said, giving her another smile—this time it was meant to reassure.

It failed.

"Well, Tremaine Knowles of Knowles Threat Solutions," she said, arching a shaped eyebrow as she locked eyes with him and took note that the connection caused a shiver to race up her spine. "Why are you on my porch and how do you know my name?"

He looked down at his booted feet and then back up at her. "I'm a private investigator and personal security expert hired to look into the discovery of the jewelry found on this property."

Alisha's gut clenched and she shifted her eyes past him to land on the bright red GMC Sierra pickup parked next to her silver 1955 Porsche 356 Speedster. She assumed the truck belonged to him.

The Del Rio family's heirloom necklace.

She winced. Her youngest brother, Marcus, and the woman who was now his fiancée, Jessica Drummond, had stumbled onto a shocking family secret—the price-less diamond, ruby and emerald necklace. It was found downstairs in a hidden room in the cellar of the 1920s family estate. But Marcus, Jessica and Alisha had all lied about the discovery location because of the letter they'd also found.

All families had secrets. The letter was theirs.

Alisha released a heavy breath.

"Can I ask you some questions? Like is there something you would like to share about the necklace, Alisha?" Tremaine asked.

Her body went stiff. With indignation. Annoyance. And a slight tinge of guilt. "Who hired you?" she asked as she settled her eyes back on him.

"The Del Rios," he admitted.

She frowned.

A foe. Sexy as hell. But a foe.

"Is there a reason you believe I am required to share any information with you?" she asked, well aware of the coldness of her tone. "And it's Ms. Winters."

He smiled. It was forced but still captivating. "I would assume you would want to clear your name in 'Diamond Gate,' *Ms.* Winters," he said.

Alisha disdained the moniker given to the whole fiasco by the press. She stood a bit taller. "Clear *my* name?" she asked, fighting the urge to ease the door closed in his face.

Tremaine nodded before looking pointedly down at the mail slot on the open section of the double doors. "It was supposedly delivered here to your home," he reminded her. "Can I come in?"

Alisha shook her head, denying his request.

He nodded in understanding. "Your brother Marcus found the envelope after it was put through the mail slot. Right?"

Yes. That's the story and I'm stuck with it.

All because of a letter written by her great-grandmother Eliza Winters, née Boudreaux, in which she'd confessed with so much remorse to secretly stealing the Del Rio family necklace when it was on loan to a Paris museum. This was back before she'd married Teddy Winters, after leaving his rival, Fernando Del Rio I, stranded at the altar. The broken engagement sparked the bitter century-old feud between the Del Rio and Winters families.

Alisha's guilt resurfaced and seemed to tug at her to reveal the letter to him, but she bit down on her bottom lip instead. The discovery that Eliza was the international jewel thief was more embarrassment than the Winters family needed to bear.

And so Eliza's secret is ours, known only to Marcus, Jessica and me.

She wished with every bone in her body that Marcus and Jessica hadn't found the hidden room. Some things were better left as secrets.

The discovery of the Del Rio necklace at the former Winters family estate had taken over the news and social media both in the US and abroad. Their plan seemed simple enough. Return the jewelry, but lie about how they found it, and keep the letter secret to maintain the reputation of the Winters family's late matriarch.

Alisha had insisted on the latter.

"There's nothing more to know, Mr. Knowles," she said, crossing her arms over her chest as she leaned in the doorway with more ease than she felt. "The necklace was given to the proper authorities until it could be sorted out."

He eyed her with far more warmth than the November chill in the air, taking her in like a delicious drink he was savoring.

If only...

The man was pure temptation. Even as a foe. Even with his affiliation with the Del Rios. Even with him on her doorstep implying that she knew more than she revealed.

Sexy. As. F—

"Ms. Winters," he said, unknowingly interrupting her thoughts as he rubbed a large hand over his mouth and beard with agile fingers.

Fingers built to please.

Her pulse raced and throbbed. Everywhere.

He is trouble. So much damn trouble.

Alisha cleared her throat and wished it was just as easy to rid herself of her desire. "I am happy for the Del Rio family that one of their heirlooms has been found. That is my official statement. I have nothing else to say," she said, stepping back to close the door.

His hand pressed against it, stopping her retreat.

Wow. He's strong.

She could visualize the muscles of his arm tensing with the move...just as they would if he was lifting her body up against his own. To hold. Tightly. As he pressed his face to her neck and kissed her with his delicious mouth, as she—

"If you have nothing to hide, why be so abrupt?" Tremaine asked.

She yanked the door open and he stumbled inside, bringing him and his scent so very close.

Too close.

Tremaine Knowles used every muscle of his body to keep from falling forward, into Alisha. She sidestepped as if to avoid that very thing happening. "Sorry," he said, even though their bodies didn't touch.

Still, he had been close enough to pick up her sweet scent and get lost in her unique vibrations. She was electric. At first sight of the beauty peeking at him out of one of the side windows that flanked the door, he had instantly felt a jolt of pure awareness. He'd come seeking answers to the discovery of the stolen necklace, but he'd found something far more beautiful.

Foolishly, he had not expected an antique dealer to be so…sultry. Not once did he envision this petite beauty with large doe brown eyes that now glared at him in reproach. Her arms were crossed over her chest and the move unintentionally emphasized her soft curves. He towered over her by nearly a foot and felt the urge to protect her, even if she was eyeing him as if he was the one from whom she needed protection.

"Listen," he began after clearing his throat. "This could be an opportunity for me to bridge the gap between the Del Rio and Winters families…and to take the glare of suspicion off of you."

"Off of me?" Alisha asked. "I thought the latest rumor was this was a publicity stunt to monetize the truce between the families with the upcoming one hundredth anniversary of the theft?"

"Surely you understand that the weight of the suspicion could lie at your doorstep—excuse the pun," he said.

"Excuse it? It wasn't clever enough to acknowledge it," she retorted before sucking air between her teeth and waving her hand in dismissal.

Tremaine bit back a smile. The woman had so much spunk. A fire that was seductive.

If it hadn't been for his best friend, Preston, recommending him to his father, Fernando Del Rio III, to look into the suspicious sudden discovery of his family's necklace, Tremaine would have asked her out on a date. Begged to be heated by her fire.

The thing was, as much as he could recognize her beauty, Tremaine had far too much experience as a former cop for the Austin Police Department to ignore what his gut told him. Alisha Winters was indeed hiding something.

He looked up at the towering cathedral ceiling of the foyer. "This truly is a beautiful home, Ms. Winters," he said, then gazed at her just in time to catch that his compliment caught her off guard.

"Th-thank you," she said with a bit of a stutter. "My grandmother Gloria left it to me. We always shared a love of the architecture and the history attached to it. I'm enjoying restoring it—just the way she would like. I believe it's why she left it to me."

She looked around as she touched her fingertips to her throat.

His eyes dropped down to watch the way she lightly stroked the skin there. It appeared soft. The caramel hue of her skin made him hunger for a sweet treat. "My father was a home builder for many years," he admitted to her.

Her eyes shifted back to lock with his.

His heart swelled and warmth filled his belly.

Damn.

Alisha's face filled with what appeared to be a sense of discovery. It lasted just a moment, but he saw it and wondered what it was about it. Feeling uncomfortable with the strong and instant effect this woman was having on him, Tremaine shifted his gaze away. Had he revealed his interest? Had she picked up on his instant desire?

Stay focused on why you're here.

But that was hard. Beautiful women were of no shortage in his life, but this particular one—this mix of brains and beauty—had an inner glow that was magnetic. It certainly was pulling him.

"You should leave, Mr. Knowles," she said.

"Tremaine," he offered.

She shook her head a little, denying the familiarity he'd put forward. "You don't know me, but I don't play games, nor do I steal," she continued, reaching again for the door handle. "I wouldn't participate in a publicity stunt."

As she spoke, she slowly pulled open one of the

double doors, making her own invitation—for him to leave.

He chuckled as he stepped out onto the porch again. He stopped and turned. "I have more questions, Ms. Winters. Can I make an appointment to come back?" he asked.

"Perhaps an appointment with Special Agent Whitlock at the Texas Department of Public Safety is what you need," she offered. "Sheriff Battle transferred the case to him."

Tremaine allowed himself to look down at her—not even the cold wind blowing around them could dim the light and warmth she seemed to radiate. He studied her face, taking note of how she notched her small chin a bit higher. Her eyes were so bright. So clever. So knowing.

And revealing.

There in the depths of her deep brown eyes was the same thing he felt. Awareness.

His heart felt as if it was being gripped inside a fist and excitement burst inside him.

"Have a good day, Mr. Knowles," she said softly, stepping back and closing the door.

Leaving him speechless and staring at the wood.

Damn.

Admitting to an attraction for someone was one thing, but knowing they felt the same allure was next level.

He raised his hand to knock again. To ask her out. To give her the Tremaine charm that had never failed him and gained him the nickname of "Lady-killer" in college. To step back into her warmth and energy.

Instead, he lightly rested the side of his fist against the wood and dropped his chin to his chest in regret.

The war between the Del Rio and Winters families was well-known. It was as big as the state of Texas. Having Preston as his best friend had made him privy—sometimes more than he wanted to be— to the conflict between two of the richest families in Royal, Texas. The whole fiasco with the dating app k!smet, which had matched up Preston's sister, Maggie, to Alisha's brother Jericho at a huge tech fair in August, had sent the Del Rio men into a tailspin at first. So much so that the next day, a meeting of both families, along with their respective attorneys, had been held at the Texas Cattleman's Club with Jack Chowdhry moderating a deal to place the feud on hold for the benefit of both families' combined multibillion-dollar ventures. In time, everyone accepted that what had begun as a technical glitch had turned into a true love match and thawed the arctic chill between the two families and business rivals.

Until the reappearance of the famous Del Rio necklace.

Tremaine stepped back from the door and turned to jog down the stone semicircle steps. Once he crossed the diamond-shaped grass-lined concrete to reach his pickup truck, he paused to look around at the gardens that flanked the long and winding driveway that led to the front gate. The property was beautiful and serene. And the house? The former estate of the

Winters family was obviously in need of continuing
repairs after more than a century in existence, but its
former beauty could not be denied even if it was fading. The three-story European structure was a rarity
in the Texas area, particularly during the time it was
built, with its millwork, stone facing, metal canopies
and wrought-iron details.

Tremaine released a heavy breath.

Inside the walls of the mansion was the secret of
just what had happened between the time of the necklace being stolen from a museum in Paris to it being
delivered nearly a century later to the once glorious
family estate of the Winters family. And he wanted
to be—needed to be—the one to provide the answers.
Such a high-profile case would secure the success of
Knowles Threat Solutions.

And for Tremaine Knowles, failure was not an option.

He'd graduated college with honors, earning his
degree in computer science, with a minor in criminal
law. With a plan in mind, he'd joined the police acad-
emy, and within nine years had moved up the ranks
to lieutenant in the cybercrimes division. During his
off-duty hours, he'd developed a reverse encryption
technology that he'd sold to a leading cryptography
firm two years ago. He left the police force, and in
exchange for the millions he was offered, he signed
a noncompete clause. Surprisingly, the break from
coding made him realize that he had been close to
total burnout.

But that left him with a need for a new challenge. A new quest. Sort of.

Obtaining his private investigation license and forming Knowles Threat Solutions had been a return to his roots as a highly decorated police officer. Over the last year, he offered cybersecurity, personal security and private investigation services. Things were going well enough, but this case would help him grow exponentially. More cases. More staff. More success.

It was his fuel.

With one last look back over his shoulder at the sprawling home, he spotted Alisha standing in the now-open doorway again. She surprised him. He tilted his chin, then eased his hands into the pockets of the leather jacket he was wearing as he leaned back against the side of his truck and continued to watch her. A bit of sunlight broke through the trees and landed directly across her face.

Simply radiant.

With a shake of her head, as if doubting herself, she stepped back and offered him entry into her home with a wave of her hand. And then she gave him just a hint of a smile that was enough to beguile him.

With a nod of his head to acknowledge her offer, Tremaine pushed his body off of the vehicle. He walked back to the home, climbed the stairs and entered the foyer, offering her a brief look.

He had two weeks to get to the bottom of the case, and nothing—not even a pretty distraction—would get in his way.

Two

Alisha sat on the bottom step of one of the dual staircases of her foyer as she watched Tremaine swiping his finger across his phone. She lightly stroked the charm bracelet she always wore on her left wrist—the one closest to her heart. The antique jewelry, with its four heart-shaped lockets, had been a true find during one of her many hunts to vintage malls, flea markets, yard sales and auctions. Each locket held a picture of someone dear to her: her mother, Camille; her stepfather, Joseph, who'd adopted her at a young age and loved her as one of his own; and her birth father, Lionel Jeffries, whom she had never met, but honored nonetheless. The last locket was empty, and she was saving it for the love of her life—the man who would meet all her needs and fill every bit of her heart with the same deep soulful love she would have for him. The one who matched her loyalty, her wit and her energy. The one with whom she would make a family.

"*The* one," she whispered, stroking the empty gold heart with her thumb.

"Alisha."

She cut her eyes up to look from her locket to the sexy private investigator, whose presence made the sizable space seem to shrink. "Yes, Mr. Knowles," she said, releasing the locket as she trembled from him walking closer to look down at her.

Their eyes met.

"I understand the envelope had your brother's name on it," Tremaine said. "Does he live here as well? Does he normally get deliveries here?"

She fought to keep her face blank.

We did not think this story through.

"My family still spends a lot of time here, perhaps the culprit assumed he did. I don't know, Mr. Knowles," she said, hating how she had to play in that gray area between the truth and a lie. She favored the former.

Eliza, why didn't you leave those people's damn necklace alone!

"You do understand how suspicious the whole thing appears?" Tremaine asked.

"Yes, I do," Alisha admitted. "But I've answered a dozen different questions and my time is precious."

He checked something on his phone as he nodded. "I can appreciate that with you owning the antique store Odds & Ends," he said, seeming to read the info off.

"I'm also an adjunct history professor at Rice University," she told him smugly.

He looked surprised by that.

"Not very good investigating then?" she queried with clear sarcasm.

He began to type onto his phone with his thumbs.

"Don't worry. Sometimes I think my family forgets that as well," she revealed.

Tremaine focused his gaze on her upturned face. "Both positions would make you the ideal candidate to purchase or sell the necklace," he said.

Alisha stiffened. "Then why turn it over?" she inquired as she pointed her index finger against her temple, imploring him to think.

"You tell me," he countered.

She chuckled, but it was bitter. "Refer back to your notes when I told you I'm not a thief. Anything else?" she asked.

Tremaine bit his bottom lip as if to keep from smiling, then dropped his head before looking at her again. "I'm only seeking the truth," he explained.

Alisha heard a tinge of annoyance in his tone. "So was the Texas Department of Public Safety when they questioned all of us," she said. "And the truth you need to accept is that DPS has concluded this a matter between the Winters and Del Rio families because the theft was nearly a hundred years ago."

"And the Winters family—"

"*My* family," she interjected with an arch of one eyebrow, daring him to say otherwise.

It was clear that she and her mother were Black and the rest of the Winters family were White. She had been very young when her mother had met her stepfather and his four children. They were truly a blended family, filled with lots of love and loyalty. Although she had a curiosity about her birth father, she would never deny the family that raised her. Even as the middle child, she knew her siblings considered her bossy and a bit opinionated, but her intention was to love and look out for them.

"I never questioned your legitimacy," he said.

"Just my involvement in a theft," she countered.

Tremaine splayed his hand and raised his shoulders as if he had no choice but to think that.

"You're mistaken," she told him, hating that her conscience would not stop the matter of the letter from rising to mind.

He locked those dark eyes on her again. "I truly hope so," he said, his voice deep and serious.

Alisha took a deep breath. Just one more step further would have him between her open legs.

Just one.

The urge to grab his waist and pull him forward surprised her.

"People may also feel an art historian and antique dealer might have access to acquiring stolen jewelry."

The urge to slap him did not.

Alisha rose to her feet. "That is insulting on so many levels," she snapped. "Get out."

Tremaine towered over her. "I said people *may* feel that way," he said.

She looked up at him as she leaned back against the railing. "And what do you think?" she asked.

He furrowed his brow a bit as his eyes searched her upturned face by the light of the antique lantern hanging above the stairwell.

His gaze landed on her eyes and then down on her mouth. The move momentarily distracted her from her anger with him.

And just what does he think of me?

"That I hope you prove them wrong," he finally answered.

His words were just the reminder she needed. The line between them was clearly drawn. Her allegiance was to her family and his was to the Del Rios, who'd hired him. With a brief nod of her head, Alisha stepped past him, about to cross the foyer.

The century-old feud raged on and was still leaving victims as its collateral damage.

"May I have something to drink?" he asked from behind her.

She released a long breath before turning to look at him. "Lunch and a nap, too?" she snapped.

He bit back a smile with his eyes twinkling with his laughter at her derision.

Alisha hated she noticed how his eyes crinkled, making him even more appealing. Her heart pounded a little as she led him down the hall to the newly renovated chef's kitchen—one of the first projects she had completed. She turned to watch Tremaine lean forward against the refurbished wooden counter block island that had a smooth quartz top and storage space.

Damn.

His handsome face was framed by the sunlight streaming in from the frameless windows over the deep sink that reached the ceiling. His brown skin gleamed. It was delectable. Sun-kissed and ready to be nuzzled, sniffed and kissed by the lips of an appreciative woman.

Me.

If only.

She turned away from him to shield her regret.

"This kitchen is amazing," he said from behind her, sounding awestruck. "It's modernized without losing its character."

She felt nervous as she paused in pulling a bottle of water from the double-sided fridge to look around at the brightly lit white kitchen, with its tall ceiling and pops of navy blue offered by the appliances and the paisley runner, which offered warmth. "My grandmother would love it. I spent many weekends here as a kid, with her teaching me about the house and the history that existed in the woodwork and the architecture. I think it inspired my love of history and antiques," she said with a soft grin at the memory of her grandmother smiling down at her and patting her cheek with love. Lots of it. "I think she knew I would love it in a way none of my siblings could. And I do."

The home was large, with two wings centered by a beautifully lit foyer. Over seven thousand square feet. Five bedrooms. Six full bathrooms and two half baths. Cellar. Attic. Study. Dining room. Game room. Living room that opened into an octagon-shaped glass solarium.

It was Alisha's favorite room to read or lounge, or grade papers—and her next project to refurbish after the wing of guest bedrooms.

"A labor of love."

The sound of his voice and the warmth of his understanding made her shiver.

"Yes," she admitted, walking over to hand him the water. "Pure love."

His eyes dropped to study hers. "It's hard to imagine someone able to express such pure love would not have integrity," he said.

His breath fanned against her face. It was fresh. And cool. She could imagine him pursing his lips and blowing a steady stream of air against her skin as he retraced licking her from the dimples just above her buttocks and up her spine to her nape.

"Tell me the truth," he insisted.

She stiffened.

Ask me no questions. I'll tell you no lies.

That quote came to mind with far too much ease. The memory of Eliza's letter, that they had chosen to hide, haunted her.

"If you're done snooping, Mr. Knowles," she said.

He gave her a smile. "Investigating," he said in correction.

"The day before Friday and the day after Wednesday are both Thursday," she said over her shoulder as she turned to lead him out of the kitchen and down the hall again. "No matter how you describe it, it's still the same thing."

Another deep masculine chuckle.

She had reached the end of the hall but turned at his continued silence.

He'd paused in the hall with his hand touching the wall as if noticing it for the first time. "This is beautiful," he said of the intricate design of the wood trim. "But—"

"It needs to go," she said. "That's the plan."

"*That* kitchen needs to be on display," he said, finally moving forward.

"I know," she said.

He stopped in front of her. The walls of the hallway sandwiched them as she looked up at him and he looked down at her. The awareness—the attraction—she felt intensified without space for it to dissipate. The force of it was undeniable.

And was being reciprocated.

The heated light of his eyes revealed that.

Alisha took a step back and felt her plushy bottom press against the wall, which meant she was unable to put any distance between them. Her entire body felt alive and electrified. Never had she felt anything like it.

Never.

With a lick of her dry lips, Alisha stepped out of the hall into the foyer and fought the urge to press her hand against the hard pounding of her heart. She did run one hand through the dense curls of her hair as she crossed the space and quickly opened the door. The cold wind that blew in around her was welcome.

She took a deep inhale of air, hoping to cool the heat of her desire. For him. This stranger. This man who was in alliance with the enemy of her beloved family. This investigator accusing her of lying.

Traitor.

She meant herself.

Tremaine stepped past her to exit.

Alisha balled one hand into a fist and pressed it to her chest to keep from reaching for him. Touching him. Stopping him from leaving. Pulling him close.

Traitor. Traitor. Traitor.

When it came to her family, she was loyal. She was protective. She was devoted.

But I'm also a woman and far from blind.

The man was gorgeous. He could be a model or an actor.

The man was fit. He took good care of his frame.

The man was charming. He could smile a pair of panties off of a nun.

The man was trouble. Big-time.

He reached inside his leather jacket and withdrew a dark brown business card. "If you remember anything else that might be helpful, please call me," he said.

She soon discovered the card felt like suede as she stroked it with her thumb. Just as soft as she imagined his skin would be. *Careful, Alisha. Very careful.* "I doubt very much we have anything else to discuss," she said, presenting the card back to him between the index and middle fingers of her right hand.

Tremaine splayed his hands. "My gut says otherwise and I always trust my gut," he said, then turned to retrace his steps back to his pickup truck.

After he climbed inside and soon drove away with one last look at her, Alisha stroked his business card and then raised it to her nose to inhale deeply of his lingering warm scent.

"Two weeks is all you have to serve me one of that enemy family, Knowles."

Tremaine stared out the balcony doors of his suite at the boutique inn where he was staying during his time in Royal, Texas. The words spoken to him just a few days ago by the patriarch of the Del Rio family were unforgettable. Fernando Del Rio III was a formidable man, much like himself, and so Tremaine knew the man would stick to his word and cut all ties with him if he didn't deliver on his promise to get to the root of the sudden reappearance of the necklace.

He squinted as he took a sip of black coffee and looked out at the gardens that were still beautiful, although a lot of the flowers had lost their bloom with the coming of winter. The converted mansion offered more comfort and solace than the larger hotels in town, which he considered too ostentatious. At the inn there was a smaller crowd, with just five tastefully designed suites and a promise of good Southern cooking that he was looking forward to enjoying for dinner later that night.

The peace offered would allow him to think. Strategize. Solve the case.

And figure out just what Alisha and the rest of the Winters family were hiding.

Perhaps they knew about the stolen jewelry longer than they are saying?

Tremaine frowned.

But what was to be gained by that? They could have just kept it and said nothing. Ever.

He took a deep sip of the brew.

Had they acquired the necklace and kept it from the Del Rios out of spite or revenge? But again, they could have just kept it and said nothing. They asked for nothing in return.

He turned from the beautiful view offered by the doors of his private balcony and crossed the hardwood floor of the sitting area, with its cream-colored linen and French country decor. He reached his laptop, which was sitting atop the lush coverlet on the wrought-iron four-poster queen-size bed. On it were his files on every bit of information he could find on the showpiece. The history of the making of the jewelry. Articles on its costliness. Photos of portraits commissioned with the Del Rio ancestors wearing the piece. News articles and think pieces on the heist. And many more on its sudden reappearance.

The sudden buzz over the necklace had made it easier for him to reach out to the chief of the Paris police for limited access to the original file on the case. It didn't offer much. He would've traveled to France, but so much time had passed since the heist that he didn't know if it would be futile or not. He did think seeing the actual museum would give him insight into how a theft was even possible, so he'd acquired the blueprints, but there had been a major revision forty years ago.

Another dead end.

Tremaine released a heavy breath as he enlarged two photos of the diamond, ruby and emerald necklace. The first was before the robbery, and the second after its recovery from the Winters estate. With nearly a century in between, there had been no changes to the piece. Nothing was missing. No damage in sight.

"From Paris, France, to Royal, Texas," he said, rubbing his thumb across the pads of his fingers as he stared off into space.

Thinking. Analyzing. Hypothesizing.

Who? What? When? Where? How? Why?

He'd learned early in life, and then again in his police career, that those questions were crucial to solving many life problems *and* criminal cases. Who stole it? Who helped? What was to gain? When did it make the journey back to the United States? Where had it been hidden for nearly a hundred years? How did it end up on the Winters estate? Had one of them been behind the original theft?

And why? Perhaps the biggest question of them all to reveal the truth—why was it stolen?

"A century ago," he said, carrying the laptop to the sitting area. He plopped down on one of the two love seats sitting across from each other. "What was happening then in comparison to now?"

A century was more than most people's lifetime. Those who could tell the story of that time were gone.

Tremaine reviewed his files again. And then once more. He double-checked the list of names of people he wanted to interview and do surveillance on. He was just missing one thing. He picked up the cell phone that he used for business.

No missed calls.

He felt foolish to have hoped that Alisha had reached out to him.

Clearing his throat, he pulled up the contact info for his executive assistant, who was manning the fort back in Austin while he was out of town.

"Knowles Threat Solutions."

"Golden. How's it going?" he asked, leaning back against the love seat as he pinched the bridge of his nose.

"Everything is just as blissful as when you left," she drawled in her mix of Mexican accent and Texas twang.

"And yet I haven't received those background reports I asked you to run on that list of names," he said.

"Oops! I got distracted with TikTok," she admitted with a giggle. "There was the most adorable guy making fresh tea and I went with the flow, you know? The universe didn't want me to miss the grand levels of happy watching that man make tea gave *to me*."

Tremaine bit back a smile, easily picturing the young woman who was small in stature, but bursting with energy and joy. She'd been the first applicant for the position of his assistant and although she had barely any office experience, Tremaine had hired her because her happiness—her joy—had been infectious. That, he loved. Golden's talk of the guidance of her angels, playing different solfeggio frequencies music to balance chakras all day, her regular breaks in work to meditate and her fully immersing herself in every emotion—even rare bouts of sadness—were more challenging for him. Still, he couldn't deny that the woman's presence—she called it her aura—was calming. As much as he pretended to ridicule Golden's spirituality, there were so many times that she just *knew* things.

Ding.

The sound of his email notification made Tremaine sit up straight to pull his laptop closer. He opened his email and retrieved the file Golden had just sent him. He looked at each of the background checks on the Winters family. He paused when he came to the info on Alisha Winters and eyed her driver's license photo.

Just beautiful.

"You two will make pretty babies, Mr. Knowles," Golden said.

"Huh?" he asked, forcing himself to scroll past her photo to the details on her.

"Alisha Winters. You are looking at her picture, aren't you? You know I be *knowing* things. My intuition tells me you two are made for each other—"

"Goodbye, Golden," he said, then ended the call and dropped the phone to the seat.

He focused on reading each detailed report.

The parents. Joseph, and his second wife, Camille. Then the children. There was Jericho Winters, the architect. Trey, who was the rancher and investor. Alisha, the antique dealer and art historian. Marcus, the designer. And Tiffany, the chocolatier. Nothing major stood out as he read through motor vehicle records, criminal record checks, credit reports and county property listings. Not that he thought he would find anything. It was a shot in the dark, and sometimes as a cop, and now a PI, the shot would hit a target.

Tremaine continued to swipe through the photos of the Winters family before he began to copy and paste the photos into a makeshift family tree. "Sometimes you have to increase the size of the bull's-eye," he said to himself.

No one in the Winters family was above suspicion. Past or present.

Tremaine picked up his phone to call Preston's cell after checking the time. As the right-hand man of his family's booming petrochemical company and the heir apparent to run the company himself, Preston was a busy man. Still, time was of the essence.

"Lady-killer! How's it going?" Preston said after answering the call.

Tremaine chuckled at his friend's use of his old nickname. "I thought we retired that," he drawled. "I've always said I would settle down once I found the right woman."

"Which is?" Preston asked.

Tremaine paused. "Someone that makes me forget any other woman exists," he answered.

The line went quiet.

"And one you can never forget," Preston added.

That took Tremaine back. "Care to share?" he asked.

Preston cleared his throat. "How's the case going?" he said, a clear redirection of their talk.

Tremaine let it rest. "Actually, that's why I called. I think it's time to widen the field," he said, turning his attention back to the family tree on the laptop.

"In what way?"

"I'd like to look into other Winters family members than the parents and kids," he said, using the tips of his index finger and thumb to zoom in on the picture of Alisha. "This is a century-old crime and the house has been in the family for almost that long. What was to be gained by someone delivering it to the old Winters estate? Why not the new estate? Why not to the Del Rios themselves?"

"Right," Preston agreed. "You're not buying the story about the mail slot?"

Tremaine smiled a bit at the hint of mischief he'd seen in Alisha's eyes. "I'm not sure. I went to the house and I met with the current owner—"

"Alisha."

"Yes," he said, accepting that his heart pounded at the mere mention of her name.

"And how'd it go?" Preston asked, sounding slightly preoccupied.

I want to see her again—and not about this case. In fact, I hate that I met her through the case.

But Tremaine refrained from sharing that information. Or that he hoped he was wrong that she was hiding something. "She was annoyed at my appearance, but she did answer some questions. Nothing really stood out. But I want to check all possibilities."

"Hold on one sec," Preston said.

The line went quiet.

In the silence, as he stared at Alisha's photo, the hard pounding of his heart seemed to echo. And that both excited and frustrated him. The desire for her, he understood and accepted. His desire to protect her even in the face of his gut telling him she was withholding something was troubling, though. He was conflicted.

"I'm back. I had to take that call," Preston said, his voice filling the line. "What can I help you with?"

Forgive me for being tempted to betray the trust you put in me.

Preston was his good friend and his de facto client.

Tremaine cleared his throat. "Send me the names of the Winters family's older generations, particularly anyone who ever lived in the home," he said, regaining his professionalism. "With your family's know-thy-enemy mantra, I figured you could get me names quickly, saving me some time having to research birth records to get them."

"I know them all," Preston said. "I'll text you a list as soon as I get out of this meeting."

"That'll work," Tremaine said, closing his laptop. "I'm headed to town to talk to the sheriff."

"Nathan Battle. Good man," Preston said. "He didn't have much to offer but maybe you can glean something from him."

"You know I follow my gut and there's no telling where it leads," Tremaine said. "And Preston?"

"Yeah."

"The one you can't forget may be the one you can't

live without," he offered, his eyes resting on Alisha's photo as he remembered with an ache the sweet scent of her perfume.

Preston didn't spill any secrets. Instead, he just laughed before ending the call.

With a slight laugh of his own, Tremaine dropped his phone onto the sofa before he began to undress. Nude, he stretched his arms high above his head as he crossed the room to pull on running pants and a long-sleeved shirt. Normally he did his daily five-mile run early in the morning, ending at Mount Bonnell, the highest point in Austin, just as the sun was rising over the city.

A jog into downtown Royal would suffice, and give him a chance to take in the large ranching town, talk to Sheriff Battle and do some surveillance of the main thoroughfare, where the shops and restaurants were located.

After slipping his feet into his custom-built running shoes and grabbing his phone, Tremaine left the suite. The carved *Honeymoon Suite* hanging on the door made him pause and look back over his shoulder into the space. The soft, creamy decor was beautiful and intimate. Just perfect for a couple lost in each other in romantic bliss. Passion. Love.

A vision played out in his mind's eye of him and Alisha snuggled together in the middle of the bed beneath the covers, sharing soft kisses. Limbs entwined. Her softness and his hardness. Lost in each other.

He frowned.

Since he'd left her home just a few hours ago, recollections of her seemed constant. Uncontrollable.

And that was troubling for a man who relished being in control.

Three

Alisha took a deep sip of her rose tea with honey from a clear glass cup as she walked out of her office in the rear of her antique store, Odds & Ends. The single-story brick warehouse located on the edge of Royal had been converted into a retail space and now housed many of the most precious of antiques that she had procured over the years. When she first saw the unique design of the exposed brick, black-painted steel windows, concrete floors and twenty-foot ceiling with rustic wood rafters, she had fallen in love. The natural light streaming from the row of skylights of the long and narrow building gave it an ethereal feel that made her happy. The place had character that, with a touch of history, made it the perfect backdrop for showcasing her inventory of antiques.

And to be the setting for her eight-week seminar on Advanced Researching for Rice University. As an adjunct professor of history and antique dealer, research was her forte. She did her doctoral thesis on the role of research in the antique culture of pre-colonial Africa. As she led senior doctoral students in their use of research in completing their dissertations, she knew her store as the backdrop was more ideal than a classroom or lecture hall. After gaining approval from the dean, she and the twelve students enjoyed their nearly hour-long weekly meetups with just two more to go before the end of the fall session.

Alisha eyed the nine-foot Moroccan mother-of-pearl armoire she had been admiring since its delivery earlier that morning. It had been costly but worth every penny for its beauty alone. She was confident that once she had it cataloged and added to her online inventory, it would be bought quickly. She even had a regular client in mind to contact about it.

"Hello, stranger."

She smiled into her teacup at the sound of her mother's voice and turned to be enveloped in a tight hug that surrounded her with the familiar scent of a custom blend of floral and fruity notes with a hint of amber. It had been a gift from Joseph—a blend designed by him, just for Camille.

That's the kind of love that I want.

"Hello, Mom," Alisha said, pressing a kiss to her smooth cheek before they separated. "Between the renovations, running the store and the seminar—"

Camille smiled. "I know. I know," she said, her

dark brown eyes twinkling with humor and love—plenty of it. "I've heard it all before."

Alisha eyed her mother, a beautiful woman who looked younger than her sixty-three years, with her toned, fit body and wrinkle-free face. It was from her mother that Alisha inherited her strong, fierce, outspoken nature. With it, Camille was a devoted player in the growth of Winters Industries alongside Joseph, and a fierce protector of her husband and all their children. Both she and Joseph had vowed to treat his kids and her daughter as *theirs*.

"I miss *both* of my girls," Camille stressed, setting the designer faux fur she was wearing over the back of a hand-painted Louis XVI accent chair. "Any idea what Tiffany is getting up to lately?"

Alisha was older than her younger sister, Tiffany, by six years, but they were close. Tiffany, as the baby of the family, was doted on by everyone—especially her overprotective brothers. The sisters often commiserated about their smothering brothers, who were *very* protective. That could be tough on a midtwenties beauty who yearned to be taken seriously.

"Between operating her confectionary during the day, and taking night classes for her MBA, she's busy, too," Alisha said, ever her little sister's defender. "But we'll have one of our spa days at Pure."

Camille smiled and shifted her long curly hair behind one shoulder with a lift of her brow. "Soon," she insisted.

"Promise."

"With all of this mess surrounding the Del Rio

necklace, I could use a distraction," Camille said, taking a step closer to stroke the seat of one of six French Henry II walnut-and-leather embossed chairs. "And a vacation."

Alisha finished her tea and turned to carry the empty cup to the rear of the store, where she had a small kitchenette space next to her office. Her locket bracelet gently rang as she moved. With a breath, she looked down the length of the building at her mother with thoughts of Tremaine and his investigative work. The very idea of that would be even more troubling to her family, but it was a reality that had to be faced. She removed the pocket watch she had in the pocket of the fitted leather waistcoat she was wearing over a sheer black shirt and wide-leg wool crepe pants, all in rich oxblood, like her lipstick. "The Del Rios hired a private investigator," she called to her mother as she made her way back to her.

Her words were as hesitant as her steps.

Camille sat down on one of the seats and kicked up one leg in the navy knee-length leather dress she was wearing with polished ankle boots that were equally as stylish. "Huh?" she asked as she continued to admire the craftsmanship of the piece.

The Del Rios have set a sexy private investigator on our trail, Alisha wanted to say.

At that moment, the very thought of him made her pulse race.

And she could easily envision Camille Winters, a consummate lover of love, focusing more on the sexiness of the man than his work. Camille was forever hopeful of having more grandchildren. Right now, Dez, Trey's smart and creative eight-year-old son, was completely doted on by both his grandparents on the Winters side.

"The Del Rios hired a private investigator," Alisha repeated when she reached her mother's side.

This time her mother heard her. Camille looked up. She looked pensive for a few moments, before forcing a smile and shaking her head a bit. "Just when I hoped the war was over," she said, trailing a finger down the seam of her dress. "Joseph is already so upset over this whole mess and now a PI snooping around as if one, or all, of us have done something wrong."

One of us did.

Love and respect couldn't change the fact that her great-grandmother Eliza was a jewelry thief.

The thought of that made Alisha wince a little.

"What's that look about?" Camille asked.

Guilt.

Alisha had never considered herself a liar—not even one by the art of omission. She forced a smile and looked over at her mother, studying her. "He came by the house yesterday and I let him look around," she said to avoid lying to her mother.

Camille nodded in understanding as she twisted her ten-carat diamond eternity band on her finger. "We have *nothing* to hide," she said.

More guilt.

"The investigator's name is Tremaine Knowles," she said, picturing him all too clearly.

"Like Beyoncé?" Camille asked with dry humor.

Her mother was refined, but she knew how to be clever and entertaining. Depending on her mood, there could be a mix of all three if she was comfortable in a person's presence.

"Yes," Alisha said.

Camille arched an eyebrow and looked intrigued. "Isn't Beyoncé from Houston, Texas?" she asked. "You think they're related?"

"I *think* he's here to look into our family and that's all that matters," Alisha said, checking her pocket watch again. "The students should be arriving soon and the university requires I close the store during the seminar sessions."

Camille rose, picked up her coat and pulled it on. "Tremaine Knowles?" she asked.

"Of Knowles Threat Solutions," Alisha added as she walked beside her mother to the front door.

"I better let Joseph know," Camille said, pausing in the now-open doorway. "Um, the original engraved sheet music—"

"By Joseph de Bologne, Chevalier de Saint-Georges?" Alisha asked, knowing her mother had admired the antique music by the eighteenth-century composer that was now beautifully displayed inside a sealed wood-and-glass shadow box. She'd acquired it several months ago.

Camille smiled. "Yes. It will make a great addition to the music room," she said. "Charge it to my account and have it delivered this week."

"Consider it sold," Alisha said, kissing both her mother's cheeks in thanks and farewell.

She hurried to close the door to block the feel of late fall as she watched her mother climb behind the wheel of her white Range Rover, then pull off with a brief honk of her horn. As she leaned the side of her body against the door, enjoying the feel of the sun through the glass, Alisha reached into the other pocket of her waistcoat and removed the brown business card. She stroked it with her thumb before tapping the corner against her chin.

Her attraction to Tremaine hadn't lessened.

In fact, after a rather erotic dream last night of deep kisses and deeper thrusts, he was on her mind even more. She wanted to call him.

To say what?

I'm intrigued by you.

I can't stop thinking of you.

I want you.

Or…

I know the truth about the necklace and I lied to you.

She looked out the glass but then focused on her reflection. There in her eyes, she saw the regret she felt and the lingering doubt over her insistence that they shield everyone else from the truth. For her, integrity was everything, especially as an antiquarian who could validate or invalidate the authenticity of pieces…and thus, their value. It was a position that required honor.

As the students began to arrive, parking their vehicles beside her Porsche, she held the door open for each of them with a welcoming smile. It brightened a bit at the sight of city workers putting the finishing touches on the Christmas decor. It was still weeks before Thanksgiving, but Royal, Texas, was already kicking off the holiday season. She did not doubt that by the end of the day, there would be beautiful white lights, garlands with red bows connecting the lampposts and a wreath on every door of the town's businesses.

She had been so busy lately that she could only hope to have the time to do the same.

Alisha froze to see Tremaine's red truck pull up next. Although the sight of him was shielded behind his tinted windows, his sudden appearance was enough to affect her. Instantly.

"Howdy, Professor Winters," said one of her male students, Rafael. "I found an interesting journal article on quantitative versus qualitative studies that I want to discuss with the group today."

Reluctantly, she took her eyes off Tremaine, who was exiting his truck, to look up at Rafael. "Great," she said, pretending her heart wasn't beating. Wildly. "Go on back to my office. I'll be right in."

Alisha stepped outside her store, letting the door swing closed. The wind cloaked her and her shiver was involuntary. "Two days in a row?" she said, dragging one hand through her wind-tossed loose curls. "I must be your prime suspect."

Tremaine slid his hands inside the pockets of the dark jeans he was wearing with a charcoal overcoat and matching thick-ribbed turtleneck sweater. "Actually, I just checked out of my suite at the inn where

I was staying because of a gas leak," he said. "I saw your car and stopped."

Her eyes filled with concern. "Wow," she said, instinctively reaching to grip his arm. "Are you okay? Is everyone all right?"

He smiled. Slow and wide. "I'm fine. Thanks for caring," he teased.

Alisha snatched her hand away, wishing his smile was not so beguiling. "Which inn?" she asked. "I may know the owners."

"Rose Hill," he said.

She nodded. "Yes. That's the Holcombs' place. Any idea on when it'll be fixed?"

"From what I understand, it's a major rehaul of the entire system, needing excavation and everything," he said, then released a yawn.

Another of her students pulled in and parked, then entered the store with a nod in greeting.

"What's your plan? Leaving Royal?" she asked, feigning hope when, in truth, she liked Tremaine Knowles...whether he was related to Beyoncé or not.

He looked away and then back at her. "I'm not at all done here," he assured her, his voice deep. "I'm here for two weeks, but I'm not up for the fancy hotel—that's why I chose to stay at the inn. So I'll just camp out in my truck until my work in Royal is done."

Alisha's eyes widened in horror. "In your *truck*?" she asked.

"I'll be fine," he said. "It shouldn't get too cold at night this time of the year."

Was money—or the lack thereof—the issue? A

room at the Bellamy, an exclusive five-star resort flush with luxury and the latest in technology, could be costly for a two-week stay.

She eyed him as she stroked one of her lockets with her thumb.

This man was in town, aligned with the Del Rios and seeking a truth that could embarrass her family further. Her love of history had taught her well that sometimes it was best to keep an enemy even closer than a friend. She could influence his investigation or at the very least be on top of just what he was discovering.

"In a show of good faith that we are not afraid of your investigation findings, on behalf of my family, I invite you to stay at the estate—in the separate wing that's still under renovations," she said, nodding as if to reassure herself of her rash decision. "There's no staff currently because of the renovations but there's plenty of space for both of us...for a little while."

"That sure is a generous offer," he said, his eyes intensely locked on her face, as if he wasn't missing one detail. "I accept."

Alisha's heart was pounding so quickly that she could only lock her knees and pray she didn't faint.

"POW!"

The sound of a gunshot was loud, even through the closed windows of Tremaine's pickup truck, as he pulled to a stop. He eyed Alisha, who was standing in her courtyard with a rifle on her hip as smoke still wafted from the double barrels pointed to the sky.

He smiled as he turned off the ignition and grabbed his leather duffel bag and matching satchel, then exited the vehicle to stand on the concrete drive. "Careful. I wouldn't want you to topple over," he teased as he strolled over to where she was standing and then looked down at her.

Alisha locked her jaw, arched one eyebrow and then cocked the rifle. "I got this. Trust and believe that. My brother Trey is a damn good shot and made sure I am, too," she said with boldness as she locked her eyes with his. "Make sure you don't become a target."

Tremaine smiled broadly as he pressed his hand to his chest. "I accepted your invite as a gentleman and I will behave as nothing less than that," he assured her.

Alisha gave him a wink and nod before turning to walk up the steps and into the house.

His eyes dipped to watch the movement of her hips, but he quickly averted them when she suddenly turned with the butt of the rifle nuzzled against her armpit and the barrel pointed to the floor. "You know where the kitchen is. I keep the fridge and pantry pretty well stocked for whenever one of my brothers drops by, so feel free," she said, then turned to climb up one set of stairs. "This wing has the guest bedrooms and it's currently under renovation."

He shifted the straps of the duffel and satchel higher on his shoulder as he took in the thick plastic dust barrier covering the entry to the hall. He looked back down the length of the walkway. "What's that way?" he asked.

"Consequences and repercussions," she said with a stern look before stepping between the plastic dust coverings.

There was a fine layer of dust and construction equipment. "What's the plan?" he asked.

"Originally there were five bedrooms and just two baths that I had converted to three full-bedroom suites, centered by this den," she explained, her voice echoing in the space that was bare-bones and in need of paint, flooring, furnishings and decor.

Tremaine looked around, enjoying the choice of molding, sconce lighting and the use of six-panel doors in the bedrooms. The fading sunlight came through double French doors leading to a wrought-iron Juliet balcony. It was a well-designed space that would be beautiful upon completion. "Nice," he said, commending her choices.

Alisha moved over to the door on the left to open it. "I got this suite ready for you. Excuse the scarcity of it all," she said.

Tremaine stepped into the bedroom, taking in the lone piece of furniture—an open rollaway bed made up with black linens and plenty of pillows. The windows were covered with blue masking tape in preparation for painting the walls that still showed the plastered spots. There was a massive wood-burning fireplace against the wall. He eyed it. It was a magnificent piece of carpentry with intricate details that had to have been carved by hand.

"I started to have it replaced with something more

modern, but I decided against it," she explained. "I think it adds warmth—and not just the heat."

Tremaine nodded. "My dad loved woodworking," he said, letting his duffel and satchel slide down his arm to softly land on the floor. Then he walked over to the wide mantel and set his hand on it. "He would have done the same thing."

"History matters. I'm all for modernizing my home but I refuse to completely get rid of its origins," Alisha added, still standing by the door as she looked around. "I hire a contractor to do the major demolishing and reconfiguring, but I tackle the smaller projects like painting and flooring."

He looked back over his shoulder at her. "I'm impressed, Professor," he said, meaning it.

"And surprised?" she asked.

"That seems to be a constant around you," Tremaine admitted. "You are…"

Alisha arched an eyebrow and waited for him to fill the silence after his words trailed off.

"An enigma," he offered, his eyes locking with hers.

A spark lit in the depths of her eyes before she rapidly blinked and broke their stare. Her grip on the rifle tightened. "I—I have some papers to review for my seminar and then I need to update the inventory list for Odds & Ends," she said. "And—and…"

She was flustered.

Tremaine liked that. A lot. The feeling was definitely mutual. As was the resistance to it.

"No worries. I will keep myself busy," he assured

her. "You go about your life just as normal. Forget I'm here."

"How?" she asked under her breath.

But he'd heard her. "Am I that unforgettable?" he asked.

Because you definitely are, he thought.

"I left a house key for you on the foyer table by the front door. You can come and go as you please." Alisha gave him a smile that was forced. "You have a good night, Tremaine," she said, her voice soft.

With a nod, he watched her turn and leave with her rifle still firmly in hand. She paused and gave him a brief look back over her shoulder before closing the door. He quickly crossed the room to open the door and stepped out into the hall to watch her walk away. The massive curls of her hair were held up in a loose topknot, but several tendrils had escaped and one was lying against her nape. Soft. Tempting.

Alisha stopped and turned, looking surprised to find him watching her. "Did you forget something you needed?" she asked.

You. I need you.

Tremaine was surprised by that thought. It flowed to him so freely. So easily.

Too easily.

And that was unsettling.

"Just looking around," he lied, before stepping back into the room. "Night."

He closed the door, then leaned back against it. Although it was a massive roof, he was beginning to rethink his acceptance in staying under that roof with Alisha. Just the two of them.

Bzzzzzz. Bzzzzzz. Bzzzzzz.

He pulled his phone from his back pocket to find Preston calling. He removed his leather coat before answering. "Preston," he said in greeting, placing the phone on speaker before sitting it atop the small bed that he wasn't quite sure would fit his frame. "Just the man I needed to talk to."

"What's going on?" Preston said.

"Just an update," Tremaine said. "Dead end with Sheriff Battle. I caught up with him at his wife's diner. He suggested a burger, that was excellent by the way, but nothing new offered outside of what's in the police report."

"And your gut?"

"He's an honest man and taking no sides in this," Tremaine replied with confidence.

"Sounds accurate."

"I also spoke to Trey Winters today. I'm meeting with Jericho tomorrow and waiting on Marcus to return my call. Nothing gained yet. Trey seems to be just as lost as you and your family about the necklace being delivered to Alisha's house."

Preston just snorted in derision.

"*But* I was able to get an invite from Alisha to stay at the estate," Tremaine said, wanting to be up-front about his moves.

"Wow. That's major. She's a tough nut to crack," Preston said, sounding surprised. "A beautiful nut."

"The Rose Hill Inn had a gas leak and she was kind

enough to offer me a place to stay while in town," he said, crossing the spacious room to open the door leading to the en suite. It, too, needed finishing. The locations for the bathtub and vanity were clearly marked but empty, with the flooring and painting needing completion. Still, there was a modern glass-enclosed double shower with beautiful glass tile and a deluxe shower system.

"I would have made the same offer *if* I knew," Preston offered.

Tremaine nodded, knowing that was true. "I know that, but here I can get closer to the truth," he said.

"And Alisha."

"I'm here to work this case, Preston," Tremaine said, removing his laptop and the growing file he had on the missing necklace from his satchel. "Nothing more."

"Look, you're my friend, but this is very important to my family, Tremaine, and Alisha Winters roaming around that mansion in nighties can be one *hell* of a distraction, friend," Preston said. "I recommended you for this case."

Tremaine frowned. "For my skills or our friendship?" he asked, unable to keep a bit of censure from his tone.

"Both."

"Well, I'm here for business, not friendship or dating," he assured him.

"Listen, I have faith in you above the neck—the practical, skillful, problem-solving you—and your heart, which is loyal and caring," Preston added. "It's the lower half of you that I don't want to take over."

Tremaine's eyes landed on the photo of Alisha and he reached to pick it up to study her face. And, ironically, the lower half of him lived up to Preston's expectations. "This plan of mine will work to get to the bottom of it. Trust me," he insisted—maybe too much.

"You? Sure. *It?* Nah," Preston said with a low laugh.

It was then Tremaine realized every muscle of his frame was taut. He chuckled himself and relaxed, tilted his head back with his eyes closed. "I'm a grown-ass man, dawg. I got this," he said.

"And the list of names I sent you?" Preston asked, not confirming or denying he believed Tremaine's declaration.

"I'm gathering info on them all," he said, removing a four-foot roll of thick cork from the side pocket of his duffel bag to secure to the wall above the mantel. It would be easy to take it down and roll it up if he needed to hide it quickly from Alisha if she came to the room.

He placed a copy of the newspaper article on the necklace's initial theft at the center with a thumbtack. "I did learn that the public offering for the k!smet app is stalled. The backlash from this scandal is not doing Trey Winters any favors as an investor. Having the company go public would mean a lot of money for him. It's almost enough to make me scratch him as a suspect altogether."

"My father has no grace or mercy for *any* of them," Preston said, his voice hard and unrelenting.

Tremaine paused in arranging photos of the Winters

family on the cork evidence board. "Understandable. But above all, my aim is to get to the truth—whatever it may be."

Silence.

"Preston?"

"None of this makes sense," he said, sounding as if he was speaking behind clenched teeth.

"It will," Tremaine promised.

Preston released a heavy breath. "I gotta go. I have to meet up with someone," he said.

"Talk soon," Tremaine said before ending the call.

Soon, he got lost in building his evidence board. He wrote new points of interest or things to be fleshed out on sticky notes with a Sharpie. Once done, he settled his hands on his hips and stepped back to study his handiwork. Around the focal point, he began with those Winters family members that were alive during the theft of the jewelry from the museum or lived in the home at some point.

Teddy Winters. Eliza Winters. Gloria Winters. Moving outward from the main names, he had some blank spots before he got to the current Winters family. He didn't know Gloria's husband, Joseph's first wife, or if Joseph had any siblings. For that, he needed to check the list Preston provided, then he could replace those sticky notes with the names. He'd also like to add any photos of them he could find.

Teddy was the original rival of the Del Rio family. Had he stolen the necklace as a means of revenge? Perhaps even gifted it to his wife, Eliza, upon their wedding? But the theft occurred in Paris. Had Teddy ever traveled there? Did he hate Fernando Del Rio that much? Was it a part of his character to steal? Like he stole the love of Fernando Del Rio's life from him?

Tremaine had those questions and many more.

There was a knock at the door.

He quickly rolled up the board before walking over to open the door. The hallway was empty. He was both disappointed and surprised. Alisha was nowhere to be seen, but a tray had been set on the floor with a hearty sandwich, a bottle of soda, a bag of chips and a small glass bowl of crudités with a white dip. Nestled among the treats was a note.

"'This isn't Rose Hill but I thought you might be hungry. Night. Alisha,'" he read aloud, loving her neat cursive handwriting with lots of swirls.

She must have run away to avoid me.

He smiled as he bent to pick up the tray before stepping back into the room. His heart hammered. At her thoughtfulness. At the thought of her at his door. At her note.

He raised it to his nose.

And at the slight scent of her still lingering on the paper.

Four

Alisha wiped the sweat from her brow with her fore-arm as she took a step back with a paintbrush in her hand. She eyed the six swatches of paint she'd placed on the wall of the bathroom. "Now which one?" she asked herself aloud, tilting her head to the left and then the right.

"Aren't they all the same?"

Alisha licked and then bit her bottom lip at Tre-maine's deep voice echoing inside the bathroom as if it was a cave. She hated that she wondered just how she looked to him in her overalls and tank top, with her curly hair held back from her face with a bright yellow bandana. She reached for her bracelet but re-membered it was safely in her jewelry case to ensure she didn't mar the antique gold with paint. She had assumed he would get back to the estate later, giving her a chance to work on the en suite bathroom of his guest bedroom. "No, this one is Rock Candy and this one is Windchill." She began pointing the paintbrush at each before glancing over at him leaning his tall frame in the doorway and looking quite handsome in a black V-neck sweater and dark jeans.

He looks good in anything...and probably even better in absolutely nothing.

She shifted her eyes back to the paint swatches.

She knew he'd entered the bathroom by the shift of energy around her. It intensified. Like a rising hum. Awareness. Within moments, he was standing beside her and every cell of her body seemed to flutter to life. Like the illumination of lightning bugs trapped in glass.

"That's gray, light gray, lighter gray, slightly lighter gray than the last—"

Alisha bumped her shoulder against his arm to stop him. "I get it. Hush," she ordered in a soft voice, wishing she wasn't so acutely aware of the hard muscles of his arm.

And his cologne. What is that? It smells so-o-o-o-o good.

She took a deep inhale of the scent of him. It made her tingle.

He chortled before he took a step forward to study the paint samples as he rubbed his chin with his hand. "I actually like this one," he said, pointing to the first one.

Alisha eyed the way his sweater stretched across

the contoured muscles of his back, ready to be stripped away. Slowly.

No. In a rush. Heated. Desperate. Crazed even. Lusty. Lost in desire. Without one damn care in the world.

Tremaine cleared his throat.

Alisha furrowed her brow as she cut her eyes up to find him looking over his shoulder at her, catching her in full lust mode. She took a step back from him and the look of amusement in his eyes.

"Careful!" he exclaimed.

But her foot had already kicked over one of the cans and caused her to fall back into the spilling paint. "Oof!" she exclaimed.

"Alisha, are you okay?" Tremaine asked, stooping down beside her and reaching to take her hand in both of his.

She covered her eyes with her free hand, flushed with so much embarrassment. "I just wish I could disappear into this wet and sticky floor right now," she wailed.

Tremaine released a snort.

She raised her arm to look at him and it was clear he was fighting not to laugh in her face. "Really?" she asked.

"*Into* the floor?" he asked, his handsome face incredulous.

They stared at one another and then broke out in laughter together—and that made them both laugh even more. That type of deep laughter from the belly that caused gasps for air, and tears to fall from their eyes. And it felt good. So good.

"Come on. Get up off this floor," he said with humor still in the deep tone of his voice.

She giggled as he rose to his full height, pulling her up to her own feet with ease. The action yanked her close to him. Very close. Her body—her softness—was against him...against his hardness. With her hand still clutched in between both of his—there between their bodies—she looked up at him as he looked down at her.

There was heat.

In the pressing of their hands together.

The look in his eyes.

Their chemistry. That bold and undeniable awareness. It had pulsed between them since that first look they'd shared when he'd shown up on her front porch.

And it throbbed with intensity in that moment. Like a rapid pulse fed by adrenaline.

Her eyes dropped to his mouth.

"Alisha," he said in warning, his grip on her hand tightening.

She dared to shift her eyes up to his.

Big mistake.

His desire for her made his eyes hungry and she got lost in the heated brown depths as she raised on her toes and eased her free hand up his muscled arm to cup the back of his head and pull him down to meet her somewhere in the space in between.

It was an invitation to kiss.

His eyes smoldered in acceptance as he took it.

The first touch of their mouths was brief but quickly followed by another that they deepened with grunts as Tremaine wrapped his arms around her waist. Alisha gripped his sweater into fists as he lifted her body up against his with ease. He turned their bodies and pressed her back against the wall by the door. A dam broke. The one holding back her desires—to be kissed and to be stroked. Thoroughly.

It had been *so* long.

And this felt so damn good.

Everything pulsed, and the way he suckled her tongue made her ache in longing. A sweet torture.

Never had Alisha felt so captive by her desire. Never. And it was delicious. She shivered as she pressed her hands to the sides of his face and took the lead, stroking his bottom lip with her tongue. She felt him shiver, and his guttural moan seemed to reverberate inside her soul.

She raised her arms high to free her hair and shake it loose before she lowered the straps of her overalls as she eyed him with a boldness that she could hardly believe. And the look of surprise and wonder on his face spurred her on. With a bite of her bottom lip, she jerked down the overalls and raised her T-shirt before arching her back and thrusting her breasts forward.

Tremaine shook his head as if to clear it and raised her body higher to press his face to her plump cleavage. "Alisha," he gasped against her flesh before pressing a kiss to the side of each of her breasts.

She gasped with each kiss. "Yes," she sighed, willing to give her approval for absolutely anything, as she wrapped her legs around his waist and rolled her hips to press the length of his desire against her intimately, admitting that she wanted those impressive inches inside her.

Stroke after stroke after stroke.

He shifted his head to lick one taut brown nipple before he deeply sucked it.

Alisha cried out as she massaged the back of his head.

So, this is mindless passion?

"Please, Tremaine," she begged in a hot whisper as her swollen bud throbbed with a life all its own. *"Please!"*

She had no shame, especially after quickly sizing him up, imagining the thickness of his inches.

He raised his head, breaking his mouth's hold on her nipple. "Please what?" he asked, his voice even thicker with his own desire.

With her breath fanning out between them, she looked up at him.

Please me.

She bit her tongue to keep from revealing just how hungry she was to finish what they'd started.

He smiled at her and waited.

Alisha's chest heaved with each breath she took as she struggled for control. But she failed because the man was handsome and his smile just increased the sexiness.

Those pretty white teeth against that brown complexion.

But—

"We can't do this," she said, finding a bit of reason, although her resolve was as shaky as her voice.

He shook his head. "No, we cannot," he said, although his regret was undeniable.

She nodded in agreement even though his body was still sandwiched between her thighs and her hands gripped the firm muscles of his upper arms—she had always been turned on by a set of broad shoulders and muscled arms.

Her clit throbbed.

They stared at one another. Temptation roared like a flame.

Just once? She knew that all it would take was for her to cross that line that had been drawn between them at their first meeting.

It would be so easy to surrender to their desire. To strip off their clothing. Step into the shower and get lost in one another as the water washed away any guilt or regrets.

So very easy.

Tremaine looked down at her still-exposed breasts and then back up to her face to study it.

Alisha wished like hell that her great-grandmother had never touched that necklace because it led to a feud that now kept her from having what could be the best sex of her life. Against a wall. With a man she wished she'd met in any other way.

"Damn," she said, puffing her cheeks before releasing the air as she lowered her head onto one of Tremaine's broad shoulders. "I am so damn loyal."

"Me, too," Tremaine said with a slight laugh before pressing a kiss to her temple.

Even *that* made her tingle.

What would a climax supplied by Tremaine Knowles feel like?

Alisha whimpered in regret and longing at the *very* thought of it.

"But let me make something very clear," Tremaine said, forcing his eyes up from her breasts. "Different time. Different place. Different circumstances."

Alisha raised her head to look at him. "And?" she asked, leaving her mouth open with bated breath.

"I would get lost *in* you," he promised with clear intent in the intensity of his eyes that he could do just that.

A shiver raced down Alisha's spine and seemed to land in the center of her core. "We would've got lost in each other," she countered.

They shared a look. A moment. Plenty of regrets.

Slowly, with so much reluctance, they moved apart.

As Alisha landed on her feet and straightened her clothing, she glanced over at Tremaine just before he turned to walk away and caught the sight of his erection straining against his jeans. She pursed her now gloss-free lips and released a stream of air that did nothing to release the pressure he'd built inside her.

"I could do this tile work," he said. "I worked with my dad's home-building business many summers doing this and plenty more."

With her hands pressed to her flushed cheeks, Alisha looked over at him standing by the stacks of tile that had been delivered that morning. "No, you don't have to do that," she said.

"And you didn't have to put me up for free for the next two weeks," he said, looking over at her. "This way I don't feel like a loafer and it's one less project you have to worry about... Professor, home renovator, store owner, antique collector, sister—"

Alisha held up a hand to stop him from listing all of her duties. "Okay. Okay. Okay," she said with a chuckle. "I am busy and it would be a big help, Tremaine. Thank you."

"I'll have to work on it during my downtime from the case, but I can knock this out for you," he assured her.

Alisha gazed around the spacious bathroom to avoid looking directly at him again. She wasn't quite sure she wouldn't get lost in his eyes, run to close the distance between them and then seduce him to fulfill the promise of passion he made.

Tremaine walked over to her instead and her pulse quickened with each long stride he took until he was standing before her and extending his hand. "We have a deal?" he asked with that charming smile of his.

She slid her hand into his and gave him a nod of acceptance. "And what just happened between us..." she began, looking over her shoulder at the wall where the paint on the bottom of her overalls had left an imprint of her buttocks.

Embarrassment flooded her.

"We'll pretend it never happened," Tremaine said, filling the silence.

She faced him again, proud of the nonchalant look she gave him, even as the feel of his fingertips on her inner wrist made her tremble.

For Alisha, that was easier said than done.

A spark had been lit.

The grumbling of Tremaine's stomach echoed inside the bedroom as he studied the evidence board over the fireplace. He had finally acquired photographs of the earlier generations of the Winters family. He had basically constructed a family tree.

As he ignored his hunger—for now—and continued to study the board, his eyes fell on Eliza Winters, née Boudreaux. She certainly was a beautiful woman and he could see how both Teddy Winters and Fernando Del Rio had fallen for her. Based on the few details his assistant, Golden, had been able to glean, either of the men would have elevated her beyond her modest New Orleans upbringing. Her love had created a century-long feud between the families and that *meant* something.

Did it play a role in the theft of the necklace or, at the very least, the acquiring of the stolen jewelry by someone else in the family?

Over the past couple of days, he'd had the opportunity to question all of the Winters family members. They were an enterprising lot. Even with being born into wealth and privilege, each of the Winters children was blazing their own trail. He eyed Jericho, the owner of RoyalGreen Architects. Then Trey, the rancher and tech-savvy business investor. Marcus, the "black sheep" of the family, ran a design firm. Tiffany owned and operated a chocolate shop while attending graduate school at night. And Alisha.

Joseph Winters had been stern and cold, but it felt more like he was offended.

Camille Winters had seemed more interested in his relationship status.

All were driven. Successful. Ambitious.

And deceptive?

Definitely defensive.

His eyes shifted to Marcus. Of them all, he had been the most guarded. The one who'd first found the jewelry. At Alisha's home. And she had been on her guard as well.

Tremaine turned to retrieve the tablet where he kept his notes.

As he read through the police report he had gotten from Sheriff Battle, he realized there was another person on-site as well. Jessica Drummond. He needed to talk to her.

He checked the time. It was nearly one in the morning. Far too late to make calls. Sometimes he had to remember that not everyone was a night owl like him. Or Alisha. There had been a couple of chance encounters that had proven they were both insomniacs.

In the kitchen, as they both made late-night snacks.

Passing each other in the foyer.

Sharing a glance as he went up the stairs leading to the wing where he was staying while she was going down the stairs from the wing where her suite was located.

"Alisha Winters roaming around that mansion in nighties can be one hell *of a distraction, friend."*

Preston's words had proven true, because each and every time he was left with lingering thoughts about what she had on.

The black satin short set with a matching bonnet covering her curls and her face makeup free.

The oversize T-shirt with the words *Like antiques, I get better with time!* along with slouchy socks and her hair up in a messy bun.

And her outfit that had sent him running for a cold shower was the fuchsia thermal set.

He grunted at the memory of the way the material clung to her. Her pear-shaped bottom and hourglass shape with her breasts firm, plump and high. Knowing just how beautiful they were when bared with her brown nipples taut and begging to be sucked made it like torture.

And she was aware of him, too.

He'd caught her eyes lingering on his arms in the black cotton T-shirt he wore with pajama bottoms. She had balled her hand into a fist as if to fight not to touch one of them. And he didn't miss when she drank down a glass of water as if the very sight of him made her parched.

Glances. Lingering touches. Held breaths. Energy. Chemistry.

It was all there and undeniable over the last couple of days.

Temptation.

Passion denied.

"We would've got lost in each other."

At that moment, her words seduced him. His inches lengthened and thickened, rising against the plaid sleep pants he wore. Aching. For her.

It was like nothing he had ever experienced before. This desire he had for Alisha Winters was intoxicating.

He swore.

Tremaine tossed his iPad onto the unmade bed and began to pace to the bathroom and back across to the fireplace. Again. And again. And again. Until his erection eased.

He released a long breath as he stretched his arms up to the ceiling and tensed his muscles. "I want her," he admitted aloud with his head tilted back and eyes closed. "I shouldn't, but I do."

"I am *really* hard to resist."

Tremaine jerked around at the sound of Alisha's voice filtering in from the en suite bathroom. He walked over to the bathroom door to look over at her standing in the doorway of the other entrance that led to the hall. He allowed himself to take her in. Thankfully, she was fully dressed in a black long-sleeved body-con dress with leather boots and her hair pulled back into a ponytail. Her jewelry consisted of thick gold hoops and her locket bracelet.

His heart pounded. In surprise. Pleasure. Desire. "Hey," he said.

"I just got back from a university mixer and wanted to see how the bathroom was coming along," she said, crossing her arms over her breasts as she leaned in the frame. "You're all done."

"I am really hard to resist."

"Uh. Yeah, I got done earlier tonight," he said, wondering if the hard pounding of his heart would ever return to its normal rhythm. "It'll take twenty-four hours before it can be stepped on."

She eyed the floor with a slowly widening smile. "It's really nice, Tremaine," she said, looking over at him. "How can I thank you?"

He raised one eyebrow, then shook his head. "Don't tease me," Tremaine warned.

"I'm not," she said with an expression of innocence as she bit back a smile before she turned and walked away.

Tremaine crossed the bedroom to open the door just as she approached it.

"Especially since you want me so bad," she said, very tongue-in-cheek, as she strolled past.

He stepped into the hall and reached for her wrist, stopping her playful and flirty retreat and causing her charms to jingle.

Alisha looked down at his hand and then up at him with an arched eyebrow.

He released her. "Tease," he told her with a lift of his chin.

She took a step closer to him, with a sexy look as she reached up to drape her arms around his neck. "I want to lick you ev-er-y-where, Tremaine Knowles," she whispered against his mouth before leaning in to lick his bottom lip.

And every part of his body stiffened.

Alisha hiccuped and then giggled before she tapped the tip of his nose with her finger.

"You're drunk," he stated, easing an arm around her waist as she wobbled a bit.

"A la-*dy* gets tip-*sy*," she said before another fit of giggles.

Tremaine smiled, then picked her up into his arms with ease. "A lady is lucky she didn't break her neck on those steps in these heels," he said, resting his chin atop her head.

"I wanted you to see me in this dress," she admitted, her words whispering against his neck and drawing shivers.

"You did?" he asked as he carried her down the hall and across the walkway.

He felt foolish that his inches were still hard, almost leading him. Her words sparked the flame and holding her body in his arms turned it up a notch.

She nodded.

Tremaine picked up the pace, wanting to remain the gentleman he promised her that he would be. With every moment of him being aware of the feel of her breath against his neck, her breasts pressed against his chest and her buttocks resting atop his arm, he was feeling less than chivalrous.

This wing of the mansion had modern and luxurious updates, with all of the bedrooms converted into a massive owner's suite lushly decorated in ivory with accents of various shades of pink. "Wow," he said, stepping into a sitting room with suede club chairs around a low-slung glass table, and a glass desk with pink glass accessories and flowers before a large fireplace. Beyond the floor-to-ceiling curtains that framed the patio doors was a private balcony. Antique artwork balanced the modern styling and was a reminder of the original creation of the home.

It was very much the private domain of Professor Alisha Winters.

The design continued beyond the double doors leading into her bedroom, with a walk-in closet to the left that led to a marbled bathroom. There was another small sitting area positioned at the foot of the bed facing a fireplace with a large television hung above it with glass bookshelves flanking them. He clearly envisioned Alisha lounging on one of the chaise lounges in front of the king-size bed, reading a book as she sipped a glass of wine.

And then him walking out of the bathroom naked and ready for her to close her book for an hour. Or two.

Alisha released a small snore.

He carried her to the bed and gently put her down.

She instantly rolled onto her side and faced him. "I want you, too," she whispered.

He had shifted to remove her boots, but paused to look over at her face. She was fast asleep.

Maybe dreaming.

Of me? Us?

The thought of that excited him. And not just sexually. Which confused him a bit.

Tremaine set her boots on the floor by the bed,

then reached for a lush dusty-rose throw draped over the foot of the bed and laid it across her. He gave in to an urge to ease her hair back from her face and fought the one to press a kiss to her forehead. With tenderness.

In a very short amount of time, he had begun to feel a tenderness toward this beautiful woman. A desire to care for her. Protect her. Talk to her. Be around her.

And, yes, he desired her like no other woman before.

It was at times unsettling just how much he was drawn to her.

With one last look back at her, Tremaine crossed the room, pausing by the entrance to dim the lights and also to turn on the fireplace, casting the room with a soft glow. As he left the suite, he glanced over at her desk in her office area. It would be very easy to search it for any clues to her involvement in Diamond Gate, but he couldn't betray her privacy in that way. Even with his gut telling him that Alisha knew more about the recovery of the jewelry than she was admitting.

His integrity was never at risk—not even for a case that could make or break his business.

He continued out of the owner's suite and crossed the walkway, quickly leaving behind the temptation to climb in bed beside Alisha just to pull her in his arms as she slept.

Five

Alisha awakened with a start, sitting up straight in bed as she looked around to get her mind right. The glow from the fireplace was warm and she slowly kicked the throw off her legs as she released a soft grunt. She had enjoyed a little too much wine at the event held at the home of the dean of history last night. Thankfully, she had caught an Uber there and back—

She gasped in horror at a hot little memory.

"I am really *hard to resist."*

And another.

"I want to lick you ev-er-y-where, Tremaine Knowles."

And another.

"Especially since you want me so bad."

And one more.

"I wanted you to see me in this dress."

She pressed her hand to her mouth in shock, then took a really deep and dramatic inhale of breath. She shifted her eyes to the left and then the right. Back and forth. She was fighting to remember if she'd said— and done—*more*. Like the naughty things she dared to dream of doing to her sexy houseguest.

Kisses.

Licks.

Sucks.

Rides—both slow and fast. Frontward and backward.

Alisha dropped her hand and sighed, as her body was now fully awake with her desire. The wine had only lowered her inhibitions, and her tipsy tongue had spoken her sober desires, especially after hearing Tremaine admit that he wanted her.

"I want him, too," she confessed aloud in a whisper, before feeling déjà vu that made her momentarily sit up a bit straighter.

And then she remembered that Tremaine had carried her to bed, thus entering her private space. She looked around. It was *her* beautiful sanctuary.

Alisha got up off the bed and crossed the bedroom to step into her sitting area/office space. Quickly, she moved to her desk and opened her laptop as she sat down on the antique Victorian gold-trimmed parlor chair. She pulled up the video from the camera inside her owner's suite and rolled it back to Tremaine carrying her inside.

She watched him lay her on the bed. Then as she shifted to her side.

"I want you, too."

Alisha gasped and flushed with heat—of embarrassment and the truth of her words. She did want him. Very much.

He was so careful as he removed her boots and covered her with a blanket before he stroked her hair. With tenderness. It was more than sexual. The look on his face was that of care and concern.

Her heart thundered.

If only...

She switched cameras as he crossed the bedroom and then the sitting room without a look over to her desk. He left the suite, closing the door behind him without taking advantage of a chance to "investigate" her private area. To violate her trust.

Alisha closed her eyes and took a large breath before rising to walk back into her bedroom. She undressed as she moved so that she was free of her clothing by the time she crossed her walk-in closet and entered the en suite bathroom. She brushed her teeth, then stepped into her steam shower. The feel of the water pulsing from the shower system felt delicious…and arousing.

Raining down on her from above.

Against her back. Her buttocks.

Pulsing against her nipples. Her belly. The plump mound down below.

She thought of Tremaine. Of his touch. His caresses. His mouth on her body.

She arched her back and cried out as she envisioned

him there with her. Surrounded by steam. Naked. Strong. Hard.

She stepped back against the wall and spread her legs as she eased one hand down between her thighs to palm her womanhood while cupping one of her breasts with the other. Lost in her vision, she thought of Tremaine's lips against her neck and his inches inside of her as she stroked the throbbing bud nestled between her lips and traced her nipple with trembling fingers.

The *very* thought of him thrilled her in a way that created a craving.

One not to be denied.

Why pretend? she asked herself. *Why can't I have the real thing?*

Without allowing a moment of hesitation and doubt, Alisha stepped out of the shower—dripping wet and feeling wild—and rushed back to her bedroom to grab condoms from the stash she kept in her nightstand drawer. She hurried out of her suite, across the walkway and beyond the plastic covering at the entry to the other wing. She didn't even allow herself to think. To deny.

Standing at the open doorway of his room, she eyed him sitting on the edge of the bed swiping his finger across his tablet. Even that subtle move made the muscles of his arm flex...and her core pulse.

Now, Alisha.

She crossed the room.

He looked up just as she reached him, and his eyes widened in surprise before smoldering in desire as he took in her nudity and the foil-wrapped condoms in her hand. His inches hardened and strained against the front of his pajamas as it grew. "Alisha—"

She shook her head and pressed her finger to his mouth as she straddled his lap. "Make me come," she begged in a whisper as she leaned in to capture his mouth with her own.

With a low grunt, Tremaine quickly used one of the condoms to sheathe himself before he wrapped his arm around her waist and lifted her up against him as he stood long enough to roughly jerk down his pajamas around his buttocks. He sat down and eased his hardness inside her, pressing his face to her cleavage as he held her tightly and his inches throbbed inside her.

Alisha arched her back, digging her fingers into the taut muscles of his shoulders at the feel of him. In her. Deeply. Each pulse of his hardness matched that of her racing heart and she knew his stillness meant he sought control to give her pleasure before he gave in to his own. But the aching was too much. She wanted release.

She needed it.

The feel of him was just what she imagined. Long and thick.

"It's so hard," she whispered, pressing her toes to the floor as she began to ride him, working her hips back and forth. Quickly.

Tremaine released a rough cry and his hold on her tightened. "Not yet," he pleaded with her. "I'm not ready to come."

Alisha paused her canter to grip his square chin and look him in the eye. "You better catch this wave or get left behind," she warned before dipping her head to give his mouth a hot lick.

This time his eyes lit with wonder.

To hell with it.

She was enjoying her boldness and was being fueled by it.

Tremaine gripped her buttocks as she began to bounce up and down on his inches as she bit her bottom lip, lost in the feel of his hardness pressing against her walls, leaving a lasting impression.

"I need this," she said with a sigh, letting her head fall back as she picked up her gallop. "I need it. I need it. I need it."

"Need what?" he asked, his voice deeper. Thicker.

She raised her head to look at him. The passion in his eyes sent a chill up her spine. "Pleasure," she admitted in a soft voice. "Release."

"You want to nut?" he asked, his eyes searching hers and being fed by whatever he saw in the depths.

Alisha rested her hands on his shoulders as she stopped the movement of her hips with her core pulsing on the tip of his hardness. She nodded, unable to find the words that spoke to her hunger for all that he offered. Chemistry. Connection. Passion.

With their eyes locked, Tremaine eased one arm across her buttocks to stroke the side of her thigh as he moved his other hand up her spine to grip the back of her neck.

She loved it.

"Ready?" he asked.

She nodded eagerly.

Tremaine began to rock his hips forward as he used his arm to lift and raise her body down onto him. It was a wicked move. So very wicked.

Alisha released a small cry of pleasure each time the base of his hardness struck her fleshy, swollen and throbbing bud. "Tremaine," she whimpered with each thrust.

Each. And. Every. Time.

"Come for me," he pleaded as his eyes searched her, as if seeking to *know* she was pleased.

And that was her undoing.

That explosion she had felt building inside her was ignited by his fast, furious thrusts. The waves of release were euphoric. "Yes," she gasped hotly, enjoying every moment of her climax.

And with even more boldness, she kept her eyes open and locked on him, feeling no shame at him seeing the pure pleasure expressed on her face. He deserved to know that he had done just what he promised. To make her nut.

Fire lit within his already heated eyes, and with her hair now in his grip, he released a rough cry and joined her in the bliss. She found the energy to circle her hips and help push him right over the edge into his own explosion. His face filled with awe. She felt powerful. Together they got lost in the passion. Their cries mingled in the air above their sex until they were spent, sweaty and gasping for breath as they clung to each other.

* * *

Tremaine awakened and raised his head from the pillow just as Alisha eased his arm from her body and got up off the bed. "You're going?" he asked, his voice still thick with sleep.

"To shower," she said, standing beside the bed with her hair disheveled.

He eyed her nudity, with her bracelet as its only adornment, and his body responded swiftly, the sheet tenting from the hardness. "Stay," he implored her, patting the empty spot where she had been beside him.

"On one condition. I've decided I would like for you to taste me…there," she said, almost shyly.

Tremaine sat up straight and arched an eyebrow. "Word?" he asked, not hiding his surprise as his heart hammered at the thought of burying his head between her thighs.

Alisha nodded. "I'll be back," she said, turning to walk away.

His eyes dipped to take in her form, loving the two dimples in the small of her back above each delicious butt cheek.

She stopped in the doorway and looked back over her shoulder. "Or you could come shower with me," she suggested with a glint in her eye.

With the enthusiasm of a young boy, Tremaine kicked away the sheets, scrambled off the bed and quickly joined her in the hall. "Ready, willing and more than able," he assured her.

Alisha laughed.

Tremaine easily scooped her up into his arms. Once again. "Let's not waste any of your energy," he said, walking them down the hall.

She stroked his neck with her hand and then pressed a kiss to his shoulder.

His gut clenched in reaction.

She was able to draw from him with ease the same reactions he evoked in her. He could feel her response to his touch and kisses. The shivers. The arching of the back. The spreading of the legs. The feel of her clutching and releasing his tool. The scent of her desire. The way she had moved in flow with his thrusts.

As if by instincts. As if connected beyond the physical.

What are we doing?

The reality of that line drawn between them by the Del Rio and Winters feud was supposed to keep this from happening. His doubts and guilt rose. But then Alisha licked a very slow and deliberate circle around the cuff of his shoulder. It was his turn to feel goose bumps race over his body.

And then all was forgotten, except for his anticipation at the taste of her against his tongue as he brought her to a climax. Or two.

"Do you like to be tasted down there?" he asked, immediately feeling her body tense for a moment.

Alisha raised her head from his shoulder. "I've never…" she began, her softly spoken words fading.

It was Tremaine's turn to pause.

"Do you like to do it?" she asked.

"Yes," he stressed. "And I'm going to *love* doing it to you."

She released a little grunt.

"Looks like it's time for the professor to be schooled."

Alisha was exhausted, but in a good way. A deliciously good way.

She raised her arms above her head and stretched her body before wiggling her toes as she released a yawn. Never had she felt so languid.

Never have I climaxed so much.

She rolled over onto her side. Tremaine was lying sprawled on the bed. Naked. Well-defined. The corner of her sheet was across his thighs, leaving him exposed. To her eyes and her curiosity. With a furtive glance at his face to ensure he was indeed sleeping, she eased into a cross-legged sitting position and leaned down slightly to study *him*. She was enthralled. His inches were darker than the rest of him. And it was thick. The tip smooth. The hair surrounding the root was tight and curly.

And it feels so good.

She fought the urge to stroke him until it was as thick and as long as when he'd stroked her to one furious climax and then the next. It had only been a few hours since she'd gone to him naked and ready to be pleased, but he had given more pleasure than she had experienced sexually in years. For *that* she felt no guilt or regret.

But...

At the thought of her parents knowing she was

lying in bed with the man sent to investigate them, her concerns resurfaced.

And my brothers? What would they say? Or do?

She covered her warming cheeks with her palms. In the midst of enjoying Tremaine's clever tongue, massaging hands and hard thrusts, she had not given a damn. Not even that he was nearly a stranger.

It all just felt...right. All of it. And not just the sex. Something in him just clicked with something in her. Naturally so.

She looked up at his face to find him quietly watching her. The flames of the lit fireplace danced in his eyes. She gave him a soft smile, accepting at that moment she could find no wrong with their connection.

Even if just for a little while.

She licked her lips and took a deep breath. "I am always so busy taking care of everyone else—even when they don't want me to—that I rarely do something *just* for me," she admitted. "I am always setting myself on fire to keep others warm—and, trust me, they would prefer if I didn't."

Tremaine sat up and placed a kiss on her shoulder before nuzzling his face against her neck, evoking a tremble.

Click.

Alisha sighed in pleasure. After he reached for one of the condoms atop her nightstand and opened it, he took both of her hands in his to roll it down the length of his tool. It was she who turned her head to lock their lips in a kiss that he deepened with a moan. His hands pressed against hers as she stroked him to hardness and lit the spark of desire for him. Once again.

"Come here," he demanded, wrapping an arm around her waist to lift her onto his lap before quickly turning them so she was lying beneath him in the middle of the bed.

Alisha gripped the muscles of his arms as he used his hips to probe her core with his tip until he found entry with one swift thrust. "Yes!" she gasped, wrapping her legs around his strong buttocks and making room for him to go even deeper.

He swore.

She smiled before gripping his chin to hotly lick at his mouth. He captured her tongue to deeply suck into his mouth. She loved it. The feel of his body atop hers. His arms around her. His inches inside pumping away. His kisses. Their connection. All of it.

As Tremaine furiously rode them both into another explosive climax, she could not find a care to give about the Del Rio necklace, the feud or what either family would think about it all.

Tremaine was lying on his side beside Alisha as he outlined the *V* shape of her mound and then up to circle her belly before tracing the divide between her breasts. He enjoyed the sight of her goose bumps as he felt her body tremble. He lightly stroked one nipple between his fingers. She arched her back. Then he did the other nipple. She turned her head to press against his neck as she moaned.

"We *just* did it," she whispered.

He smiled and dipped his head to press kisses to her shoulder. "That was just to release the pressure," he said, already feeling his inches hardening and as he raised the sheet that covered their bodies.

"Each time?" Alisha mused.

"Yes," he stressed.

Alisha shifted her head to look up at him. "And this?" she asked softly.

Surprised at the tenderness he felt for her at that moment, Tremaine gave in to the urge to kiss her. Slowly. He savored the feel of her mouth and tongue. The connection. His entire body felt more energized than ever and yet, there was a calmness and ease to lying there with her in the bed. So he lightly took her chin in his hand and raised her face just enough to look down into her eyes. "This is *more* than that," he said.

"More?" she asked.

"Much *more*," he promised.

Her eyes softened and she bit back a smile. "Oh?" she asked.

"Oh, yes," he assured her as he lowered his head to kiss her again.

It was delicious.

His heart pounded. His body felt electric. Her kisses warmed his soul.

They would face whatever consequences tomorrow, but for the rest of the night, he wanted to enjoy what was truly the most magnetic connection he had ever felt. In it was not just pleasure, but joy. A thrill. Wonder.

With restraint, he enjoyed the taste of her body. The

sweet smell of the soap on her skin blended with the subtle salt of her sweat. Her neck and shoulders. The valley between the delicate swells of the sides of her breasts. He lingered there before shifting to lick and then suck each taut brown nipple.

"Yes!" Alisha exclaimed as her hands gripped the back of his head.

Wanting her pleasure—and being fueled by it—Tremaine wrapped his arms around her body to arch her back and he tickled one thickened nipple with the tip of his tongue. Feather-light flickers made her shiver and whimper.

The sounds of pleasure. Satisfaction.

He lost count of the minutes that passed as he feasted on her breasts. From one to another. Back and forth.

He was reluctant to leave them, but there was more he wanted to taste. He *had* to.

Her navel. Each curved hip. The plump mound of her intimacy.

With a deep moan, he pressed his face against it, took a deep inhale of her scent and then rubbed his beard against her.

Alisha released a low and deep sexy chuckle that made him smile against the plump mound.

He shifted lower to lie flat on his belly between her open legs. With a lick of his lips, he eyed Alisha. Her lips. Her core. Her fleshy bud.

She propped up on the pillows. "More?" she asked, her eyes glassy with desire as she eased her legs open with boldness.

Tremaine smiled again before he indulged. He could never get enough. The taste of her was fresh and sweet. He kept his eyes locked on her face as he slowly feasted, pulling her bud into his mouth. Her hands clutched her hair. Her back was arched and her mouth was open as she released heated breaths.

Again, time was lost. His only concern was bringing her to a climax. Twice he succeeded, enjoying her cries and the writhing of her body as he did. With the taste of her still on his mouth and his hardness leaning heavily from his body, Tremaine shifted up to press his body down atop hers. The way her body molded to his as she rubbed the back of his legs with the soft heels of her feet made him want to take his time with her. To not rush their connection in search of the climax, but to move slowly through their passion. To savor it and miss nothing.

Alisha looked up into Tremaine's face, enjoying not just his good looks, but the intensity as he used his hips to guide his hard inches inside her slowly. She gasped with each thrust until she took as much of him as she could. She felt her mouth quiver as she pulled in a deep steadying breath. One hand was splayed on his back and the other gripped one of his firm buttocks. She saw in the tight lock of his jaw that he, too, struggled for control.

To not hurt her.

To not release deep, fast, furious strokes.

To not climax.

They held each other's stares as they began to move.

His slow thrusts to the slight wind of her circle. In unison. Connected.

At times, they shared kisses. Some deep. Others tender.

When Tremaine whispered his praise of just what he loved about the feel of her, Alisha found the boldness to do the same even as her cheeks warmed with a blush from the naughtiness.

She felt the pounding of his heart in his chest in rhythm with her own. She matched that tempo as she clutched and released his tool with her walls.

"I feel that," he told her. "Wait."

She paused.

He withdrew his inches until just his throbbing tip was inside her. "Kiss it," he demanded.

She did.

They shared a laugh. But it was brief.

Tremaine stroked inside her again. Filling her. They replaced the laughter with kisses, which quickly shifted the mood. He slid one arm under one of her legs to lift it as he deepened his thrusts, but not the pace.

There was no rush.

Their passion deserved all the time in the world.

Alisha pressed her palm to his face, and although she knew it was a tender gesture—one shared by those in love—she couldn't resist. His slow strokes were reverberating through her soul, bringing forth not just pleasure but emotions. And when he turned his head to press a kiss to her palm, she closed her eyes to keep the tears that rose from falling and revealing that what had begun as a very physical act had taken on a deeper meaning for her.

It was *much* more.

She had no clue of what was to come, but presently she felt a connection to Tremaine that was unexplainable and undeniable. It almost felt as if she had known him for a lifetime and not less than a week. And as he slowly stroked them to a climax that evoked rough cries and trembles as they came together, she wondered if she would ever be able to forget him.

Six

Tremaine enjoyed the feel of the crisp, cool air filling his lungs as he ran at full speed down the main street of Royal. It was early morning, with the sun just beginning to break up the darkness of night in the sky. The closed stores were darkened, with only the light of the Christmas decorations to offer illumination. There was a potted Christmas tree on every corner. He slowed to running in place as he leaned forward to inhale deeply of the scent of pine. With a smile, he began to whistle "It's Beginning to Look a Lot Like Christmas" as he turned to jog back up the street.

He was just glad to have found the energy to complete his morning ritual. During nearly his entire run from Alisha's estate, he had allowed heated recollections of their night to replay in his head. His hunger for her had been so great that he had been able to perform several times in one night—a first. He knew that giving in to their attraction was a rare treat he would never be blessed with again and he hadn't wanted to miss any opportunities to have her again. And again. And again.

He could only hope she wasn't too tender and tired, knowing her busy schedule. He thanked God for youth and fitness to maintain the stamina needed last night.

And early this morning.

Leaving her bed with one last kiss to the corner of her mouth just as she released a tiny snore had made him yearn to climb back under the covers beside her. Instead, he'd fought his urge to lie with her in his arms, then taken a shower and allowed himself a well-deserved quick nap before forcing himself to rise to keep his date running.

He thought of her. The look of her. The many sides to her.

While laughing.

While being stern.

While thinking. Grading papers. Smiling.

And making love.

Wild hair. Glassy eyes. Brown skin flushed with heat. Lips plump from kissing.

It was intoxicating.

"Damn," he said as his heart pounded and that now familiar electricity shimmied over his body.

Last night still had not been enough.

Professor Alisha Winters was in his system.

The Del Rio necklace was a blessing and a curse

for him. Were it not for his allegiance to Preston and his desire to grow Knowles Threat Solutions, he would pursue more with Alisha.

More.

That word made him smile.

But he meant more than sex. He would ask her out on a date. Woo her. Romance her. And—

"And more," he said aloud, the breath of his words swirling in the cold air.

Much more.

It felt unfair.

To meet the right woman but be unable to pursue more because of a line of war drawn by her family and that of the relatives of his friend. A theft that occurred a century ago was a wedge between him and a woman that offered him the most incredible chemistry he had ever encountered. The light touch of her fingers to his skin made him tremble with goose bumps. The fine hairs on his body stood on end at just a look at her that lingered a bit longer than it should have. The palms of his hands itched to caress her.

His phone vibrated.

He reached inside the pocket of the heated jacket he was wearing for his phone. "Golden?" he asked, his surprise obvious. "You're up?"

His assistant cleared her throat. "Not by choice," she answered, her voice thick and rough with sleep. "Mrs. Knowles is worried because you never called her back last night, so she decided to call me."

Ma.

During his sexual escapades with Alisha, his phone

had been in his bedroom and he'd missed several calls and voice mails from his mother. "I...was busy last night," he said, biting back an impish smile. "But I planned to call her back at a reasonable hour."

Golden released a clearly sarcastic snort.

"My apologies for my mother's early wake-up call," he said. "I'll call her since she's up."

"Oh, she's definitely *wide*-awake," Golden drawled. "And now, so am I."

He laughed.

"But the real big deal is you up running after being so *busy* last night," she said, sounding smug.

His smile faded. He had yet to get used to Golden and her gift of knowing things. The woman's intuition was on point. Always. He swore she could make a living from it. She always *knew* things. She insisted it was the wisdom from the many past lives of her soul and the guidance of her angels, ancestors and spirit guides.

"We are souls in a body having a human experience," Golden had reminded him time and time again before going into one of her long spiels on soulmates.

After last night, Tremaine could almost believe she was right because his connection with Alisha had felt perfectly aligned. Time had faded and never had he felt so much stamina in one night. As much as he feasted on her, he had still felt starved for...

More.

He slowed to run in place. The thunderous roar of his heart had nothing to do with exertion. He cleared his throat and rotated his shoulders to remove his sudden unease.

There was no room for more. No possibility of it.

"Get some sleep, Golden," he said.

She chuckled. "You, too, *cowboy*," she said with another soft laugh of mocking delight.

He shook his head and ended the call before dialing his mother. It rang just once. He took a breath to prepare himself for the emotional ride to come from Nora Knowles.

"Tremaine Lamont Knowles!" his mother exclaimed in relief.

He bit back a smile. "Full legal name?" he asked.

"Better for me to say then to have it on your death certificate after you were discovered lying dead in a ditch from an accident," Nora said.

"I'm not in a ditch and definitely not dead, Ma," he said, resuming his run toward the other end of town.

"Too bad I didn't know that all night long," she countered as smoothly as an oil slick.

He imagined her right eyebrow arched and her tongue in her cheek, as if she had made a clever chess move. "I was born twenty-eight years ago. I think you were there," he reminded her.

"I was there. *Nine* stitches to prove it," she reminded him.

Tremaine winced. "Yes, I've heard about those stitches plenty," he drawled. "They've healed. Or at least, I hope so."

His mother laughed.

It made him smile. "Listen, you have to stop worrying about me and have a little faith that the boy you raised into a man can take care of himself," he said. "I won't always be able to answer the phone each time you call, and you have got to stop killing me off every time you worry."

"I guess," Nora said with reluctance. "So-o-o-o-o, was it a case or some girl's cookies?"

Both.

"Boundaries, Ma," he said.

"And will these…*boundaries* allow you to join the family for Thanksgiving dinner this year?" Nora asked.

Tremaine came to a stop and flung his head back to release a hearty belly laugh. Once in college, he'd spent Thanksgiving with Preston and the Del Rios. Once. Ten years ago. But that question came every holiday like clockwork. "God willing and the creek don't rise."

Something his father used to say often.

The line remained quiet.

"Ma," he said, nudging her to reply, trying to gauge where she was.

"I miss my Ernie," she said, her voice soft.

His heart tugged. "Same," he agreed.

It had been just a few years since his father—and his mother's beloved—had passed away from prostate cancer. There was more healing to be done. Their grief lingered. But every year was better than the year before. Bit by bit.

"Until we meet again," Nora said.

Tremaine smiled. "Well, I'm not Dad, but you and

I will see each other for turkey day. I promise," he added.

"Then I will be sure to have two sweet potato pies set aside just for you," she promised.

Just like always. Even that one time I didn't make it home for Thanksgiving.

"Ma. I love you like crazy," he told her, coming to the last lamppost on the road that he used for his turnaround point every morning. "I'm gonna finish my run. I'll call you later."

"All my love," Nora said, then ended the call.

Tremaine put the phone back in his pocket and set off for the other end of town. This time he was determined to cut his time nearly in half. And with no distractions, he did just that.

He checked the time on his phone as he noticed the vehicles parked outside of Odds & Ends, including Alisha's flashy Porsche. The sun was now high in the sky, but it was still outside the store's business hours. He was intrigued and a bit worried that something was wrong for there to be such a gathering.

Although breakfast at the Royal Diner had been his plan, he instead headed toward the converted warehouse on the edge of town housing Odds & Ends and opened the door. The bell above it signaled his entry. Tremaine paused as all activity and conversation stopped. Trey, Jericho and Marcus Winters, all of them with Christmas decorations in their hands, eyed him with open hostility.

"What the hell do you want now?" Trey barked.

Tremaine's body stiffened as he wondered if he

was going to have to fight all three brothers. He felt no fear. "I saw the light on and wanted to make sure Alisha was okay," he said, hating the need to explain, when just last night he had been buried inside her. Deeply.

Marcus dropped the lit garland he was holding to the floor. "Listen, you don't need to harass our sister—"

"Harass?" Tremaine asked, feeling his face shape into a scowl. "I would hardly consider coming to her store harassment when I'm staying at her house."

"What!" the three men exclaimed in unison.

"Oh," Tremaine said, nodding in sudden under-standing. "You didn't know."

"No, they didn't."

Alisha eased between the shoulders of Marcus and Jericho. Her bracelet made its familiar ring as she crossed her arms over her chest and gave him a hard leer meant to reprimand him for sharing too much.

He bit back a smile. Somehow, even with her eyes lit with annoyance at him and clearly wanting to hide him away like mold, she was beautiful.

"What the hell is going on, Lish?" Jericho asked.

With one last glare and curl of her lip at him, Ali-sha forced a smile and turned to face her brothers. "Mr. Knowles was one of the guests displaced from the Rose Hill Inn and I generously offered him one of the rooms in the guest wing during his brief time in Royal," she explained.

The three men all frowned as they eyed each other in disbelief.

"He's not staying with you anymore!" Trey spouted.

"Have you lost your entire mind?" Marcus asked.

"Why the secrecy?" Jericho asked.

"Wait a damn minute!" Alisha snapped, holding up both hands.

Uh-oh.

Tremaine knew that meant trouble for her brothers.

"Secrecy implies I owe any of you a direct vote or input on *my* home," she said, her voice stern. "Let's get *that* straight first."

"Alisha—"

"Second—and we've had this conversation before—Lionel Jeffries made me and Joseph Winters raised me. None of you are Lionel or Joseph, so handle me accordingly," she said with lots of attitude.

"Says the bossy little sister?" Jericho drawled.

"Yes, but *I'm* usually right," she countered, pressing her fingertips to her chest.

"Did you really just say that?" Marcus drawled.

Tremaine looked on quietly, amazed at their rapport. Alisha was an African American woman, but her dynamic with these three white men—to whom she was related legally, if not biologically—was sibling loving. Pure. Protective. Teasing. Loving.

He liked that for her, and that she was strong enough to stand up for herself with them.

"And I'm right about this," she added, finally glancing back over her shoulder at him. "This was a good faith move to prove the Winterses have nothing to hide—especially me, since I live in the residence where the necklace was delivered."

Her brief look hit him in the gut like a punch.

He wished her brothers had not been there because it would've been so easy to turn her around into his arms to lift her up and kiss her deeply with his hands woven through her curls as he massaged her scalp the way he'd learned that she loved.

She made him ravenous for her.

"Do our parents know about this?" Marcus asked.

Tremaine watched her body stiffen from behind. She raised her head to sniff the air. "Am I smelling snitch in the air? Are we in our thirties or our teens?" she asked, her tone slightly mocking. "What they do know is that it is now *my* home, left to *me*, by *our* grandmother. And what I know is I have enough secrets buried in me to cause lots of family meetings."

"You wouldn't," Trey replied.

"No. *Y'all* wouldn't," she warned. "Don't start none, won't be none."

Tremaine hung his head to keep the men from seeing his delight at the way she handled them with ease.

"Now. Thank you for helping to decorate the store with me," she said to her brothers, clasping her hands together before turning to face Tremaine. "Thank you for checking on me. All is well. I'm safe. As you can see, my brothers are *very* protective of me. Please enjoy your day, Mr. Knowles."

Mr. Knowles, huh?

Aware of her brothers' stares and wanting to protect her privacy, Tremaine gave her a perfunctory nod and turned to open the door.

"Keep your hands off our sister, Knowles," one of the brothers warned with a heavy Texas drawl.

Too late.

He left the store without looking back.

"Mr. Knowles, huh?"

Alisha looked up from the papers laid out beside her on the double chaise lounge where she was sitting. Tremaine was leaning in the doorway, wearing his leather coat over a red sweater and jeans. She removed her glasses and shifted on the seat to look over at him. "Yes," she said, feeling playful with him. "I thought it was more suitable than *lover*."

He nodded in understanding as he pushed off the frame and entered the room with his hands inside the pockets of his coat. "*Lover* sounds great, but Tremaine would've sufficed," he said with a chuckle as he paused in the center of the room to look up at the glass ceiling.

Alisha followed his gaze with her own and was taken aback by the sight of the full moon blazing through the dark sky and the break in the leaves and branches of one of the towering live oak trees on the property. It was a magical sight, and one of the reasons she loved the glass-enclosed solarium. With the renovations she had planned, the area would be truly transformed.

"Aren't you cold?" he asked, looking at her and the bulky sweater she was wearing over a long-sleeved T-shirt and wide-leg jeans with comfy socks.

"I never got around to lighting the fireplace," she admitted, raising her chin toward the mantel on the other side of the room. "It's on my to-do list for this room."

Tremaine removed his leather coat and tossed it over to her to catch before striding across the room to the fireplace. She let her eyes watch his body as he moved. She bit her bottom lip and released a shaky breath as she remembered the feel of his moves the night before. Her body lit up as if a switch had been flicked. She tingled.

Soon, the crackle of the lit fire echoed into the silence and gave the space a warm glow.

Tremaine remained standing there, looking down into the flames.

It was a glorious sight.

An urge to join him in front of the fireplace and strip him of his clothing filled her.

But we can't.

Not again.

Can we?

Tremaine looked over at her. The reflection of the flames against his face was intense.

She shivered. "We can't," she said softly.

This man had spent the day investigating her family for the theft of the Del Rio necklace. Even with the bravado she'd exhibited when speaking to her brothers earlier that day, she knew they would feel her dalliance with Tremaine was a betrayal.

But...

He walked over to her.

She watched him closely, feeling her heart rate increase with each step that brought him nearer to her. And when he lowered to his knees in front of her, she raised her hands to grasp both sides of his handsome face. His hands gripped her hips. Together, they locked gazes and leaned in toward each other to feed the hunger in their eyes. And just a second before their lips touched…

The doorbell rang.

Tremaine leaned back on his legs and Alisha jumped to her feet, flooded with shock at the intrusion, and guilt. She reached for her phone, which was atop the papers, and opened the app for surveillance as her heart pounded. She smiled a bit at seeing her younger sister, Tiffany. She felt a mix of pleasure and regret.

"Excuse me," she said, briefly touching his broad shoulder as she eased past him. "It's my sister."

She paused when he reached for her hand. His touch was warm. Electric. Addictive.

"I'll go up to my room," he said, rising to his feet with ease as he stroked the back of her hand with his thumb. "Maybe her arrival was for the best."

Alisha looked up at him. "Maybe so," she lied.

They left the solarium with their fingertips lightly touching. In the foyer, when they reached the stairwell on the right, Tremaine raised her hand to kiss her palm before freeing her and jogging up the stairs. Alisha watched his retreat as she stroked the spot he'd kissed. It still tingled. The urge to press her lips to the same spot consumed her.

Instead, she walked over to the double front doors to unlock them and open one. She smiled at her sister, a brown-haired, brown-eyed beauty with curly hair and an athletic frame, but she frowned at the small bag she was carrying. "Hey, Tiff," she said with hesitance. "Everything…okay?"

Tiffany stepped inside the foyer and set the overnight bag on the floor. "Definitely not," she said, her Texas accent just as prominent as the rest of the family's. "Our brothers are in an uproar about your houseguest—"

"There's nothing going on they should be concerned about," Alisha said, closing the door.

"Liar, liar, pants on fire," Tiffany said in a singsong voice.

Alisha froze before she turned to eye her sister as she leaned back against the door.

"If I had arrived five minutes later I might've caught you two midstroke. Did I at least catch you in midkiss?" Tiffany asked, very tongue-in-cheek.

Alisha turned her lips downward and arched an eyebrow as she stared at her sister's smug face. She reached for Tiffany's wrist to tug her behind her.

"Hey! Careful!" Tiffany exclaimed as Alisha crossed the foyer and pulled her into the hall leading to the kitchen.

"Do you see how good he looks?" Alisha asked, releasing her sister's wrist and spinning to eye her.

"Definitely. He's irresistible, huh?" Tiffany asked with a look that was part sympathy and part understanding of Tremaine's appeal.

"And *trust* me, he's even better in bed than he looks."

"Oh. Okay then," Tiffany said. "TMI."

Alisha began to pace as she rubbed her bottom

lip with her thumb. In truth, she had to tell her sister. She *had* to tell someone. It had been that good. His kisses. The touches. His strokes. All of it. She grunted in pleasure. "So good," she said with a shake of her head.

"Lish."

She looked over at Tiffany. "Huh?" she said softly.

"Listen, your business is just that. I won't be sharing it with anyone, but you have to know this won't end well," Tiffany said.

"If you didn't interrupt, it would have ended *very* well," Alisha said with a hard, wide-eyed meaningful stare.

Tiffany laughed. "Look, I'm not really in a position to judge. *Trust* me—"

"What does *that* mean?" Alisha asked, looking on at her sister as she crossed the kitchen, opened the dark blue Viking refrigerator and pulled out a bottle of water.

"Nothing," Tiffany said.

Alisha continued to watch her, and her eyes widened when her sister's cheeks flushed with a rose-colored blush. "Hmm," she said, slowly crossing the kitchen to stand before her. "Not in any position to judge…"

Tiffany shifted her gaze away.

"Someone has a secret," Alisha said, her voice softly teasing.

"Yes, *you*," Tiffany said, sitting the bottle of water down on the top of the island. "And exactly what is going on with you and Tremaine…except playing with fire?"

Hot memories of the sex they'd shared played in her mind in a rapid-fire sequence.

"Just fun. And lots of it," Alisha answered, but it felt like a lie.

Today in her store, she had been surprised by the instant desire to stand beside Tremaine against her brothers' failed attempts at bullying. She had wanted to defend him and hated pretending that there was nothing between them but cordiality. Everything with Tremaine felt like more than just fun. All of it—all of him—was *so* good. And not just the physical aspect. The chemistry. The conversation. The way she thought of him often and the way she caught him giving her a brooding stare or an innocent touch lingering on her just a bit longer than necessary. And making her feel he was drawn to her as well for more than glorious sex.

It was becoming a lot more than just a careless fling.

In fact, she was beginning to care quite a bit.

Their connection was so intense. So very addictive.

Even now she craved his kisses and touches. His strokes. And then there was the pure pleasure of lying beside him in bed, sweaty and spent with their bodies touching.

"Nothing good can come of the fun you and Tremaine are having. Trust me on this," Tiffany advised her, finally leveling her eyes with her sister. "Is a fling worth making the family feel betrayed?"

Alisha arched an eyebrow. "And is *your* secret worth it, little sister?" she asked. "Let's talk about it."

Tiffany took a deep drink of water and gazed out the window for long moments, then looked back at her sister. "Okay, but first pajamas, and I brought chocolate, of course," Tiffany assured her.

"*Of* course," Alisha agreed, wrapping her arm around her sister's as they walked out of the kitchen and down the hall to retrieve her overnight bag from the foyer. "There is nothing better than a sleepover with my little sister."

"Not even your *lover*?" Tiffany asked with obvious dramatics as they climbed the stairs together.

"Good evening, ladies."

They both looked over to find Tremaine descending the other stairs.

"Oh, my," Tiffany said under her breath as she observed him.

"Oh, my" was right.

He was fully dressed, but the clothing accentuated his strong build and made anyone wonder about the nudity beneath.

"I was going to grab a sandwich," he explained.

Eat me instead.

"Okay," Alisha said aloud as she paused on the steps and watched his descent.

Every move.

Her heart pounded in total awareness.

Tremaine had paused on the stairs as well. "Tiffany, it's good to meet you," he said.

"Same," she replied.

"Listen, I'm sure you know I'm in town to investigate the reappearance of the Del Rio necklace. I'd like to give you a call to talk about it."

"Sure, but I don't know anything," Tiffany replied.

He smiled. It was broad and contagious. Meant to put someone at ease. He just gave her sister a shrug of one broad shoulder before continuing down the stairs. "Alisha, should I turn off the fireplace?" he asked, stopping on the bottom step to look over at them.

At me.

His eyes are on me.

Warmth flooded her body.

"Yes! I forgot. Thank you, Tremaine," she said, pressing a hand to her face at what could have been a disaster.

"Don't worry," he said, locking his eyes with hers. "I got you."

She looked back at him over her shoulder, liking the sound of that. He smiled as he crossed the foyer.

"Night-night, Mr. Knowles," Tiffany said with the sweetness of saccharine before tugging Alisha's arm for them to continue up the stairs.

She moved with reluctance.

"You got it bad, sister," Tiffany drawled.

I sure do.

"And so did I…for his best friend."

"Preston? O-o-ooh, no! He's a Del Rio!" Alisha said, picturing the handsome and highly ambitious man with a bit of a ruthless streak in business. "Is *he* your little secret?"

Tiffany looked sheepish. "Him and…our baby on the way," she said, pressing a hand to her belly.

Shocked, Alisha took in a deep inhale that sounded harsh. "What!" she exclaimed with wide, incredulous eyes.

"We have a lot to talk about, sis," Tiffany stressed as they reached the top of the stairs.

"Yes, we sure as hell do," Alisha insisted, dragging her little sister into her bedroom suite.

Seven

Tremaine stood before the fireplace in his bedroom studying his evidence board. He looked down at the photo of Eliza Boudreaux that he held. She had been a beautiful woman and it was obvious why such beauty would cause a century-old feud, because she had captured the hearts of two powerful men.

His eyes shifted to the first. Fernando Del Rio.

And then to the second. Teddy Winters.

Eliza had been the girlfriend of Fernando at the time of the theft that occurred in Paris.

As an investigator, it only made sense to not just focus on the current events but the ones of the past as well—back to the time the necklace was first stolen. Was there a correlation? He wasn't ready to dismiss that possibility.

The necklace theft and its return a century later didn't make sense. Tremaine took a step forward to use a thumbtack to attach the copy of the black-and-white photo on the board on the Winters side—between the photos of Fernando, who was at the helm of the Del Rio lineage, and Teddy, the patriarch of the Winters family.

Knock, knock.

He looked over his shoulder at the door.

"Tremaine? You awake?"

He smiled and started toward the door to let Alisha in, but paused to turn and roll the evidence board first. At the moment just before he opened the door, he felt that all too familiar mix of desire and guilt. His desire won yet again.

And there she stood. Beautiful. Bright-eyed. Hair in a curly ponytail. Dressed in overalls covered in teddy bears.

"Cute," he said, eyeing her and taking note that the comfy nightwear did absolutely nothing to hide *all* her curves.

Alisha did a little curtsy.

He grinned as he leaned in the doorway.

"Did I wake you?" she asked, looking past him to his made bed.

"No," he said. "Did your sister leave?"

Alisha shook her head. "She's sleeping," she said.

They locked eyes on one another.

That electric awareness shimmied between them.

"She knows about us," Alisha said, shifting her gaze down to the floor for a moment.

It was just long enough to break the spell she cast

upon him without even trying. Still, he shivered, remembering the night they'd shared lost in each other. "I'm sure that wasn't an easy conversation," he said.

"No—no, it wasn't," she admitted, easing past him to enter the bedroom. "But even now I want you."

Tremaine turned, closing the door as he did. "As much as I love hearing that, I don't think that is why you are here," he said.

She crossed her arms over her chest. "It must stop. This must stop," she said, turning to face him.

Tremaine did not miss the irony that the very thing that stood between them was symbolized by the evidence board in the background behind her. "I know," he said.

"We both have so much to lose," she said with a conviction that seemed forced.

Tremaine felt she was truly trying to convince herself and not him. "The success of Knowles Threat Solutions is very important to me," he said, crossing the room to sit on the edge of the bed. "Coding used to be my thing. Even when my parents encouraged me to attend college, I knew it had to be in that field. I had been doing it since my early teens."

Alisha's face filled with surprise.

"Even when I was working in cybercrimes on the police force, I was still coding at night and developed a technology that made me a lot of money, but meant signing a noncompete clause that left me needing a new challenge," he explained.

"Wow," she said, sounding impressed. "That's cool, Tremaine."

"Thanks," he told her, surprised she made him feel bashful.

Alisha came to sit beside him on the bed. "So part-time builder, a coder, a cybercrimes detective and now a private investigator?" she asked.

"Knowles Threat Solutions offers all the things I'm good at—cybersecurity, personal security and private investigation services," he said. "I want it to work, and this case would help establish that."

Alisha released a little grunt and looked contemplative. "You succeeded at so much at a young age. I assume you're financially set," she said, shifting on the bed to now face his profile. "Why is this business venture so important?"

Tremaine shrugged one shoulder. "I've never failed before," he said.

She tilted her head to the side and gave him a chastising look. "And if you did, why would one stumble matter when you've had so many wins in this race called life?" she asked.

He looked over at her, but then focused on the unlit fireplace as he pondered a very valid question. "I've always done well," he said.

She shrugged. "Cool, but perfection is hard to maintain," she said. "And a desire to do so reveals some deeper stuff."

"Oh, yeah?" he asked.

She nodded.

"And you're not just trying to get me off the case, are you?" he asked.

She pressed a hand to her chest and feigned offense. "The nerve!" she exclaimed.

He playfully smirked.

They fell silent.

It was comfortable.

"I should go," she said. Softly.

He watched her.

She shifted her gaze away from him, then back again. "But I don't want to," she admitted.

"I don't want you to," he confessed, his heart pounding with his truth.

Her eyes filled with anguish.

Tremaine saw it—he felt it. The pain that radiated across his chest surprised him. He looked away from her as if he wished he could escape the feeling. When she released a small sigh, he held his breath.

We can't.

But his body stirred just from her nearness.

The bed made a slight noise and his body tingled as she drew nearer. Her soft lips pressing to his cheek made his heart pound.

I can't.

But at the same moment of his thought, he turned his head to lock his mouth with hers. To kiss her. Taste her. Have her.

When he felt nothing but air, Tremaine opened his eyes just as she left the bedroom and him behind. He jumped to his feet but stopped. He fought the urge to go after her.

To kiss her again. Taste her again. Have her again.

"Damn," he said as regret settled on his shoulders so heavily that they slumped.

Alisha paused in the doorway of her bedroom to find her sister sitting up in bed, wide-awake. "Why are you up?" she asked, crossing the room with just the light of the fireplace to guide her.

Tiffany gave her a chastising look as she slowly shook her head at her. "You horny, horny girl," she teased.

I wish.

Alisha lifted the covers on the bed.

Tiffany frowned. "Shower first, please," she said.

"We didn't have sex," she snapped.

Her sister's face filled with mocking disbelief.

Alisha gave her little sister a stern look before climbing onto the bed and turning on her side to face away from her.

"Oh," Tiffany said.

I should be beneath Tremaine, being stroked. Over and over and over again.

Alisha closed her eyes and smiled into her pillow as she clutched it tightly, remembering the time Tremaine had whispered in her ear that he loved being deep inside of her as he made love to her.

That could have been us right now, if not for...

Tiffany tapped her shoulder. "But what were y'all doing this time of the night?" she asked.

Alisha opened one eye and gritted her teeth. Truthfully, she was a little annoyed at her sister's intrusion, because if not for her sudden appearance, Alisha knew Tremaine would have been delivering her a second—maybe third—climax.

"Ending things once and for all, Tiffany," she said.

"Oh," Tiffany said again.

Alisha snuggled down under the covers and closed her eyes, smiling at a vision of Tremaine walking toward her, naked and hard.

"It's for the best," Tiffany added.

With a snort of derision, she looked back over her shoulder at her sister. "Take your own advice, sis," she drawled with a look of "so there."

Tiffany frowned and perhaps regretted sharing her own secret with her older sister. "Good night," she said, flopping back down onto the bed and turning her back to Alisha.

Don't start none, won't be none.

She settled her head back on her pillow. Time seemed to tick slowly. Long after Tiffany's deep breaths of sleep filled the air, Alisha was still awake. Still wished things between her and Tremaine could be different. Still debated rushing over to the other side of her home to climb into his bed with him.

But it was more than just sex. She truly liked Tremaine. Last night, in between bouts of glorious sex, they had lain with their limbs entwined. Laughed together. Showered. Ate snacks in the buff in the kitchen. Fallen asleep together with his arm over her waist.

She loved her sister, but Tiffany's appearance popped that bubble of isolation they'd created. A bubble Alisha had not been ready to leave, but her sister was a reminder that she had to do just that.

Still, Alisha lay awake all night. Unable to sleep. She fought the childish urge to roll over and press her feet to her sister's buttocks to nudge her out of the bed and onto the floor. But she wouldn't ever do anything to hurt her sister, and knew that Tiffany didn't intend to hurt her in any way. It wasn't how they were treated or raised. Loyalty was always key.

It is why she would heed her sister's advice and let things with Tremaine cool.

And she wouldn't completely overlook Marcus's concern about Tremaine staying with her.

Nor would she stop shielding their great-grandmother Eliza's greatest shame.

Family sticks together. Always.

Long after the sun rose and a new day began, Alisha had to keep reminding herself of that. After she hugged her sister and waved her goodbye as she drove away, again and again, she had to repeat it like a mantra during meditation.

Family sticks together. Always.
Family sticks together. Always.
Family sticks together. Always.

"Family sticks together. Always," Alisha repeated out loud as she closed the front door and then turned to lean back against it as her eyes traveled up the stairs to the plastic barrier covering the entry to the guest wing.

It opened and Tremaine emerged in his running attire.

Handsome as ever.

"Mornin'," he said with a bright smile. "You're up early."

"My sister left. She likes to get an early start on making the chocolate for her shop," she said, watching every move of his muscles as he jogged down the stairs. "Plus, I didn't really sleep."

Tremaine came to a stop in front of her and looked down at her upturned face. "Maybe you should go back to bed," he suggested.

She bit her bottom lip to keep from saying "Not without you."

When he smiled and lowered his head, she felt like he read her mind.

"Tremaine, I—"

"Am asking for trouble if you keep looking at me like that," he warned, looking down at her. "Try to avoid that if we're going to stick to what we talked about last night."

"I don't want to avoid you for the rest of your stay, Tremaine," she said, still using the door for support as he towered over her and made her entire body feel awakened by his unique energy.

"Should I leave?" he asked.

Don't you dare. Not yet.

"That's not necessary," she said, ignoring that what she felt was alarm at the very thought of him leaving.

"Then what do we do?" he asked.

"Get it out of our systems," Alisha said.

"Word?" Tremaine asked, already reaching to undo the zipper of his lightweight jacket.

She reached out to hold his hand and stop his undressing. "I meant…we spend some time together—nonsexual time—and get used to each other *that* way," she said.

Tremaine's face filled with understanding, some obvious regret and then acceptance as he rezipped his jacket.

Alisha let her hand drop from his as he did. "Maybe I can join you for your run?" she suggested.

Tremaine chuckled and it grew into a laugh.

She playfully swiped at his arm. "Are you laughing at me?" she asked. "Do you *think* I can't keep up with you?"

"No, no. No!" he stressed, even though there was still mirth in the depths of his eyes. "Although I do run daily and fitness is my thing—"

"And yet that night you fell asleep first, Mr. Fitness," she retorted as she looked up at him with a smug expression. "Your snores serenaded me while I was ready for a second round."

Tremaine's eyes darkened. "Unless I lost count, there were three rounds…and nary a complaint," he said.

The heat in his eyes made her breathless with desire. "Nary?" she teased him, seeking some levity.

He appeared amused. "I wanted to impress you, Professor," he said.

Alisha licked her lips, finding them parched. "Trust me, you left one hell of an impression that night," she said. "An unforgettable one."

Tremaine's eyes widened and he tossed his hands up in the air as he strode away from her, paced the foyer and then strode back over to loom over her. There was no denying the desire in the brown depths of his eyes. "You can't tease me and flirt and not expect me to want to give you just what you know we both want," he said.

Alisha took a step back but felt nothing but the un- relenting wood of the double front doors. "I wasn't—"

"Weren't you?" Tremaine asked with a little mock- ing tone.

Her heart pounded so loudly she heard it in her ears. "I wasn't," she insisted, but knew she was lying.

And knew that he knew that as well.

Tremaine leaned down closer to her, and his eyes dropped to her mouth before slowly shifting back up to her eyes. "Weren't you?" he asked again.

This time so softly.

Their breaths—the shaky ones that revealed so much of what they felt and what they fought—echoed in the short distance between them.

"The choice is yours, Alisha," he said, after what seemed the longest time. "Run? Or more?"

More.

Alisha closed her eyes and took a breath.

Family sticks together. Always.

"Run," she said, sounding resigned. "Just run."

Alisha opened her eyes just as Tremaine pressed a light kiss to her forehead that seemed to make her soul shiver.

"Then run it is," he said with obvious regret.

She crossed her arms over her chest to hide that her taut nipples pressed against the thin shirt she was wearing.

"You better go get dressed," Tremaine said, stepping away from her.

And with every step she took away from him and up the stairs, Alisha kept repeating her mantra in her head and fighting like hell to remember it.

Family sticks together. Always.
Family sticks together. Always.
Family sticks together. Always.

Tremaine entered the Royal Diner and blew extra heat into his cupped hands before removing the leather jacket he had on. He paused in hanging his coat on the black rack by the door. The high level of chatter that filled the air when he entered had become noticeably quiet.

He turned and nearly every eye was on him, many with open curiosity and speculation. He forced a smile and gave a brief wave to many of the patrons as he made his way across the black-and-white checkerboard linoleum floor of the 1950s-inspired diner to slide into one of the red faux-leather booths.

"Howdy."

Tremaine looked up at Amanda Battle, who was standing beside his booth with a container of coffee in one hand and a menu in the other. She was the wife of the sheriff and the owner of the diner. He gave her a smile. "Hello," he said, accepting the menu she handed him as she turned over the cup sitting atop his table to fill it.

"Don't mind the stares—everyone is very aware of

who you are and why you're in town," Amanda said. "Not much escapes the people in town."

"Oh, yeah?" Tremaine asked, leaning back to look past her at the eyes still openly studying him.

"*Oh*, yeah," she stressed with a chuckle. "I'll be back to take your order."

He nodded as she strolled away to refill the cups of other patrons.

"Pssst."

Tremaine frowned a bit as he looked back over his left shoulder to find an older bearded man with fiery red hair looking at him over the rim of his spectacles. "Yes?" he asked.

"The Winterses are a good solid family and well respected 'round these parts," the man said.

"Thanks for the information," Tremaine said before turning back forward.

"Pssst."

Tremaine closed his eyes and hung his head, then shifted in the booth seat to sit sideways and look at the man again. "Yes?" he repeated politely.

"So who else are you looking into…except the Winterses?" the stranger asked before taking a big bite of a spoonful of a steaming bowl of chili.

"You have any insight you want to share?" Tremaine inquired. "Because I don't."

The man paused and then released a chortle. "You're an ornery son of a gun, huh?" he asked, before raising his napkin to swipe it left and then right across his mouth.

Tremaine shrugged. "Just honest. That's all," he told the man.

That admission received a snort.

Tremaine turned back around in his seat just as Amanda walked up to his table. "I'll have two brisket burgers with the works and chili fries," he requested, handing her the menu.

"Two?" the redheaded stranger questioned from behind him. "Somebody's made a friend."

Amanda shot the man a chastising look. "Mind your business and your manners, Earl," she drawled.

"Can I get them to go, actually?" Tremaine asked, reaching for a few packets of sugar to sweeten his coffee.

"Sure can," Amanda said with a warm smile.

Between Earl's nosiness and the open stares from the rest of customers, Tremaine was feeling less inclined for a public outing.

"Pssst."

Nope.

"Pssst."

Tremaine took a deep sip of his coffee.

Earl cleared his throat. Twice.

After one last gulp of the brew, Tremaine set his cup on the saucer and rose to his feet to stride across the restaurant to stand at the counter.

"Pssst."

What the...?

Tremaine turned and then had to look down to find Earl standing there, nearly a foot shorter than him. "You're pretty persistent, huh, Earl?" he asked.

"Closed mouths don't get fed," Earl remarked, shifting past Tremaine to take a seat on one of the stools lining the counter.

Small-town gossip spread faster than ants to spilled sugar.

"Really?" Tremaine reached in the back pocket of his jeans for his wallet to remove one of his bank cards to hand to Amanda.

"The necklace fiasco has put Royal, Texas, on the world stage," Earl noted.

Tremaine showed no reaction and said nothing to the man as he accepted the brown paper take-out bag, his receipt and his card from Amanda.

"Enjoy it," she said.

"I'm sure I will," Tremaine assured her, turning to grab his coat with his free hand before pushing the diner's door open with his back. "Bye, Earl."

The man frowned.

Tremaine shook his head as he left the restaurant—and especially Earl—behind. He stopped short as he almost walked directly into Alisha. The urge to pull her close for a kiss to her mouth came swiftly. "Evenin', Professor Winters," he stated with a polite nod.

She looked confused at his formality, but her eyes then filled with understanding. "Same to you, Mr. Knowles," she replied as he stepped back to hold the door open for her.

"I got you a burger and chili fries," he whispered to her as she passed.

"Then I'll get dessert," she whispered back.

"Deal."

"Let the lady through without you quizzing her!" a familiar male voice declared.

Earl.

Several other townspeople inside the diner rallied him on.

"Yeah!"

"Leave the lady alone!"

"Pick on someone your own size!"

Alisha turned and walked backward inside the diner with an impish twinkle in her eyes. "Yes! Let me eat in *peace*, Mr. Knowles," she said with feigned anger, but then gave him a playful wink that no one but him saw.

Delicious images of him laying a nude Alisha over his lap as he lightly slapped her bottom gave him far too much satisfaction as he turned and made his way to his pickup truck.

Bam! Bam! Bam!

Alisha was awakened by a sudden banging and shot up in bed, alarmed. "Am I dreaming?" she asked, her heart pounding.

The pounding continued.

"I guess not," she muttered, answering her own question as she flung back the covers and rose from her bed.

Bam! Bam! Bam!

Fearful it was an intruder, she pondered what to do. Go search…with her rifle? Call the police…with her rifle? Sit it out and wait…with her rifle?

"Where *is* my rifle?" she asked aloud, looking left and right.

The noise, combined with the darkness of night, rattled her nerves, especially since she lived alone.

But I'm not alone...

"Tremaine!" she gasped, thankful she was not by herself in the big rambling mansion.

Alisha raced across the bedroom and then her sitting area to reach the double doors of her suite. She could hardly believe she was doing the ultimate no-no in horror movies by going toward possible danger. As she eased the doors open, all she knew was that she wanted to get to Tremaine.

A tall figure loomed over her in the darkness.

She released a high-pitched squeal and turned to flee.

"Alisha," Tremaine said as he pulled her trembling body close to his.

She wrapped her arms around his waist and held him tight. "Thank God, it's you," she said, sighing in relief, enjoying the strong feel of his body.

"I'm here. I got you," he promised, his deep voice seeming to echo inside his chest.

"What the hell was that?" she asked, her heart pounding in fear.

She was hardly a damsel in distress, but it felt good to have Tremaine offering security and protection. She appreciated him for that, especially after the trick she'd played on him earlier that night at the diner. Thankfully, they had laughed over her little stunt as they enjoyed their meal together, followed by Southern buttermilk pie.

"The late-night wind whipped an open shutter back

and forth. I just fixed it. I can do a proper job in the morning, but this should hold for tonight," he explained as he gave her back comforting rubs.

She bit her bottom lip to keep the moan she started to release from coming out. Realizing how tightly she was holding him and was pressing her softness against him, Alisha let her hands fall to her sides as she took a step back from him. And her awareness of him.

"Get some rest," he said, stepping back into the hall.

She nodded in agreement. "Thanks," she said, reaching for the door handle.

"Night," he said, then turned to cross the walkway.

Alisha watched him before releasing a grunt of pure appreciation as she closed her bedroom doors. She turned and pressed her back to them, still trembling from Tremaine's closeness.

Still longing for him.

Memories of the night they'd shared stepped forward and claimed her, nudging her to stop denying herself the passion. Never had she experienced such blinding electricity and heat.

And I may never feel it again.

"But I can't," she said, fighting to convince herself and to remember…

Family sticks together. Always.

As her womanhood pulsed to life and electricity shimmied over her body, the strength of her mantra was fading fast and her want of Tremaine Knowles was rising faster.

Just once more.

She always put her family first. Always. Problem-solving. Building up. Speaking truth. Interfering because she wanted the best for her siblings.

"Well, now I want the *best* for me," she said aloud, rushing across the suite to retrieve a condom before retracing her hurried steps to twist the knobs and fling the double doors open. Wide.

Tremaine, who was halfway across the walkway, paused.

Alisha pressed her hand to her throat and felt her pounding pulse as she stepped into the hall.

He looked back over his broad shoulder.

"Come here," she demanded softly, feeling emboldened.

His face filled with doubts. "Your family. My business," he said. "Alisha, we can't."

She walked over to him, removing her nightgown as she did.

"Alisha," he moaned in a sort of agony as he eyed the sway of her breasts and her hips as she moved to him.

"We have to," she urged him, reaching to press the condom in her hand to his bared chest. "Once more."

Tremaine looked down into her upturned face. "We said that the last time," he reminded her.

"But we'll get it out of our systems *this* time," she said, reaching down with her free hand to touch him there and finding it hard.

They both gasped.

With a harsh curse, Tremaine lifted Alisha up by her waist and turned her to press her back to the wall. She pressed her hands to his face as they deeply kissed while Tremaine used quick movements to lower the sleeping pants he was wearing to free his hardness to cover it with the condom.

Alisha cried out and pressed her face against his neck as he entered her with an upward thrust of his hips. Filling her. Satisfying her. And completing her.

She clung to him with her arms and legs as she enjoyed each deep and delicious stroke. Every rotation of his hips. Each pause as he struggled not to climax. His kisses. The tender bites from one shoulder to the next. The deep suckle of one of the pulse points at the base of her neck.

"Alisha, Alisha, Alisha," he moaned against her collarbone, his voice filled with both passion and a bit of torture.

She understood it well and felt it deeply.

But as he stroked them both to a riotous climax, she clung to the joy of the passion and ignored the torture of nothing real being born from their amazing chemistry. Nothing that would lead to *more*. Nothing that would last forever.

Eight

"I was hoping for more results at this point."

Tremaine picked up his snifter of aged scotch to take a deep sip before eyeing Fernando Del Rio III across the table of their prime seating at RCW Steakhouse. The nearly sixty-year-old man with dark hair streaked with gray and a beard was as stern in person as he was over the phone—perhaps more so. The man had the aura of a formidable businessman with killer instincts and shrewd eyes that were currently studying him. "So was I, Mr. Del Rio," he revealed. "It's baffling. There was nothing for the Winters family to gain by suddenly giving back an item they were culpable of stealing or hiding. In fact, they're taking a huge hit in the press, and with dissolving business ventures. I even got an inside word that k!smet's meteoric rise in new membership has slowed since the scandal, and they've lost existing members as well. Trey Winters and Misha Law are halting going forward with an IPO for the app."

Fernando shifted his eyes to look around at the dark wood furnishings and heavy drapes.

It was clear he was thinking carefully before he spoke. "I must admit, the truce suited my business interests more than the continuing of the feud," he said, tapping his fingers against the top of the table. "Business allies that were made with Winters and me are retreating as well."

"Yes, I know," Tremaine confessed with honesty, wanting his client to know that he was, in fact, on top of most issues surrounding those involved with the feud and the jewelry—all except how it ended up on the Winters estate. "The accusations and insults you and Joseph Winters keep flinging at each other in the press play a huge factor in that."

"I need to know the truth about the necklace," Fernando said, as if reading his thoughts. "And according to our contract, you have just one week to get me the answer."

Tremaine clenched his jaw even as he nodded in agreement.

"I'm sure you understand this can make or break Knowles Threat Solutions, based on my recommendation," Fernando said, his voice as cold and unrelenting as his stare.

Tremaine met his stare with one of his own, as he was never one to back down, not even with the man Preston had spoken of many times over the years. Growing up, Fernando the businessman was far more present in the lives of his daughter and son than Fernando the father. Preston often said not even the warmth of their mother's love could diminish Fernando's coldness. But as he grew older, Preston thought Fernando was mellowing. Tremaine couldn't see it. If this was mellow, what was he like before?

And that made Tremaine grateful for his father, who had provided far more love and guidance than money. For him, the former far outweighed the latter.

"Mr. Del Rio, I don't fail," Tremaine assured him.

Fernando gave him a look that said he better not. "My wife had a meeting, but she should be joining us for dessert and coffee," he said, lifting his snifter of scotch to take a sip.

"Actually, I have a lead I want to check out," Tremaine said, giving his stomach a light pat before reaching inside the black suede blazer over a matching silk shirt for his wallet to withdraw two crisp hundred-dollar bills to set on the table. He picked up his black Stetson from the seat of the empty chair beside him. "That porterhouse steak and side of goat cheese grits has me stuffed."

"Dinner is on me, Knowles," Fernando said, waving his hand dismissively.

"Thank you kindly, sir," he said, hearing his own Texas twang and drawing a smile. "But I always pay my way."

"No arguments, Fernando, because you would do the same," a woman's voice said.

Tremaine looked on in surprise as some of the hard lines on Fernando's face softened a bit as he looked up at his wife, who was now standing beside where he was sitting.

Love has a way of warming the coldest of hearts.

"It's good to see you, Mrs. Del Rio," Tremaine said, bending to press a polite kiss to the cheek of the dark-haired woman of average height who favored the actress Sandra Bullock. "Enjoy your dessert, but I doubt you'll find anything as good as the hummingbird cake you made the year I came home with Preston for Thanksgiving."

Gayle Del Rio laughed and gave him a bright smile that made her dark eyes twinkle. "And it is on the menu this year as well, Tremaine," she said as she bent slightly to press a warm kiss to Fernando's silver temples before claiming the seat next to her husband. "Will you be joining us again? You are more than welcome."

"Hopefully, he will not be in town because his work will be completed before then," Fernando said, handing his wife the leather-bound dessert menu. "Right, Knowles?"

Tremaine forced a smile. "Enjoy your dessert," he said to them, then turned to make his way past the other diners in the restaurant that served beef straight from the cattle ranch of the family of the owner, Rafe Cortes-Williams. As soon as he stepped outside the brick structure, he slid on his Stetson and dug his hands into the pockets of his blazer.

A trio of women came walking up the street toward him with their giggles echoing around them. He tipped his hat to them. "Evenin', ladies," he said.

"*Hey*, cowboy," they all said in flirty unison as the one closest to him trailed her fingernails across his chest as they passed, sending them all into another fit of giggles and bold glances back at him.

He just beamed before walking up the street. He was far from a cowboy, but the Stetson and his polished black boots let it be known he was all Texas, all the time. He reached his red truck, which was parked on the street, but paused before unlocking the door to look down the length of the street at the bright white Christmas lights. A brisk chill blew in and whipped against his cheeks and beard.

He shivered as he blew heat into his hands, then entered his vehicle. He was thankful for the heat that soon rose from the vents and his leather seats.

Tremaine tapped his knuckles against the steering wheel as he eyed the residents and visitors of Royal, Texas, enjoying late-night shopping at those businesses still open. It was a different pace from Dallas or Austin. A nice, relaxed one. Folks lingered over a cup of coffee and hot chocolate. Knew each other. Took care of each other. Not perfection, but definitely peaceful.

And especially Alisha.

Being in her presence, her aura—or her *energy*, as Golden put it—was calming.

He could be annoyed at a prospect leading nowhere, but seeing Alisha, being in the same room as her, just walking past her on the stairs, made him feel better. Lighter. Happier. Less stressed.

She was a shot of pure serotonin for him.

Even now, as he drove toward her home, he felt anticipation. But in a week, he would be gone back to his life in Austin—whether he solved the case of Diamond Gate or not. And if he proved the Winterses were complicit in the theft, it would be the nail in the coffin of possibly ever having a relationship with Alisha, because he would not conceal the truth no matter who was involved.

Not even Alisha.

He eyed her softly lit home in the distance as he turned down her street and felt pensive. Their dalliance was affecting his work. Pre-Alisha Tremaine would have searched the laptop she frequently left lying around her home, but he couldn't bring himself to violate her in that way. Staying at her estate had been solely to check more deeply into her, and he'd spent more time in her bed than searching through her files. Even though he knew she was keeping *something* from him.

Maybe it's time to ask her for the truth.

Tremaine frowned, surprised at the fear he felt if the truth tore them apart.

But there was no *them.*

There was no future.

Hell, I don't even know if we'll ever make love again.
Or if we should.

Tremaine was a clever man with great instincts. He knew that Alisha was just as intrigued by him as he was by her. He also knew her heart was tender. The last thing he wanted was to leave her hurt by their dalliance.

And he couldn't overlook that his integrity could be put in question.

"And according to our contract, you have just one week to get me the answer."

And my business.

"I'm sure you understand this can make or break Knowles Threat Solutions, based on my recommendation."

He pulled his truck to a stop next to Alisha's silver Porsche in front of her home. The windows were lit, giving it a warm and welcoming vibe. His eyes shifted to the solarium on the right of the house. His heart hammered as he saw her sitting there twisting her beloved locket on her wrist as she leaned in to look at the screen of her laptop. Her curly hair was up in a messy bun with a pencil—or two—stuck inside it. She was wearing a bulky sweater over her clothes and thick socks with rabbit ears. Her lips moved as she read something. Suddenly her eyes widened, and she bit her full bottom lip as she bounced on the chaise lounge and struck the air with her fist in what appeared to be victory or celebration.

For a moment he allowed himself to imagine he was coming to her this night just as he did every night before. That made his insides melt. He could see himself lying on the chaise beside her watching her as she worked—on the papers of those she taught as a professor, handling the business side of Odds & Ends or researching the history of some antique piece. It didn't matter. Just being near her was enough. And when her work was done, he would sit up, remove the pencils from her hair and dig his fingers through the curls to massage her sweetly scented scalp as he pressed her body down beneath his and kissed away any thought of work.

Alisha looked up suddenly and her face lit with surprise at seeing his truck sitting there. She smiled and waved at him with her fingertips. It was clear she was happy to see him, matching his mood.

Hell with it.

Tremaine climbed from the truck and gave her a wave as he made his way around it to walk over to the solarium entrance. Every fiber of his being knew that he had to free himself of his distraction with Professor Alisha Winters, but with every step that drew him closer to her, he could not find the will to do so.

"Have a good night, Professor Winters."

Alisha gave her last student a smile as he opened the door to Odds & Ends and exited. With just one more session, she would be saying goodbye to the group of people she had come to enjoy guiding through their theses on precolonial Africa. Research was a cornerstone of their future career and she felt honored to play a role in their journey. It also meant she could focus on a new course she wanted to present to the dean of history that built upon her own doctoral thesis on the role of research in the antique culture of precolonial Africa.

Lining the brick walls were beautiful photographs

of ancient relics from African empires. Rock art, sculptures, pottery, masks, furniture, weapons and tools. She longed to purchase more pieces but those would be for her personal collection. Right now, a good chunk of her finances was tied up in her antique store and the renovation of the estate.

One day, though.

With a slight yawn, Alisha removed her round tortoiseshell spectacles before she began to finish closing down her store. She turned off the lights and checked that the rear door was locked, then set the alarm and left the store. She had just climbed behind the wheel of her car when her cell phone lit up and vibrated. She smiled at a picture of her brother Marcus on the screen.

She answered with a smile, putting the phone on speaker. "Hey, little brother," she said.

"By two whole years," he reminded her with a drawl.

"Absolutely," she assured him, cranking the car and wishing her vintage baby had an automatic start, since the chill of fall during the night made her shiver. "Two years of wisdom and experience."

Marcus grunted.

"But that's not why you called," she told him.

"No. No, it's not," he admitted, sounding solemn.

Alisha sat back in the driver's seat. "Okay," she said.

"Maybe it's time to tell the truth about Eliza and the necklace, Lish," he stated.

She let her head fall back against the rest and pinched the bridge of her nose. "Marcus—"

"Listen, this thing is getting out of hand and the

reputation—and business—of the family is taking a beating while we protect someone we loved…but also the same someone who stole the necklace," he pronounced.

There *was* validity in what he said.

But…

"What if revealing the truth makes it worse than it is now," she said, tapping the tips of her almond-shaped neutral nails against the steering wheel.

"What if the private investigator living in your house finds out about the letter?" he asked. "I've hidden it well, but still…"

Tremaine.

Last night, there in her solarium, Alisha had set aside any concerns about the necklace, the letter or either family in the century-long feud. She'd straddled Tremaine's lap and removed his Stetson as they shared a long kiss as his hands settled on the curve of her buttocks. Again. The bliss of their sex—their connection—had outweighed it *all*.

"Alisha? You there?" Marcus asked.

The vision of her wearing his hat as she slowly rode Tremaine with his pants down around the top of his cowboy boots disappeared.

"Huh?" she asked with a shake of her head. "Marcus, I need you to bring me the letter."

"I buried it at Eliza's grave."

"You what?"

"Don't worry—I put it in a plastic baggie. I'll grab it tonight, but what if Knowles finds it, Alisha?" he asked.

"He wouldn't check my things, Marcus," she said, not hiding her defense of the sexy private investigator. "But I'll put it in the safe at my store."

Marcus's silence was lengthy.

"You still there?" she asked, reaching to turn up the heat.

"Why all the faith in a man you've only known a week?" he asked.

Not this again.

"Video surveillance," she said, telling a half-truth as she checked behind her before reversing out of her parking spot.

The full truth was she trusted Tremaine. She was the one who'd concealed a theft from him.

"You gotta get him out of there," Marcus said. "And don't give me the line about your house and your privacy. Concealing that letter from our family involves *me* because I'm the one who hid it."

True.

As Alisha drove down the street, the white Christmas lights twinkled against the windows of her car. On the day after Thanksgiving, the city would erect the official Christmas tree and truly kick off the holiday season that swelled with the joy of both giving and receiving. Christmas carols. Family and friends gathering. Delicious meals. The squeals of children's joy at their gifts from Santa. All of it rang of the magic of Christmas and made her smile a little.

"Fernando hired him for just two weeks and then Trem—*Mr. Knowles* is headed back to Austin," she said as her smile faded. "Just one more week."

The thought of never seeing him again was sobering. *What have I started?*

It was pure folly to put her own pleasure ahead of family loyalty, but with her feelings toward Tremaine Knowles, that made her a fool.

"I gotta go, Marcus," she said, her brow furrowing. "Bring the letter to the store tomorrow, first thing."

"Alisha—"

"Let's just stay the course. *Please*," she stressed, before ending the call with a tap of her finger on the screen.

During her entire drive home, Alisha knew she had to set things back to rights with Tremaine. No matter how delicious, sex had to be off the table. It was clear, as her heart ached at the thought of him leaving, that their liaison had become "complicated."

"For me, anyway," she admitted aloud softly with a tender pang of hurt.

Then she released a quiet curse.

"No more, Alisha," she reprimanded herself. "I will get this all straight as soon as I lay eyes on him."

But the sex.

"Doesn't matter," she said aloud, answering her own thought.

And the contagious laughter we share.

"Nope."

Or the talks we have in that warm afterglow after sharing fiery climaxes.

"No sex means no climaxes means no afterglow and thus no talks," she affirmed firmly as she turned down the street she lived on. "So that solves *that*."

But then a memory surfaced...

"The softness of your skin is addictive," Tremaine had whispered against her nape one night as he was lying behind her in the middle of her bed.

Then he'd pressed a kiss where his words had caressed the sensitive skin, evoking goose bumps and a shiver.

Alisha pulled her car to a stop beside Tremaine's truck. Her seminar session meant getting home later than normal but she was still surprised to find him home first.

Not. Not home. This is not his home.

She reached for her bag and briefcase before exiting her car. As she crossed the courtyard, she paused when the lights of the foyer suddenly shut off. "Ummmm," she said, arching an eyebrow and feeling some trepidation.

One of the double doors opened and Tremaine stepped onto the porch.

He looked delicious in dark jeans, a black V-neck sweater and a matching beanie pulled low over his eyes. He smiled and his white teeth beamed against his beard.

Sexy mother—

"Everything okay?" she asked as she continued forward.

"You look especially good today," he said, his eyes taking in the flared faux-leather dress she was wearing with high-heeled ankle booties and patterned sheer stockings.

"Thank you," she said with a slight curtsy.

He jogged down the steps to take her bags into one

of his hands as he stood behind her. "Okay, close your eyes before I cover them," he said.

And she did because she did indeed trust him.

"What's going on?" she asked as he guided her forward.

"A surprise. Duh," he joked.

She smiled.

"Careful of the step," he said. "And one more."

The scent of his cologne on his wrist teased her. It was warm, spicy, and she knew it well. She resisted the urge to free her tongue and lick his pulse.

"Okay. Open your eyes."

Alisha did and immediately gasped in surprise and pleasure at the towering, elaborately decorated tree stationed between the landing of the double steps leading to the second floor. The bright white light twinkled like the stars against the inky darkness of the unlit foyer. She pressed her hands together under her chin. "It's beautiful," she whispered, taking in the elaborate ornaments and long lengths of ribbons running down the sides to the floor. Down the length of both banisters were lit garlands, and a huge wreath hung from the banister of the second-floor walkway. It was more than she could have ever imagined for her first real holiday in her home.

"The guy I usually get my tree from in Austin drove this big boy here as a favor, and his wife decorated it," Tremaine said, stepping up to stand beside her to look up at the towering Virginia pine tree. "I know you've been so busy with Odds & Ends, your duties as a professor and renovating this house that

I figured someone who loved Christmas as much as you must not have the time to do this for herself. You like it? Is it okay?"

See? This is why it's so hard to deny myself this man.

"Watching a Christmas movie—either *Jingle Jangle: A Christmas Journey* or *A Christmas Story*, to be exact—while sipping peppermint hot chocolate would make this night complete," she said, tilting her head back to take in the sweet-faced gold angel atop the tree.

"Done," he said. "Especially since there are also smaller trees in the solarium, the den and your bedroom."

"Seriously?" she asked him, bashfully looking down at the tips of her boots.

"Yes," he assured her.

She had to wrap her arms around herself to keep from clutching at him. "Thank you so much. This is my first Christmas here, you know," she said, feeling immensely touched by the kind gesture.

"Then that makes all of this all the more better," he said. "Right?"

This man she had once pegged as an enemy had proven her wrong again and again.

Alisha dared to look at him.

Big mistake.

She was completely charmed by the twinkle in his eyes and his smile as he awaited confirmation of her happiness.

With one step and lifting on the toes of her boots, she wrapped her arms around his neck and gave his lips a hot lick before kissing him deeply. Soon, his hands were at her sides and lifting her body up against him as he released a grunt of pleasure that echoed in his chest.

She tugged her head back to break the kiss before she rested her forehead against his. "We can't keep doing this, Tremaine," she whispered, even as she longed to taste his mouth again.

"I know," he admitted.

She took a deep breath and nodded several times, trying to convince herself that they were right and their desire for each other was wrong. Her obligation to her family and his to his business had to be uppermost.

"This is not easy," she admitted, looking into the deep brown of his eyes and seeing the same conflict she felt. "I need you to know that."

Tremaine brought up his hand to softly massage her nape as he guided her head down until her face was nestled against his neck. He pressed a kiss to her cheek. "It's not easy for me, either, Alisha," he said.

She didn't quite know how long they stood there holding each other with the lights from the holiday decor breaking up the darkness. She didn't want to let him go—physically or otherwise—but in time, Tremaine set her back down on her heels and released her with obvious reluctance. They each took a step back, even as their eyes remained locked on each other.

Tremaine eased past her to jog up the stairs.

She watched him as she ran her fingers through her hair.

He paused and hung his head.

She tensed, knowing he was about to say something he didn't want to, but felt he *had* to.

It was a reminder that the truth about the necklace lingered there between them, pushing them apart.

"Alisha, my gut tells me there is something you're not telling me about the necklace," he said, not looking back at her.

It was the first time since he had been staying on the estate that he'd mentioned the discovered jewelry to her again. The lie she told him then, as compared to now, felt different. Like a betrayal. In just one week, everything between them had changed. She closed her eyes and turned away from him to look out one of the side windows beside the doors.

"Listen, this thing is getting out of hand and the reputation—and business—of the family is taking a beating while we protect someone we loved...but also the same someone who stole the necklace."

As Marcus's words replayed, she felt tempted to follow his guidance. To tell the truth.

"Alisha?" Tremaine said.

At this point, the truth would only make things worse.

She didn't turn to see if he was now looking at her. "No, there's nothing," she lied, ignoring the guilt that pierced her gut.

"I wish I could believe that," he said.

It was not in her nature to be deceptive.

Alisha continued to look out at the courtyard. When she looked up at the stairs, he was still standing there. Still not looking directly at her. Still waiting for her to tell the truth.

She bit down on her bottom lip to prevent doing just that. She crossed the foyer and quickly scurried up the other set of stairs to make her way to her suite. Once she closed the doors, she leaned back against the wood, covering her face with her hands.

Everything in her world was completely upside down.

With the weariest of sighs, she took heavy steps across her suite to fall face-first across the middle of the bed. Somehow, the perfect guy had come into her life in the worst possible way.

"Damn," she said, giving in to the tender ache of her heart and letting her tears of sadness and regret rise and then fall as she turned on her side to reach for a pillow to clutch.

Tremaine's hand gripped the banister as he fought not to follow her retreating frame with his body as he did with his eyes. He was torn between wanting to comfort her and needing to know if his gut was correct that Alisha was hiding something from him. Tonight, her actions just confirmed that for him. Her answer had been damning.

He felt tense.

More than just his investigative work for the Del Rios, the idea of Alisha lying to him was unsettling. It wasn't in alignment with whom he hoped—thought— she was. Not after the week they'd shared.

The passion.

The connection.

Clenching his jaw, he looked back over his shoulder and his gaze landed on her briefcase, which he'd set on the table in the foyer. Her laptop could be in it. He released a heavy breath.

In any other scenario as an investigator and former police officer, he would have checked the devices of those linked to the case. He had to be honest that his involvement with Alisha—his attraction to her—had caused a lapse in judgment. Even a lack of integrity.

He cleared his throat.

The Del Rios had hired—and paid him—to investigate, not to become enamored of Alisha Winters. They trusted him. His friend Preston trusted him.

But Alisha.

He literally shook his head. That was his flaw. This week he had taken more consideration of Alisha than of his clients.

Yet another heavy breath freed itself from him as he continued to eye the briefcase.

Whom do I choose?

The Del Rios or Alisha?

Where does my loyalty lie?

Business or pleasure.

The rubber had met the road.

Nine

Alisha rolled over in her bed and opened her eyes with her line of view falling on the lit tree next to her unlit fireplace. She thought of Tremaine. It was hard not to. Her regrets were many.

The letter Marcus had hid. The lie she'd told. The secret she would not tell. And, above them all, truthfully, was that there could never be more for her and this man who had very quickly come to mean something to her.

Tremaine was just doing the job that he'd been hired to do.

I'm the one lying. Someone in my family was in the wrong. Not the Del Rios. And not Tremaine.

And the truth was that she genuinely liked him. His laughter came with ease. His smile stayed ready.

His humor. The scent of his cologne. His insight. His charm. Intelligence. Sex appeal. Those eyes.

There wasn't a thing about him she didn't like—except his role investigating the sudden reappearance of the Del Rio necklace. And only because it kept them from—from...

From what?

Even without the line drawn by the Del Rio and Winters feud, who said there was a future?

Tremaine lives in Austin. And who said he even wanted a serious relationship with me, or anyone?

Alisha rose from the bed and walked over to open the floor-length curtains at the windows that flanked the fireplace. There was an early morning frost on the ground, but the afternoon Texas sun would eventually melt any sign of it away easily. She glanced over to the courtyard, looking down at his red pickup truck parked next to her Porsche.

And what would I want in a perfect world?

She wrapped her arms around herself as she leaned against the window's frame.

Love. Kids. My own little family.

Alisha had never run from the idea of falling in love. She just had yet to find the man who could match her energy. Someone to make her laugh. Hold her when she was crying. Understand her when she stepped into full scholarly mode or spent hours chasing down one antique. Protect her when she was afraid. Challenge her strength. Match her sexually.

Until Tremaine.

She took a deep inhale and released it through

pursed lips—the breath steamed against the glass pane as she reckoned with the truth. Somehow, in such a short amount of time, she had come to care very deeply for Tremaine Knowles. Against all odds.

He was everything she had ever looked for in a man, and above all, in his presence, she just felt more alive. As if he completed her. Elevated her. Made her whole. A missing piece.

"Damn," she whispered, letting her forehead lightly rest against the glass as she closed her eyes and felt her heart swell with all of the emotions she experienced.

The joy at even finding him and enjoying him for a little while. The sadness at having to let him go before she truly began to consider all of the what-ifs.

She smiled a bit at the vision of her looking down at a beautiful dark-skinned baby boy with his eyes so much like Tremaine's.

Or a daughter. A sweet baby girl.

At that moment, it all felt so very possible.

She couldn't believe she was even able to envision building a life—a family—with a man she had not known for very long, but he was the first man to break past the shield she placed around herself as she sorted through suitors to find—

At the sound of the front door being slammed echoing throughout the house, Alisha opened her eyes to see Tremaine striding toward his truck.

"The one," she whispered, reaching out to press her hand against the glass as if to actually touch him.

He was so tall. So strong. Handsome.

Just perfect.

It could never be.

"Alisha, my gut tells me there is something you're not telling me about the necklace," he'd said.

"No, there's nothing," she had lied.

"I wish I could believe that," he had said.

As she watched him open the driver's-side door, her heart ached. What would he do if he discovered that she had hidden the truth from him the whole time? Even as she invited him into her home to stay?

She saw firsthand the long hours he put into his investigation. She shared seduction with him. And had formed a friendship of sorts. She knew of the importance of the investigation to his business and still, she'd said nothing.

Tremaine paused in getting into his truck and looked directly at her window. The fall sun lit upon his face and seemed to make the tips of his long lashes glisten. His dark skin gleamed and the whites of his eyes were brilliant...almost as much as his smile.

The man was beautiful—inside and out.

Tremaine gave her a brief wave that she returned before he climbed in his truck and soon pulled away with a roar of his engine.

Alisha stepped back from the window and closed the curtain. "What a mess," she said, releasing a deep breath.

She looked down at the clothes she'd worn yesterday, having slept in them—including the ankle boots—and found them to be horribly wrinkled. With a shake of her head, she spread her arms wide and fell face-first onto the middle of her bed. "An entire mess," she mumbled into the covers with her face pressed into them.

She didn't know that covering for their great-grandmother would leave her a victim of the collateral damage. A true ache of her heart. She turned her head to the side on the bed, but pressed her eyes closed as she wrestled with the nervous anxiousness she felt. The sadness. Her guilt. Her fear of the truth being exposed.

All of it.

Never had she thought she would be so overwhelmed by it all. So affected.

She raised her head to look for her cell phone, but remembered she'd left it and the rest of her things downstairs. With all the strength she could muster, she climbed off the bed and made her way out of her bedroom to her desk in the outer room of the suite. She picked up her cordless landline to call the only person she could tell the absolute truth to and know she would have a soft place to land.

The phone rang twice before it was answered.

It was time for some truth to be told.

"Mom," Alisha said, her voice filled with the troubles of her emotions. "I need you."

"On my way," Camille promised without hesitation.

She nodded as if her mother could see her. And once the line disconnected, she remained sitting there, looking off into the distance but not really focusing or seeing anything. Just running over everything in her mind. The good and bad. The highs and lows.

Tremaine Knowles's entry into the game had changed

everything, including the carefully laid rules she'd made for herself.

The sound of the doorbell echoing jarred her and made her realize just how long she had been sitting in a daze. She rose and left the suite. The towering Christmas tree glowed as bright as the morning sun and the scent of the tree was heavy in the air. As Alisha made her way down the stairs, she found it hard to take her eyes off the beauty of it and not remember the gesture Tremaine had made in surprising her with it. But not even it could erase the truth of the divide between them. The obligations neither could deny. And so, the night of a wonderful surprise had ended with a distance between them.

When we should've made love on the floor as the lights from the tree flashed against our sweaty bodies, she thought, allowing herself the vision of it, if not the true lasting memory.

As soon as Alisha opened the door, Camille stepped inside and pulled her close. "What's going on?" she asked. "What happened?"

For a moment, Alisha allowed herself to cling to her mother and wish for the days of childhood with no real worries. She stepped back and turned to sit on the steps as she rested her head against the banister and stared at the lit tree. Slowly, and holding nothing back, she told her mother the story of her and Tremaine. At some point, Camille sat beside her on the step and pressed a consoling hand to her knee.

"I never knew I could feel so much so quickly for someone," she confessed with softness.

"Oh, Alisha," Camille said with a sigh.

"And a part of me believes he feels the same way, too," Alisha admitted, her line of vision blurred by the tears that rose.

Camille rubbed her back. "There is a...*lot* to unpack," she said.

Alisha nodded. "Like Eliza's letter," she revealed, then told her mom the truth—how Marcus and Jessica found the necklace and letter in the hidden cellar room and the discussion about what to do after the discovery. "I thought we were doing what was best for the family—just like I always do."

"And just like I always tell you, daughter, stop taking the weight of the family on your shoulders," Camille said, moving her hand to Alisha's chin to raise it and force her to meet her eye. "You can't survive setting yourself on fire to keep others warm, my child."

Alisha felt contrite.

"This was not your problem to solve," Camille continued. "Especially with a lie."

Alisha nodded in agreement.

"This is too big. I can't keep this from your father."

Alisha jumped to her feet in alarm. "No!" she exclaimed.

"Calm down," Camille assured her, tugging her daughter's wrist to pull her back down to sit. "Not your personal business—you never owe anyone a look under your clothes no matter the circumstance."

Alisha was able to muster a smile. "Under your clothes" was something her mother's mother would say referring to someone's sexual history, and she loved when her mother used one of Granny's adages.

"But I must tell him about what Eliza did...and the letter," Camille said. "I will not place a lie between your father and me."

Alisha looked over at the Christmas tree. "Trust me, I understand now more than ever," she said, her voice sounding hollow to her own ears. "It is the lie that lingers."

Camille groaned in dismay. "That sounds like a great Lifetime movie, but a horrible Hallmark one," she said.

Alisha feigned a pained expression although she did laugh a little.

"Your dad will want to see the letter."

"Okay."

They fell silent. Alisha was glad for the comfort of her mother.

"Tremaine Knowles *is* a divinely handsome man," Camille said, filling the silence.

Yes. Yes, he is.

"And an enemy of the family by association," Alisha said as if to remind herself of something she had forgotten.

"There should be no enemies," Camille said, giving her daughter's shoulder a squeeze before rising to cross the foyer. "To be honest, a century-long feud, because a woman chose to love one man over another, is the height of male ego."

"A desire to be with someone will make you do some crazy things," Alisha said, referring to both her attraction to Tremaine and the love both men held for her great-grandmother Eliza.

Camille moved to stand in front of the tree, tilting her head back to take in every foot. "You do love Christmas," she said, glancing over at her daughter with a smile. "This may perhaps be one of the sweetest things ever done by a man that cares for a woman."

Alisha rose from the step and moved over to stand beside her. "I wish I could have met him under different circumstances," she admitted.

"Everything is just as it is supposed to be," Camille said.

"What have I done?" Alisha asked.

"Fallen in love," her mother said before pulling her daughter's head to her shoulders and then pressing a kiss to the top of her head amid the bundle of curls.

Alisha looked down at her bracelet and lightly touched each of the metal heart-shaped lockets. Each of the loves of her life. Her mother. Her stepfather. Her birth father. And the last one left empty for the one she would give her heart…and hoped they would give theirs back in return.

Do I love Tremaine? I like him a lot. But love?

Oddly, the refrain from the song "Could You Be Loved" by Bob Marley & the Wailers played in her head: "Could you be, could you be loved?"

Could I? Am I?

"Listen, go upstairs and get freshened up and I will make you some of my grandmother's honeybun pancakes," Camille said.

"In that?" Alisha asked, taking in the ivory leather

trench coat adorned with gold buttons that her mother was wearing over a matching tailored wool pantsuit that screamed designer runway.

Camille pressed a hand to her chest, and her massive diamond ring sparkled. "A mother is a mother no matter what she wears," she said with feigned haughtiness. "But I will use an apron."

"Of course, Queen," Alisha said with a slightly mocking bow before turning to retrieve her purse and briefcase from the foyer table, still surprised she had left both downstairs last night. She paused. In his search for the truth, had Tremaine been tempted to check her laptop? She shook her head in refusal of that notion.

He wouldn't violate my privacy like that. Not after everything we've shared.

"And we'll talk some more about Eliza, her two men, the necklace and this letter you and your brother kept from us," her mother added.

"For those pancakes, I'll tell *all* my secrets," she said, climbing the stairs as her mother made her way toward the hall leading into the kitchen.

Camille's laughter echoed behind her.

Tremaine was wrestling with his conscience so he followed the urge to get away. From Alisha. Her home. The Winters family and the Del Rios. The entire town of Royal. Hopefully, the three-hour drive to Austin would give him the courage he needed to actually view the files and discover if Alisha was lying to him the way his instincts told him that she was.

I don't want to be right. Not this time.

He looked down at the flash drive in his left hand as he steered with his right. He stroked it with his thumb.

What would it mean if he discovered that she had been playing him the whole time? That it was the reason for the invite to stay at her home? Seduce him to distraction.

"No," he said aloud.

The passion between them had been real.

Hadn't it?

His grip on the flash drive tightened and he was almost tempted to break it in half to toss the remnants out of the window onto Interstate 35. But he couldn't. He had just received his weekly payment from the Del Rios for his work. Accessing Alisha's files was a part of that.

"Damn," he said, then tossed the flash drive onto the passenger seat atop his briefcase and accelerated forward.

He pressed the button to activate the phone system. "Call the office," he ordered.

It rang far too many times.

"Knowles Threat Solutions," Golden said when she finally answered. "How can we be of service?"

"By answering the phone in a timely manner, Golden," he said, switching lanes with ease.

She giggled, bubbly as ever. "Anything meant to be, will be. No need to force anything. Remember to…" she began.

"Go with the flow," they said in unison, with his voice dripping in sarcasm.

"Yes! You got it," Golden enthused.

"Let's see if the flow of unemployment is easy to go with," he drawled.

"Not cool, boss," Golden said. "And also not possible. I did a tarot card reading on myself and there was nothing on a change in employment."

"And were you warned that I was headed into the office today?" he asked.

The line went silent.

"So that's what that warning was about?" she said.

He shook his head, ever the skeptic. "Be there in about an hour," he said.

"Oh. Oh? O-kay," Golden said before ending the call.

Tremaine was sure she would use the time to correct whatever she'd implemented in his absence. She was a testament to the fact that he was loyal. Perhaps to a fault.

His loyalty to not just his business, but his friend Preston, may very well be keeping him from following his inclination—no, his desire—to have more with Alisha. And he did want more.

More of her.

Her smiles. Her touches. Her kisses. Her sighs of pleasure as he stroked inside of her.

But not just that.

Her wisdom. Her eyes twinkling at him as she laughed. Her fiery spirit and protective nature. Her love of her family. Her uniqueness. Her honor and respect for both of her fathers. Her love of books and history. Her desire to learn. To fix. To improve everything.

And everyone.

Alisha Winters—the beautiful professor with the bright eyes and smile—seemed to be exactly everything he wanted in a woman. Everything he had always said would make him settle down.

The right one.

His eyes darted over to the flash drive. He couldn't ignore or escape the feeling of foreboding.

Just as strongly as his gut had told him there was something Alisha was keeping from him, that same instinct said that this connection between them was real. How could both things be right? He could never see himself with a woman involved in a robbery in any way. Or one who lied to him. And not just when they'd first met, when she had no obligation to tell him anything, but after everything they shared.

We shared sex, he thought, but he knew that was a lie.

There had been more. Much more.

And I want even more than that.

But how?

How to overcome the obligations of her family for Alisha and his to his business and friendship. A full-blown relationship may give the notion of impropriety to his investigation. And that, along with the wrath of Fernando Del Rio, could destroy his business before it ever really began.

And who says Alisha even wants more?

Gripping the wheel and shifting to get more comfortable in his seat, Tremaine made the rest of the drive in silence. His thoughts focused on the traffic and he purposefully avoided any further contemplation of Alisha and any hopes for a future.

He was glad to make the final turn into the crowded parking lot outside of the massive four-story office complex in downtown Austin. He stretched his tall frame as soon as he climbed from the vehicle. He went around to the passenger side and opened the door, looking down at the flash drive before grabbing it and his briefcase. He entered the building that housed an abundance of office spaces, coworking units and retail units. The corner offices of Knowles Threat Solutions were on the second floor, and soon he was striding into the stylish modern three-room suite that was thankfully free of whatever incense, candles and crystals his bubbly assistant surely had lying around in his absence.

Golden jumped to her feet. "Welcome back," she said. "I ordered in your favorite acai fruit bowl and green smoothie you love."

His stomach grumbled as he took the items from her. "Thank you. I'll admit I have not been eating as healthy in Royal," he said, moving past her cluttered desk to his spacious office.

"Do you need anything?" Golden asked from the doorway, having followed him.

Alisha.

He shook his head. "Some peace. No calls. It's like I'm still in Royal," he said, setting his briefcase, the flash drive and his late breakfast atop his large ebony desk before claiming his seat. He leaned back against it and looked up at the ceiling.

Even at that moment, being far away from her, Tremaine missed Alisha.

He smiled as a memory of her laughing at something he'd said played so clearly in his head.

Bzzzzzz. Bzzzzzz. Bzzzzzz.

He shifted his head on the rest of his leather office chair to look at his briefcase. Inside, his cell phone vibrated loudly. He leaned over to reach for it and check the screen.

Preston.

He set the phone back atop his desk after silencing the ring.

He looked at the flash drive. There was no need to talk. Not yet.

With a heavy breath, Tremaine reached for the drive and plugged it into his twenty-two-inch all-in-one monitor. What he felt as he logged into the secure system and began to download the files was nervous—a feeling not familiar to him. But never had the stakes felt so high.

Slowly—methodically—Tremaine began to go through each file. Most were related to her work. He felt more and more scurrilous. There was nothing. He had betrayed her trust for nothing.

Tremaine looked up and did a double take to find Golden standing in the doorway watching him with a look of sadness in her eyes. "What's wrong?" he asked.

"Just checking on you," she said. All of her usual light and bubbly nature was gone and solemnity remained. "I'm here if you need me."

And then he knew that something was indeed off. So wrong that his intuitive assistant was at the ready. His heart pounded and dread filled his bones. Golden *knew* things—whether he liked it or not.

"Could you get me a cup of coffee?" he asked, turning his attention back to the computer screen.

"Boss—"

"Thanks, Golden," he said with more firmness than was needed.

He felt contrite when he saw nothing but more concern on her face. Golden was a firm believer that grudges and other low vibrational feelings were roadblocks to progress and purpose in life. With one last look of concern, she walked away.

With his gut clenched, Tremaine refocused on sifting through the files and came upon a folder of downloaded bank statements. One by one. Month by month.

"Damn," he said softly at a large money transfer during the same time of the discovery of the necklace.

It was sizable.

And condemning.

Tremaine jumped up from his seat and turned to look out the window at the view of downtown Austin, but he didn't truly focus on anything except for the tight feeling in his gut. He slid his hands into the pockets of the leather coat he was still wearing. He tightened and released his jaw as he tried to make the new pieces to the puzzle fit.

What could that money be for?

The Winterses were a wealthy family, and it was

clear from her records that Alisha was a woman of means, but transactions of that size were not common for her. It stuck out—particularly with the timing around the discovery of the necklace.

Had she purchased the necklace the way he'd first thought?

But to what end?

To resell it at Odds & Ends for profit.

Then why turn it over to the Del Rios?

Tremaine frowned before he turned and removed the rolled evidence board from his briefcase to open it atop his desk. With his hands pressed down on either side of it, he leaned down to look at the cast of players in the mystery of the missing jewelry. "Make it make sense," he whispered as he moved his eyes to each person, ultimately lingering on Alisha.

Everything pointed to her involvement.

Her house.

Her money.

Her antique store.

Her lies?

That stung like the piercing of the hot blade of a knife. Deep and visceral.

Grabbing the small bronze statue on the corner of his desk, Tremaine used it and a photo of his parents to hold down the sides of the board. He stepped back and leaned against the windowsill as he stroked his beard. His eyes shifted from the evidence board to the download of the bank statement still open on his computer screen. He then looked back to Alisha, her brother Marcus and his fiancée, Jessica. And then back to the screen.

The story was Marcus had arrived at the house and there was a package slipped through the mail slot. No video cameras on the property at that time. How convenient.

Did Marcus find the package meant for Alisha by accident? Then Alisha convinced Marcus to lie for her? Family protecting family?

Perhaps Alisha had just wanted to possess the jewelry so closely tied to the history of her family?

Each scenario he came up with, Alisha was at the root of it all.

"Alisha, my gut tells me there is something you're not telling me about the necklace," he had said to her.

"No, there's nothing," she had said.

"I wish I could believe that," he had replied.

And what if it all had been a lie, including her desire for him? Had her seduction been more about distracting him?

It had worked. He had nearly gotten so lost in her that he had missed a huge clue that had been right there all along.

Fool.

In his life, he had been deceived, and at times had done the deceiving in the search for truth in a case. His mother would always tell him that people loved a fool because they could use a fool.

"So don't be nobody's fool, son."

"Too late," he muttered.

He needed to talk to Alisha and report his findings to the Del Rio family.

But first, the energy building up in him—of frustration, doubts, anger and indecision—made him feel caged.

He strode out of his office and past Golden's desk. "I'm headed home to change and then go for a long run," he said over his shoulder, reaching for the handle of the door.

"Wait? What's wrong? I just feel like something is off," Golden called behind him. "What happened?"

Tremaine paused in the open doorway with a snort of derision, so lost in his negative emotions that not even that aura of positivity that he loved about her could shift his dark mood. "Don't you and your angels *know*?" he asked, his voice dripping with sarcasm, before he stepped into the hall and slammed the door behind him.

Ten

The next evening, after a long day that ended in a bubble bath, Alisha was in her kitchen making herself hot chocolate by melting pieces of her sister's handmade bittersweet chocolate in whole milk with sugar, fresh vanilla, almond extract and cinnamon. She added a generous pour of Amaretto for a nice kick. She poured herself a cup and turned to lean against the counter as she held it in both palms before taking a sip. The same question that had plagued her since the day before lingered.

Have I come to love Tremaine?

More than twenty-four hours later and she was still reluctant to give just what she felt for him that name.

That's not how love works. Is it?

She thought of him, and a warmth spread over her

body like a heated blanket pulled up to shield her from the most brutal chill of winter.

The thought of never seeing him again filled her with melancholy.

Even his disappearance had her feeling the type of concern that spoke of more than just lust. All last night she had checked her bedroom window to see if his truck had parked beside her vehicle. She had been unable to focus on any of the many tasks on her to-do list. Her sleep had been difficult. Imaginings of accidents and him being hurt troubled her. All day today, concern for him lingered as she worked at the store.

Since staying at the estate, it was the first time he had been gone for more than twenty-four hours.

He's not obligated to check in with me. He's my guest, not my—

Alisha paused in taking another sip of her cocoa. "My what?" she whispered into the steam as it softly kissed her lips.

The sound of the door of a vehicle closing echoed from outside.

Alisha's heart pounded. She sat her cup atop the counter and turned to look out to see Tremaine's truck parked in the courtyard. She hung her head for a bit, feeling relief that he was okay. Her concern had been real.

And now her curiosity had replaced it.

She tightened the straps of her black robe, embroidered with flowers, that she wore over a floor-length black slip. As she left the kitchen, she removed the satin bonnet she had on to protect her curls during

sleep and fluffed her curls with the tips of her fingernails. By the time she climbed the stairs and eased
through the protective plastic barrier, her heart rate
had slowed a bit. She was anxious to see him.

Just to lay eyes on him. To see his smile. To have
him say something to make her smile.

Or blush.

But the last time they'd seen each other, things had
been tense.

Where do we stand now?

Alisha was nervous as she stepped in front of his
open bedroom doorway. He was packing.

"Oh," she said, leaning against the door frame.

He looked over at her and there was a coolness in
his eyes that chilled her.

"You're leaving?" she asked.

He gave her a stiff nod. "Yes, I think it's for the best,
considering," he said, his tone colder than his look.

"Considering what?" she asked, stepping into the
room to stand at the foot of the bed.

Tremaine shoved the folded clothes he held into
his leather duffel before looking over at her. His eyes
were filled with turbulence. "Were you involved in
the reappearance of the necklace?" he asked. "Other
than what you've already said?"

Yes.

She forced herself not to break the hold of their eyes.
To not appear as guilty as she felt. "Maybe it is best
you leave if you plan to spend every moment question-
ing me," she said.

"Nice way to avoid the question, Alisha," he said

with a shake of his head as he returned his focus to packing his clothing.

She eyed him carefully. There was a difference. The man before her was not curious, but angry. Something had changed him. "I think it would be fair to tell me what's going on right now, Tremaine," she said.

He tossed the clothes he was holding onto the bed before walking away to pace as he rubbed his hand over his mouth and beard. "I don't want you to lie to me anymore, Alisha," he said, looking over at her with such intensity, then walking over to stand before her. "I am avoiding giving you another chance to look me in my face and lie because then everything we shared might be a damn lie, too."

This time, she did shift her gaze away for a moment. It was a revelation she instantly regretted.

He swore and stepped back from her, before turning to pace once again. This time when he stopped, his eyes were filled with some emotion she couldn't decipher. Not until he spoke. "Was everything between us just your way of distracting me off the case?" he asked, not shielding his disappointment in her and disgust of her.

Wow.

"My body is not for sale for anyone or anything," she said, feeling her annoyance with him rise.

He snorted in derision before turning away.

She walked over to grab his arm and turn him back toward her. "What is your problem?" she snapped.

His eyes searched her face. "What's wrong with me?

Even now I just want to kiss you," he said, and then deeply frowned. "Even now I feel like *I* betrayed *you*."

"Betrayed me how?" she asked in confusion.

"I checked your laptop," he admitted.

Alisha felt a chill and now she stepped away from him. "Why?" she asked, her voice sounding hollow.

"Because I know you're lying to me," he countered.

"But you were a guest in my home," she retorted. "You violated the trust I put in you."

"And you watched me chase down the culprits in this case and all the while you knew more than you said," he told her swiftly.

They stared at one another. Both of their chests heaved. Chaotic energy was charged around them. But there was also sadness.

Just this morning, I pondered loving him. What a fool am I?

"You accuse me of selling myself to distract you," she said. "When you used me not just for my body, but for access to my home. My things. My privacy. That is the height of hypocrisy."

She looked away from him, unable to see him in a new way, and unwilling to show him the hurt she felt that was weakening her knees.

"I never used you, Alisha," he said. "I never lied about my reason for being in Royal and I won't ignore my instincts anymore that you are hiding something from me. I put you—us—before the case I was hired to investigate."

"There is no us. There never was," she said, crossing her arms over her chest to comfort herself as she felt her heart slowly shatter.

And there never will be.

"Your instincts were right about one thing," she said, moving to the door of the bedroom. "You need to get the hell out of my house."

She hated the "hurt"ache that she felt across her chest and the tears threatening to rise.

"Alisha."

At the feel of his firm grip on her arm, she stiffened.

"On my behalf, everything we shared was real. More real than anything I've ever felt," Tremaine said.

She pressed her eyes closed as a wave of pain nearly rocked her on her feet. With a courage she didn't know she possessed, Alisha looked back over her shoulder at him—this man she dared to consider loving.

In his eyes she saw the doubt he had in her. It matched the way she felt about him.

"I have to report my findings to the Del Rios," he said.

Alisha scoffed. "What findings?" she asked with attitude.

"The large transfer of money you made just before the necklace was found," he said.

She eyed him with a shake of her head. "That's what this is about?" she said, still shaking her head. "I gave you far too much credit for being a smart man, Tremaine Knowles. Far too much credit."

"Alisha, what was it for?" he asked.

She looked up at him with a shocked expression.

"I don't owe you anything. Not answers to your questions. Not a place to stay. Not even any more of my time or attention," she said, raising her hand to poke her finger into his chest as she spoke. "Get out of my house. Stay the hell away from me. And pray I don't load my gun quick enough to send you the hell away from here with shots ringing out around your head."

Tremaine held her hand with both of his.

She hated that she still found warmth and electricity from his touch.

"Alisha, I didn't want to invade your privacy," he stressed. "But I knew—*know*—you are lying to me. Tell me the truth. Let me help you if I can."

"Still on the case, detective?" she asked sarcastically, snatching her hand away from him. "Get out of my house. Now!"

Their eyes met.

She refused to look away or back down. And she refused to believe in the pain she saw in the brown depths of his eyes. He believed what he believed, and she knew what she knew.

Where they had clung to each other in passion, they now stood with so much emotional distance between them built on mistrust.

It is what it is.

He looked grim as he turned and finished shoving his clothes into his bag before zipping it closed and putting the strap onto his broad shoulder. She led him out of the bedroom and then down the hall. They moved in silence as they descended the stairs and crossed the foyer.

"Alisha."

She ignored him and snatched one of the double front doors open.

Tremaine paused in the foyer. "You know I came to Royal to find the truth," he said, handing back his house key.

She took it and laughed bitterly, sparing him a withering glance. "Was it between my thighs?" she asked in condescension.

He walked past her to step onto the porch. "Trying to hide the truth of your lies kept you focused between mine," he countered.

"Focused?" Alisha snapped, looking up at him with storm-filled eyes. "Your ego is almost as big as you, Tremaine Knowles. We both enjoyed it and now it's over."

"Damn right it is," he said.

That stung. So deeply. She didn't even try to keep the tears from welling in her eyes. "How could I be so wrong about you?" she asked softly, barely louder than a whisper.

And that stung him. She saw it in his eyes.

"Trust me, I wanted like hell to believe I was wrong for doubting you," he said, clenching his jaw.

"You are," she insisted.

"Prove me wrong, Alisha," he said with urgency as his eyes searched hers. *"Please."*

"I have nothing to prove to you or those damn Del Rios," she said, her eyes and tone chilled by the hurt she felt at his betrayal.

He wouldn't violate my privacy like that. Not after everything we've shared.

That's what she'd once thought.

Like a fool!

"I wish I could send all of you, that necklace and this damn Christmas tree to the darkest side of hell," she spluttered before swinging the door closed hard enough to shake the entire house.

She turned and pressed her back to the door as her tears fell, blurring her vision of the lit Christmas tree. She pressed her hand to her mouth as she allowed her body to slide to the floor. She pulled her knees to her chest and settled her chin on the groove between them, then let the tears flow as the pain came in searing waves. Never had she felt such profound regret and loss.

Tremaine had given her many first experiences, and it was clear that the last one was both betrayal and pure heartbreak.

With his hand pressed to the wood of Alisha's front door, Tremaine heard her cries, and each one tore at his gut with the savagery of a wild animal. Even amid his anger and disappointment with her, and in knowing she lied to him, he had never felt so compelled to tear a door from the hinges to get to her. Hold her. Rock her. Press kisses to her temple. Swear to fix it.

"Damn," he said, forcing himself to turn and walk away.

His feelings were based on an illusion, and he refused to be misguided by them anymore.

Still...

He paused in walking to his truck.

Even if it had all been a ruse on her behalf, his feelings had been real and raw, even if seemingly rushed.

But she hadn't explained the transfer.

I still believe she's lying to me about something.

I no longer trust her.

And she no longer trusts me.

He continued forward to his truck, tossing his duffel onto the passenger seat before climbing inside to start the engine and turn up the heat. As he drove away, he did not allow himself to look back. He couldn't.

Last night, as he sat on the balcony of his corner condo overlooking downtown Austin, sipping on scotch, his anger beat out the alcohol and outdoor fireplace in keeping him heated. There he remained, nursing his drink and his doubts. One fueling the other.

After working from the KTS offices for most of the day, he finally made the drive back to Royal, clinging to hope that she would offer a reasonable explanation and tell him the truth.

His grip on the steering wheel tightened because none of that had happened.

In truth, he wanted nothing more than his suspicions to be assuaged. To not feel that he imagined everything he'd experienced with Alisha over nearly two weeks. That he had been duped.

He picked up his iPhone and called Preston, knowing he could not delay the inevitable anymore. He had wanted to question Alisha first and let him know his intention before contacting Preston or his parents about his discovery. There was no room for more delay.

His integrity was at risk.

The phone rang several times before Preston answered.

"Evening, Lady-killer," he said.

Tremaine grimaced. "Trust me, those days are getting further and further behind me with each passing year," he said.

"Me, too. More than you know," Preston drawled. "So what's going on with the case?"

He pulled his truck to a stop at a red light. "That's why I called. I have an update," he said.

"I'm headed to RCW for dinner. Join me," he offered.

"Done deal. On the way," Tremaine said, already making the right turn at the corner.

Their call ended and he dropped the phone back onto the passenger seat before focusing on making it to the steakhouse. Once he was parked, he hesitated to leave his truck because he knew he was about to serve Alisha up on a plate. He was not eager to do it. Not at all.

Even as he finally made his way inside the restaurant and was led to Preston's table, he wished things could be different. "Hey, Preston," he said, then claimed the seat across from him.

"So what's going on?" Preston asked.

Their waitress came to their table. She was petite and cute, with bright red hair and wide blue eyes.

"My name is Penny. I'll be taking your orders this

evening," she said with a bright and friendly smile. "Can I start you both off with a drink and appetizers?"

"Penny, I'll have a double scotch on the rocks," Tremaine said.

"Of course," she said. "And for you, Mr. Del Rio?"

"Same," Preston said.

"Are you ready to order your entrées?" she asked.

Both men ordered medium-well steaks with sides.

Preston settled back in his seat to eye him across the table. "Fill me in," he said.

"It's nothing definitive," Tremaine began. "But just before the discovery of the necklace, one of the Winterses made a large transfer of money. I have a forensic accountant following the money trail. He should be getting back to me tomorrow."

Preston drummed his fingertips atop the table. He was silent and appeared calm, but it was clear his mind was racing. "Perhaps one or all of them were in on purchasing the necklace?" he asked aloud. "But then why expose that they have it?"

"It doesn't make much sense, but I wanted to share the info with you," Tremaine said, sitting back a bit as their waitress set their drinks on the table before them.

"You seem reluctant to do it," Preston observed.

Tremaine said nothing and just took a deep sip of his drink. The rattling of the ice in the glass reminded him of the constant jingle of Alisha's beloved charm bracelet.

Preston drummed his fingers some more as he looked off at some spot across the restaurant.

Tremaine looked down into the amber liquid in his glass, wishing he could forget Alisha. The scent of her. The taste of her. The feel of—

"Which Winters?"

He looked up from his drink to find Preston's eyes now firmly locked on him.

Tremaine cleared his throat. "Alisha," he said, then finished his drink in one gulp and motioned for the waitress to bring him another.

"Ah," Preston said, nodding in understanding. "The pretty professor-slash-antiquarian who offered you shelter."

And much more.

Tremaine clenched and unclenched his jaw, hating that his desire for her lingered even in the face of her playing him like a fiddle. "Which made the discovery possible," he said.

"We've been friends—good friends—since college," Preston said. "But I recommended your firm to my father because I know firsthand that you have integrity and killer instincts."

"Accurate as ever," Tremaine said.

"I hope that's still true."

The men stared at one another. It felt like a standoff at high noon in a Western movie.

"We're friends and you're my client, but don't question my integrity, Preston," he said, his voice strong and unrelenting.

Preston gave him a smile that seemed forced before taking the first sip of his drink. "Same here, friend," he countered. "So don't you question my intelligence."

Then they gave each other a begrudging smile before leaning in to touch their glasses in a toast.

"I have just as much invested in this case as you do, Tremaine," Preston said, settling back against his seat. "It's no secret I want to step into leadership at the Del Rio Group once my father decides to step down. My father doesn't believe in nepotism. The last thing I need is a show of failure on my part because you were compromised by a pretty face and curvy legs."

Actually, I'm more of a butt man and Alisha's is truly glorious.

But he said nothing, feeling no need to explain himself further. He had long since left behind the childish ways of bragging about his sexual conquests to friends.

What happened between Alisha and me is no one's business—friend/client or not.

They both fell silent as their waitress and another server set their steaming plates in front of them. Even once they were alone at the table again, they focused on their meal.

"How's everything going?" Penny asked a few minutes later.

"My friend has a lot on his mind," Preston said, wiping his mouth with his linen napkin. "Another round of drinks, please."

"Right away," she said before turning to walk away.

"Listen, Tremaine, let's set the case aside for a minute," Preston said.

Tremaine eyed him as he sliced a thin piece of

porterhouse before dipping it into a spicy steak sauce and enjoying the bite.

"We're friends and it's clear something—or someone—is troubling you," Preston said.

"Just thinking about the case," he said, deliberately evasive.

Getting involved with Alisha had been the height of unprofessionalism. Admitting that he had been duped by her wiles was foolish. He didn't want to admit to any of it. To anyone.

Not even myself.

Penny set their drinks on the table before slipping away.

"I understand the attraction to a Winters woman," Preston admitted as soon as Penny was out of earshot.

Tremaine eyed his friend and then thought of Alisha's sister, Tiffany. Although they were of no blood relation, both women were stunning. "Has the younger Winters sister caught your wandering eye?" he asked.

Preston released a snarky grunt. "She's all I can think about since we hooked up at my sister's engagement party," he said before raising his new drink to his lips.

"A Winters?" Tremaine asked in disbelief, knowing how deep the divide between the two families ran for the last century. Preston had spoken of it enough over the years.

"Right," he drawled.

The irony was not lost that the best friends were both battling their desires for a set of sisters.

"So I understand letting your guard down. Women can be any man's Achilles' heel, my friend," Preston said.

Don't I know it.

"But this case is directly tied to my destiny at the Del Rio Group, so I need you to either get your head back in the game or tap out, my friend," Preston said, his eyes unflinching.

"I'm on top of it, Preston, and I will finish getting to the bottom of this," Tremaine promised him. "It's just as important to me as it is to you."

Even more so.

If Alisha Winters played him for a fool by seduction to keep him from discovering the truth, all she'd accomplished was to make him more determined than ever.

Eleven

"Professor Winters. Professor Winters?"

Alisha slightly shook her head as she refocused her attention on her student Olivia looking at her with a curious expression with her iPad still nervously clutched in her hands. "Very good, Olivia," she said, although she admittedly had missed a good chunk of the woman's presentation of the rough draft of her thesis. Luckily, Alisha had each of her seminar students send the second stage of their papers to her before the class for her review. The presentation was primarily for the opinion and input of her classmates.

She took a sip of her matcha latte and eyed each of the twelve doctoral candidates where they were seated at the rear of Odds & Ends. "Any input for Olivia?" Alisha asked.

Everyone offered nothing but praise.

"And I agree," Alisha said, rising from the 1800s wooden desk chair to stand before them. "In fact, I am proud of the work all of you have placed in your thesis. Please review the email I've sent each of you with any minor notes but know that I could find no major fault in any of your work. Which is great since our time together has come to an end."

Many of them laughed or smiled.

"Thank you for the opportunity to help guide you on this part of your journey in receiving your doctorate," she said with a genuine smile of her own. "Please enjoy the rest of your day and if I don't see any of you before Thanksgiving in a couple of weeks, *please* enjoy the break. Feel free to reach out to me if you have any further questions or need guidance."

As her students rose and began to gather their items, she began to clean up their cups of hot chocolate and the pastry treats she'd offered them. They each said their goodbyes to her before taking their leave, and soon she was alone. She walked to the front door to turn on the sign signaling the store was open and paused to look out at the street. There was a slight drizzle of rain, but thankfully it was not quite cold enough to worry about it freezing over into black ice. Still, the dreariness fit her mood.

She vacillated between anger at Tremaine for violating her privacy and sadness that she had misjudged him.

And what we shared.

She had never counted on their connection lasting,

but to learn it had been a farce had stung and there was no denying that. She longed for the days when she never thought of him at all.

To hell with Tremaine Knowles.

Alisha moved back across the store and had just taken a seat at her desk when the bell over the door sounded off. "I'll be right with you," she yelled, taking a sip of her hot chocolate with Amaretto before rising to leave her office.

She paused to see her parents standing just inside the entrance. The looks on their faces revealed it all. Camille looked apologetic, meaning she had indeed told her husband about Eliza's letter of confession. Joseph's stern expression meant he was not pleased with the revelation.

Here we go.

It was the last thing she needed as she continued to replay everything she and Tremaine had said yesterday. It was on a loop.

"Trust me, I wanted like hell to believe I was wrong for doubting you."

"You are."

"Prove me wrong, Alisha. Please."

"I have nothing to prove to you or those damn Del Rios."

That and so much more replayed and tormented her.

Setting aside her broken heart, Alisha stepped back inside her office and walked over to the Victorian-era bookcase against the brick wall. She turned one of the many handles, seemingly meant to be pulled, and heard the click as one of many secret compartments was opened. The bookshelves were a door that she opened to reveal that behind it was a working safe. She used the key to unlock it and removed the letter that sat atop other valuable or memorable items she kept secured there. It was a piece she had no plans to sell because of the clever design.

As she walked out of the office and to the front of the store, where her parents awaited her, Alisha stroked her thumb over the letter that she had fought so hard to conceal.

"Alisha, your mother told me you can explain the mystery behind the appearance of that damn Del Rio necklace. Something about a letter you found? Can I see it?" Joseph asked, easing his hands inside the pockets of the gray cashmere topcoat he wore over a matching sweater and slacks that brought out the gray hairs lightly streaked through his blond hair and beard.

She could see why her mother had fallen so hard for him. The man resembled Brad Pitt and had a bundle of charm. And he adored her mother just as much as she loved him. That was clear.

And it is what Alisha had imagined having for herself. A good, warmhearted, loving man who also had the ferocity, when needed, to protect his family and its legacy. Joseph Winters was not a man to take lightly.

Nor was he one to disappoint.

And at that moment, Alisha felt she had done just that.

"Yes," she admitted as she continued to walk toward them. "It's a letter written by your grandmother Eliza confessing that she is the one who stole the jewelry while it was on display at a museum in Paris. I've had the letter authenticated by calling in a favor to get it done quickly. The certification is in the envelope as well."

He held out his hand and Alisha gave it to him. A glance at Camille's face showed it was filled with love and assurance even as she rubbed light circles on her husband's back as he opened the letter and read it with a grim expression.

Joseph nodded as he cut his eyes up from the letter to stare at her with a steady gaze. "I would have preferred it brought to my attention as soon as it was discovered," he said.

"Of course," Alisha said.

"Who knows about this?" Joseph asked as he refolded the letter to slide back inside the envelope.

Alisha opened her mouth but couldn't bring herself to draw Marcus under Joseph's ire as well.

"Honesty, Alisha," Camille gently said to her. "As I told you, no more setting yourself on fire to keep others warm."

She released a shaky breath, admitting that her first instinct had been to take the entire blame and shield Marcus—much like she had done for her siblings over the years. "Marcus and Jessica discovered the necklace and letter in a hidden room while searching the family archives in the cellar," she admitted, closing her eyes as she did. When she was done, she opened one to gauge her father's reaction.

"What?" Joseph said, much louder than necessary.

"So Marcus lied about the package delivery knowing the necklace was in the basement the whole time?"

"Yes," Alisha replied quietly.

Joseph frowned.

"It was my idea to conceal the letter," she said with a look at Camille as she twisted her charm bracelet around her wrist. "I thought its revelation would only make matters worse. My intention was to protect the family from further scandal."

Joseph took a long time, but then finally nodded. "I understand," he admitted before handing the letter back to Alisha.

The move surprised her.

"I'll put it back in the safe," she said.

Both Camille and Joseph shook their heads at her.

"It's time to bring this Diamond Gate fiasco to an end," Joseph said. "I won't have the entire family scandalized over a foolish act from over a century ago."

She thought of Tremaine's accusation of her being the culprit and it pierced her.

"Grandmother Eliza would not want her actions to stain the family's legacy in that way," Joseph said, reaching to take one of Camille's hands in one of his own. "With Del Rio's private investigator digging into our family business behind this, I want the entire matter resolved and over."

"And perhaps the feud can end again," Camille said as she looked up at her handsome husband with soft eyes. "It's time. For the sake of Jericho and Maggie, Joseph."

And Tiffany, Alisha thought, wondering what her

parents' feelings would be when Tiffany told them she was pregnant with Preston Del Rio's baby.

Joseph just frowned and released a grunt.

"Don't forget the business," Camille added, reminding him of the effect of Diamond Gate on valuable deals made with Winters Industries and the Del Rio Group that were on the brink of ending.

Another grunt.

Camille raised up on her toes in the gray leather boots she wore to press a kiss to the corner of her husband's mouth. Joseph gave her a begrudging smile.

That's what love will do. Calm the beast. Real love, anyway.

"We better be going, Alisha. Your father and I are going to Trey's ranch," Camille said. "Dez wants us to be in a new video he's directing for TikTok."

Her eight-year-old nephew was on a mission to one day become a film director, and she had to admit the cute mini-twin of her brother Trey posted really good content. "I look forward to seeing what he has come up with on my feed," she said, feeling so much love for him. "My curiosity is piqued."

"Mine, too," Joseph drawled before bending to press a kiss to her temple. "I trust that you can handle the letter?"

"Yes. I will," she promised.

"Good," he said, turning to open the front door.

The bell jangled.

"I'll be right out," Camille said, turning to stand beside Alisha. "I need to ask our daughter something."

With one final brief wave, Joseph left the shop.

"How are you?" Camille asked, wrapping an arm around her shoulders to pull her close to her side.

Alisha rested her head on her mother's shoulder and took an inhale of her familiar scent. "Not good at all," she revealed, hearing her own sadness.

She filled in her mother on the divide between her and Tremaine that had been created by him invading her privacy because he believed she was lying to him. "I am pissed," she confessed. "But I must admit it will feel good to show him the proof that he was wrong to accuse me."

"Sometimes anger is confused for hurt, Alisha," Camille said, turning her daughter by her shoulders to face her. "Don't let it consume you."

As if in confirmation, a deep pang of emotion radiated across her chest. "That or love," she said with a hollow tone.

"Oh, no," Camille sighed, pulling her close for a hug.

Alisha closed her eyes as tears rose like a flood. "I feel like a fool," she confessed in a whisper as she wrapped her arms around her mother's waist and clung to her.

"Here's the best advice a mother could give her child that is hurting," Camille said. "Everything happens for a reason. It will either propel you forward as you learn the lesson of it, or it will destroy you. Choose wisely. Nothing can destroy you unless you allow it. This, too, shall pass."

Alisha nodded.

"Now, should I have your father ruin him?" Camille asked.

Alisha leaned back to look at her mother. "No!" she exclaimed in alarm.

Camille gave her a soft smile. *"Exactly,"* she stressed. "I was just making sure you remembered that."

Alisha nodded. "And this, too, shall pass," she said.

Camille raised her hands to give her tiny air claps. "Now, take *all* of the evidence you have to answer the questions of the sexy—although duplicitous—detective once and for all," she said. "Should I go with you?"

Alisha shook her head.

"Come stay with us tonight," Camille said, removing gray leather gloves from the pocket of her fur to ease onto her hands. "In fact, maybe it's time for the entire family to have a sleepover. We don't have to wait for the holidays to come together."

Alisha had to admit that the idea of not going back to her home, which felt decidedly lonelier of late, made her feel better. "You don't have to do that," she said.

Camille arched an eyebrow. "Of course I do," she said, reaching to stroke her chin. "That's what family is for."

"And Dez will love it," Alisha admitted.

With one last smile, Camille turned and left the shop.

Alisha crossed her arms over her chest as she made her way back to her office. She took the seat behind her desk and picked up her cup of hot chocolate that had chilled, but was still delicious. She eyed the envelope now sitting atop the open ledgers on her desk.

Yesterday she had banished Tremaine from her life.

What little feelings she had left for him—those she planned to purge ASAP—made her nervous about what she had to do. With a lick of her lips, she picked up her phone.

"And this, too, shall pass."

She closed her eyes as the ringing seemed to echo in her head.

"Alisha."

She released a breath. "Mr. Knowles, we need to meet," she said, her voice stern and cold. "It's time for the truth to be told."

A few moments of silence passed by.

"Finally," he said.

She rolled her eyes. "Meet me at the Texas Cattleman's Club," she said. "There are private rooms there where we can speak alone, because I want you nowhere near my home again."

More silence.

"Whatever you want, Ms. Winters. Just like always," he said.

"Tonight. At seven," she said, before ending the call.

Tremaine was standing at the large window of one of the private rooms in the Texas Cattleman's Club, a men's club with its paneled walls lined with hunting trophies and historical artifacts. He looked out at the tennis courts as he awaited Alisha's arrival.

He had to admit his interest was piqued. What was the truth she would provide?

That she lied and manipulated me? Not hardly.

Still, with his deadline to solve the case just a few days away, he was ready to get to the truth.

And get the hell away from Royal, Texas.

He checked the time on his phone. The professor was running late.

"I'm here."

He looked up and his eyes fell on her reflection in the glass as she stood in the doorway. She wore a black leather pantsuit with her hair pulled back into a sleek bun with dark makeup. As he turned to watch her walk into the room, closing the door behind her, he felt as if her garb had been specific. He just wasn't sure if it was to serve as armor or as a movie-like revelation that she had been the villainess all along.

One thing was sure. Alisha Winters was one beautiful woman, even in anger.

His eyes dropped to the envelope and documents in her hand.

"Let's get right to it," she said, coming to a stop a brief distance in front of him and extending her hand to offer him what she held. "I'll admit that the transfer of money might look incriminating, but it was money my brother Jericho borrowed to buy a large parcel of land just outside of Royal as a surprise gift for Maggie."

Tremaine looked down at the bank receipt that included a copy of a deposited check before his eyes shifted up to her face.

"He didn't want her to catch on to the surprise he had for her so he used my money and wrote me a check the very same day of the transfer—that I admittedly just deposited today," she said with a hard glint in her eyes. "There was no rush when I knew the check was good and didn't know I needed to prove myself to someone I trusted in my home."

Oh, no.

Guilt over snooping in her laptop made his gut clench.

Or is this a ruse to hide the truth?

She released a sarcastic laugh. "I see you still don't believe me," she said, then handed him an envelope that was faded and worn at the edges with a tint to it that hinted it was aged.

Tremaine took that as well and opened it as his heart hammered with the might of a sledgehammer.

"What you are reading is a letter that was discovered along with the necklace," she said.

As he read the handwritten letter, Tremaine's eyebrows deepened into a frown. It was a confession.

"My great-grandmother Eliza, in a decidedly bold and foolish move, stole it a century ago," Alisha continued.

"Eliza," Tremaine said in surprise, thinking of the photo he had of the woman and how his instinct on it somehow being about her was right.

Just like it had been about Alisha concealing something from him, but the moment didn't feel right to throw that into her face. Not when it meant he had betrayed her trust for nothing.

Well, almost nothing.

"So you had this all along while you watched me

spend countless hours looking for the answer?" he asked, forging ahead with his concerns.

"And I'm only showing it to you to clear both my and my family's reputation in this," she said. "There's a certificate of authenticity if you don't believe the letter is real."

"I believe you," he said.

She then told him the real story of how the necklace and letter had been discovered by Marcus and Jessica. When she was done, Alisha looked down at her feet and then back up at him. "And no, I did not sleep with you because of that damn necklace and letter," she said.

The conviction in her eyes touched him deeply. It seared into his gut.

"Yes, I protected the truth of what Eliza did for my family. Yes, I did that, and if put in the same situation, I might do it again because it's what family do."

"Even when they commit a crime, Alisha?" he asked.

"A hundred years ago!" she exclaimed. "Fine. And she lived with the shame of her actions all those years. It's there in the letter. But none of the current Winters family members have done anything wrong."

"Except cover up her crime," he said.

Alisha released a bitter laugh. "Rigid indignation is the hill you want to die on right now after snooping through my private things. Really, Tremaine? Really?" she asked with an incredulous expression.

She's right.

"I have regrets, Alisha," he confessed.

She released a short little laugh that was so telling. "So do I," she admitted in a whisper before reaching to take the documents from his hand. "I'll send copies of these to your email address. Goodbye, Tremaine. I'm sure you'll report all of this to your clients."

He watched as she turned and walked away from him.

It felt like it was the last time he would see her.

"Alisha," he called behind her.

She paused with obvious reluctance, but she did not face him.

"What happened between us was real for me," he admitted. "I risked so much just for the time we shared together, and I would risk it again. Believe *that*."

"I wish I could," she replied before leaving the room without looking back.

Tremaine turned and looked out the window again.

A few minutes later, his phone vibrated. An email notification.

He pulled his phone from the inner pocket of the blazer he was wearing to check the screen. Alisha had indeed sent him the copies—possibly right out in the parking lot.

The investigation was over. He had succeeded in his mission.

And possibly lost so much more in the process.

He looked down at his phone and considered whether to reach out to Fernando yet. The sooner, the better. He was ready to go home, so despite it all, he was grateful to make the call.

"Fernando Del Rio."

"Evenin'. This is Knowles. The case is over," he said, leaving the room.

"Hold on. I'll put you on speaker. My wife and children are here with me," Fernando said.

Tremaine was soon walking out of the single-story dark stone-and-wood clubhouse and toward the parking lot.

"Go ahead, Tremaine," Preston said.

But as he unlocked his truck and climbed behind the steering wheel, he hesitated in revealing the entire truth. "It seems Eliza Winters, the grandmother of Joseph—"

"We're *very* familiar with her," Fernando said with clear disdain.

Tremaine started his truck. "She was the original cat burglar of the necklace in Paris—"

"What!" both Maggie and Gayle exclaimed.

Fernando released an expletive. "When will that woman cease to being a headache for this family!" he roared.

Tremaine held the phone away from his ear before also placing it on speaker.

"Calm down, Fernando," Gayle soothed him.

"Go ahead, Tremaine," Preston repeated, sounding closer to the phone than before.

"In a letter, Eliza confesses to hiding the necklace at the Winters estate. It's been hidden away in a secret room in the cellar all this time until the current Winters family discovered it. Marcus lied about it being left at the front door. I imagine he was worried about no one believing him until the letter was authenticated. He wanted to get the necklace back to your family as soon as possible," Tremaine said, driving out of the parking lot and soon exiting the property. "I'm going to head to Austin and compile my report and evidence to have to you tomorrow."

"Wait—hold on. Joseph Winters is calling my father," Preston said with his father still in the background roaring with anger.

"Listen, take his call," Tremaine said. "But remember, they did what was right in revealing what they found out."

"Okay, Tremaine," Preston said. "Thank you for this. Be safe on the road. We'll talk tomorrow."

"Okay."

Tremaine could only hope they calmed Fernando down further before they answered the call.

As he made the drive out of Royal and headed toward home, he played Christmas music and tried to convince himself that everything would be okay. Tried. And failed.

He made the trip in record time, shaving nearly thirty minutes off his usual time, and was thankful to pull into his reserved parking spot. He left the truck and stretched his frame before grabbing his duffel bag and making his way to the elevator. It was late. He was tired and mentally worn out. He just wanted to shower and sleep.

Tomorrow he would resume his normal life. Focus on cases. Enjoy the Austin nightlife. Maybe even call a pretty friend for some laughs and fun.

I will get Alisha Winters out of my system in no time.

The elevator opened and a pretty woman with thin waist-length braids rushed forward to step onto the elevator beside him. He'd seen her in the building before. With two full floors of amenities, including a fitness center, a wine cellar, a bar, heated infinity pool, outdoor lounge, movie theater, grocery store and even an activity room for kids and grooming station for dogs, the building was a world within itself. They'd seen each other and shared those types of lingering looks that let each other know they were interested.

"Hi, stranger," she said, her voice soft and husky, like she could whisper naughty things or sing the blues. "Haven't seen you around. I thought you moved out on us."

He gave her a smile. "Nah. Never that. I love it here," he said as the doors closed. "I was out of town for work the last couple of weeks."

"We've never done the formalities," she said, extending her hand and spreading her smile. "Ginger Kaplan."

He enclosed her soft hand in his. "Tremaine Knowles. No relation to Beyoncé and Solange," he added for good measure, and then instantly thought of Alisha and how she would tease him about that.

"Their loss," Ginger said with an appreciative look up at him as she stroked his hand between both of hers.

The move was warm, but there was no fire. Not even a spark.

Not like Alisha.

Just being in the same room with her made him

feel more alive. A look thrilled him. A touch was electrifying.

And when they made love?

That was indescribable.

"Damn," he said.

Ginger eyed him and then her face filled with understanding. "It's always the sexy ones with the drama," she said, giving his hand one last squeeze before she released him. "Y'all are either on a quest to conquer every woman you sniff in a ten-mile radius or mending a heart broken by your *Boomerang* girl."

"*Boomerang*?" he asked in confusion. "Like the movie?"

In it, the playboy played by Eddie Murphy finally falls for a woman played by Robin Givens, who gave it to him as good as he normally dished it out.

She nodded. "Absolutely," she said. "And I am not trying to be the woman to help clean up that mess."

Tremaine made a face, feeling offended. "I am not a mess and Alisha is not my boomerang."

"Ding! Ding! Ding! We have a name, ladies and gentlemen," she said, pumping the air with her fist and then clapping as if on a game show. "Boomerang!"

Tremaine eyed her. "I don't know whether to be upset because you're insulting me or to like you because you're hilarious," he admitted.

"Friend-zoned," she said dryly.

Tremaine chuckled at her self-deprecating comical expression.

Ding.

The elevator slid to a stop. "Listen, you can find

me in apartment 506 in three months when you have gotten *A-lish-a* out of your system—"

"Three months?" he said, balking.

The elevator doors slid open.

Ginger eyed him. "Matter of fact...make it six months," she said before turning with her two fingers up in the peace sign as she strolled off the elevator.

He watched her in astonishment until the doors closed her off from his view.

"Three months," he said, balking again. "Me? Tremaine Knowles? Lady-killer? Please."

He was still mumbling in indignation when the elevator stopped on the top floor and he stepped off to make his way to his corner condo. "Somebody better let her know," he scoffed to himself, using his thumb to press against the biometric lock to enter his home.

He waved his hand over the switch to raise the lighting that lined the twelve-foot tray ceiling. He had just swung his duffel onto the low-slung dark gray suede sofa when his phone began to vibrate.

Bzzzzzz. Bzzzzzz. Bzzzzzz.

He pulled it from the inner pocket of his blazer, surprised to see Golden calling. He tossed his phone onto the sofa and walked away, choosing a shower over a chat with his assistant.

Bzzzzzz. Bzzzzzz. Bzzzzzz.

He paused because Golden never called after business hours. Turning on the heels of his boots, Tremaine leaned down to pick up the phone and answer.

"Welcome home, boss," Golden said.

"How did you— Never mind," he said, not bothering to ask how she knew.

"Listen. Sorry to bother you but we got a new trial prep case," she said. "And they offered double your rate if you could jump right on it."

"A new case?" he asked, rubbing his beard with his free hand.

"And I figured you could use the distraction to help you boomerang back to your old self," Golden said.

He stiffened. "Did you say *boomerang*?" he asked.

"Yeah. Why?"

A coincidence hearing that word twice? Golden wouldn't think so. She was always speaking of synchronicities being a sign from the universe.

But a sign of what?

I don't know and I don't want to know.

He was not willing to stir Golden up about her spiritual journey. He'd already tucked his tail and apologized for snapping at her and his slick remark about her angels with paid Fridays off for a month.

"Send me the details and let's get to work," he said, indeed glad for the distraction.

"Boss?"

This time it was his turn to just *know*. His assistant did not want to speak business. "Not now, Golden," he said.

"Yes. Now," she insisted. "If there's one thing I am learning on this journey of mine, it's that love comes easy. We feel it. We know it. But it's the mind that puts up all the blocks to really feeling it fully. We stick restrictions like past experiences, hurt feelings, high expectations and how long we've known someone to block ourselves from the yummy goodness that is love."

Tremaine crossed the living room and opened the French door leading out to his balcony.

"What if the whole purpose of even existing is to be in, know, give and receive...*love*?" she asked, finishing with a soft tone. "In spite of it all. Resentment. Grudges. Bad times. Unforgiveness."

As Tremaine looked out at the bright lights of surrounding downtown Austin as the chill of the night swirled around him, he thought of the days he'd spent in Royal. With Alisha. He smiled thinking of her smile. Suddenly, he felt a warmth in his belly that spread across his body.

From the moment he'd met Alisha, he had felt drawn to her. Connected in a way he had never known before.

And maybe never would again.

Boomerang.

Twelve

Five days later

Alisha rose from her seat in her parents' living room of the sprawling mansion and grounds that had become the new estate of the Winters family. She looked down at her charm bracelet and opened each of the heart-shaped lockets, lingering on the one that was empty. The one she saved for the love of her life.

Tremaine.

At the thought of him—a constant over the last week—she snapped the empty locket closed.

If only she could cut him out of her life with the same ease.

Not even her anger at him could erase the scoundrel from her daily thoughts and nightly dreams.

I just can't escape him.

Alisha frowned as she recalled the memory of him turning around to face her as she stood in the doorway of one of the private rooms in the TCC clubhouse. She had been lingering there, watching his profile, and wishing things could have turned out differently for them. That he hadn't betrayed her trust.

"We need to talk."

She glanced back over her shoulder at her father, who was strolling into the room carrying two cups with steam rising from both. She gave him a smile. "Have I overstayed my welcome?" she asked as he joined her at the window and handed her what she discovered to be hot chocolate.

"Never," Joseph said. *"But..."*

She took a sip and felt almost as warmed as she did by Tremaine's touch.

"Your mother and I encourage you all to think of this as your home, but not your escape," Joseph told her.

Alisha avoided his gaze. She had not been back to her home since the first night her mother planned the family sleepover. Somehow, the home she loved now felt different. It was a reminder of the hurt she felt. And a haunting of everything she shared with Tremaine there and even the dream she'd once had that there could be *more*.

"Tell me," Joseph said with a steady gaze on her over the rim of the cup.

"Tell you what?" she asked.

"Whatever it is that your mother and you are keeping from me," he said. "The reason why you are sad and hanging out here with us and putting your entire life on pause. You haven't opened your shop and have barely left the estate."

True.

"Exactly who or what are you running from?" he asked.

Alisha hesitated.

Joseph had been understanding of her shielding his grandmother's crime and letter of confession, but how would he feel about her sleeping with the enemy?

"I can head home," she said.

"Don't miss the mark, Alisha," Joseph said, his voice slightly stern. "That was not the reason for this conversation."

"I know," she admitted, looking out at the night wind that caused the leaves of the trees to flutter.

"I've fallen in love with the wrong guy," she admitted.

And Joseph listened on patiently as she filled him in on her short-lived relationship with Tremaine— leaving out the sordid details but speaking from her heart. "I had felt like meeting him was meant to be," she said, moving to set her cup atop a ceramic coaster before claiming a seat on the sofa. "It all just clicked."

That all too familiar pang of loss and regret radiated as she stroked her forehead with her fingertips. She closed her eyes to keep any more tears from falling. She was sure she was near dehydration from weeping so much.

Noting Joseph's continued silence, she looked up

to see him studying her from across the room. She immediately felt he was upset. She cleared her throat. She had told the truth, and after everything of late, she wanted to live in her truth.

"Your silence is damning," she said.

Joseph gave her a slight smile. "I am not happy about you inviting a stranger to live in your home," he said. "But you're an adult. An intelligent woman. And you have one helluva good aim."

"Absolutely," she assured him, chuckling as she told him about Tremaine pulling up to the house while she was awaiting him with her rifle.

"That's my girl," Joseph said with a nod as he came over to sit on the sofa opposite her.

"He promised to behave as nothing less than a gentleman," she recalled. "But he didn't."

Joseph frowned deeply.

Alisha shook her head. "I meant him snooping through my computer. It just felt like such a violation," she said.

"As I'm sure you lying to him when he asked you for the truth felt the same to him," Joseph offered as he shifted his tall frame on the seat as if to find comfort.

She arched an eyebrow in shock.

Joseph's look was admonishing. "I had hoped Camille and I taught you all about seeing things from another point of view," he said. "He was absolutely wrong for invading your privacy—"

"Yes," she stressed.

"And you were wrong to invite the man to stay there knowing you were hiding the truth about the case you knew very well he was in town to investigate," Joseph offered. "*Two* wrongs."

"Whose side are you on?" she asked.

"Truth. Always," he assured her. "And love."

Alisha felt conflicted.

"You should see the look on your face when you talk about him...especially him surprising you with the Christmas tree," he said. "Do you love him, Alisha?"

"In less than two weeks? How?" she asked.

Joseph shrugged one shoulder. "At the very least you may discover you have something to build on and to grow," he said. "Maybe."

Alisha felt doubtful.

"Make a choice and be okay with it," Joseph said, rising to his feet. "Come off pause, Alisha."

She nodded in understanding.

Joseph rose and came over to give one of her shoulders a comforting squeeze before leaving her alone again.

She tucked her sock-covered feet beneath her bottom and cupped the mug as she looked over to her parents' massive tree, which was as wide as it was tall. She had hardly known Tremaine Knowles for two weeks and yet he made such a huge impact on her life.

So much pleasure.

So much happiness.

So much laughter.

And then, so much pain.

How can I trust him?

She thought of the wisdom of her father.

And to be fair, how could he trust me?

She sighed as she ran her fingers through her curls. Her father was right; she had to stop running from moving her life forward. But what kept her stuck was the idea of life without him. The last week had made it clear that his effect on her still clung—not even anger at him could weaken that she—

Ding.

Breaking the hold her eyes had on the embers in the lit fireplace, she picked up her phone from the end table. It was a text from Tiffany with a link.

"'I'm glad this is all finally over thanks to your sexy PI!'" she said, reading the message aloud.

Tremaine.

And off went her heart pounding so quickly, as if it was in a race all its own.

What now? she wondered as she opened the link.

Soon a video filled the screen, and she turned her phone sideways to watch Tremaine walking up to his parked truck amid a crowd of reporters.

"We have the private investigator looking into the sudden reappearance of the Del Rio necklace that was missing for the past century from a museum in Paris," a voice said before a microphone and cameras were pressed closer to Tremaine's handsome face. "His website purports him to be an acclaimed tech developer and former lieutenant with the Austin Police Department."

Alisha bit down on her bottom lip as she eyed Tremaine looking confident and poised.

And so handsome.

"I thought it best to make it clear, considering the

public and press interest in this case, to ensure the truth be told with the approval of the Del Rio family, who hired me," he said. "I have concluded that the current Winters family had no involvement in the jewelry theft. In fact, in the interest of justice, it was because of the cooperation of the Winters family that I was able to close the case so quickly."

Alisha sobered quickly as she eased forward to sit on the edge of the sofa.

Not only was Tremaine publicly clearing the air of the scandal involving Diamond Gate, but he was also ensuring that the actions of her great-grandmother were kept private.

And me. He's covering me about concealing the letter!

"And the feud between the Del Rio and Winters families? Where are they in continuing this century-long war?" a reporter asked.

"Listen, the parameters of what I was hired to do did not include a kumbaya moment between these families," he said. "You'll have to check with them for that part of it and any further details of the case, which I consider private. My role in all of this is done."

"Your firm, Knowles Threat Solutions, is in Austin," another reporter said. "So why are you back in Royal, Mr. Knowles?"

She rose to her feet with the phone clutched in her hands.

In Royal? Tremaine was in Royal?

She felt light-headed.

Maybe he was in town to finish up his business with the Del Rios.

Tremaine gave them a charming smile as he opened the door to his truck. "That is private as well. Take care," he said, then climbed inside his vehicle as the camera lights continued to flash around him before he pulled away.

She checked the time of the video. It had just been posted a few hours ago.

Was he already headed back to Austin?

It was clear he had not wished to meet up with her since he had not called or sought her out. Her father was right. It was time to shift her life forward, off of pause. Alisha crossed the spacious room to head up the stairs to the guest room where she had been hiding to pack her things and go restart her life.

There was a knock at his door.

Tremaine looked up from his laptop, surprised by the intrusion. Setting the computer on the sofa, he rose to cross the living room and open the door. He smiled at Alisha standing there, looking beautiful in a Kelly green sweater dress with a deep V that exposed the brown swell of each of her full breasts and thigh-high black leather boots.

"Alisha."

"I saw all of the press you did about Diamond Gate," she said as she strolled in with her finger trailing across his chest over the T-shirt he was wearing with plaid sleep pants.

"It was the truth," he said, closing the door and

watching the curve of her buttocks against the sweater as she moved before she turned to lean back against the couch.

"I just wanted to thank you in person," she said, tilting her head to the side as she eyed him with heated gaze. "And see if we can make amends, Tremaine."

The thrill of being near her again excited him, but he paced himself as he walked closer, not wanting to appear anxious because he wasn't confident about just where they stood anymore. "Amends?" he asked. "In what way?"

Alisha gave him a slow smile and reached down to grip the edge of the sweater dress up her body, slowly revealing her nudity beneath it until she flung the garment away. "The best way," she said, taking a step forward in her boots to grip the back of his neck and pull him down for a kiss.

Following her lead, Tremaine deepened the kiss as he wrapped an arm around her waist and lifted her to crush her body against his.

"I've missed you, Tremaine," she whispered against his mouth. "I missed you so much."

Tremaine leaned back a bit to look down at her. This beautiful woman had both fiery passion and cool wit. "And I need you, Alisha," he told her with honesty as he walked her down the hall to his bedroom.

"You do?" she asked as she pressed kisses to his neck.

"In every way," he promised her.

Alisha raised her head to look deeply into his eyes

as she stroked the back of his head. In her eyes, he saw her feelings for him. "More, huh?" she asked.

"Much more," he promised her.

She nodded in agreement. "Is this thing between us real?"

"As real as it gets," Tremaine told her before setting her down on the king-size bed so he could quickly shed his clothes.

"So we get to do this forever?" she asked as she eyed every inch of him.

Tremaine smiled as he lay down on the bed beside her and began to trace light circles around each of her nipples until they were taut.

Alisha gasped and arched her back.

His eyes devoured the pleasure on her face as he continued to enjoy the feel of her soft skin against his fingertips and the way she shivered. Her eyes sparkled. Her cheeks flushed. Her hair was spread out around her face. "Beautiful," he moaned, looking down into her face before lowering his head to lick at her trembling mouth. "So beautiful."

She pressed her hand to the side of his face. "We will make beautiful babies," she said.

Tremaine nodded in agreement as he continued to explore her body. He drew from her a tremble, moan or sigh with each spot where he lingered. The underside of her breasts and her cleavage. Her navel. Each hip. And when he reached her mound, he looked down into her eyes and saw she was anticipating his touch. With a smile that hinted at the wildness she stirred in him, he eased his hand between her thighs to palm her.

Alisha stretched her arms high above her head on the bed as she spread her legs for him.

"That feels like an invitation," he said against her temple before kissing her there.

"It is," she whispered, turning her head and lifting her chin to press a kiss to the corner of his mouth.

Tremaine drew her tongue into his mouth as he eased his middle finger inside. She was tight, warm and wet. The growl he released was primal and his hunger to fill her consumed him. "Ready?" he asked.

"Are you?" she asked as she reached out to wrap her fingers around his hardness to stroke him.

"Always."

"Always," she repeated.

"Always," he repeated as he moved to lie atop her.

"Al-ways," she agreed as she wrapped her legs around his waist.

"Always," he said again as he connected their bodies and seemingly their souls.

"Always," she gasped, digging her fingers into the muscled flesh of his shoulders as he stroked away. Deeply. Swiftly.

Knock, knock.

"Always. Always. Always."

"Tremaine," a woman's voice said, rousing him from his dream.

Knock, knock.

"Tremaine!"

Knock, knock, knock, knock.

"Always," he shouted out as he was snatched from sleep and one hell of a dream. "Huh? What?"

He looked to his left and jumped in surprise at Alisha standing there with her fist raised to knock again. With his heart pounding from a mix of shock and surprise at seeing her, he lowered the driver's-side window. "Hey," he said.

The wind whipped her hair about her face. "You're still in town?" she asked.

"I've been waiting on you to get home," Tremaine said. "I went by the store—"

"You've been here for hours?" she asked, looking cute in a V-neck sweater and wide-leg denim pants with her beloved charm bracelet in place on her left arm.

The one closest to my heart, she had once told him about the keepsake.

"You didn't call," Alisha said, stepping back as he opened the truck's door to step onto the paved courtyard.

"I wanted to surprise you," he said, studying her closely.

"I saw the interview you did," she said, looking everywhere but at him. "Thank you for that."

"The details didn't need to be shared," Tremaine said. "And I didn't want to see your reputation muddied. You didn't deserve that."

That drew her stare.

He matched it with his own.

"The day before everything blew up I was actually considering being in love with you, Tremaine," she admitted, her eyes filling with hurt that lingered.

It wrenched at him.

"That's how I felt when I realized you lied to me," he said, reaching for her hand.

She snatched it away. "You were thinking you love me?" she asked, and then shook her head in disbelief.

"I didn't call it that then, but I know that is exactly what I feel about you," he said, reaching for her and not letting her shake him off as he held on tight and pressed kisses to the side of her face. "I love you. Somehow. Someway. I fell in love with you. To hell with times and rules. Right or wrong. Family or business—to hell with it all."

She shook her head even as she left it pressed against his shoulder.

He rubbed her back, feeling hopeful. Feeling loved. It warmed him. "I know what I feel. I know how you make me feel."

Her hands rose from her sides to land on his back.

Tremaine smiled at the move. "I want to see where this goes, Alisha," he said. "I want to try our hands and our hearts at forever."

"Me, too," she whispered.

Beneath his jacket, her hands gripped his shirt and she held on to him so tightly.

"Are we crazy?" she whispered, with her fear causing her voice to tremble.

"Absolutely," he said. "And we have been since the first day we met."

Alisha leaned back to look up at him. "No more snooping," she said.

"Agreed. I apologize for that," he said. "And no more dancing around the truth."

She nodded in approval. "Nice word usage," she said. "And I'm sorry for keeping the letter away from you."

"But Eliza's actions brought us together in the end," he said.

"Destiny, huh?" she asked.

"You have got to meet my assistant, Golden," he said. "She loves you for me, by the way."

Alisha looked confused. "She does? But we've never met," she said.

"You'll get it once you talk to her. Trust me," he assured her.

They stared at each other and smiled as the wind swirled around them.

"How are we going to figure this out," she said. "Long-distance dating?"

"At first," he said, turning to wrap an arm around her shoulders and guide her forward. "Besides, we have a lot of unfinished business."

"We do?" she asked, sliding her arm around his waist. "Like what?"

"Hiring a full-time contractor to finish the renovations, for one," he said as they both stopped to look up at the sprawling home.

"And what else?" she asked.

"I was in the middle of one helluva dream when you woke me up," Tremaine said.

"Really?" she asked, looking intrigued.

"You were in it."

Alisha wiggled her feet and laughed as she leaned down long enough to unlock the front doors. "And what were we doing?"

Tremaine bent a bit to lift her up into his arms with ease. "Naughty things that I definitely want to make a reality," he said, stepping inside the foyer and closing the front door with a nudge of his foot.

* * * * *

"One Minute" Survey

You get up to **FOUR books** <u>and</u> a Mystery Gift...

ABSOLUTELY FREE!

SIZZLING ROMANCE

PASSIONATE ROMANCE

YOU pick your books – WE pay for everything!

See inside for details.

YOU pick your books –
WE pay for everything.
You get up to FOUR new books and a Mystery Gift...
absolutely FREE!
Total retail value: Over $20!

Dear Reader,

Your opinions are important to us. So if you'll participate in our fast and free "One Minute" Survey, YOU can pick up to four wonderful books that WE pay for when you try the Harlequin Reader Service!

As a leading publisher of women's fiction, we'd love to hear from you. That's why we promise to reward you for completing our survey.

IMPORTANT: Please complete the survey and return it. We'll send your Free Books and a Free Mystery Gift right away. And we pay for shipping and handling too! ← *We pay for EVERYTHING!*

Try **Harlequin® Desire** and get 2 books featuring the worlds of the American elite with juicy plot twists, delicious sensuality and intriguing scandal.

Try **Harlequin Presents® Larger-Print** and get 2 books featuring the glamourous lives of royals and billionaires in a world of exotic locations, where passion knows no bounds.

Or TRY BOTH!

Thank you again for participating in our "One Minute" Survey. It really takes just a minute (or less) to complete the survey… and your free books and gift will be well worth it!

If you continue with your subscription, you can look forward to curated monthly shipments of brand-new books from your selected series, always at a discount off the cover price! Plus you can cancel any time. So don't miss out, return your One Minute Survey today to get your Free books.

Pam Powers

"One Minute" Survey

GET YOUR FREE BOOKS AND A FREE GIFT!

✓ Complete this Survey   ✓ Return this survey

▼ DETACH AND MAIL CARD TODAY! ▼

1 Do you try to find time to read every day?
☐ YES   ☐ NO

2 Do you prefer stories with happy endings?
☐ YES   ☐ NO

3 Do you enjoy having books delivered to your home?
☐ YES   ☐ NO

4 Do you share your favorite books with friends?
☐ YES   ☐ NO

YES! I have completed the above "One Minute" Survey. Please send me m
Free Books and a Free Mystery Gift (worth over $20 retail). I understand that I am
under no obligation to buy anything, as explained on the back of this card.

☐ **Harlequin Desire®**
225/326 CTI G2AF

☐ **Harlequin Presents® Larger-Print**
176/376 CTI G2AF

☐ **BOTH**
(225/326 & 176/376)
CTI G2AG

FIRST NAME   LAST NAME

ADDRESS

APT.#   CITY

STATE/PROV.   ZIP/POSTAL CODE

EMAIL ☐ Please check this box if you would like to receive newsletters and promotional emails from
Harlequin Enterprises ULC and its affiliates. You can unsubscribe anytime.

Your Privacy—Your information is being collected by Harlequin Enterprises ULC, operating as Harlequin Reader Service. For a complete summary of the information we collect, how we use this information and to whom it is disclosed, please visit our privacy notice located at https://corporate.harlequin.com/privacy-notice. From time to time we may also exchange your personal information with reputable third parties. If you wish to opt out of this sharing of your personal information, please visit www.readerservice.com/consumerschoice or call 1-800-873-8635. Notice to California Residents—Under California law, you have specific rights to control and access your data. For more information on these rights and how to exercise them, visit https:// corporate.harlequin.com/california-privacy.

HD/HP-1123-OM

© 2023 HARLEQUIN ENTERPRISES ULC
™ and ® are trademarks owned by Harlequin Enterprises ULC. Printed in the U.S.A.

◆ HARLEQUIN Reader Service — **Here's how it works:**

Accepting your 2 free books and free gift (gift valued at approximately $10.00 retail) places you under no obligation to buy anything. You may keep the books and gift and return the shipping statement marked "cancel." If you do not cancel, approximately one month later we'll send you more books from the series you have chosen, and bill you at our low, subscribers-only discount price. Harlequin Presents® Larger-Print books consist of 6 books each month and cost $6.80 each in the U.S. or $6.99 each in Canada, a savings of at least 6% off the cover price. Harlequin Desire® books consist of 3 books (2in1 editions) each month and cost just $7.83 each in the U.S. or $8.43 each in Canada, a savings of at least 12% off the cover price. It's quite a bargain! Shipping and handling is just 50¢ per book in the U.S. and $1.25 per book in Canada*. You may return any shipment at our expense and cancel at any time by contacting customer service — or you may continue to receive monthly shipments at our low, subscribers-only discount price plus shipping and handling.

▲ If offer card is missing write to: Harlequin Reader Service, P.O. Box 1341, Buffalo, NY 14240-8531 or visit www.ReaderService.com ▲

BUSINESS REPLY MAIL
FIRST-CLASS MAIL   PERMIT NO. 717   BUFFALO, NY

POSTAGE WILL BE PAID BY ADDRESSEE

HARLEQUIN READER SERVICE
PO BOX 1341
BUFFALO NY 14240-8571

NO POSTAGE
NECESSARY
IF MAILED
IN THE
UNITED STATES

Cynthia St. Aubin wrote her first play at age eight and made her brothers perform it for the admission price of gum wrappers. When she was tall enough to reach the top drawer of her parents' dresser, she began pilfering her mother's secret stash of romance novels and has been in love with love ever since. A confirmed cheese addict, she lives in Texas with a handsome musician.

Books by Cynthia St. Aubin

Harlequin Desire

The Kane Heirs

Corner Office Confessions
Secret Lives After Hours
Bad Boy with Benefits

The Renaud Brothers

Blue Blood Meets Blue Collar
Trapped with Temptation

Texas Cattleman's Club: Diamonds & Dating Apps

Keeping a Little Secret

Visit the Author Profile page
at Harlequin.com for more titles.

You can also find Cynthia St. Aubin on Facebook,
along with other Harlequin Desire authors,
at Facebook.com/HarlequinDesireAuthors!

Dear Reader,

They had me at chocolate.

Having never written in a continuity series before, I'll admit to being a little bit nervous about the idea of working with preexisting characters. *What if they don't like me? What if I scare them away with the weird faces I make while I'm writing?* But when I heard that Tiffany Winters was a chocolatier whose impulsive decisions occasionally caused her a bit of trouble, let's just say that I knew we were going to get along *just* fine.

Of course, Tiffany wasn't the only cook making a mess of the kitchen. Ambitious CEO-to-be Preston Del Rio has never been one to stand on ceremony when he sees something he wants, and he's been wanting Tiffany for a *very* long time. Because everything is bigger in Texas—even the family feuds—Preston seizes his chance at his sister's engagement party and he and Tiffany turn up the heat big-time. Only now that she's had a taste, Tiffany's craving for the Del Rio Romeo refuses to be ignored, and what their night of passion created could be either the sweetest of surprises or a recipe for disaster.

Happy reading!

Cynthia

KEEPING A LITTLE SECRET

Cynthia St. Aubin

To anyone who's ever found their calling after trying to make all the wrong ones fit, and to those who are still looking. Curiosity is your copilot. Grab some snacks and enjoy the ride!

Acknowledgments

First and foremost, my undying gratitude to my incredibly patient husband, Ted, world's best cat dad, breakfast maker and song writer. I love you with my whole squishy heart. #Fated

Sincere gratitude to Stacy Boyd, my magnificent editor, for her patience, vision and enthusiasm.

My enthusiastic thanks to Kerrigan Byrne, my critique partner, emotional support human, platonic life partner and co-owner of wild dreams. Angus and Fergus await! Me and Thee.

My endless appreciation for my talented agent lady and momma pit bull, Christine Witthohn, for feeding me in every way possible.

Finally, my heartfelt appreciation for readers everywhere who make it possible for me to keep my cats in kibble. Your love is everything.

One

We need to talk.

Preston Del Rio's stomach knotted as he read the text glowing beneath the rosewood table in his father's corner office.

He hated surprises.

Ever since the new dating app k!smet's "SurpriseMe!" function had set off the chain of events that led to his sister getting engaged to the second eldest son of their family's bitter rival, it had been one unwelcome revelation after another.

The heirloom Del Rio necklace being found in the basement of the Winters ancestral estate.

The letter explaining how it got there.

The implosion of the tenuous truce between the Winterses and Del Rios.

And now this.

Stuck in an endless one-on-one meeting, listening to his father drone on while his brain whipped itself into a frenzy over a text from his recent one-night stand.

Before Preston could reply, his phone vibrated with a second message.

Cattleman's Club. 8:00 p.m. by the statue. You know the one.

Oh, he knew it all right.

Six weeks earlier, in the patch of shadow cast by the statue's imposing form, he had kissed Tiffany Winters.

If kissing had been *all* they'd done the night of Maggie's engagement party to Jericho Winters, Tiffany might not be texting him at all.

But what had started as a flirtatious reprisal of the role that had earned him the nickname Romeo Del Rio in high school had ended with them making out behind the Cattleman's Club's iconic bronze Texas longhorn.

From there, they'd barely made it to her house before their clothing disappeared along with their sanity.

Preston's blood heated at the memory as his hand tightened on the phone.

I'll be there, he texted in return.

"Coffee?" A gentle tap on Preston's shoulder brought his attention back to the present, where his father's executive assistant held a copper carafe in the golden afternoon light. Though it gleamed like manna from heaven, Preston shook his head.

His half-finished mug of black brew had turned into acid, eating at his gut. His third of the meeting, it failed to deliver the jolt he needed after another night of less than five hours' sleep. Despite the family feud, he'd been counting on using this evening to catch up on the notes Jericho Winters had given him regarding their shared refinery optimization project.

Staring down at Tiffany's message, he felt those hopes evaporating.

"…son?"

Preston realized—too late—that his father had asked him a question. He glanced up to find Fernando Del Rio III looking at him expectantly. In his late fifties, he still had the face of a king. Wise, but shrewd. The crinkles at the corners of his eyes did nothing to soften his iron gaze. Ditto for the subtle patches of silver sprouting at his temples and flecking the dark goatee framing his downturned mouth.

"I'm sorry, Dad." Preston set his phone facedown on his lap. "Can you repeat that?"

His father rested his forearms on the table where they always sat for these weekly chats. He had taken off his suit jacket and rolled the sleeves of his custom dress shirt to his elbows. His habit when the two of them were alone.

"Is the subject of my retirement failing to keep your attention, son?"

Oh, the acute irony of his father having to ask this. Since he'd sat on his father's lap at his first board meeting for the petrochemical company Fernando had turned into an empire, all Preston had wanted was to someday sit at the head of the table. He'd wanted it so much, he'd welded himself to his father's footsteps. Choosing the same alma mater, the same major, playing the positions on the same sports teams and mirroring the same monkish devotion to his drive.

Here he was, poised for the very moment he'd been dreaming of, and all he could think about was how good Tiffany Winters had felt in his arms.

"Of course not, Dad. I've just had a lot on my plate now that Diamond Gate put Project Optima on hold."

Saying the name the press had chosen for the on-going battle involving the Del Rio family jewels set Preston's teeth on edge. The discovery of their family heirloom in the basement of the Winterses' ancestral estate had been the death knell to the brief cease-fire that his sister's engagement to Jericho Winters had wrought. And the mediation required to broker peace, as good as a brick wall for the energy optimization project Preston and Jericho had been working on together.

"That's exactly what I wanted to talk to you about, son." Fernando leaned back in his chair. The smile that slid onto his face did nothing to release the tension gathering in Preston's chest. "I think I found somebody else to help us get Project Optima off the ground."

Preston stared at his father. "You know Maggie is still engaged to Jericho Winters, right?"

"But not married yet. And especially with how

quickly they rushed into things…well. As we know, a lot can happen between a proposal and the walk down the aisle."

Preston couldn't believe what he was hearing. Or he could, but thought that at least where Maggie was concerned, their father had put his feelings about the Winters family aside.

"You're suggesting that we cut Maggie's fiancé out of a project he came up with for our benefit?" Preston asked.

"I'm suggesting that, with a project as important and vital as Optima, you have to be willing to look past familial concerns to identify the best potential partner."

Familial concerns.

A wild understatement for the generations-long feud that had begun with Preston's great-grandfather Fernando the first, and Teddy Winters, his much-loathed adversary.

"And what if I think Jericho is the best potential partner?"

His father's expression hardened. "Then I'd say your soft spot for the Winters family makes me concerned about whether you're truly ready to step into the role of CEO."

Retirement. The carrot his father had been dangling in front of him as long as Preston could remember.

A finish line that seemed to recede into the distance no matter how hard Preston ran to reach it. All through college, he had given up friends. A social life. Even relationships, save for one completely disastrous and short-lived engagement to a classmate he'd met through his father's friend.

To have doubts about his commitment to the company thrown in his face after all that left Preston bitter and hollow.

"There's certainly been a good deal of talk about your and Tiffany Winters's interaction at your sister's engagement party."

Preston's palms began to sweat against the wooden arms of the chair.

"There's always been a good deal of talk about everything concerning our interactions with the Winterses. Maybe I just recognize that prolonging this ridiculous feud is only poisoning the well we all drink from here in Royal, Texas."

Preston knew this wasn't strictly the truth, but neither was it a lie. When it came to the Winters family, his father's ability to see clearly would always be suspect.

"It seems you're not in the right frame of mind to discuss this at the moment." The icy calm in his father's voice preceded an inevitable dismissal. "Why don't you call it a day. Go for a run. Give you time to sort out your thoughts."

Priorities, more like. Suggesting both solitude and physical exercise had ever been his father's resolution to conflict. Or to give him the chance to realize that he was the source of it.

Preston had no intention of taking his father's suggestion, but knew to argue with him further would be pointless. Better to take the opportunity to make a smooth exit.

"Sounds good," he said. "See you tomorrow."

"You're not coming over for dinner tonight?"

Shit. He'd entirely forgotten the plans his mother and Maggie had made earlier via their WhatsApp family thread.

"I'm afraid I can't," Preston said, tucking his phone in his pocket. "I have some work to catch up on. I'll let Mom know."

Fernando studied him, his dark brows lowered over narrowed eyes. "All right, son."

Preston was at the door to his father's cavernous office, nearly home free when a coda was added.

"Think about what I said."

As if he hadn't already.

As if he hadn't been thinking about it since he was just a boy, when his father stood beside him before the windows of this very office, looking out over their vast oil refinery and the flat sprawl of Texas countryside beyond.

As if he didn't know exactly how much he stood to lose if he lost his father's faith.

Preston glanced at the digital readout as he slid behind the wheel of his Alfa Romeo. Just after 6:00 p.m.

He'd stop by home first.

Shower the day off him and change out of his *Future CEO of Del Rio Group* attire.

Two hours had seemed an eternity, and yet, the fizz of excitement made the minutes pass in a blur once he'd arrived home.

Every time he glanced at the clock on his phone and found more minutes gone, Preston was taken aback by the fierce pulse of pleasure.

He'd known that he wanted to see Tiffany Winters again.

But until her text, he just hadn't known how much.

Two

Tiffany Winters sat in the parking lot outside the Texas Cattleman's Club, keeping her eyes trained skyward until she saw the first star wink into existence.

She noticed things like this now. The first hint of red on the old oak tree. Sunset's last wisp of orange. Things she would have missed in the hustle and bustle of the life she'd forever think about as *before*.

Before she knew she was pregnant with Preston Del Rio's baby.

Looking back, there had been at least a dozen signs she'd also overlooked in the daily whirl of work, family and school.

Signs, like brown sugar fudge.

Long one of her favorite staples at Chocolate Fix, it had been the first time she'd experienced a strong repulsion to a familiar and formerly loved smell. So strong, she'd dumped a whole batch from the steam kettle before starting over and nearly dumping a second when she was interrupted by Moira, who arrived for work and insisted she neither smelled nor tasted anything different.

Then, it had been the dizzy spells.

She'd be standing there at the counter, packing an order of truffles, when the brightly colored array of confections would start to swim like fractals in a kaleidoscope and she had to brace herself to avoid sliding sideways off the planet.

Her eating habits had never been stellar and her sleep cycles less than reliable, and when she began devoting late nights to working on her MBA, Tiffany had begun to suspect it might be her ever-erratic schedule had finally caught up with her.

But…no.

She had received the final word on the matter three days after her missed period. Out of desperation, after work she drove thirty miles out of town to buy a pregnancy test.

Because God forbid any of the Royal locals see it in her shopping basket at the Kroger's.

Impatient creature she had always been, Tiffany had elected to take the test in the women's restroom before even leaving the store.

Three minutes and two pink lines later, her life changed forever.

Tonight, she'd be changing Preston's.

The thought brought her a pang of guilt as she

watched his black sports car pull into the parking lot. From her vantage, she could just make him out through the tinted glass, finishing a conversation on his phone. Two minutes passed before he disconnected, opened the driver's-side door and walked to the appointed spot.

Tiffany bit her lower lip, experiencing a keen ache in her middle that had nothing to do with her pelvis expanding to make room for the life growing there.

Preston Del Rio moved like a man who owned the world.

And why wouldn't he?

Poised to take over a suite of companies conservatively valued in the billions, he could buy a good chunk of it. Already, he'd earned a reputation as a worthy successor to his father, Fernando Del Rio III. Shrewd as he was ruthless. Brutal as he was brilliant.

For one glorious night, she'd tasted it all.

She supposed it was time to pay the piper.

Flipping her sun visor down, she checked herself in the anemic glow of the car's interior light.

Was it her imagination that painted smudges beneath her brown eyes? Only her imagination that thickened her eyelids and leached color from her normally golden complexion? She honestly couldn't tell.

That was the thing about secrets.

They transformed you from the inside out.

Fluffing her hair and pinching her cheeks, she dropped her keys into her purse and got on with it.

Whether out of politeness or ceremony, Preston didn't turn to face her until she was a couple of yards away.

When he did, Tiffany felt the bottom drop out of her stomach for a second time.

That damn lopsided grin. The silky Belgian cocoa hair falling into his hazel eyes. The cocky smirk lifting one corner of lips she could remember meeting hers for the first time in this very spot.

Now, they shaped the word *wow*, before he caught himself, cleared his throat and straightened.

This had to be a kindness on his part. Tiffany felt about as far from wow as a body could get in the billowy high-waisted black palazzo pants, plain white tank and chunky cardigan that had become her uniform when she was in town. Though she knew for a fact she wasn't yet showing, she couldn't shake the fact that a glowing neon sign blinked over her head.

"Thanks for coming," she said. "I'm sorry for the short notice."

"You didn't give me much of a choice."

He was correct, she knew. Her message had been deliberately vague. Provocative enough as to ensure his compliance.

"Should we walk?" she asked, cutting her eyes toward the building. The TCC would be quiet on a weekday night, but what represented neutral ground gave no guarantees of staying that way as the night wore on.

"Depends."

He leaned in, and she was overcome with an ambrosiac mix of his cologne, laundry detergent and clean, impossibly smooth skin. That this had replaced brown sugar fudge as her favorite smell in the entire world had to be down to some kind of oxytocin-induced mania.

"On what?" she asked.

"Whether this walk will be ending the way our last one did." He flashed her a smile that threatened to turn her knees to water.

"That's kind of what I need to talk to you about." Tiffany hugged her cardigan tighter around her, her palm pressed against her still-flat abdomen as she turned and started to walk before his scent could drive her to acts of desperation.

Preston's dark hair fell in his eyes as he cast a sideways glance at her. "I'm game if you are."

"I'm pregnant." The words fell from her lips, completely preempting the careful speech she had labored over for hours, days even.

Preston stopped in his tracks. "What?"

"I'm pregnant, Preston."

In the waning light from the clubhouse that had been Royal's social hub for generations, he turned to her.

"You're…"

"Pregnant," she said quickly, beyond ready to have this part of the evening out of the way so they could make a plan.

He reached up to brush his hair out of his face. "But how?"

Tiffany arched an eyebrow at him. "Do you honestly not remember, or are you asking me to explain the mechanics to you?"

"It was only the one time," he said. "And I, *we*—"

"Had unprotected sex?" she finished for him. "You want to guess how many babies have been conceived the same way?" That the memory should fill her with such smug pleasure felt entirely inappropriate to the gravity of the moment. "And anyway, it wasn't one time, it was one *night*."

A night she remembered all too well.

Their conversation at the bar after a sumptuous dinner. How effortlessly it had turned into a flirtation. From a flirtation into a dance. A dance that turned into a stroll in the balmy late September evening. How the stroll had turned into a kiss. How the kiss had become...*more*. Hands everywhere, a brushfire burning out of control. Unsatisfied with frenzied groping, they had stumbled to his car and laid down several feet of rubber exiting the parking lot.

Luckily, the event had coincided with the commencement of the fireworks that had drawn everyone onto the sprawling deck and sloping field beyond the clubhouse.

What had occurred at her house after that, she couldn't bear to think about, lest she lose her nerve.

Only the most memorable night of her entire life.

Until the one she'd spent cradling a positive pregnancy test in her hand.

They'd been so stupid. So incredibly reckless.

"You're pregnant," Preston repeated.

"Yes."

He took a step closer, his breath warm on her cheeks as he gazed down into her eyes. "You're pregnant with *my* baby?"

How she wished those words didn't turn her insides to melted butter. How she wished she could erase the flash of fear in his eyes when she nodded. "I am.

"I'm going to have it," she added before he could betray anything else. "But how involved you want to be is entirely up to you."

"You're sure?"

It was almost cute, his naïvety.

Like she hadn't spent every single minute of her life thinking about this from the second she knew.

"I'm sure." Tiffany forced her boots to begin moving toward the creek. "I feel like we shouldn't announce it before Maggie and Jericho's wedding. I don't want to steal their thunder."

"Agreed," he said, falling into step beside her again. "How far along, exactly?"

"Six weeks," she said.

"Have you been to a doctor yet?"

"Not yet," she admitted. "HIPAA laws notwithstanding, I wanted to talk with you before anyone spotted me in the ob-gyn's office on a regular basis."

Was it relief, this easing of tension on his face? Relief that it was still a secret? Or maybe relief that she'd approached this so tactically.

"Does anyone else know?" he asked, answering her question.

"Alisha."

The corner of his mouth curled upward. "And she hasn't tried to run me over with her Speedster yet, so that's a good sign."

"Don't take this the wrong way, but she wouldn't consider that worth risking her custom paint job." She smirked at him. "Also, I swore her to secrecy."

"We both know how good she is at that." He slid her a sideways glance.

Tiffany didn't know if he intended it to be a dig, but it certainly felt like one. That Alisha and their brother Marcus had originally lied, not only about the appearance of the Del Rio necklace, but the confession letter from Eliza Boudreaux explaining how it came to be in the basement of the Winters ancestral home was the reason the ugly wound between their families had been torn open afresh. The upcoming negotiation that Jack Chowdhry had stepped up to assist with did little to ease her mind.

"She and Tremaine seem to be doing well," Preston said after an awkward silence.

Tiffany felt a twinge of uncharacteristic envy at the mention of the new man in her big sister's life. Six years Tiffany's senior, her beautiful, brilliant sister always seemed to be so much further ahead. From her long-legged stride to her voracious appetite for knowledge and her keen head for business. Tiffany couldn't help but feel she was forever scrambling in her wake, gratefully following the path she'd already blazed.

But then, this was the case with all her siblings. Jericho had his thriving green architecture firm and was soon to be married to the love of his life. Trey had his ranch and now had Misha, a wildly tech-savvy partner, to go with it. Even Marcus, and his own successful luxury home goods business, had a new passionate partner by his side with Jessica.

Meanwhile, Tiffany had done things backward as usual. The business before the MBA. The baby before the relationship. Not that Preston had even grazed against that idea.

"They're ridiculously happy, all right."

Preston slowed at her side. "I'm sorry," he said. "I haven't even asked you how you're feeling about all this." The genuine concern in his dark, intelligent eyes was a balm for her aching heart.

"Freaked out. Tired. Excited. Incredibly irresponsible." Treacherous tears glazed her eyes and she turned away to look out on the crystalline trickle of water.

Warm hands landed on her shoulders and turned her to face Preston. "It took two of us to create this situation, and there will two of us working together to figure out the best possible solution. I know I don't have the best track record, but I promise you I'm going to be here for you, Tiffany."

She wished she could believe him.

But he was right. An ever-changing cast of Royal's most beautiful debutantes had been his leading ladies throughout high school. And though she'd relied on the gossip mill for information about his exploits in college, she was aware of his engagement to the iconic Instagram influencer Sunny Rothschild. Even that hadn't stuck.

"I'm okay, Preston. Really, I am. I'll have plenty of help. Alisha has already assigned herself favorite aunt status, and my mom has been hinting about more grandbabies because Trey's son, Dez, is such an amazing kid. This doesn't need to affect your career plans in any way."

Tiffany didn't fail to notice the subtle bob of his Adam's apple nor the flexing of his jaw.

He hadn't made it this far in his considerations yet. Now that he had, the fear was plain in his face. It didn't take a psychic to figure out how his father would react to this news.

"Just let me know how I can help," he said.

Hold me, she silently willed him. *Take me in your arms and make me feel like everything will be all right.* It was a silly, romantic whimsy to wish for this. Longing to be in his arms was exactly what put her in this position.

"I will," she said. Her phone chirped in the pocket of her cardigan and Tiffany drew it out to see a text from Alisha.

All good? Because I'm at the diner and I can be there in five minutes.

Tiffany smiled down at the screen. This was just like her sister. Despite her insistence that she didn't need backup, Alisha had stationed herself at the Royal Diner in case she needed to swoop to the rescue.

As she so often had.

All good, Tiffany quickly answered. Will stop by after.

"Everything okay?" Preston asked.

Feeling her insides flutter at the sexy rasp in his

voice, Tiffany resolved to get herself out of here sooner than later.

"Yep." She dropped the device back into her pocket and forced a smile onto her face. "I do need to get back to Chocolate Fix, though."

He lifted a dark eyebrow. "This late? And I thought I was a workaholic."

Tiffany turned and began strolling back toward the parking lot. "I'm afraid so. I've got a huge order coming up for Misha's employee appreciation party at the k!smet headquarters."

Technically, not a lie. But not the full truth, either. She needed to stop back by the shop, only to make sure Moira and Steph had their marching orders for the mountain of prep that needed to happen.

"Things at the shop going well?" he asked.

This felt like a bone tossed in her direction. Compared to a petrochemical business behemoth like the Del Rio Group, Chocolate Fix might as well be a lemonade stand.

But she'd had hopes it wouldn't always be that way. Getting her MBA was only part of the phased rollout she had expanding her little shop to a national brand.

Licensing to put her chocolates in high-end restaurants. Gourmet grocery outlets. Finally, the thing she was most excited about, the nonprofit she planned to establish to provide financial support to female cocoa farmers in underdeveloped communities.

All her carefully laid plans. Her life just taking a shape that resembled her. To make her mark not only within the Winters family, but the world.

Once again, she'd managed to derail herself.

"Going good," she said. "Super busy, but I'm not complaining."

"That's great," he said. They both slowed when they had once again reached the statue where all their troubles began.

A lone cricket that had survived the first freeze chirred from a clump of ornamental sweet grass bordering the gigantic bronze bull.

Singing its heart out for no one.

The thought pierced her with acute sorrow she decided to blame on hormones.

Preston's eyes lit with an odd glow as he captured a tendril of brown hair and tucked it behind her ear. Electricity danced on her skin at the contact.

"Well, there's one thing I know for sure," he said, leaning in until she was washed with another heady wave of his intoxicating scent on the cool night breeze.

"What's that?"

He fixed her with a boyish grin that revealed the dimple in his chin to full, devastating effect. "This is going to be one good-looking kid."

Tension made them both laugh harder than the joke deserved, but it felt good to share this one, warm thing.

"Preston, I—"

"I was thinking," he said at the exact same moment.

Tiffany's heart beat at the base of her throat. "Go ahead," she insisted.

"Why don't I wait here for a second?" he said. "Let you leave first? Just in case…"

"Right," she said preemptively.

Preston didn't need to finish the sentence. All it would take was for one of the many Royal gossip mavens to spot them out on a romantic stroll together and the rumor mill would begin working overtime.

Hell, she'd scarcely stilled the tongues that had been wagging since they both went missing from Maggie and Jericho's engagement party.

But it still stung.

Tiffany located her keys in her cardigan pocket. "I guess I'll be in touch then?"

"Sounds good," he said.

Her bottom lip began to quiver the second her back was to him. By the time she reached her car, her cheeks were wet with tears.

A fresh wave came as she turned over the engine, unable to banish the question that made her heart feel like a lump of lead in her chest.

She wondered just how much of this journey she would walk alone.

Three

Preston sat in his car, watching the foot traffic at the edge of Royal's quaint downtown area and psyching himself up for the task ahead.

His stomach growled its protest at having been neglected in favor of squeezing in a couple more meetings last minute. Lack of sleep and warm air blasting from the car vents made his eyes feel grainy and dry.

Running on empty had become his default setting in the last year of attempting to prove his readiness to take on the role of CEO, but he owed last night's restlessness to a completely different cause.

Tiffany Winters.

Pregnant.

His mind still refused to wrap itself around this fact. Which was why he was parked outside Odds & Ends,

Alisha Winters's sharply curated antique furniture/ consignment shop.

Enough procrastinating.

He killed the engine and got out, taking a deep breath of the cool autumn evening air before facing his fate.

"Well, well, well. If it isn't Romeo Del Rio." Alisha Winters stood behind the counter, the angular set of her jaw and arms folded across her chest confirming what he already suspected to be the case.

He had royally blown it with Tiffany.

"Please don't call me that," he said, attempting to summon the proper amount of contrition to the request.

"Would you prefer *father-to-be*?"

Preston winced.

Words that were so familiar but completely abstract had taken on new meaning.

"I'd prefer Preston."

"I know what I'd like to call you," she muttered under her breath. Turning her gaze back to the paperwork and iPad she'd been focused on when he came in, she allowed him to stand there, squirming for several awkward moments.

Preston planted his hands on the counter, refusing to be dismissed. "Can you please just tear me a new asshole and get it over with?"

Alisha finally looked him in the eye. "You *want* me to eviscerate you?"

"Immediately," Preston said. "If not sooner."

"Why?" she demanded.

"Because I really need to talk."

He had arrived at the idea of coming here by process of elimination. Maggie had always been his compass and his confidant. Both roles she largely had to abdicate during the course of her whirlwind courtship and subsequent engagement to Jericho.

She hadn't even busted him for missing dinner last night. An offense that would have earned him at least a WTF text during any other phase of their lives.

He had thought about reaching out to Tremaine. They'd met in college and stayed best friends after. Preston had always valued his analytical mind and no bullshit approach to life. But bringing him into the loop would mean one more person who knew, and that only meant more opportunity for word of Tiffany's pregnancy to get out.

Which was when the idea popped into his head.

Why not talk to somebody who *already* knew?

If he couldn't talk to his own sister, he'd do the next best thing.

He'd talk to Tiffany's.

Standing in Alisha's arctic chill, he was rapidly reconsidering this sentiment.

"You need to talk?" She set the iPad aside hard enough for Preston to worry about the delicate components. "Cool. Let's talk. How about you start by telling me what the hell you were thinking when you slept with my sister?"

"I wasn't," he ventured.

"Damn right you weren't." Alisha's tawny skin took on a more russet hue as her cheeks flushed.

She came around the counter, her face mask-tight and hands balled into fists at her sides. "Look, I get it. It was a wild night. The dancing, the drinking… But with all the women available at the engagement party, you seriously thought of Tiffany as the best option for a random hookup?"

"It may have been a hookup," he admitted, pushing a hand through his hair. "But it wasn't random."

She cocked her head of onyx curls. "You're saying you were interested in Tiffany *before* you were both full of champagne and stupid?"

His chest deflated with a long exhale.

He'd come this far. "Just because our families have let this ridiculous animosity fester for generations doesn't mean I'm blind, Alisha. Tiffany has always done her own thing and I really admire that."

She studied him with leonine eyes that gave him the eerie feeling she could see straight through his skull. "And how long have you been admiring? Because I'm really hoping the answer isn't something like 'after the hors d'oeuvres but before the soup course' at the engagement party."

Funny thing was, he actually remembered when it had started.

With the senior drama class he'd taken to get out of honors English Lit. He hadn't known Tiffany Winters was also enrolled in the drama program until halfway through the semester when Mr. Overton, their instructor, announced that Tiffany needed volunteers to help build the set for the updated version of Shakespeare's *Romeo and Juliet* she was student directing for her freshman class. The strength of Preston's reaction to the tragedy had surprised him. He'd even earned detention by walking out in the middle of a rehearsal.

Only later had he identified its source.

His unrequited crush on the doe-eyed beauty who had always smiled shyly at him despite their family's rancor. Knowing that he couldn't so much as wave to Tiffany without both their fathers finding out made Preston want to break things.

Starting with the stupid rule that Del Rios didn't date Winterses.

As always, his sister had beaten him to the punch. Not only dating a Winters, but getting engaged to one. Preston had been naive enough to believe that might actually change something. At Maggie's engagement party, he'd been foolish enough to act on the magnetic attraction that had drawn him toward Tiffany for years. Only for their families to resume their endless wrangling in the aftermath.

Maybe they'd both known it was inevitable.

Maybe that was why they'd gone as far and as fast as they had.

Because the idea of unpacking this entire story made him feel instantly exhausted, Preston simply said, "Before I left for college."

Alisha's icy demeanor softened at this. "You're telling me you had a crush on Tiffany when she was a teenager?"

"We were both teenagers, if you'll remember."

Alisha glared at him. "I remember you showing up

at every single dance and football game with a different debutante on your arm."

"Most of them the daughters of whichever oil baron my father happened to be courting at the time," Preston pointed out.

"As sorry as I am that was the case, this isn't high school anymore, Preston. And there's a lot more at stake than a date to the homecoming dance."

Irritation singed the edges of his fraying patience. "Why do you think I'm here?"

"Because you need my help redeeming yourself from the absolute shit show of a performance the other night?"

He didn't bother denying it.

"I guess I was kind of caught off guard? I'm not exactly sure how you're supposed to react when you get that kind of news."

Alisha snorted. "Not acting like a goddamn robot would have been a good start."

It hadn't been the first time he'd experienced this problem.

When he'd broken things off with Sunny, his one failed attempt at a long-term relationship, he'd been so concerned about sparing her feelings, she hadn't actually understood that he was breaking up with her. She'd shown up at his door the following morning with coffee in hand and a solicitous expression on her face.

Round two hadn't been nearly so amicable.

"Okay. Yes. I think we've thoroughly established that I fucked up. What I need to know is how *not* to do that." Preston held out his hands in supplication. "You know her better than anyone in the world, Alisha. I don't want to force my way into her life, but I want to be there for her. And for my child."

My child.

This was the first time he'd spoken these words aloud and doing so filled him with a gust of protective warmth. He wanted to be there in ways his father never had been. He just had no idea how he was going to do that *and* take over running the Del Rio Group.

"Step one," she said. "Tiffany is trying to run a business *while* getting her MBA. Now she's going to be doing both those things while trying to gestate your child. She doesn't need a man. She needs a co-parent."

"Co-parent," Preston repeated. "Got it."

"Step two," Alisha said. "Follow me."

Preston did as ordered, trailing her toward the back of her shop where a long glass case of jewelry and other smaller but expensive items were displayed. His heart began to hammer in his chest when she unlocked the case holding a small selection of diamond engagement rings. He felt a rush of relief when Alisha bypassed them and picked up a gleaming silver rattle.

She held it up by the intricately carved handle.

"Step two. You're going to tell me what incredibly thoughtful sentiment you would like engraved on this and then you're going to come back in half an hour to find it gift wrapped and ready to deliver to a woman who is currently testing out different colors of beige for a nursery."

The mental image slammed into him with such a fierce tenderness, it rocked him back on his heels. "You really think she won't mind my showing up unannounced?"

"Showing up unannounced *with a present*." She shrugged her elegant shoulders. "It worked for the magi."

Preston followed her up to the counter where Alisha waited with a pencil in hand to take down the requested sentiment. He dragged the sleep-deprived depths of his mind and was about to resort to an internet search when Friar Lawrence rode to the rescue. Preston recited the line with slight alterations for context. "May 'this alliance may so happy prove, to turn our households' rancor to pure love.'"

Alisha blinked at him. "And here I was hoping you didn't serve up a *Fight Club* quote." Alisha snatched an Odds & Ends branded notepad and scratched a hasty scrawl onto the first page.

"Sometimes I even surprise myself." He reached into his back pocket to pull out his wallet. "How much do I owe you?"

Returning to her station behind the counter, she set the rattle on a padded black velvet jewelry board. "You're in luck," she said. "You qualify for the father-to-be discount."

Heat baked from beneath his collar. They finished the transaction and he walked to The Eatery for a mood-enhancing coffee while he waited. Alisha was with another customer when he returned, but cut her eyes toward a box on the counter, beautifully wrapped with a silver bow and mint-green ribbon.

Neutral colors.

He ducked his head in gratitude and saw her mouth two words on his way to the door. "Good luck."

He sure as hell needed it.

Pulling up to the curb in front of Tiffany's home, Preston endured a tidal wave of sensory memory. As her house was closer to the Texas Cattleman's Club than his own, they had opted to drive here, fueled by their impatient, mad passion. He hadn't truly appreciated how beautiful it was, his attention being otherwise engaged when they had arrived that night.

The ivy crawling up either side of the main bank of windows had just begun to go shades of red and gold at the edges. Roses grew wild on trellises in the side yard. The brick had been treated with a technique he recognized from the home-flipping shows he sometimes watched when he couldn't sleep. Chalky white in some places with patches of red and brown in others. Against freshly painted black shutters, the effect was cozy and bewitching. Cottagecore at its finest.

He turned off the engine and opened the door, grinning as he heard the bass thump of nightclub music drifting from the open windows. Gift in hand, he approached the front door with the nervous gait of a prom date.

How might their lives have been different if he'd been allowed to ask her? She had been a freshman when he was a senior and the gap would have raised some eyebrows, but not enough to stop him had his father not been the source of his hesitation.

He pressed the glowing blue circle of the app-based doorbell and was surprised when no chime sounded. He tried again to the same effect.

Preston tapped on the glass door and waited, but no answer came.

Trying the door handle, he found it unlocked.

How could she just leave the front of her house un-protected like this? The window was wide open, and the music loud enough that she couldn't even hear if someone just decided to let himself in.

Instead of going inside, Preston stalked around the side of the house to where the loudest of the music seemed to be emanating.

There, just outside the golden beam of light spill-ing from another open window, he spotted Tiffany Winters.

Dancing.

He stood transfixed, unable to tear his eyes away from the sight before him even to announce him-self. Her hips rolling and undulating in an earthy rhythm, her thighs flexing beneath the frayed ends of her denim cutoffs. Her breasts swaying beneath the thin fabric of her white tank top. Chocolate-brown tendrils of hair whipping free of the messy pile atop her head, her cheeks flushed against the dark cres-cents of lashes fanning against them.

Tiffany wasn't just glowing, she was *radiating*. Giving off waves of sensual earth goddess energy as she moved her body like an enchantress. The song hit its bridge and her lips parted, the blunt edge of a paintbrush rising to hover before her mouth like a microphone.

He couldn't much hear her above the thumping bass, but he smiled anyway, intensely grateful that he had taken Alisha's advice to drop by.

The song ended, and with it the spell.

Tiffany's eyelids fluttered open. She looked straight at Preston, leaped back about a yard and emitted an ear-piercing shriek. Preston fumbled the box, nearly dropping it before he recovered his coordination.

The music ceased abruptly as Tiffany stamped over to the window. A radioactive wash of red stretched from her forehead to her chest.

"What the hell do you think you're doing?" she demanded.

Preston opened his mouth to speak, but she kept rolling, stabbing the air with the paintbrush for emphasis. "You can't just sneak up on me like that. And why are you just lurking there outside my window? Do you have any idea how creepy that is?"

"I—the front door—I rang, but—"

"Wait. Where are you parked?"

"On the curb out front—"

"Shit!" She disappeared from the window and reappeared seconds later, flustered and breathless. "Well, come on. We need to get your car off the street before the neighbors see it."

Preston sprinted back to the front of her house and unlocked his car with the key fob before pulling it in next to her Jeep in the garage. The door leading from the garage to the kitchen stood ajar.

He found her standing in front of the open fridge, guzzling what looked like sweet tea from a Mason jar. She was breathing hard when she finished, holding the tea out to him in silent invitation.

Preston accepted it more out of solidarity than thirst but found the brew to be strong and lightly sweet…unlike the tea-flavored sugar syrup that many of the restaurants in Royal favored.

"Thanks," he said, handing it back to her. Tiffany took several more swallows before placing it back in the fridge.

"Last time, I had to tell everyone that my Jeep hadn't started, and you'd been kind enough to loan me your car so I could get home."

It took him a moment to realize she was talking about the engagement party and her having to explain to nosy neighbors what his car had been doing in her driveway. They'd been so mad for each other it hadn't even occurred to them.

As if strung together on a fishing line, memories of that night came in quick succession, prompted by the surroundings in which they had occurred. The granite counter of the large kitchen island where they now stood—where he had set her down to align their mouths. The wall connecting her dining room to the living room—where they nearly knocked a family picture off the wall while fumbling at each other's buttons and zippers. The leather living room couch—where they'd landed first but ended up rolling to the floor in their frenzy. The hallway leading to her bedroom, which had seemed miles long in their haste to reach a large horizontal surface.

He was glad he at least had the presence of mind to stop what they started outside the Cattleman's Club. The thought of his future son or daughter having been conceived against a wall set his teeth on edge.

"What's wrong with your doorbell?" he asked.

"My doorbell?" she asked.

"I rang your doorbell when I got here but it didn't make a sound."

"Huh," she said, fishing her phone from the back pocket of her cutoffs. "That's odd."

"And why wasn't your door locked?" he asked, tearing his eyes away from the ample curve of her ass.

"It was," she said distractedly, squinting at something on her phone.

"Oh really?" He marched into her living room and waited until she was within his eyeline to demonstrate by swinging the glass door outward.

"I *thought* it was." She shook her head. "I'm so scatterbrained these days, I swear."

An answer that comforted him not at all.

"With you back there and the music blaring like that, anyone could have just walked right in here and you would never know."

She looked up from her phone, her eyes narrowing slightly. "Well, I guess I'm lucky that someone just watched me from the window instead."

The tips of his ears flamed like someone had taken

a match to them. "Where I wouldn't have been if your doorbell actually worked."

He knew what he was doing and suspected she did too. Picking a fight to dispel the tension thickening the air between them. Behind it, a desire to protect her he had absolutely no right to.

"What do you think I'm trying to do here? It looks like the device came unpaired from my app." She returned her gaze to the phone and frowned.

"Do you want me to look at it?" he offered.

"Because your male brain is superior at all things technological?"

"Because you keep squinting and I'm assuming you removed your contacts to paint," he said.

With a warm, intelligent mother and a brilliant, creative sister like Maggie, the male tendency to assume any kind of superiority had never taken root.

"Oh," she said, shifting on her bare feet. "Thanks."

The phone was warm in his hand as he opened the settings and reset the pairing with minimal trouble. "Done," he said, returning it to her.

"Thanks." Tiffany slipped the phone back into her pocket and folded her arms under her breasts. "Is that for me?"

Her eyes lit on the box Preston had all but forgotten he had slipped under his arm when he reached for her phone. That she wore no bra under the tank top did nothing to aid his concentration.

"Right. Yes. It's actually for *both* of you." His gaze flicked to her belly as he held it out.

"Then we should open it in the nursery," she said, taking the box from his hands.

He followed her down the hallway and into the room she'd been painting. She lifted a large plastic sheet covering a pile of items he guessed had been part of a guest room and she perched on a box.

Preston pretended to busy himself examining the freshly painted walls.

"I'm keeping it neutral," she said from behind him. "I want it to be a surprise."

"Won't that make it difficult to pick out clothes and…things?" he asked, embarrassingly bereft in his knowledge on this topic.

"Not really." The wrapping paper crinkled. "There's actually a wealth of gender-neutral—*oh*!" Her gasp made him whirl around sharply.

Her fingertips were pressed to her lips, her eyes wide and shining. She lifted them from the gleaming silver rattle to his face. "Preston. It's so beautiful. I… I…" She laughed. "I may need you to read it to me."

He recited it instead.

The tears welling in her eyes spilled down her cheeks and he imagined roots growing from the soles of his shoes to keep him from crossing the room to hold her.

"Now that I've interrupted your night, startled you *and* made you cry…" He trailed off.

"Please." She snorted. "*Everything* makes me cry these days. You should have seen me bawling in the walk-in fridge earlier this morning because there was a shriveled strawberry I couldn't use."

"And you were sorry to waste it?" he asked.

"I was sorry that all its friends got to be beautiful chocolate-dipped strawberries and it got left behind."

Preston felt like he'd been mule-kicked directly in the sternum. "I happen to know a guy with a ranch and would be happy to take up a collection of any fruit unsuitable for human consumption. Goats aren't nearly so picky."

Tiffany gently placed the rattle back in its protective box and stood. "You would do that?"

He placed a hand over his chest. "It would be my honor," he said with exaggerated chivalry. "As gladly as I would take on any other quests, errands or general missions to keep you from dehydrating through your eye sockets."

Tiffany chuckled and wiped her cheeks with the tail of her tank top. The flash of her smooth plane of a stomach revealed no visible changes.

"You really don't have to do all this, Preston. I meant what I said at the TCC. I don't want this to be an imposition on your life."

He took a step toward her. "That's actually what I came here to talk to you about."

"What about it?" she asked.

"How I blew it mostly. My dad and I had had a big blowup earlier that afternoon, and I was already keyed up about the upcoming mediation with Jack Chowdhry over that damn necklace. When I got your text, I didn't know what to think. I went into it trying to stay neutral and ended up coming off like a goddamn robot." Deliberate thievery of Alisha's assessment.

"I wouldn't say a robot. Now a cyborg maybe…" She returned to her paint tray and bent to work the roller over the pan.

"Do you want some help?"

She glanced at him over her shoulder, blowing a lock of hair away from her face. "You're not exactly dressed for it."

Her divided attention resulted in her dropping the handle of the roller into the puddle of creamy beige.

"Shit," she hissed under her breath as she fished it out, searching for a rag.

"Let me." He lifted one from a pile near her other supplies and brought it to her.

Tiffany wiped her hand, then the handle before pushing her hair out of her eyes again and smudging her cheek in the process.

Preston grabbed another rag. "Come here. I need to get that before it dries and you have to find makeup to match Desert Sand."

"This is Alpaca Mist, I'll have you know."

"I don't know what's funnier," he said, dabbing at the smudge. "That someone in marketing actually signed off on naming a paint color after a ruminant, or that with all the options available to you, you decided that you wanted alpaca-colored walls."

Her chin brushed against his fingers as she laughed. "I was actually thinking alpacas could be the whole theme."

"Theme?"

"You know, for the nursery? Bedding, clothes, decor, etcetera. Alisha was telling me they have this huge outlet in Coleman."

Preston caught the scent of vanilla and lavender rising from her warm skin. "I could go with you sometime."

She blinked up at him. "Really?"

He nodded. "I think Coleman is far enough from Royal's rumor mill we might even be able to park out in the open and walk in together. What do you think?"

Her lips pursed and her brow furrowed as if in deep contemplation. "Sounds plausible. After the k!smet employee party is over, I might even be able to take an actual vacation day."

Preston felt a band of anxiety tighten around his ribs. The odds that his father wouldn't notice his taking a vacation day were next to none.

But he wanted this. He wanted to spend an entire day with Tiffany Winters away from prying eyes. Unconcerned about the stories they might tell. Feeling the way he felt the one night their family history hadn't mattered.

He tossed aside the soiled cloth and captured the tendril of her hair that kept falling in her face before gently tucking it back into the pile on top of her head.

"Sounds like a plan," he said.

Neither of them moved.

Standing there, Preston could still remember the exact spot her warm breath had cooled the sweat on his chest. The place on his ribs her curled fist had tucked against. The precise location on his leg where her knee pressed and her ankle hooked. She had fallen asleep right on top of him and he'd lain there stroking the silky curve of her bare back. Knowing it was a moment too beautiful to last.

But together they made something that would.

And now, he had to figure out how to care for his child without falling desperately in love with its mother or compromising the future he'd worked and sacrificed for his entire adult life.

He took a step backward to retain his sanity.

"Promise me you'll let me know how I can help."

"I promise," Tiffany said.

Preston made his way back to the garage. "Lock the door after me?"

Because everyone and everything in his world depended upon it, Preston found the strength to turn, and leave.

Winding through the familiar roads of Royal beneath the darkened sky, Preston couldn't get the sound of her adorably pitchy laugh out of his ears or her intoxicating scent out of his lungs.

Four

The shrilling of her phone woke Tiffany out of a dead sleep and the most delicious dream she'd ever had. She batted about in the darkness, searching her nightstand even as she still felt the phantom weight of Preston's body on hers. Her hand closed over the familiar shape. She blinked and rubbed her eyes, and seeing the name on the screen, quickly answered the call.

"Hey, Moira," she said. "What's up?"

"I am so, so sorry to call you this early."

Hearing the thick sound of tears in her employee's voice, Tiffany sat straight up in bed. "Are you okay?"

There was a sniffle on the other line. "Steph and I went out for drinks last night, and I don't know if it was something we ate, but we've both been sick all night."

"Food poisoning?"

"We think so. I can try to find someone else to fill in for me today, but—" A retch cut off the rest of the sentence. The line went muffled, but what she heard in the background was unmistakable.

A toilet flushed, and Tiffany waited through several moments of silence until Moira's croaking voice came back on the line.

"I'm so, so sorry," she said again. "I know today is going to be the final push for the k!smet employee party, and we haven't even started prepping the chocolate fountain trays—" Moira coughed and blew out an audible exhale. Tiffany imagined her sitting very still, trying to breathe through another wave of nausea.

"It's okay, Moira. I promise. I'll figure something out."

"But—"

"Listen, if you've got any ginger, try making yourself some ginger tea. Cutting off a little piece to put under your tongue will help as well." Or so Tiffany had read in many of the forums for newly expecting moms she'd been exploring since she found out.

"Okay," Moira said after another sniffle.

"You get some rest," Tiffany said. "I'll call to check on you later."

"Okay. Thanks, Tiff."

Moira disconnected and Tiffany flopped back against the pillows to stare up at the ceiling. Dawn hadn't yet begun to creep through the blinds.

Just after 4:00 a.m. They had planned to meet at Chocolate Fix at 6:00 a.m. to get started.

Calling one of her brothers would likely earn her a

long day of listening to their unsolicited critiques of her business plan. Alisha had her own store to run and had already shared plans about closing up early to go for a day trip to a bed-and-breakfast with Tremaine. No way was Tiffany about to mess that up for her.

Her mother would come to help if she called, but then Tiffany would have to explain why she'd been keeping her distance as of late. Declining family invitations and inventing reasons to miss any events that would offer the bright, observant Camille the opportunity to notice something.

The local temp staff agency wouldn't even open until nine.

As far as she could see, this left her with only one option.

Promise me you'll let me know how I can help.

Preston not only said it the night he'd brought her the silver baby rattle, he texted it at least six times in the couple days since his surprise visit.

Her cheeks burned in the darkness remembering the moment when they had locked eyes through the window. The hungry way he'd looked at her. She felt a delicate flutter in her middle at the memory.

He hadn't touched her. Hadn't kissed her.

But he had wanted to.

Every time his gaze fixed on her lips or skimmed downward to breasts she hadn't remembered were braless until after his departure, she could see it written all over his face.

She only hoped the same hadn't been true in reverse.

Because it had taken every ounce of her self-restraint

not to pounce on him like a starved lioness. Food cravings had been fairly minimal up until this point. The same could not be said for her libido.

Whether it was a side effect of her raging hormones or the volatile chemistry that had brought them together the night of Maggie and Jericho's engagement party didn't matter. She walked around the rest of that night with her body humming like a tuning fork.

Dreams like the one she'd just had didn't help.

But her fear of what might happen between them was no match for the anxiety she felt at the idea of failing to fulfill the order in time for Misha's employee party.

Pulling in a deep breath, she plucked up her courage, picked up her phone and pressed the call button.

Preston answered on the second ring, his voice deepened by sleep and somehow even sexier as a result.

"Hey," she said, already feeling foolish. "It's Tiffany."

"Tiffany." All traces of his fogginess evaporated. "Are you okay?"

"I'm fine," she said. "Everything's fine—I just have a bit of a problem I was hoping you might be able to help me with."

"What is it?"

"Remember how I was telling you about the big order for k!smet's employee party?"

Muffled rustling. A quiet click. "Yeah?"

"Well, I just got off of the phone with Moira, and

both she and Steph have food poisoning. I know this is short notice, but—"

"What time do you need me there?" The solid warmth and reassurance of his question made her want to cry. Which, given her recent history, was far from a surprise.

Tiffany cleared her throat. "The plan was for us to meet up at six, but I can go ahead and get started if you want to come in sometime after—"

"Wouldn't we need to get started sooner than that if there's only two of us?" he asked.

"I mean, that wouldn't be the worst idea." Squeezing her eyes shut, she bit her knuckles to keep from grinning so hard he could hear it through the phone.

"It's what…" She heard a scratchy sound like he was pulling the phone away from his face to check the time. "Just after four? I can be at Chocolate Fix in about twenty minutes?"

"I'm afraid it's going to take me at least half an hour. I move a little slower these days."

"4:45 then?"

"Perfect," she said, already peeling back the covers.

"See you then."

After hurrying for a shower and a very basic makeup routine, Tiffany bundled her hair into a messy topknot and dressed in the jeans and T-shirt she always wore when she had a long day of work ahead. After throwing on an oversize sweater, she stepped into comfortable sneakers, grabbed her purse and keys and locked up before heading out through the garage.

Preston was already waiting for her when she arrived, white bag and two coffees in hand.

The combination of his overnight stubble, rugged flannel shirt and work boots created a surge of ardor that careened into her like a freight train.

Tiffany levered herself out of the car and grabbed her things before walking to meet him.

"Morning," she said fighting a yawn.

"Morning," he replied.

Dredging her bag for the shop keys, she glanced at the sidewalk and the empty parking places in front of the shop.

"I parked in the alley," he said.

"Are you always this thoughtful before 5:00 a.m.?"

He gave her a roguish grin. "Depends on what kind of thoughts we're talking about."

I am in big, big trouble, was the one currently in her head.

She wrestled the notoriously sticky lock open, and he held the door for her with his elbow before following her in. The cool, cocoa-tinged air was a welcome greeting. As were the pristine glass cases bearing orderly rows of her handmade chocolates.

Preston's nostrils flared.

"If heaven doesn't smell like this, I don't want to go," he said, setting their coffee on the counter.

"I concur wholeheartedly." Tiffany left the after-hours light on in the main shop before walking behind the counter. If running her own business had taught her one thing, it was that people never read the hours posted on the door. If the lights were on, the audacity was in full effect. "You can come back here to the prep area."

She hip-checked the swinging door that led to the small industrial kitchen and immediately felt her heart rate stabilize. The gleaming chrome appliances and spotless white counters always filled her with this Zen-like sense of calm.

"Office, walk-in fridge, blast chiller, steam kettles," she said, pointing out the highlights by way of a tour.

"Let me just stash my stuff and we'll get started." As was her habit, she placed her purse in a drawer under her desk and tucked her phone in her pocket before changing into her white chef's coat. She then proceeded to the employee sink to wash her hands before drying them off with the paper towel then reaching into the white box mounted on the wall to pull out two hairnets. She donned one before dangling the other on a finger held out to him.

If nothing else, they might prove the libido inhibitor she desperately needed.

Preston eyed it warily. "Really?"

"Here at Chocolate Fix, we take our food safety requirements very seriously."

His sensuous lips pursed as he stretched out the hairnet and pulled it over his head. Several tufts of his dark hair stuck out from the bottom and side.

"Have you really never worn one of these?" she teased, ducking behind him to tuck in the stray pieces.

"Negative," he said. "I have a reputation to uphold. If word of this ever gets out, I'll be ruined."

"Better your reputation than my truffles." She took

longer than she needed to tuck the net's elastic edges behind his ears. Proportionally small and set high above his long, smooth neck, they reminded her of a river otter's.

Tiffany found herself imagining a much tinier version attached to a downy little head resting in the crook of her arm.

"You gave me a hickey you know."

She quickly finished securing the hair at his nape and turned to the linen shelf to conceal her flushing face. "Excuse me?"

"The night we were together. I woke up the next morning and had a hickey the size of a silver dollar right about here." He brushed his index finger over the spot just to the right of his Adam's apple where a single freckle stood out above his collar.

Tiffany remembered having fixated on that exact spot as they stood talking near the bar at the engagement party. She couldn't stop wondering if it felt as smooth as it looked.

"Huh," she said. "We have to keep it pretty cool in here for the chocolate, but if you're likely to get overheated, you might want to take your flannel off before you put an apron on."

Preston unbuttoned his shirt and hung it on one of the coat hooks next to the hand-washing sink. "I had to wear my collar popped for a week," he said. "My team thought I was having an identity crisis."

Coming around behind him, she slipped the apron's loop over his head and adjusted it to the right length. "If only a popped collar would conceal what you gave me," she said, giving the apron strings an extra hard tug before tying them around his lean waist.

"Touché." Preston clapped his hands and rubbed his palms together, making a papery sound. "So, what's up first on the agenda? Will I be filling cream puffs? Dipping strawberries?"

"The strawberries will be dipped, but not by us." Dropping an apron over her own head, Tiffany's muscle memory took over to tie it. "We need to make batches of white and milk chocolate fondue for the fountains as well as cut up fruit and angel food cake for the skewers. But before any of that, I'm going to chug about half of this coffee."

They stood in companionable silence, taking several slugs of the delicious brew.

"Better," she said. "Let's get this show on the road."

With his help, she prepared two cutting stations on the large stainless-steel table in the prep area. Preston insisted on carrying everything from the walk-in fridge, and in the process of delivering her instructions, Tiffany was surprised to note that he already knew how to deconstruct pineapple.

"My mom was big on gender equity, especially where kitchen labor was concerned," he told her with a wry grin.

Tiffany placed a loaf of angel food cake onto her cutting board and began dividing it into snowy cubes. "I always imagined the Del Rios having a personal chef."

"We do," he said. "But only during the week. Weekends, Mom cooks, and if we're home, we help."

When she glanced up from her board, she noticed that he had already cut twice as much cake as she had and already started on the stack of homemade marshmallows.

"You're just one of those incredibly annoying people who manages to be good at everything from the second you try it, aren't you?" she asked.

"And you're not?" His chuckle was a rich, warm sound, and drawing it from him felt like a special accomplishment. "I seem to remember someone getting parts in every school play, winning 4-H contests, making the swim team, taking home debate ribbons left and right…"

"I had no idea that you had followed my accomplishments so closely."

Preston looked at her from under his obscenely long lashes, suddenly shy and boyish. "Oh, I did."

Her knife froze midchop. If he had told her he had secret ambitions of becoming a CIA agent, she would have been less surprised.

"Please. You just feel bad about my being the least impressive Winters and you're trying to give me some sort of distinction."

"Tell yourself that if you want to." He shrugged and dropped the handful of marshmallow cubes onto one of the silver trays she set out beside the work area.

"You're being serious?"

"When have you known me to be anything but?" he asked.

"Speaking of," she said, resuming her work. "When is your father retiring?"

Preston's shoulders slumped as his jaw tightened. "When he's finally finished putting me through this ridiculous gauntlet to prove myself."

Tiffany snorted out a breath. "Our fathers have a surprising amount in common. If they could just figure out how to stop hating each other, they could probably take over the entire state of Texas."

"That's no lie," he said.

"How do you think he's going to react?" Her question seemed to drain a little of the light from the room, reminding them both of the challenges that lay ahead of a day that had been mostly fun and flirtatious.

He kept his eyes trained on his blade. "He won't be thrilled."

She suspected this might be an understatement of epic proportions.

"How about yours?" he asked, dropping the ball back into her court.

"Hard to say," she said. "With Maggie and Jericho getting married, it's not like he isn't aware that there's going to be a connection between our families. It's just that…" She paused to find the correct words. "The rules have always been a little different for me."

"Because you're the youngest?"

"Probably." Tiffany finished prepping the last of her angel food cake and started tidying the fondue tray. "With Alisha, Trey, Marcus and Jericho watching over me, it's more like I never had the opportunity to scandalize the family."

"I'd say we certainly made up for lost time."

She grabbed a chunk of angel food cake and lobbed

it at Preston, but he batted it out of the air before it could hit him in the chest.

"Careful, or I'm going to tell Misha. I'm not sure she'd tolerate this kind of unprofessionalism in her caterer."

"Be my guest," Tiffany said. "If she can find somebody else to make chocolate fountains for two hundred between now and 3:00 p.m., she's welcome to try."

"How is it already noon?" Preston asked. "We haven't even started the chocolate yet."

The concern in his voice was irresistibly endearing.

"We're actually ahead of schedule," she said, amazed at what she could accomplish with a Closed for Catering Event sign and Preston's capable hands. "In fact," she continued, "if your dad refuses to retire, just know you always have a place here."

"It would certainly cut down on the drama and bullshit egos." Preston aimed a killer grin at her.

"Don't count on it," Tiffany said. "Last week, a customer came in and demanded a refund for a single chocolate because she didn't like it after she'd already eaten half."

"Please tell me you're kidding."

"Nope. She even demanded the free sample I always give people when they come in even though she'd already been in earlier that day."

"I'll remember that for later," he said, a wicked gleam in his eyes.

Before she could turn into a soft center herself, Tiffany crouched down to turn on the steam kettles for the chocolate fondue fountains and felt the world go wavy when she stood up.

She braced herself against the waist-high cauldron, taking a deep breath and pressing her fingertips against her eyelids.

Preston was at her side in a flash; his eyes were wild with alarm. "Are you okay?"

The brushed metal rim of the kettle warmed beneath her palm as the steam made the base knock and hiss. "Totally fine," she said. "I just stood up too fast."

A crease appeared in the center of his forehead. "Have you been to see the doctor yet?"

Tiffany used his offered arm to resume her place at the counter. "My first appointment is next week."

"When?" he asked.

"Why?" she countered.

"Because I'm going with you."

"You really don't need to do that. If you thought people seeing us walk together in a parking lot was bad, just wait until we're spotted together at Dr. Everett's office."

"Hell with that," he said with enough force to startle her. "If it means we have to tell our families before then, so be it. I'm not missing out because I'm afraid one of the Royal busybodies might go to tattle to my father."

Her heart felt like it had swollen six times its normal size in her chest. "Thursday, 11:00 a.m. at Royal Memorial."

"I'll be there."

"Fine," she agreed. "Now will you kindly get back

to assembling those trays before Misha's minions arrive and have to walk away empty-handed?"

"I think you should go sit down in the office and eat something. You're looking really pale."

"It's the chef's coat," she insisted. "Really, this won't take me long and then I promise I'll take a break."

"I'm holding you to that, Winters." He lightly tapped his fingertip against her chest. The single point of skin seemed to glow like an ember beneath her T-shirt.

She rolled her eyes at him. "It just drives me crazy when you call me by my last name," she said in a terrible Mae West drawl.

"And when have I ever done that?" he asked.

Tiffany blinked at him. "You really don't remember?"

"Negative," he said.

"You only did it the entire time you were helping build the set for *Romeo and Juliet.*"

He stared out into the middle distance as if searching his memory. "I'll be damned," he said. "You're right."

She felt a keen sense of disorientation that a fact so significant to her should have made so little an impression on him. Tiffany peeled the lid off a small tub of pure coconut oil and coaxed the solid glob into the kettle, where it liquefied on contact.

"I always thought it was because a Winters was the only thing you saw me as."

Preston looked at her intently. "It's how I reminded myself that you were off-limits."

Tiffany's heart beat faster in her chest. She reached

for the oversize silver whisk from a hanging rack overhead and beat the last opaque blobs of coconut oil into the translucent pool. This kind of admission was the very last thing she ever would have expected. She thought him a player in high school, a superficial snob in college and a single-minded workaholic since. None of these identities comfortably coexisted with the clever, charismatic man who had made a day of grueling work fly by. For the very first time, she let herself imagine co-parenting might be a possibility between them. He was obviously still obsessed with his ascension. But also protective, caring and observant. Qualities that would make him an excellent father.

"Do you need the chocolate?" Preston asked, drawing her out of her reverie.

"I got it," she said, grateful for the opportunity to escape to the dry storage.

Tiffany spent an extra moment there with her back against the door, willing her body's hormones to get themselves under control. Preston Del Rio had thrown a couple compliments her way, and she was already mooning and swooning like some kind of lovesick teenager.

After pulling her phone from her pocket, she checked the time.

If she could just get through the next ninety minutes, Misha's crew would come to pick up their order and she could get the hell out of here and into a cold shower at home.

Alone.

Tiffany reached for the industrial-size block of bittersweet Belgian chocolate and flipped off the light before returning to the prep area.

Preston had four trays assembled and was wrapping the last with cellophane. Despite her otherwise conflicted feelings, she felt a swell of pride at how beautiful they looked lined up there on the counter. Bright green fig leaves. Tumbles of ruby-red strawberries. Clouds of snowy marshmallows. Succulent stacks of pineapple stamped into golden little hearts by the cookie cutters she'd bought from the kitchen supply store in a stroke of inspiration. All ready for Misha's employees to build their own skewers and plunge them into the silky curtains of chocolate that would cascade from two fountains that would be the reception's centerpieces.

"If you wouldn't mind putting those in the walk-in, I'll have you start on chopping the white chocolate."

Preston saluted her and lifted the first two trays.

When he was out of sight, she checked her phone, surprised to find a text from Alisha.

Just heard Moira and Steph got food poisoning. You OK? Do I need to send reinforcements?

Totally fine, she texted back with great haste. I got an early start.

If you're sure. PS. You're gonna have to see Mom sometime. She's starting to wonder what's up.

Forget the shower, Tiffany resolved to go straight over to her parents' house once the order had been picked up. The quicker she got out of that shop—and away from Preston—the better.

After trading her serrated knife for the chef's knife, she made quick work of the bittersweet chocolate.

"I know I'm not exactly the expert here," Preston said, peeking over her shoulder. "But I thought the point was even chunks."

"For the dipping components, yes. The chocolate is just going to get melted down." She carried the boardful of brown rubble over to the steam kettle and dumped the contents in. After letting the heat work for a moment, she whisked vigorously. The primordial-looking sludge quickly smoothed out into a glossy lake.

"You were saying?"

"I was saying I was gonna shut my mouth and get back to work. The white chocolate getting the same treatment?" he asked.

"If you please."

She prepped the next kettle over with the coconut oil and collected four one-gallon stainless-steel buckets to receive the finished product.

The white chocolate came together just as quickly, and by the time Misha's staff showed up—twenty minutes early no less—they had just placed all four in the bain-marie.

With Preston's help, they loaded the order into their van, enduring her repeated admonishments to make sure they preheated the fountains before pouring the chocolate in.

"I give it half an hour before I get a text from Misha about the chocolate seizing up," Tiffany said as she closed the van doors. "How much you wanna bet?"

They watched the van back out of the loading area and turn onto Main Street.

"I bet if you text Trey, he'll make sure they do exactly what you said." Preston stood beside her still wearing his apron but sans the hairnet he ditched at the first appropriate second.

Tiffany reached up and removed hers, massaging the spot on her forehead where the elastic had been rubbing all morning. "Not a bad idea," she agreed.

"He always seemed like the protective type."

"Overprotective, more like," she said as she quickly fired off a text message to him. "No wonder I never got any dates in high school."

"I seem to remember you having no problems in that arena," he said.

"For the year that you were still around."

They turned and walked back into the shop before closing and locking the door to the back entrance after them. "I'd only been asked to one homecoming dance by the time you were engaged to Sunny Rothschild."

The smile abandoned his face, and she instantly regretted bringing it up. "Your homecoming corsage probably lasted longer than our engagement did. I knew it was a mistake before I even proposed."

"Then why did you?" she asked.

Preston leaned back against the counter, his hands anchored on the rounded edge. "Because her father is an East Coast steel magnate, and my father practically shoved the family diamond in my hand."

Tiffany had always thought the Del Rio family patriarch was a very handsome, if somewhat intimidating, man. His animosity toward her father had been so famous that it never occurred to her to wonder what dynamics might be on the other side of the brick wall surrounding the Del Rio estate.

"He kept promising that once I'd set a date for the wedding, we could discuss a time frame for my taking over control of Del Rio enterprises. Then I woke up one morning and realized I wasn't counting down to the wedding, I was counting down to my father's retirement. I just couldn't go through with it."

"Maybe you should try to get him to set an official date *before* we tell him," she suggested, turning her back to him to untie her apron strings.

His warm hand covered hers, arresting her progress.

"Not so fast, Winters." To hear his voice so close to her ear and feel his skin against hers sent a chill dancing up her spine.

"I believe I'm owed a sample."

Tiffany waved a hand toward the door to the front of the shop. "Help yourself."

"That's the problem." He tugged the strings clutched in her hands and she felt her apron loosen. She stood frozen as he lifted the neck strap over her head and draped the apron over the counter. "I *can't.*"

Five

Impulsiveness.

Hadn't he learned his lesson yet?

Preston had known it was a bad idea when he brought up the sample instead of just collecting his things and getting the hell out of there the second Misha's company van pulled away.

Every minute he spent in Tiffany's presence, the danger of his breaking his promise to Alisha grew.

This entire day had felt like foreplay.

Their bodies moving in concert around Tiffany's sweet-smelling kitchen. The parade of aphrodisiac foods. The way she stood there looking up at him like she expected his mouth to lower to hers at any second.

Preston cleared his throat to break the moment.

"I can't help myself if I don't know what the flavors are," he explained.

Tiffany blinked and offered him an embarrassed smile.

"Right," she said. "Of course. This way, good sir."

He hung back for a moment purely to appreciate the sight of her backside in the well-worn jeans that fit her like bark on a tree and bit his lip when she hip-checked the swinging door open. The practiced grace in this simple gesture was one of many he'd witnessed over the course of this day.

"All right," she said, turning to face him. "There are important questions that need to be considered if I am to curate the perfect sampling experience for you."

"Hit me," he said.

"Milk or dark?"

"Dark," he answered without hesitation.

"Are you saying that because you actually like dark chocolate or because you think pretending to be a cocoa snob will get you bonus points?" she asked.

"Can't it be both?"

Tiffany rolled her eyes at him. "Chewy or melty?"

"Melty."

"Boozy or fruity?"

"Again, is both an option?" he asked.

"Actually," she said, approaching the case at the far end of the counter, "yes."

Pulling out two separate boxes, she placed them on the counter before him.

Preston found himself genuinely taken aback by the beauty and delicacy of the small, glossy domes lined up in neat rows. One set was Jackson Pollock splattered with streaks of marigold orange and glittering with gold dust. The other, molded in gem-like facets and the shimmering burgundy of a fairy-tale velvet throne.

He picked up the small gold card stationed in front of one to try and read the delicate script. "'Orange You Glad'?"

"Valrhona chocolate ganache with a salted caramel Grand Marnier center."

He nodded and picked up the other card on the tray. "'Pop the Cherry'?"

She gave him the full force of the slow, sexy grin that had caused them both so much trouble.

"Chili-spiced dark chocolate mousse with a Luxardo Maraschino marzipan center."

"I think I'm going to need you to decide for me," Preston said.

Tiffany began to swivel her finger back and forth between the trays, attempting to select at random.

"Not like that," Preston said, plucking one of the orange truffles from its small paper cup. "Like this."

She shook her head. "No thanks. I only ate about a thousand of them as I was trying to perfect the flavor."

The cool chocolate began to melt between his fingers. "That's how you're going to help me decide. By watching you react."

"You know what? Just take one of each. Hell, you can fill a whole pound-sized box if you want to. It's the least I can do to thank you."

"What if watching you eat them is the thanks I'd prefer?"

Their eyes met.

Her lips parted, and he slid the chocolate between them. He watched her intently as she chewed, white teeth dimpling her full lower lip for the briefest of moments.

"Option two," he said.

His pulse thundered in his ears as he brought the cherry truffle to her lips, brushing it slowly from corner to corner. She opened her mouth, and he gently pushed it onto her tongue. She chewed slowly this time, her eyes slightly closed.

Preston felt the familiar heaviness gathering in his groin but couldn't make himself look away. Pleasure lay across her beautiful features like a veil, transforming her.

When her eyes opened again, they smoldered from beneath the dark fringe of her lashes.

The sweet-scented air between them vibrated with the unspoken question.

She answered it by clutching handfuls of his T-shirt and pulling him to her.

Their mouths met and melded in a decadent rush of sweetness and spice that their tangling tongues only served to enhance. Her breasts molded against his chest and Tiffany moaned, adding her urgency to the heady mélange on their shared palates. Preston's grip on her tightened as he hauled her up his body, her legs wrapping around his waist.

He shouldered them through the swinging door

and into her office. Reaching behind her, he cleared a space on her desk and lifted her onto it. Tiffany reached out and yanked the cord to close the blinds as he bent at the waist and unbuckled his belt. They separated just long enough for her to strip his T-shirt off before shedding her own. Preston didn't even bother to unhook her bra, opting instead to push it up to free her breasts.

They were warm in his hands, firmer and heavier than he remembered. Tearing his mouth from hers, he then moved it to the dusky, turgid peaks of her nipples. Her back arched on an urgent cry that filled him with savage pleasure.

He was transported back to their first night together.

Both of them so desperate to have each other that they moved only what was strictly necessary for their joining. Tiffany quickly unbuttoned her jeans, before shimmying them down her hips and taking her panties with them.

Preston trailed his hand down her stomach and found her already soaked. Slick beneath his fingertips. He had barely begun to explore the taut bundle of nerves within the silken petals of her sex when she cried out and bucked against him.

"Please," she said, shaking with the aftershocks of her explosion. "I need you."

"I… I don't have anything with me." He said now what he should have said then, feeling a flicker of guilt.

Tiffany flicked her eyes downward. "It's a little late for that."

"I won't…hurt anything?" he asked.

Tiffany gave him a softly indulgent look that he imagined countless men receiving from countless women over the centuries. Ignorant as they had the luxury to be, of this most basic building block of life.

"No," she said. "You won't hurt anything."

His hesitance boiled away, leaving something primal and possessive in its wake. He freed his arousal and pressed her back against the desktop. Widening her knees as much as the jeans still bunched around her calves would allow, he filled her with one thrust and stilled.

He folded forward to kiss her, grazing her cheek with his jaw. Nuzzling his lips against her ear. "I've wanted you like this for so long," he breathed.

She scored his back with her short nails and buried her face in his shoulder.

"You can have me, Preston. As much of me as you want, as often as you want it."

He wanted it all.

He wanted it always.

Preston rocked back and filled her again, curling his hips to delve deep within her wet heat.

"More," she whispered.

The hands spanning her rib cage moved to her shoulders to anchor her.

Preston obliged. The heat between them ignited a firestorm of desire and he let himself be taken by it. Let it burn its way into him through their joined bodies, a roaring devouring thing that incinerated everything in its path. It obliterated the last of his caution and he was driving into her with enough force to send her desk scraping across the office floor. Tiffany's hips rose to meet his every thrust, spurring him onward until he felt her contracting around him.

Tiffany called his name and sent him careening over the edge. He lost himself inside her with the intense searing pulses.

Neither of them moved or spoke in the aftermath.

Preston didn't know which made him more of a fool. The fact that he had just torn through the paper-thin illusion that their relationship had only been a one-night stand. Or that he'd ever entertained that as a possibility in the first place. That he'd honestly ever thought he could remain neutral and platonically co-parent.

Giving in to his desire had landed them in a giant gray area where the lines weren't just muddy, they were nonexistent.

Maybe his father had been right.

When it came to Tiffany Winters, he didn't have a soft spot.

He had a blind spot.

Preston pushed himself up on his palms and gazed down at her, not having the faintest idea what to say or do next.

Tiffany pushed a sweaty lock of hair away from his forehead, her heavy-lidded eyes fixed on his.

"We'll figure it out, Preston," she said, answering the question he'd been too afraid to ask.

He was surprised by just how much that statement comforted him.

He helped her to sit up and turned to pull up his

pants so she'd have a chance to do the same without his watching.

"What do you have going on for the rest of the day?" He hated how artificially casual this question sounded given the intimacy they'd just shared.

"First, a nap," she said. "Then dinner at my parents'. I've mostly managed to avoid them for the last few weeks and Alisha told me I owe an appearance."

Preston felt a pang of guilt. In all his pondering over the past week, he hadn't once thought about what strains or pressures holding this secret inside her might create between her and her parents.

"Do you really think it will be possible to wait until after Maggie and Jericho's wedding to make the announcement?" he asked, handing her T-shirt to her.

Tiffany quickly pulled it over her head and gathered her hair back into its bun. "Provided that I'm not showing a ton. I'm planning on wearing a lot of oversize sweaters and flowy tunics this winter."

Not for the first time, it occurred to him just how disparate the division of labor was in this proposition, both literally and figuratively. Her body would be the one to undergo the physical changes, her life, the greatest impact.

"I'm not sure what that will help. You could wear one of those flour sacks and you'd still draw attention." Preston stooped to pick up the papers they had avalanched to the floor. As he tapped the papers into a neat stack, his eye reflexively skimmed down the top page. A profit and loss statement—the figures showing mostly the latter.

"Please." Tiffany pulled out a desk drawer and smoothed balm on her kiss-swollen lips. "It's not like I have suitors lining up at the door. And a few months from now, I suspect the dating pool is going to get *very* shallow."

The thought of her as she would look six or even seven months pregnant was having quite the opposite effect on him. Her athletic frame filling out with new curves, glowing like a goddess.

He notched a finger under her chin and planted a soft kiss on her minty lips. "I'm only ever a text away. Day…or night."

Tiffany grabbed her sweater from the hook on the back of the door and shrugged into it before grabbing her purse and keys. "I guess we'll just have to see how things go between now and the appointment on Thursday."

From his present vantage, that sounded like an eternity.

He followed her into the shop, where she took a small gold box from the cupboard below the counter and quickly filled it with a selection of chocolates from the assorted cases. "For my mom," she explained. "Truffles go a long way toward smoothing over daughterly neglect."

"And how about brotherly neglect?"

"I hear they're even better on that score." She put her box aside and picked up a second. "Maggie likes the fruit creams, if I remember correctly."

"How did you know?"

"Jericho comes in to get them from time to time."

"Really?" he asked.

"Yep. And often hauling a giant bouquet into the shop so it doesn't wilt in the five minutes he'd have to leave it in the car." She moved to a different case and began loading the box. "I've never seen Jericho so smitten."

It had taken Preston a minute to get away from the gut-level flinch he had always felt hearing the name. Lately, he'd even detected a growing appreciation. He liked the idea of his sister being engaged to a man who paid attention to the kind of things she liked and thought to bring them to her.

Preston certainly hadn't been that sort of boyfriend.

Or fiancé. Sunny had never expressed any contention about it and Preston had always been too busy with work to notice if that was the case. The regret he felt now wasn't that their relationship had ended, but that the version of himself he had been with her hadn't doted on her the way so many other men would have. If anything, the time spent in Tiffany's presence had made it clear just how unfair to Sunny he had been.

"Red, black or gold?" Tiffany directed his attention to the drawer full of decorative metallic elastics below the cash register.

"Gold."

With nimble fingers, she snapped the bow into place and handed him the box.

"What do I owe you?" he asked.

"Not a thing." Tiffany turned off the lights to the kitchen and engaged the security system before approaching the front door. "Oh shoot," she said. "I forgot you're parked in the alley. Do you want me to let you out the back door?"

Her willingness to do this for his sake made him all the more determined not to take advantage of the offer.

"Nope," he said. "I'll walk around."

"But what if somebody sees you leaving my shop?" she asked.

Preston leaned in and kissed her cheek. "Then I sure hope they enjoy the view."

The determined look on her face did him a wealth of good.

He waited right there on the sidewalk in front of God and everyone while she locked up, then followed her to her Jeep to open her door.

"Such service." She laughed. "See you Thursday morning, then?"

"Unless you feel compelled to call me before then," Preston said.

"Thanks again for all your help today," she said, buckling herself in and then starting the engine.

"Anytime." He shut her door and watched as she backed out of her parking space and motored down Main Street.

Only when the Jeep had turned at the corner did he notice the figure standing on the sidewalk halfway up the street.

Royal's premier gossipmonger.

Mandee Meriweather.

Six

After an epic nap that left her wondering what year it was, Tiffany stumbled into the shower and stayed there until the hot spray lifted the fog from her eyes.

If only her mind could be cleared so easily.

Once again, Preston had joined her in her dreams. She'd woken up with her nipples hard and her panties wet. As if they hadn't done enough damage for one day.

Once is an accident.

Twice is an experiment.

Her mom's oft-uttered saying returned to her as she toweled off outside her shower.

In other words, what had happened between her and Preston could no longer be considered a one-night stand.

Catching a glimpse of herself in the somewhat

fogged vanity mirror, she was relieved to see minimal evidence of their passionate encounter. Slight dappling on her chin and around her mouth. A small suck mark on her breast that clothing would easily cover. Her stomach remained mostly flat, but her breasts had grown heavier. Her nipples, a darker version of their normal auburn color.

The only signs of a pregnancy she could yet identify.

All in all, nothing makeup and a carefully chosen outfit couldn't take care of. Suddenly ravenous, Tiffany wrapped herself in the towel and headed to the kitchen, where she chugged what felt like a gallon of orange juice while waiting for a slice of bread to toast. Enough to stave off the light-headed feeling she had, but not so much as to ruin one of her mom's excellent dinners.

She knew her brother Trey would be at Misha's party, but Tiffany had tried to covertly find out whether any of her other siblings might be stopping by the Winters estate this evening, but the reply she had received from her mom was somewhat vague.

"Oh, honey, between the wedding planners, landscape designers, calligraphers, florists, I never know who's going to show up here these days."

Tiffany hoped tonight might be the exception.

She hurried toward her bedroom, before stopping when she caught sight of the small silver rattle sitting on top of the snowy white blanket she'd hauled out of a box in her closet right after she'd gotten home with positive pregnancy test in hand.

The blanket had been hers.

One of the few items she felt still carried an energetic connection to the mother who had died shortly after she was born. Seeing them together, the rattle and the blanket, woke an ache in her chest. She couldn't ask for a better upbringing than she'd had with her father and Camille, who had been nothing but kind and warm and loving to her from the very beginning. Her mom in every sense of the word. And to inherit an older sister in the transaction had proved to be an added bonus. Tiffany turned the rattle over in her hand, rubbing her thumb across the inscription.

God, she hoped it proved to be prophetic.

She had been taken aback by bitterness in Preston's voice when he talked about his father. This couldn't come at a worse time for him, and she knew it. If they could only get through the wedding and the Diamond Gate mediation, there might just be a shot.

Thirty minutes later, her Jeep crunched over the gravel in the circular drive of her parents' home.

The familiar scent of her childhood washed over her in an almost overwhelming wave as she let herself in the front door. The baked-good-scented candles that her mom favored. Cleaning products from their housekeeper. Beneath it all, she recognized a scent that in any other situation would have been the most welcome of all. Her mom's signature lasagna.

With her newly enhanced sense of smell, the combination made her feel a little weepy.

"Hello?" Her greeting echoed in their cavernous

foyer but was met with no reply. She hadn't seen any other cars in the driveway, but it was also possible they had parked in the three-car garage.

Tiffany took the familiar path into the kitchen, stopping in front of the stainless-steel double-wide refrigerator, where Jericho and Maggie's save-the-date card was secured with a magnet. She leaned in to study it, feeling an acute sense of longing at the joy so obviously glowing in their faces.

So in love, they beamed at each other like flood-lights.

Tiffany opened the fridge not so much out of hunger as a desire to break the hold the beautiful black-and-white photo had over her.

The contents hinted at preparations for some of her winter and fall favorites. Hearty soups that her mom often made and chilled before freezing. Pie crusts and oatmeal crumble that would be used to top delectable pumpkin and apple crisps.

Food had played a significant role within their blended family.

Tiffany couldn't help but wonder if similar efforts might be in her future if she and Preston figured out how to raise this child together, but separately.

Her baby could have half-siblings. Or stepbrothers and stepsisters. A stepmother.

Tiffany was so caught up in her tailspin, she jumped about half a foot when she closed the refrigerator door and found her mom standing on the other side of it. Dressed in black leggings and a white cashmere sweaterdress, her skin glowed a burnished mahogany from her afternoon run.

"That's for Thanksgiving," she said, glancing at the disk of pie crust in Tiffany's hand. "I'm just chilling them before they go in the freezer."

"You don't usually start the prep until a few days before," Tiffany pointed out.

"Well, now that all your siblings have a plus-one, we'll be probably having a few extra guests this year," she said.

No sooner had she said it than the next phase of Tiffany's own personal pregnancy panic dream entered her head.

Oh God.

She hadn't even thought about holidays.

How would those work? Would both families come together? Would they trade off? The thought of her child spending half of its holidays in a different home made her stomach feel tight and cold.

And that was to say nothing of birthday parties. Sleepovers. Family vacations.

"I had no idea you were hosting everyone," Tiffany said, returning the pie crust to the shelf.

"That may be because you have been scarce around these parts as of late," her mom teased. "And now that you're here, you're acting like a stranger. You haven't even hugged me yet."

Her mother held out her arms. Tiffany dissolved into them, grateful for her strength and her softness. For the familiar amber scent of her perfume.

"I'm so sorry, Mom." Tears filled her eyes. "I just finished that huge order for k!smet and I'm exhausted."

Her mother smoothed a hand over Tiffany's hair and patted her back.

"It's all right, sweetie. We've certainly had plenty going on around here with the wedding plans and all."

"How's that going by the way?" Tiffany asked against her shoulder.

Camille released her embrace and blew out a breath.

"If I never hear the words *seating arrangement* again, it will be too soon."

She reached into the fridge and pulled out a bottle of Tiffany's favorite Chardonnay.

Knowing her mother had probably bought it in anticipation of her presence made Tiffany feel like the worst kind of neglectful daughter.

"Trying to figure out where to put wedding guests from families who've spent generations avoiding each other has been a headache I can't even begin to describe." Camille opened a drawer and took out a corkscrew. "It's enough to make me wish I could reach back in time and slap that sparkly necklace out of Eliza Boudreaux's sticky fingers."

Camille opened the cabinet and set two white wineglasses on the counter.

Tiffany's mouth watered thinking of the cool, crisp wine and how good it would taste in her sour, acidic mouth. She waited until her mom had poured one glass to stop her.

"I think I might wait just a bit," she said. "My stomach's been a little iffy today."

And every day for the last month.

Her mother's face creased with concern as she placed both the bottle and the glass down on the counter.

"You do look a little pale," she said, placing the back of her hand against Tiffany's forehead. "Do you think it might be the same bug that Moira and Steph caught?"

"They had food poisoning," Tiffany reported. "And I'm okay, really. I didn't sleep very well last night."

"Because you were worried about the k!smet order?"

Of all the things Tiffany appreciated about her stepmother, this had to be near the top. She had a talent for providing the easiest path out of a difficult situation.

Tiffany nodded. "The shop has been kicking my butt lately."

Camille brushed Tiffany's hair away from her cheek. "I think you've been working too hard. Your sister told me you were there at the crack of dawn this morning finishing that whole order by yourself."

Half-true, at least.

Her mother opened the fridge and brought out a bottle of ginger ale, just as she had every time Tiffany complained of any stomach-related ailment when she was a child. She could still remember the crisp bite of the soda and how it had soothed when she was sick early on in Camille's courtship with Tiffany's father.

They'd still had a live-in nanny at that point, but Camille insisted they cancel their date so she could stay in and help take care of Tiffany.

The strength of the affection she felt for this woman who had raised her like her very own made tears rise to Tiffany's eyes as the bubbling glass arrived in front of her. A development that her mother did not miss.

"Baby, what's wrong? You look like you're about to cry."

The kindness unstitched the last of her resolve.

Her face dropped into her hands, and she began to sob. All her fears, her worries, her embarrassment, her shame, poured out of her in hot tears. Abandoning both glasses, her mother came around the counter to pull her in for another hug.

When Tiffany's silent sobs died down to a watery sniffle, her mother drew back and looked at her. "I'm guessing this isn't just about the k!smet order."

Tiffany's eyes swam down toward her shoes as Camille reached into her pocket and retrieved a tissue to dab away the last of her tears.

"You don't have to tell me anything you don't want to. But I'm here to listen if you do."

Tiffany studied the veins in the marble countertop, feeling exhausted all over again and hollow, unable to meet her mother's eyes.

"I'm pregnant," she said. "I have absolutely no idea what I'm going to do, but I've decided I'm going to have the baby."

The silence stretched on forever.

A warm fingertip under her chin brought Tiffany back to Camille's warm, soft gaze.

What she read in her mother's face was a complete

and total departure from the look of utter disappointment she had imagined.

"You're telling me... I'm going to be a grandmother again?"

Tiffany sniffed through tear-swollen sinuses. "Not tomorrow, but yes."

Camille's shriek of delight startled Tiffany out of her sadness.

Throwing up her hands, her mother did an impromptu dance with a lot of hips and air punches. "Take *that*, Gayle Del Rio." She slapped the counter for emphasis. "You may have the biggest estate, you may have a set of diamonds worth almost as much as the crown jewels, but I have grandbaby number two on the way."

Apparently the carefully cultivated neutrality she had always modeled wasn't quite so neutral after all.

Tiffany cleared her throat. "You're not that far ahead of Gayle Del Rio."

Her mother's eyes widened. "You mean... Maggie?"

"I mean Preston," she said. "He's the father."

Having raised three stepsons through their adolescence, Camille was no stranger to shocking revelations. Tiffany's brothers had gotten into their share of trouble on the way to adulthood. Never in all that time had Tiffany seen her mother's mouth drop open and stay that way through multiple eye blinks.

"You...and Preston?"

Tiffany nodded.

"You two are..." her mom trailed off, inviting her to insert the appropriate term. Trouble was, Tiffany wasn't sure what the correct term describing their current situation might be.

"We're not together. It was just the one time."

Ish.

"The night of Maggie and Jericho's engagement party?"

Tiffany's eyebrows lifted in surprise.

"It required all my creative wiles to keep your father from noticing the two of you dancing together." Her mother reached for her wine and took a gulp. "Does Preston know?"

Tiffany sat down on a bar stool at the counter.

"He knows," she said. "But we both feel it would be best not to announce it until after the wedding."

She saw the ripple of unease move over her mother's face. "You're sure? The mediation session for the necklace is coming up. I can't help but think—"

"The last thing I want is for this pregnancy to be used as some kind of bargaining chip." Tiffany sipped her ginger ale. "Until Diamond Gate and the wedding are over, no one can know about this."

"Know about what?"

The sound of Joseph Winters's voice from the kitchen entryway made them both jump. In addition to the ZZ Top T-shirt and faded jeans her brothers had joked about making him look like a roadie, her father wore the brushed suede slippers that made his progress through the house surprisingly stealthy.

"The surprise that Tiffany is planning for Maggie and Jericho," her mother said without missing a beat.

"Oh." He fished in the pocket of his sweater and

came back with a handkerchief to polish the glasses he only wore when at home. "Did someone scream? I thought I heard someone scream."

Tiffany and her mother exchanged the kind of look women had been passing back and forth down the ages.

"I did," her mother said. "I just got an email from the wedding planner about the Del Rios changing the seating chart for the reception."

Her father's concern quickly melted away to annoyance. "Again?" he demanded.

All these battles that had taken place without her having been aware of them.

"I'm afraid so," her mother said.

Her father stomped off, trailing a string of curses in his wake. Camille turned to her once he was out of earshot.

"However you decide you want to tell your father, maybe make sure I'm there too?"

They heard the door to the liquor cabinet slam and snatches of words muttered from the other room.

"...thinks he owns the goddamn world...bastard is going to apologize if it's the last thing I do."

Her mother took another sip of her wine. "On second thought, maybe you and Preston shouldn't be anywhere near him when he finds out."

"What are you suggesting?" Tiffany asked.

"Your father and I are taking a trip to the Amalfi Coast after the wedding. I'm thinking that may be the time to tell him."

"When strangling Preston would require a transatlantic flight?"

"Exactly," her mother said. "Everything sounds better with a belly full of calamari."

Her father's voice grew louder again as he made his way back to the kitchen.

"...if he thinks I'm just going to sit here like a stallion while he profits off of *my* son's idea, he's got another thing coming." He gestured with his glass, sloshing amber liquid up the side. "What's going on with you two anyway?"

"What do you mean?" Camille swiveled and met her husband with such a look of confident innocence that even Tiffany herself was tempted to believe it.

Her father's blue eyes narrowed. "You look like you're plotting something."

"I believe you mean *planning* something," Camille shot back. "You're the one plotting. And I'll be damned if it's going to affect our son's wedding, so unless you're trying to volunteer to help me rework these seating charts, I advise you to take yourself off until dinner is ready."

Her father ran a hand through his dark blond hair. "I need to head to the TCC for my dinner meeting. But I should be back by the time you ladies are having dessert."

Tiffany sagged with relief when he was gone.

Camille's warm, fragrant palm molded itself to her cheek.

"It's going to be okay, Tiffany." The steadiness in her voice was enough to lower Tiffany's blood pressure by several points. "This child is going to be loved,

and that's what matters. Everything else, we can figure out along the way."

Her eyes stung once more. "Thanks, Mom."

Her mother glanced down at Tiffany's abdomen as
if just now registering the physical aspect of her condition. "Have you seen an ob-gyn yet? Do you need
one outside of Royal?"

The forethought was more touching than anything
Tiffany could possibly have imagined at that particular moment.

"I have an appointment with Dr. Everett at 11:00 a.m.
this Thursday."

"Is someone coming with you?" An exceedingly
subtle way to determine who that "someone" was.

She nodded. "Preston."

Camille gave a stiff nod of approval and squeezed
her shoulder. "Good. Now drink your ginger ale. Alisha should be here any minute."

Tiffany picked up her glass and swiveled on her bar
stool to face the kitchen. Watching her mother cook
had always been one of her favorite things.

"Alexa, play Etta James."

The sultry tones spilled from the kitchen's sound
system, instantly lightening the mood. Camille opened
the fridge and pulled out a block of pancetta. Setting
it on the cutting board, she began slicing it into neat
little cubes as she smiled wistfully to herself.

Tiffany could practically see the chubby-fisted toddler wandering around behind her eyes.

The front door opened, and she heard Alisha call
out as she headed toward the kitchen, "Sorry I'm late."

Breezing into the kitchen, Alisha set her bag and keys down on the counter. "I had to finish up grading essays for my Northern Renaissance seminar."

The charm bracelet around her sister's wrist winked beneath the pendant lights as she massaged a spot on her forehead.

"That bad?" Tiffany asked, being well acquainted with the challenges of Alisha's part-time gig as an adjunct art history professor.

"One of the students from my night class actually spent five double-spaced pages talking about how Leonardo shouldn't have been included as one of the *Teenage Mutant Ninja Turtles.*"

"And you don't agree?" their mother asked, dropping the pancetta into the pan.

"Hell no," Alisha said. "If there was an odd reptile out, it was Donatello. He was already sixty-six when Leonardo was born."

"You learn something new every day." Their mother turned from the stove and started on the celery.

"Oh shoot," Camille said, pausing midchop. "Tiff, could you grab the pearl onions out of the freezer? I've still got pancetta grease all over my hands."

"Of course." Tiffany shot up from her stool and went to the fridge, before squatting to open the freezer drawer. She located the small bag near the front and elbowed the compartment closed before standing.

"Here you—oh." No sooner had she taken a single step toward her mother than the floor skated beneath her feet.

The soulful music took on a muted, faraway quality. A strange gray twilight rushed into the edges of her vision as her knees turned to water.

"Tiffany!" The knife clattered to the counter and Camille launched herself toward Tiffany as a red curtain dropped over the whole show.

Seven

Another meeting. Another text. Another unwelcome surprise.

Preston felt like he'd been sitting at the long, glossy table in the boardroom of the Del Rio Group's corporate office for a solid year. The scent of furniture polish had brought on a gnawing headache. The voices had all faded into a numbing drone. No matter how hard he tried, he couldn't make himself focus on the current discussion.

Considering how his weekend had dragged on, he wasn't entirely surprised. The chocolates that Tiffany had lovingly picked out for Maggie still sat on the kitchen table of his bachelor pad home. His intended mea culpa for missing their family dinner the other night foiled by yet another wedding-related emergency. He was quickly losing patience with this entire process and the ridiculous feud that had started it.

And now this.

Hey, you! I'm in town for a week. I was really hoping we could get together.

The hopeful tone of Sunny's unexpected text gutted him.

Why now?

His father had risen from the head of the table, folding his hands behind his lower back and taking up the slow cadence he favored when about to make an important announcement. Preston wrenched his eyes away from his phone and tried to refocus his attention in the present.

"When my great-great-grandfather originally purchased this land, he had a simple dream."

Preston could recite the rest by memory. *With only twenty-five dollars in his pocket...*

He couldn't help but feel envy for a life he imagined to be far simpler than his current predicament. He'd been born into money and seen firsthand the ways it warped the mind. This obsession with legacy that turned otherwise reasonable men like his father into peacock-proud combatants. Preston had always considered it his legacy as well and spent so long chasing after it he'd never even paused to think about whether he really wanted it. Whether his desire to take over the Del Rio Group was born of a personal passion or was just a mirror for his father's blind ambition. His relationship with Sunny had similarly twisted roots.

He owed her closure at least. After what had happened between him and Tiffany at her shop, he felt like he needed to formally resolve all ties before he could think about his next steps.

He was composing his reply to Sunny when sudden thunderous applause brought him up short.

Everyone was looking at him.

He dredged his recent memory for a word or phrase that might help him but came back empty-handed.

He was losing it.

"January 1." The man seated next to him clapped him on the back. "How does it feel to finally have an official transition date?"

Preston glanced at his father, whose broad smile didn't quite reach his eyes.

Fernando Del Rio had announced his official retirement date.

At the moment he had waited for, prepared for and worked for his entire life, Preston had been ruminating about an ex-girlfriend.

And his lack of focus had clearly been noted.

A cold sinking feeling invaded his chest.

Fernando turned his attention back to the audience of board members held in his thrall. "I hope you'll all join me tonight at the Glass House to celebrate this momentous occasion."

Preston cleared his throat. "Actually, I don't know if tonight will work so well for me."

His father's self-satisfied smile dissolved into a

scowl. "But you're the guest of honor. What could you possibly find more important than celebrating your ascension to the post of CEO at the Del Rio Group?"

He wouldn't like the honest answer to this question.

Preston had planned to stop by Tiffany Winters's house.

Not only had she not texted him all weekend, but she also hadn't answered his text this morning confirming the ob-gyn appointment.

The board members began to shift in their seats as the tension in the room mounted.

He could put in half an hour at the reception. Shake some hands and present his back for slapping, and then head straight over to Tiffany's house afterward.

"Not a thing." Preston forced a triumphant smile onto his face. "Who wants to pick me up? Because I know I certainly won't be driving home."

This display of nauseating swagger was met with a chorus of masculine approval. Though Preston loathed this kind of fraternal mischief, it managed to restore his father's good humor.

"6:00?" Fernando proposed. "The first round is on me. The second, on the man poised to inherit the most lucrative business in ten counties."

The group noisily pushed back from the table and got to their feet.

One by one, he received their handshakes and congratulations, all of it leaving him hollow and dissatisfied.

His father was the last to leave, making his way

over to Preston in a slow procession that made the moisture evaporate from this throat.

"You're pleased with this announcement I hope."

Preston closed his laptop and tucked it under his arm. "Of course I am."

Fernando pushed the chair Preston had vacated flush with the table. "I only ask because you seem very distracted."

"I've had a lot on my mind." He offered no additional explanation.

"Like the upcoming Diamond Gate negotiations with Jack Chowdhry?" His father crossed his arms over his chest. "Because I'm expecting you to be there. Now that the word is out that you'll be taking over as CEO, people will be watching our family very closely, Preston. It's vital that we present a united front."

The very cadence of these words irked him. Whether or not he and his father resolved any of the issues complicating their relationship, they must always appear solid to everyone else.

A message that had been emphasized to him since his acquisition of language.

It wasn't like he had ever been asked to be perfect.

Only to make sure everyone else thought he was. Having personal problems was acceptable provided nobody else was ever aware of them. Years of maintaining this front left him exhausted and edgy.

Burned out.

"I'll be there," he said.

"Good." His father passed him in a wave of cologne and clothing starch. "You wouldn't think about canceling tonight at the last minute."

It wasn't so much a question as a warning.

"It would be disappointing to some of our most important associates if you didn't show."

"I understand, Dad," Preston said.

"Their faith in us is the reason that Del Rio Group exists. Without that faith—"

"I'll be there," he repeated, cutting him off.

His father's eyes lingered on his long enough for him to know he was being assessed. "We'll talk tonight."

Preston replied with a curt nod and fled the conference room like his ass was on fire. What would normally be a ten-second walk to his office took several minutes as he was forced to stop and receive the enthusiastic congratulations of every single person he passed.

When he finally reached it, he shut the door and slumped back against it, thinking he was safe until his phone buzzed in his pocket. Sunny, he expected, accepting his invitation to meet for coffee later that week.

But he'd been wrong.

Congratulations, Pres! Though seeing a text from his sister lifted his heart, the context dampened his spirit.

Word sure travels fast, he replied.

I knew he would be announcing it today—I just didn't know when until Amanda Battle asked me what I thought when I stopped by the diner.

How the hell would she know already?

You know she has sources within every building in a sixty-mile radius.

LOL. Are you coming to Dad's little shindig at the Glass House?

Can't. Having the 76th fitting for my dress. She accompanied the message with a GIF of a cartoon character beating its head against a wall.

And here I thought your life was nothing but conjugal bliss, Preston replied.

You have my permission to find the love of your life, but please don't ever plan a wedding. For the love of God, elope.

Preston felt like someone had just shot an arrow into his chest.

The love of his life.

He couldn't even figure out how to have a relationship that lasted more than a year. The one woman he'd managed to sustain any kind of interest in was completely off-limits, but now carrying his child. Any future for the two of them forever altered by that fact.

You have my word, Preston texted back.

He shuffled over to his desk and sank into the leather chair, the back warmed by the sun pouring through the floor-to-ceiling window. He spun a slow circle to look out over the sprawling Texas landscape.

His kingdom, or so he'd been raised to believe.

Tonight would merely be an extension of that fantasy.

The repetition of tired phrases shouldn't surprise him. After all, Preston had been hearing them since puberty.

It was only a matter of time.

Wasn't everything?

Here comes the future CEO.

As if he'd had a choice.

You're the spitting image of your father.

Like there had been any effort on his part in that matter.

For half an hour, he'd allowed his father to steer him around the Glass House's outdoor patio, letting party guests pick at his psyche like an appetizer.

The atmosphere was festive, the music, lights and outdoor space heaters lending the gathering an intimate air despite the concentration of bodies.

None of it felt real.

Only when he spotted his mother and Maggie waiting patiently at the back of the crowd did his anxiety ease.

Gayle Del Rio was positively beaming, her pride evident in her glowing smile. Maggie, who had canceled her fitting at the last minute, was a different story. The second their eyes locked, her demeanor changed from congratulatory to concerned.

Preston worked his way over to them and was quickly joined by his father, who made sure their handshake was captured by the photographer who'd been making the rounds.

For his part, Fernando played the role perfectly. Standing alongside Preston with a properly proud smile on his face.

Preston blinked to dispel the corona of blue from a camera flash.

"I'm getting a drink," he announced, slipping away from his family.

At the bar, he had chugged half a bottled water and ordered a Scotch when a familiar scent drifted into his nostrils. Jasmine and vanilla.

Sunny's signature.

Now Maggie's expression made sense.

He should have known that Sunny texting him the same day his father announced his ascension to the role of CEO wasn't just a coincidence.

"You didn't think I would miss your big moment, did you?" Sunny placed a lip-gloss-sticky kiss on his cheek.

She was as beautiful as she had ever been. Long, dark hair. Wide brown eyes. Smooth umber skin. Everything that had once attracted him still present and yet, completely and totally uninteresting. A condition that seemed to be his alone as every man in the room stole glances at her in her fire-engine red body-hugging cocktail dress.

His father had clearly orchestrated her unveiling like a showgirl popping out of a cake. Sandwiching her between layers of colleagues and contacts.

"I can't believe it's finally happening."

A white-shirted bartender handed him his Scotch, and Preston dropped a twenty in the tip jar.

"You and me both," he said. "I thought the old man would end up staying at the head of the Del Rio Group until he had to be propped at the boardroom table like a scarecrow."

"I meant us," she said, looking at him beneath a fringe of dark lashes.

The hopes he'd harbored of this being a cordial conversation resulting in mutual closure quickly evaporated.

"You want to take a walk?" he asked.

What he had to say, he didn't want to be overheard by the entire goddamn town.

"It would be my pleasure," she purred.

The bartender had brought her a fresh martini without even being asked. She took it and thanked him with a sexy smile that made the man's ears turn crimson.

They wove through the crowd to the side of the patio and down a set of stairs to landscaped grounds of the Bellamy hotel.

Preston slowed when they reached a pocket of privacy created by a screen of hedges.

He'd been rehearsing what he might say since he received her text, but now they were alone, his mind went blank.

"My father invited you, didn't he?"

"Yes," she said. "But that's not why I came."

"Then why did you?"

Sunny took a step closer to him. "Because I miss you."

Preston's heart dropped into his guts. The last thing he'd wanted to do was hurt her *more*. "Sunny—"

"Please." She held up a hand. "I need to say this before I lose my nerve. Ever since we broke up, I haven't been able to stop thinking about what you said. How you couldn't marry me because your career would always come first, and that wouldn't be fair to me. I realize now that I wasn't as supportive as I could have been. That maybe if I had spent less time dragging you to trendy places and taking pictures of us being the perfect couple, we might have had the chance to be one in real life."

"No," Preston interrupted. "The only one to blame for our breakup is me."

"How so?" Her perfectly shaped eyebrows lifted.

"I wasn't being honest with you," he said. "Or myself."

Sunny hugged her arms tighter around herself. "What do you mean?"

The distant sound of the party drifted over on a breeze that rattled the leaves in an old scrub oak.

"My father kept dropping hints that he thought it was time I settled down. That having a family to continue the Del Rio line was part of what it meant to carry on his legacy. I thought if we got engaged, he might think I was ready to take on the role of CEO."

The sheen of tears caught the golden fairy lights overhead. "But…when you proposed, you said you couldn't imagine your future without me in it. You said—"

"I didn't realize how fixated I was on following

in my father's footsteps. Or how it was affecting my decisions." He stared out at the tangled silhouette of branches in the distant tree line. "I cared about you deeply, Sunny. I tried to convince myself that would be enough. That I'd be a good husband even though I couldn't seem to feel what you felt."

"You made me *feel* loved, Preston." She placed a hand on his forearm. "That *is* enough for me."

Preston placed his hand over hers. "It really isn't. Remember all the dates I broke? The trips we never took. All the things you wanted but never got. I watched you pretend that none of it mattered. But it did. It mattered, and I let you down in every way possible. You just wanted us to work so bad that you didn't see it."

Her dark hair fell forward around her face as she looked down at the cobblestones.

"You know I'm right," he said, feeling the weight of that truth within his bones. "You're going to find someone who can give you the kind of love I never could. I know you will."

She lifted shining eyes to Preston. Her hands pressed his chest through the fabric of his shirt, and she lifted on the toes of her strappy sandals to press a kiss against his lips.

"Thank you, Preston."

"For what?" he asked.

"For telling me the truth. Even when it hurts." She gave him a watery smile. "Especially then."

He brushed a tear away from her cheekbone. "Promise me you'll be happy."

Sunny pulled his hand away from her cheek and squeezed it. "I promise you I'll try."

He looked at her for what felt like an eternity, glad for this poignant moment despite his father having been its architect.

She drew in a deep breath and released it in a sigh. "I think I'm going to head out. Will you give your mother and sister my best?"

"I will," he said.

He watched her cross the grass to the parking lot, listening to the muffled sounds of people celebrating. Not really celebrating him, but themselves. Their connection to what they hoped would be a profitable company under his leadership.

He needed to confront his father about inviting Sunny, but knew this wasn't the time.

And anyway, her presence had been unintentionally helpful. Remembering their relationship had made the contrast between his present circumstances and what he felt for Sunny that much more vibrant.

He knew what he needed to do.

Pulling his phone from his pocket, he opened his family's WhatsApp chat and quickly typed in a message. Small emergency I need to take care of. Please apologize for me.

His chest filled with cement as the app registered that his sister, mother and father read the message. A tiny trail of bouncing bubbles indicating his father typing a message appeared and disappeared several times.

His mother and sister beat him to the punch with simultaneous replies.

Mom: Of course, son. Go take care of what you need to.

Maggie: We've got it covered, Pres.

His father's typing stopped, and Preston felt a rush of gratitude for the strong, courageous women in his life.

He laid down several feet of rubber as he screeched out of the parking lot and pointed his car toward Tiffany's home.

Preston needed to see her. To talk to her.

Not because he harbored an adult version of the unrequited crush that had tormented him in high school.

Because after tonight, he knew he was falling for Tiffany Winters.

And if he wasn't careful, those feelings could cost them both dearly.

Eight

"You do know, Miss Winters, what the consequences of your irresponsible choices will be?" the stern-faced judge demanded in a voice that sounded eerily like Fernando Del Rio's.

Tiffany frantically searched her memory but couldn't think of anything that would have landed her in court. Every time she opened her mouth to answer, he pounded his gavel.

Her hands balled into fists at her sides, she finally got irritated enough to shout back at him.

The sound of her own strangled moan ripped through the fabric of her dream.

She had fallen asleep on the couch.

The economics book she'd been reading before she crashed lay on her chest. The Netflix logo lazily swam around her TV screen against a black field. The phone she'd silenced when she settled in to study for her upcoming quiz bore several missed call notifications.

The most recent from Preston.

Which was when the pounding on her front door made sense.

Her body felt like a giant block of concrete, and raising it from the couch required significant effort.

"Coming," she called as she shuffled over to the door.

Preston's handsome face was kissed with sweat, his eyes wide with worry. The expression of naked relief evaporated and was replaced with irritation.

"You scared the shit out of me," he said. "I was seconds away from calling 911."

Tiffany moved to the side, rubbing her bleary eyes. "What are you even doing here?"

"Aside from panicking you mean?" he asked, walking inside.

"Panicking about what?" A yawn ate half of the last word.

"You didn't answer my calls, then I get here, and I can see your Jeep in the garage and all the lights are on, but you're not answering the door."

"Because I was asleep." She gestured toward the couch.

"How was I supposed to know that?" he demanded.

"You weren't," she said. "You were supposed to be at your house or a restaurant or whatever it is you usually do with your evenings."

His lean, muscular form crackled with energy as he paced the length of her living room.

"From now on, I don't think you should turn the ringer on your phone off when you're alone."

"Why is that?" Tiffany folded her arms across her chest, very aware of her braless state.

"Because I need to be able to make sure you're safe," he said. "What if you had passed out and hit your head?"

Adrenaline swept away the last of her sleep fog. "Then chances are, I wouldn't be able to get to the phone even if the ringer *was* on."

Preston's lips flattened into a line, his face turning a rosier shade of its usual beachy brown as he pulled his phone from his pocket and began typing.

"What are you doing?" she asked.

"Buying you one of those Life Alert systems," he said without looking up.

"Why don't you just install security cameras? Then you can watch me anytime you want," she muttered under her breath.

His scowl softened as he glanced around her living room. "That's not a bad idea."

"I was kidding," she said.

"After what happened the other day, can you honestly tell me I shouldn't be worried?"

Her irritation blazed into out-and-out anger. "What did Alisha tell you?"

Preston's eyes narrowed. "What do you mean, *what did Alisha tell me*? Did something happen?"

"Answer my question then I'll answer yours." She

crossed into the kitchen and went to the fridge. Taking out a bottle of the extra-strong ginger ale Camille had stocked there, she offered one to Preston, who refused.

"Alisha didn't tell me anything. I was talking about you getting dizzy and almost falling at Chocolate Fix."

Tiffany took a sip of the spicy brew and blew out a resigned breath. "It's called hyperemesis gravidarum, and it's not serious." She walked back into the living room and plopped down on the couch.

Preston followed but remained standing.

"Dr. Everett says it's actually very common and—"

"Dr. Everett? I thought your appointment wasn't until Thursday."

"It was," she said, already thinking of how she could state the next part without further alarming him. "I stopped by to see my parents, and my mom recommended moving it up." This didn't come out quite as casually as she hoped it would.

"Wait, Camille knows too, now?"

Tiffany nodded.

"She took one look at me, and I knew there was no point in trying to hide anything from her. She agrees that we should wait until after the wedding and she's a good ally to have."

He was silent as he digested this. "Why did she recommend moving the appointment up?"

So much for hopes of her mom knowing their secret derailing him from this line of reasoning.

"I had one of my spells when I was in their kitchen. I didn't faint this time—"

"*This* time?" His voice had risen by an entire octave. "You mean you fainted before?"

"Barely," she said, tucking her knees under her on the couch. "It was more like a brownout."

Preston's angular nostrils flared. "And you didn't think to let me know?"

"What purpose would that have served?" she asked.

"The purpose of making me aware of potential health problems with the mother of my child."

"Is that my official title now?" She set her bottle of ginger ale on the coffee table. "Because if it is, I guess I need an idea of exactly what the role entails. Is it all my personal health information that you're now entitled to? Or just things that you're afraid might affect the pregnancy?"

"That's not what I was trying to say."

"Then what *were* you trying to say?"

His posture slackened as some of the anger went out of him. "I was trying to say that I care about what's going on with you. I want to know so that I can be there for you."

"You *can't*." She hadn't meant to say it quite so forcefully and immediately wanted to soothe the hurt she read in his eyes. "I love that you want to be helpful—I really do. But this is just reality, Preston. You can't be there for me all the time. You can't come running over to my house every time I won't answer my phone. You can't act like something we're not."

Preston shuffled over to the window—it looked out to the street where his car was parked at the curb.

She felt an acute longing to press her cheek against

the broad plain of his back. To hear the muffled ticking of his heart within his sturdy torso. To know the thoughts looping through the coils of his keen mind.

When he faced her again, she could see the protective fire had dimmed to an ember. "I'm a shitty partner, Tiffany. I know myself well enough to admit that. I've never managed to put anything but my work first." His hands relaxed at his sides. "I don't want to be like that with you. I don't want anything to get in the way of putting our child first."

"That's what I want too, Preston," she said.

"And you're right. I need to be more respectful of your privacy. Which is why I think it's best that we keep things strictly platonic going forward."

The hope rising in her heart collapsed like a startled soufflé.

"I see," she said.

"I'm sorry that I let things get out of control at the shop the other day. I let my libido get the best of me and I made things more difficult in the process."

"That was a two-person effort," she said. "If I remember correctly, I'm the one who suggested a repeat performance."

"As much as I would like that, and I really would, for the sake of both our families and careers, we shouldn't play with that particular fire."

He wasn't saying anything Tiffany hadn't thought in the aftermath of their time together. They still needed to have deeper, more difficult discussions, but the idea of doing so now made her feel even more exhausted.

She scooted forward on the couch and yawned.

"In the interest of putting down the matches, do you want to get out of here so I can shower and fall into bed?"

"No," he said. "But I'm happy to supervise your shower so you *don't* fall and then tuck you into bed."

Part of her wanted to refuse on principle. To prove she could turn him away just as easily as he could dismiss the possibility of their having a physical relationship.

But tonight, she didn't want to be alone.

Her mom and Alisha had both offered to come stay with her for a week or so until the medication that Dr. Everett had started her on had a chance to get her symptoms under control, but she couldn't bear the thought of separating them from their beloved homes and partners. Not to mention putting them in the position of having to manufacture an excuse that didn't involve her pregnancy.

It was more than that too.

Preston's proximity made her feel safe.

She wanted him here. Wanted him all to herself. Knowing her possessiveness was completely irrational did nothing to alter its existence.

"Whatever will make you sleep easier," she said as if she agreed only for his benefit.

Reaching for the remote, she turned the TV off and stacked her book avalanche on the coffee table. Tiffany pushed herself up from the couch before dragging her leaden bones down the hallway.

Preston hovered a step behind her. Close enough

to grab her should she begin to fall, but far enough to give her space.

She stopped in her bedroom, where she fished clean underthings and an oversize T-shirt out of her dresser drawer. Preston hung back in the doorway, waiting until she proceeded to the en suite bathroom before he followed suit. Leaning against the sink, with his arms folded across his chest, and an endearingly serious expression on his face.

"We should get you a shower bench," he said, glancing through the glass wall.

We.

That word again.

Even if it was only temporary, she allowed herself to enjoy it.

Tiffany opened the shower door and turned the handle to start the spray. "I'm sure I can find something to that effect online."

His phone was out of his pocket and in his hand in a flash. He turned the screen toward her. "How about something like this?"

"That's really nice actually," she said, looking at the classic teakwood bench. "Will you send me the link?"

"It will be here by tomorrow between 2:00 to 5:00 p.m.," he reported with a grin.

"Preston," she scolded. "You didn't have to do that."

"I wanted to," he said. "I'll feel better knowing that you have it."

"When you're not available for shower supervision duty?" After gathering her hair into a messy pile at the top of her head, she secured it with an elastic.

"So that you have somewhere to sit while I'm supervising."

She laughed, turning her back to him as she stripped off her T-shirt. "Surely you're not planning on being here every single night."

When he didn't answer, she glanced over her shoulder to find his gaze fixed on her bare back, his lip caught between his teeth. She cleared her throat and his eyes flicked back toward the ceiling.

"Would that bother you?" he asked.

"It wouldn't bother me. I just find it extremely unlikely."

"Because?"

"I know how many social engagements your father signs you up for. How important networking is. How you're easily the most eligible bachelor for ten counties. I can't expect you to surrender your entire social life to play shower sentinel to a schlub."

Preston pushed himself off the counter before taking a step toward her. "You are the furthest thing from a schlub."

Tiffany glanced down at her faded, baggy sweats. Complete with bleach stains and a hole in the knee, both acquired over the years in the course of cleaning. "Glamour personified right here."

"If you're aiming for frumpy, you're gonna have to try a hell of a lot harder than that."

"You say that now, but just wait until there're various baby-generated stains added to the mix."

"I intend to." He said this with the fervency of a

vow. "Now get in there before you waste all the hot water."

Never particularly self-conscious, she stripped off her sweats and kicked the pile toward the wicker hamper.

The heated spray felt delicious on her skin.

She stood there and let it beat down on her and rolled her neck to release the tension. "What was the highlight of your day?"

A question asked to dispel the awkwardness of his being present for what was usually such a solitary ritual. Loading her loofah with bodywash, she then set about her usual ablutions.

"My father announced his retirement date."

The sudsy puff froze in its journey over her collarbone. "Really?"

"Really," he said. "As of January 1, you're looking at the new CEO of the Del Rio Group and its various holdings."

"Why don't you sound happy about that?"

"Because I feel like there's an ulterior motive for him having finally chosen a date."

"Such as?" Setting the loofah aside, she reached for her face wash.

"Such as, I don't know, but I plan to find out."

"You don't think there's any chance that he decided you were ready?"

The dark shape of his body moved in her peripheral vision. "Fernando Del Rio doesn't up and change his mind. He's famously stubborn and twice as proud."

"You come by it honestly then." Letting her head

fall backward, she rinsed the foam from her throat and chest.

"And what's that supposed to mean?" His voice was closer than she expected and sent a little jolt of electricity through her middle.

"It's not supposed to mean anything," she said. "It's just a general observation."

"If we're handing out unsolicited observations, I don't think you're eating enough."

Tiffany massaged the foamy cleanser into her cheeks. "You ought to look in my pantry. There's a gigantic bag of chocolate-dipped potato chips that only yesterday was full to the brim."

Preston shuddered. "Talk about a bizarre pregnancy craving."

"If that's true, then half of Royal must be secretly knocked up." Tiffany let the spray pellet her face. "They're one of my bestselling items. That and the brown sugar fudge. How did Maggie like her chocolates, by the way?"

"I haven't given them to her yet."

"You haven't seen her?" she asked.

"I saw her tonight, but I didn't have them with me."

"At your parents' house?"

"At the Glass House," he said.

It wasn't so much the revelation as the tone of voice it was delivered in that made her antennae twitch. "You went there for dinner?"

His silence lasted a few too many seconds. "It was an informal get-together to celebrate the announcement."

Tiffany swiped her fingers over her eyes to clear them so she could look at him. "And it was over in time for you to be banging on my door by seven o'clock?"

Preston shifted in his boots, his eyes fixed on the tile floor. "Not exactly."

Tiffany cut the water and yanked open the shower door.

"You left your own party just to drive over here and check on me?"

Preston's eyes swept up her naked body then quickly back to the floor.

He pulled the towel from the hook and held it out to her. "Yes."

"Why would you do that?"

Only when she had wrapped herself in the towel did he look her in the eye. "Because I had to know you were okay."

Preston had left a party celebrating the very thing he'd been working toward for the last decade of his life just to check on her. Her remorse at having been so salty to him was instant and powerful.

"Why didn't you just call Alisha? You could have told her that you weren't able to get hold of me and that you were worried. You didn't have to—"

"Yes," he said emphatically. "Yes, I did. I couldn't stand there another second with a smile pasted on my face, shaking hands and making small talk, pretending I gave a shit about what any of them had to say when I thought you might be hurt or in trouble."

A hard lump formed at the base of her throat, cutting off any words she had wanted to say.

"To answer your earlier question, it's not just pregnancy-related information I'm interested in. I want everything. I want to know how you're feeling. What you're thinking. What scares you. What excites you. I want to know *all* of it, Tiffany. All of it. All the time."

He was breathing hard. The skin of his throat stretching over his Adam's apple as he swallowed.

There were so many things she wanted to say to him. So many questions she wanted to ask. But fear got the better of her and she settled for something far less revealing. "I'm scared that I'm going to lose my shop, or flunk out of my MBA program, or both. I was just starting to get some momentum, and now it feels like someone has tied bricks to my ankles."

She stepped onto the cushioned bath mat and secured the towel under her arm.

Preston scooted out of the way to give her access to her vanity. "I meant what I said. I really want to help."

Tiffany opened the mirror cabinet and took out the moisturizer Alisha gave her that was meant to help with hormone-related breakouts. "Are you offering to do my homework for me?" she asked.

"Any kind of work that might be required in your home or otherwise."

"Just not the kind of work you did in my office," she teased.

Preston's boots shifted on the tile floor again. "We're in this together, Tiffany," he said, leaping over her comment entirely. "I need you to know that."

She wanted to. More than anything, she wanted

to quell the nagging voice that insisted on reminding her that at the end of the day, what was happening was happening to her body alone.

The only obligation he had to her or to their child was moral.

Preston was the kind of man who would want to "do the right thing."

But Tiffany wasn't sure that there was any one thing that would be right for everyone involved.

"Thank you for being here tonight," she said. "I promise it won't be so dramatic once the medication starts working in earnest."

"Is that my cue to leave?" he asked.

"Were you wanting to stay?"

"As I recall, I offered to tuck you into bed. I intend for this to be a full-service experience."

"You really don't need to do that," she said.

"And what if I want to?"

She could see that arguing with Preston Del Rio was unlikely to yield any results. "Just give me a minute to change into my pajamas."

When she opened her door a few minutes later, Preston was standing there with the tray from her kitchen. Glancing at its contents, Tiffany felt her heart threatening to melt right out of her chest.

A bottled water and a ginger ale from the fridge. Her lip balm. A sleeve of saltine crackers.

Annoyingly ever-ready tears stung her eyes.

"What is it?" Preston asked. "Did I forget something?"

"You're just being so…so… Nice to me."

He gave her a boyish grin. "I'll try to work on that."

Tiffany wiped her tears on the sleeve of her pajama shirt. "I was so rude to you earlier, and here you are putting together this amazingly thoughtful bedside tray." Her voice wobbled on the last word.

"Definitely bedtime for you." He nudged her forward, and Tiffany shuffled toward the bed. After placing the tray down on her nightstand, he began divesting the comforter of throw pillows.

"You can just toss them in the corner," she said.

"Is that why they call them throw pillows?" he asked. "Because all you really do with them is throw them in a corner?"

"They're decorative," she said, feeling a little foolish at the sheer volume.

Preston peeled back the covers in a neat triangle and made a show of fluffing her feather pillow before stepping out of her way. "In you get."

Tiffany sat down and slid her legs under the covers Preston held up.

"Not so fast," he said when she began to lie back.

She hugged the down comforter to her chest. "What am I waiting for exactly?"

Preston reached behind her to adjust the pillows. "It's all about the sink."

"The sink?" she asked.

"Yeah. There's nothing like sinking into a freshly fluffed pillow. But you have to take it slow to get the full effect."

Her abdominal muscles tightened as she laughed. This whole region of her body was prone to strange twinges and tugs, already making room for the tiny life growing within her. "And where did you come up with this theory?"

He shrugged and scratched the back of his neck. "Just something Maggie and I used to do as kids."

Tiffany could easily imagine them. A dark-haired boy and girl with giant long-lashed eyes and impish expressions.

She'd been so focused on what role Preston might play in this child's life that she hadn't paused to think about what role his sister might.

Aunt Maggie. Uncle Jericho.

No matter what happened—or didn't—between her and Preston, this baby would have a family. The thought brought her some comfort.

She so badly wished this could be enough to stop her mind from churning out awful scenarios. To keep her heart from bleeding ridiculous wishes.

Wishes she didn't dare share with him.

Tiffany sank back against the pillows at a speed that felt processional. The second her head hit the pillow her eyelids began to droop. Exhaustion stalked her like a leopard these days. There was no telling when it would pounce.

Preston nodded approvingly. "Much better," he said. "Is there anything else I can bring you?"

She fought an epic yawn and lost. "I'm…good." Her bedside lamp clicked off. "To lock the front door, you just…punch the thingy and wait for a beep."

"Punch the thingy," Preston repeated. "Got it."

The second lamp clicked off, and in the velvet

dark, Tiffany felt the comforter being pulled higher to cover her shoulder. Preston's delicious scent washed over her, followed by a whisper that chased her down into her dreams.

"Good night, Juliet."

Nine

Preston couldn't move.

His fingers tingled from lack of blood flow, his arms crushing into his ribs. His knees jutted against something unyielding, and his lower back ached from being immobilized. Through the maze of legs, he could barely make out an emerald-green football field.

Only then did he realize where he was.

The Royal, Texas, stadium at the fairgrounds that housed Friday night high school football games. Only, instead of being on the field, he was trapped under the bleachers. No wonder they were calling his name through the loudspeaker.

He grunted with the effort of trying to wrench himself out from under the metal benches. Straining to get into the stadium lights. He was so close, he could smell it.

The crisp fall air was alive with freshly mowed grass, hot dogs and popcorn from the concession stands and…

Coffee?

"Preston." The loudspeaker softened into a familiar voice. Something warm brushed his forehead and his eyes fluttered open.

The unfamiliar surroundings were disorienting at first. A coffee table. A stack of books. And Tiffany standing over him with a steaming mug in her hand.

"Is this an angel I see before me?" His voice was little more than a croak.

"I'm pretty sure angels would have something better than standard Colombian coffee to offer you," she said, setting down the mug on the coffee table.

Preston winced as he pushed himself upright on the sofa, entire body stiff and sore. "Thanks," he said.

"I wasn't sure how you take yours, so I made it like I make mine."

"Black, and usually from a plastic pod, so this is a significant improvement," he said, blowing away the steam to take a sip. "Oh wow. What did you put in here?"

"Brown sugar, homemade Madagascar vanilla bean simple syrup and a splash of half-n-half." She smiled and reached for her own mug, which was sporting a cap of pillowy whipped cream.

"How come mine doesn't have any?" he teased.

"I stopped short of inflicting my full sweet tooth on you." She pushed herself up off the couch and padded into the kitchen, returning with a spray can. "Occupational hazard."

Preston held out his mug and received a swirl. The result was decadent, delicious and something he never would have chosen for himself.

He cradled the warm mug between his palms in the early morning light and watched Tiffany return to the kitchen. From the couch, he had the perfect vantage to observe her bustling around the well-appointed space.

His own contained nothing but the barest essentials. He typically grabbed breakfast after the gym, ate lunch at work and had dinner with clients or his family. His place didn't reflect him the way Tiffany's reflected her. She had made this a home.

The word woke an ache in his chest.

His parents' house would always hold a nostalgic allure, but it was no longer his place. No longer the center of his daily life. For the past several years he had lived inside his head and the hopes that lived there.

Was this what they meant by nesting? The desire to create a warm, welcoming space to where the rest of the world could be shut out.

Preston rose from the couch, feeling every stiff muscle as he did so. Walking into the kitchen with his coffee, he propped one hand against the doorframe overhead for a stretch.

"You could have just slept in the bed, you know." Tiffany looked at him over the rim of her coffee cup.

"I know," he said. Not that there would have been any chance of his doing so. He'd had a hard enough time getting his brain to turn off while lying on her couch. The image of her naked and wet danced through his mind until almost dawn.

"Or, you know, your bed."

"I know," he said again.

He had gotten as far as the living room last night before turning back to check on her. Finding her breathing even and deep, he'd turned to leave and stopped again when he heard a rustling outside her front window. It had only been an opossum, but this had led to him checking the backyard. The alley. The garage. He'd decided he was *really* leaving this time when he noticed the bathroom window was slightly ajar. Which led him to checking all her window locks.

Discovering that two of them didn't even work, he stationed himself on her couch.

"I hope your day isn't too hectic at least."

Hectic didn't begin to cover it.

The day after such a big announcement, his father was sure to wring the maximum impact out of the news. Preston hadn't yet looked at his phone but knew that as soon as he did it would be confetti with notifications.

The mere thought of it made him even more tired.

"I'll be fine," he said. "How about you?"

Tiffany went to the cupboard and came back with a brightly colored tin that she placed on the counter between them. She popped the lid to reveal neat little stacks of shortbread in scalloped paper cups.

Lifting one up, she dunked it in her coffee and bit into it. "The usual," she said.

He raised an eyebrow at her. "Cookies for breakfast?"

"It's not a cookie—it's shortbread."

"What's the difference?" he asked.

"A couple of eggs, some baking soda and my talent for justification."

She nudged the tin toward him, and Preston took one. It dissolved in his mouth like delicious sand.

Sweetness.

Sweetness had been in very short supply in his life lately. Every moment spent in her presence felt like a reward. A holiday. A treat.

"I have an idea," he said.

Tiffany popped the last of the shortbread in her mouth and dusted her fingers. "What's that?"

"We should play hooky today."

Her lightly freckled nose wrinkled. "Hooky? Seriously?"

"Seriously," he said, liking the idea more every minute. "When's the last time you did?"

Her lips pursed and she leaned against the counter. "Never?"

"You never played hooky," he repeated.

She shook her head of adorably sleep-rumpled curls. "Nope."

"Not even in high school?" he asked.

"Especially not then. Marcus was always the troublemaker. There wasn't really room for any of the rest of us."

"Then it's settled. We're getting out of Royal, and

we're going to go shopping for every possible baby-related thing your heart desires."

If Preston could freeze her delighted expression in time, he would have given up years of his life.

"Are you sure you can?" she asked. "With the announcement—"

"I haven't taken a day off in over a year. I don't think the company will fall apart completely in my absence. How about you?" he asked. "Do you think the girls can hold down the fort?"

"I think they should be able to manage it," she said.

"Perfect. How about this for a plan then? We finish our coffee, I go home and get cleaned up and I come back to pick you up in an hour."

Tiffany raised her mug to clink with his. "Sounds like a date...er—deal," she quickly corrected.

Preston far preferred the former to the latter but kept his mouth shut in the interest of their discussion from the night before.

Once at home, Preston hurried through his usual rituals. Fueled by a sense of excitement like he hadn't felt for as long as he could remember. He had finished all of his chores and even invented a few new ones before facing the one he knew he was putting off.

Texting his father.

He stared at his phone for a solid five minutes before deciding on a simple Working from home today.

After he pressed the send button, Preston set his phone on the counter and ran away from it like it was a bomb. The reply waiting for him when he got out of the shower left him staring at his own stunned reflection in the mirror.

No worries. We'll hit it hard tomorrow.

Preston almost would have preferred that his father reacted with the outrage he had expected.

He decided not to look a gift horse in the mouth and replied with liking the message before getting dressed and heading back to Tiffany's.

She met him at the door with a smile and a truffle. "That was fast," she said, shrugging her purse over her shoulder.

"What's this?" he asked, looking down at the mirror-polished tiny red dome topped with a sculpted poison-green leaf.

"Just a little something I've been working on." She stepped out onto the porch and shut her screen door.

"Don't forget to press the thingy," Preston teased, before popping the chocolate in his mouth.

Tiffany shot him a look as she engaged the lock. "I can't believe I went down so hard last night."

"I can. You looked—oh wow." The chocolate was silk on his tongue, releasing a complex bouquet of flavors as it warmed. "What's this one called?"

"The Bad Apple. Persipan, Madagascar vanilla bean white chocolate ganache and apple jelly spiked with a Ceylon cinnamon whiskey."

"Persipan?" he asked.

"Like marzipan but made with apple seeds instead of almonds. Is it a keeper?"

"Definitely," he said. "I could eat about thirty of those."

"Amateur like you?" she asked. "That would make you sick."

The word triggered his memory of her pale, peaked face above the steam kettle.

"I didn't even ask how you were feeling this morning. Are you sure you're up for this?"

"Positive," she said. "I don't know if it's the pills or a solid night's sleep, but I feel great."

"I'm so glad," Preston said.

The brick that had been sitting on his chest lost a few crumbs.

Her street was blessedly quiet and empty of other occupants as they walked down the front path to his car. Preston held the passenger-side door for her then walked around to his side and slid behind the wheel. "Think we can get out of town without anybody spotting us?"

"Just let me know if you spot anybody you recognize, and I'll lay my seat back." She fastened her seat belt and Preston ignited the engine.

He glanced at her as they pulled away from the curb. "Look, I'm sorry I've been so paranoid. It's just, my dad—"

"You don't have to apologize," she said. "I may not understand what it's like to be my family's golden child, but I know enough about the pressure from family."

"You feel pressure?"

Tiffany shrugged. "All my other siblings have these

wildly successful businesses and stable relationships, and I'm over here accidentally pregnant and barely able to keep up a tiny chocolate shop."

"But you're building something from the ground up," he pointed out. "It was an idea that you came up with yourself and you made it happen. That takes a lot of courage."

"Or delusion," she muttered. "Marcus and Jericho did the same, but their businesses were successful right from the start."

"We're supposed to be playing hooky here. Which means talk of business, work, family feuds, stolen necklaces or other adult-related responsibilities is strictly forbidden."

"That narrows the topics of discussion considerably," she said. Leaning forward, Tiffany pulled out a tube of lip balm and flipped down the visor mirror to apply it.

The scent of the vanilla drifted over to him. He really wished he didn't know exactly how it would taste if he pulled the car over and kissed her.

And God did he want to. No matter how many times he told himself that theirs had to remain a platonic relationship for the benefit of their future child, he couldn't stop reliving the soul-ensnaring ecstasy of being inside her.

"So where to first?" he asked. "Baby Barn? Baby Mart? Baby Depot?"

Tiffany flipped the visor back up. "That's a toughie. I've always loved trains."

"Baby Depot it is."

* * *

A short time later they pulled into the shopping center, relatively quiet on a weekday. Despite Thanksgiving being just around the corner, the giant retail stores were donning their holiday finery. Ribbons and lights. Wreaths, bells, elves and reindeer.

The festive atmosphere combined with Tiffany's excitement was almost enough to make Preston forget that every smile was bought with stolen time.

He followed her from display to display, refusing to take his phone from his pocket to check it for messages.

"Oh my God, would you look at these!" Tiffany held up the tiniest set of pajamas Preston had ever seen. Pale buttery yellow with minuscule llamas, they came with a matching bathrobe whose hood sported a set of perky ears, large lashy eyes and a black button nose.

Preston took the itty-bitty slippers in his hand. Imagining the foot tiny enough to fit into them felt completely impossible.

"I'm sorry," he said, keeping his face deadpan. "We can't buy these."

"Why not?"

"These are *llamas*. I distinctly remember you saying the nursery was going to be alpaca themed."

Tiffany batted him with a tube of rolled-up receiving blankets. "Close enough."

Preston added the set to a shopping cart already piled with other items.

An hour later, and there was no room left in either Preston's trunk or his backseat.

Tiffany stood next to the car hugging her coat around her and watching Preston attempt to rearrange the items to make room for the oversize stuffed llama who had found its way into the cart at the last boutique.

"Think we might have overdone it just a touch?" she asked.

"Nonsense," he said. "I hear maximalism is all the rage these days."

"Well, this is about as maxed out as it gets. Of course, whatever doesn't fit in the baby's room at my house we can always put in the baby's room at yours."

Preston nearly smacked his head on the doorframe.

How had this not occurred to him?

All the pondering he had done about the future and none of it had been focused on the actual day-to-day reality of sharing a child outside a relationship. Like everything else in his world, there would need to be paperwork. Official documents governing resources, time and responsibilities. The idea that punctured what remained of his jovial mood. He stood up, his arms still full of bags as he stared into the back of the car.

"Hey," Tiffany said, her brown eyes wide. "Are you okay?"

"I'm fine," he said. "I was just thinking."

"Thinking about what?" Tiffany leaned back against the car. They weren't going anywhere until he gave her a satisfactory answer.

"How are we gonna do this?"

She peeked through the window. "I think if we pulled out the Diaper Genie, the humidifier and mini bounce house, we could actually stack the boxes and—"

The rest of her words faded away as he looked across the parking lot and saw a man somersaulting a blond toddler onto his shoulders as they walked toward a Mercedes SUV, the child's mother following close behind.

Preston didn't want to be the kind of father who was never home on a random Friday afternoon. The kind of father who canceled on baseball games. Or football games. Or any other of life's small but important moments.

He knew what it felt like to be on the receiving end of that kind of defensible neglect.

The sound of Tiffany clearing her throat returned him to the present moment.

"Can we just stop for a moment to appreciate the mastery of my work here?"

While he had been gathering wool, she had reorganized the entire backseat.

"Color me impressed," he said.

Tiffany slurped the last of the Frappuccino she had insisted wasn't for her, but for the baby. "You know what I think we should do next?"

Preston certainly knew what he *wished* they could do. Walking through all the stores, constantly being mistaken for a couple had had a strangely aphrodisiac effect.

"What's that?"

"I think we should see a movie."

"A movie?" he asked.

"I've been craving popcorn like mad, and there just happens to be a giant mega multiplex right there across the parking lot."

"I don't even know what's playing," he said. He couldn't even remember the last time he'd set foot in a movie theater.

"I guess we'll have to find out then."

The options were comfortingly predictable. Rom-com. Superhero movie. Fantasy epic. Live-action remake of an animated classic. Recycled horror. Action adventure. Tearjerker.

They settled on the rom-com. Tiffany insisted it was the least likely to make her eyes leak. You never knew when they would sneak in a pet in peril in some of the other genres.

"I'll grab the tickets if you want to be on snack duty," Preston suggested.

"Deal," she said.

As soon as she was through the doors, Preston turned back to the kid behind the plate glass window. "How many tickets have you sold for the 11:30 of *Love, Linda*?"

The kid consulted the monitor parked in front of him. "None so far."

"How much would it cost to buy out the theater?"

Behind his smudged glasses, the kid's eyes widened. "The *whole* theater?"

"The whole theater," Preston repeated.

"Just one moment and I'll call my manager." The

kid picked up the phone and mumbled into the receiver before pressing it to his bird-boned sternum. "He says it will be—" he gulped audibly "—two thousand dollars plus tax and cleaning fees."

Preston pulled his wallet from his back pocket and slid his platinum card into the brushed metal trough below the glass.

The kid's eyes were as large as duck eggs as he processed the transaction. He folded Preston's card into the receipt and slid it back to him. "Enjoy the show, sir."

Opening his billfold, Preston pulled out a crisp hundred and tucked it through the slot. "Appreciate your help—" he squinted to read the name tag "—Doug."

"You're very welcome, sir! Happy Holidays!" Doug's cheeks were patchy pink. The tips of his ears nearly scarlet. He looked like he might be on the verge of breaking out in a Tiny Tim leap.

Popcorn-scented air whooshed over Preston as he pushed through the doors to find Tiffany at the concessions stand, loading up a carrying caddy.

"That's quite the array," he said, unzipping his coat.

Tiffany grabbed a handful of napkins and set them on the tray. "Extra-large popcorn, butter and salt layered of course. Licorice, gummy bears and chocolate malted milk balls."

"What are those?" he asked, pointing at the three small white cups perched atop the popcorn.

"Ranch," she said. "For the popcorn."

"Now I *know* that's got to be a craving."

She gave him a sheepish smile. "Actually, I always eat ranch with my popcorn."

"Why am I not surprised." Preston relieved her of the tray and walked toward the podium, where another kid with a barcode scanner snapped to attention.

"You'll be in theater seven," she said brightly. "You just turn right down that first hallway, and it will be halfway down on your left."

"Thanks so much," Preston said. He stood still long enough for Tiffany to get a couple steps ahead, then dropped the folded hundred-dollar bill he'd concealed in his palm.

His chest warmed at the expression of absolute wonder on a face that had looked too young to be so jaded only seconds before.

Stepping into the dim theater, he felt a strange sense of déjà vu, having squired many a high school and college date through similar rituals. They sat down just as the previews were beginning.

Tiffany folded out a tray table and set out all the various items.

"You know the seats recline, right?" She reached across his lap to press a glowing blue button. Preston's legs began to lift as the seat whined backward.

"Why are you whispering?" Preston asked. "We're the only two people in here."

He tried very, very hard not to notice the proximity of her forearm to the part of him beginning to stir at her nearness.

"Theater etiquette is very important," she said, biting into a licorice rope. "Regardless of whether other patrons are present."

Preston lifted the popcorn bucket and set it down on his lap. A gesture more practical than anything else.

It felt like a strange reimagining of a life he'd only lived in dreams. Tiffany Winters's beautiful profile lit up from the movie's flickering glow. He couldn't help but think how much easier his life might have been, both of their lives might have been, had they the chance to do this when they were teenagers. To be silly. Irresponsible. Impractical. Selfish. To get into trouble they could then get themselves out of.

Had this been a date, now would be the time when he was thinking of a way to get closer to her. Nothing so obvious as the arm around the shoulder bit, but maybe a whispered question like—

"Did you see him in that *Hamlet* remake?" Tiffany's breast brushed his arm as she leaned in to grab a handful of popcorn.

"I didn't," he said.

"You should. He was better in *Titus*, but I really think you'd like it."

"I'll have to look that up."

Images moved on the screen, but his entire awareness centered around the bare half inch where the side of her hand touched his on the armrest.

It really was like being in high school.

Complete with an inconvenient erection he was unsuccessfully attempting to think away. His father's rules had precluded him dating anyone steadily until he was old enough to have his driver's license. And on the day he'd earned it, Fernando had insisted they go for a drive down one of Royal, Texas's many back roads. While they bumped through the scrub mesquite collecting a patina of dust, Fernando gave him his version of *the talk*.

Not about the actual mechanics—he'd been pretty clear on those for a while at that point—but about the consequences. Parked on one of the rare vistas granting a view of their family's land, Fernando had impressed the importance of using protection.

"It's an awesome power, son. Having any kind of power at all is a privilege. You can tell a lot about a man by how he chooses to use it and who he chooses to share it with."

At the time, Preston had been so taken aback by his father's use of the word *man* that he hadn't given the proper weight to the true meaning of his words.

It wasn't just about avoiding a teenage pregnancy.

It was about their family's legacy.

And Preston's obligation to continue it responsibly. He had failed this most basic of tests and would have to tell his father about it.

Tiffany's elbow nudged his on the armrest. "Pass the gummy bears?"

On-screen, the hero and heroine leaned toward one another. Their faces doing the tension-heightening hover-pause before their lips met.

Preston located the box of candy and passed it to Tiffany, whose eyes stayed riveted on the screen. She opened it by feel alone, chewing absently as the kiss got serious.

The back of Preston's neck felt hot. His groin heavy. He debated excusing himself to go to the bathroom, but only desperate thoughts about how to resolve the situation once he got there followed.

Preston didn't know how he was going to survive the next hour, let alone the next seven months.

The couple fell into bed together, dramatically rolling across the mattress and tearing clothes away from each other's bodies.

A fine film of sweat broke out across Preston's forehead. "Are you sure this is a romantic comedy?"

Tiffany nodded as she stared at the screen, her hand first missing her mouth with a bite of popcorn, then missing the bucket as she reached to retrieve another.

Preston shoved the bucket toward her, knocking into the vat of soda in the cup holder between them. They both bent to secure it and managed to bump heads.

"Shit." Preston rubbed his scalp at the site of impact. "I'm so sorry."

"*I'm* sorry." Tiffany's eyes crinkled at the corners as she winced. "I'm the one who insisted on getting all these snacks."

"Let me feel." Preston sank his hand into the cloud of her hair and tenderly probed her scalp. No lumps or bumps, to his great relief.

Tiffany's eyelashes were feathered against her cheeks, her head tilted toward his touch.

"That feels nice," she said dreamily.

"Good." He was barely breathing. Gently kneading his way downward toward her nape.

"Mmmmm." Her head lolled forward on a quiet moan that lanced Preston straight through the gut. He closed his eyes to home his attention to her hair moving through his fingers like warm silk. He wanted hours—days—to map every single part of her body this way. To learn what made her giggle, sigh, scream and sing.

He wanted to pull her into his lap right here in this theater and—

"Preston?"

He opened his eyes to find Tiffany looking at him. "Hmm?"

The mysterious magnet that had drawn them together the night of Maggie's engagement party and again in her shop woke once again. Their mouths drifted closer. Brushed. Brushed again.

Met.

Fused.

His hand tightened in her hair, releasing another small moan. He drank its honey sweetness as she opened her mouth to him. The sensuous dance of their tongues grew urgent. Demanding. Their bodies sought contact despite the physical barriers determined to separate them. Elbows making awkward introductions to the seat backs, the armrest, the tray tables in their haste. Teeth bumping. Smiling against each other's lips at their awkwardness.

"You want to get out of here?" Tiffany's lips gleamed in the light from the screen.

He'd been afraid to ask this question. Afraid that daylight would burn away their passion and restore them to their senses. Afraid of what might happen if it didn't.

"Yes."

They hastily gathered their things, depositing the remainder of the snacks in the popcorn bucket that Preston used as a shield as they quickly made their way through the lobby.

Preston trotted ahead to get the door. Glancing back at Tiffany, the bottom dropped out of his stomach.

She stood frozen like a statue, her face ghost white.

He thought she might be having a fainting spell until a familiar voice rushed into the foyer on a gust of chilly air scented with a familiar heavily floral perfume.

"Well, what are the odds!" Mandee Meriweather bustled past him to give Tiffany a hug. Her short cabernet-colored pixie cut stuck up in odd whorls, a casualty of the constant Texas wind. Bird-bright eyes flicked between them. "What on earth are the two of you doing here?"

Tiffany's mouth opened, but sound failed to come out.

"Concessions," Preston blurted out. "Tiffany has been working on getting her chocolates into local retailers. I just happened to know the manager of the movie theater, so—"

Preston looked back toward the ticket counter just outside the doors, where the first kid he'd given a hundred spot to lifted a hand as if on cue.

"Oh," Mandee said primly. "Isn't that nice of you. That must be what the two of you were talking about in front of your shop the other day."

"It sure was," Tiffany chimed in.

Preston was relieved to see that she'd recovered some of her color along with her voice.

"It was awfully nice of them to give you snacks for the road." Mandee's penciled brows rose. Another subtle attempt to call their bluff.

"Yep," Preston replied, offering no further explanation. "What about you? Did you come to catch a solo matinee?"

"Goodness no. I'm on a fundraising committee. We're going to do a charity raffle at the TCC and the theater has agreed to donate a movie night basket. I'm just here to pick it up."

"We'll let you get to it then." He nodded to Tiffany.

"Good to see you," she said, smiling at the *Royal Tonight* reporter.

They were almost home free when Mandee called after them. "You know the proceeds of the raffle are going to Furry Friends Animal League. And of course, there's always the option to give *anonymously*," she said, emphasizing the last word.

Preston and Tiffany traded a knowing look.

"I'd be more than happy to put together a goody basket for you," Tiffany said.

"You're such a dear. I hope you didn't take that as my hinting. I'd never want anyone to feel pressured."

"Not at all," Tiffany said. "I'm happy to help."

"Of course you are. It is a wonderful cause. All those poor, sweet creatures, just looking for a bit of warmth during the cold, dark—"

"I'm sure the Del Rio Group could come up with something as well," Preston cut in before Mandee could break out her phone to pull up one of the posts with pictures of pets in need of adoption that she was always sharing and he agreed to foster a dozen of them.

"Oh, bless your heart, you kind, wonderful man." Mandee fished a hand into her purse and came back with her phone. "I actually have a Venmo QR code for the raffle if that works."

Preston blinked at her.

"Um, sure." Handing off the popcorn bucket he no longer needed for coverage, he pulled out his phone and scanned the code.

"Of course, it's up to you how much you'd like to donate, but every little bit helps. Did you know that even five dollars can feed a homeless pet for up to a week?"

"I didn't," Preston said, typing numbers into the payment field.

"Just think of how many pets five hundred dollars would feed," Mandee added. "Or even a thousand."

Preston deleted the number he had been typing and doubled it before pressing Send.

The reporter's phone pinged, stopping her mid-monologue about the importance of checking in wheel wells and undercarriage this time of year lest they be harboring a stray seeking shelter.

"Oh, Preston." She pressed a manicured hand to her matronly bosom. "How can I ever thank you?"

"Don't say another word about it," he reassured her. "We were happy to help."

Mandee mimed zipping her fuchsia lips and throwing away the key. "You two enjoy the rest of your day."

Preston ducked his head and shifted toward the parking lot to signal their imminent departure.

They turned to each other once she was safely out of sight.

"Did I just get fleeced?" Preston asked. "Because I feel like I just got fleeced."

"I didn't want to say anything," Tiffany said gravely. "But you just got fleeced."

Preston pressed his key fob to unlock the car and held the door open for Tiffany.

"It could have been worse, I guess," she said.

He shut the door and walked around to the driver's side. "How so?" he asked.

"She could have caught us coming out of Baby Depot," Tiffany said. "Or asked you to be part of a bachelor auction."

Just the mere idea of their having avoided either of these possibilities left him woozy with relief.

"You okay?" Tiffany pressed a cool hand to his clammy cheek. "You're looking a little peaked."

Preston sagged forward to rest his forehead against the steering wheel's smooth, well-worn leather.

"Hell with Jack Chowdhry," he grumbled. "We should have hired her to be the mediator for Diamond Gate."

"When is the meeting happening about that, anyway?"

He sat up and started the engine. "Tomorrow morning." The wall he'd constructed between this day and the rest of his life had begun to crack, occasional drips of dread seeping in.

"How do you feel like it's going to go?"

Preston stepped on the gas as they hit the freeway entrance ramp. "I thought we agreed not to talk about any adult responsibilities."

She was silent for a protracted moment, staring out at the orderly diagonals of an alfalfa field after the harvest.

"It seems like they're determined to find us whether we talk about them or not."

"Seems you're right."

They rode in silence most of the way back to Royal.

Preston had driven these roads a million times, but rarely had he really looked at the modest brick houses situated between the tall rows of trees planted as windbreaks on the individual plots of farmland. He had never wondered who lived in them. What the parents did for a living. Whether the sales from the yearly crop were enough to cover the costs, or if they had to supplement with full-time jobs at one of his father's refineries. Whether their teenage sons and daughters worked at movie theaters, delighted by a hundred-dollar bill.

"You mind if I turn the heat up?" Tiffany shivered.

"Not at all."

The endless Texas sky had turned from a crisp blue to a gunmetal gray, the meteorologists calling for a cold snap that the power grids were ill-equipped to handle. Glancing at his dashboard, Preston could see the temperature had already dropped by ten degrees.

He thought longingly of the wood-burning fireplace in Tiffany's living room.

Even if seeing Mandee Meriweather had let the air out of their amorous tires, at least they could sit together in front of it for a while.

If he could just have that, he promised himself he'd be content to walk through whatever consequences tomorrow might bring.

Their luck held on the drive into town, and they were able to glide straight into Tiffany's garage without any additional unwelcome encounters. Preston killed the engine and ordered Tiffany inside to put her feet up while he unloaded the car.

"I promise that both my legs and arms still work perfectly well. I can at least carry the clothes."

"It's not a question of whether you can," he said, herding her toward the garage door. "I'm here to help, so let me help."

"But what about when you're not here?" She set her purse on the counter and followed him into the nursery.

Preston bent at the knees to deposit his armload of boxes, bags and free-range stuffed animals too large for either.

"What if I was always here?" Preston's pulse pounded in his ears. His arms and heart relieved of a burden that left him feeling instantly lighter.

Tiffany's brow furrowed. "You mean like, move in together?"

Preston took a step toward her, gazing down into her big, beautiful brown eyes.

"Yes," he said. "That's exactly what I mean."

Ten

Tiffany stared up at Preston, not quite believing she'd heard him correctly.

"Wait," she said, sitting down on one of the boxes in her pile. "Wait, wait, *wait*. As of this morning you were still afraid to be seen with me. But now you think we should move in together?"

The mere idea of it gave her emotional whiplash.

Preston walked over to the window, planting his hands on the sill and looking out at the spot where he had startled her while she was painting.

"I don't want our baby to have two separate rooms. I don't want to have to decide which clothing goes where, who gets what lamp. Whether we both have the right brand of diapers." He looked at her over his shoulder.

"Are you talking about living together platonically to raise our child? Or something else?"

"Look, I don't want to pressure you. I think we can both agree that if there's any way this baby could have two loving parents in the same home, it would only be to the good. I don't want to be there just when it's my weekend, or my turn. I don't want to miss any part of this."

Even a day ago, he'd be saying the exact words she wanted to hear.

But now, what he *wasn't* saying spoke the loudest.

"Preston, I really appreciate you being willing to do this. But I meant what I said the first time we talked about this. I don't want you rearranging your entire life for me."

The quick jerk of his shoulders upward could have been lack of enthusiasm on his part or fear of that possibility on hers. "Just promise me you'll think about it."

She blew out a breath and rose from her box.

"I'm not going to lie—I've been a little afraid of what it was going to feel like when I was bloated and exhausted watching you out on the town with some supermodel."

His dark brows lowered. "Do you honestly think I would do that?"

Tiffany searched his face, looking for the answer to his question.

"I don't know, Preston. Maybe that's not the answer I'm supposed to give you, but it's the truth. I have no idea whether I'm being reasonable or ridiculous. I have no idea what I'm doing, or how not to feel jealous when I think of you with someone else. I have no right to want you to myself, but I do, and there you have it."

Tiffany's heart sank as Preston folded his arms across his chest and stared at his shoes.

Treacherous tears welled up in her eyes and she turned before they could spill down her cheeks.

The air shifted on the back of her neck as he came up behind her. His hands found her hips and drew her backward until her shoulders were pressed against his chest. He wrapped his arms around her and held her there, not saying a word until she relaxed into him.

"I'm here, Tiffany." His sandpapery cheek grazed against hers. "There's no one else but me and you."

He nuzzled against her neck, sending a tide of goose bumps spilling down her arms. She sighed and let her eyelids fall closed. Warm tears slipped down her cheeks and landed on the muscled forearm resting across her chest.

"Tell me you're not doing this out of pity." Her voice was tight.

She felt Preston pull away and turned in the circle of his arms. The wounded look in his hazel eyes only drove the pain deeper.

"Is that what you think?" he asked.

"What am I supposed to think? We both know how this started out. It was supposed to be a one-night stand. If it wasn't for my accidentally getting pregnant, you wouldn't even be standing here right now."

Preston brushed a tear away from her cheekbone

with the rough pad of his thumb. "You don't know that."

"Really?" she challenged. "In what universe would Preston Del Rio, only son of my father's bitter enemy, be standing in my spare bedroom after an entire lifetime of not even knowing I existed?"

"I knew you existed, Tiffany."

She shook her head. "This isn't about my ego, Preston. We were feeling it, we went for it and now we'll be forever connected by the consequences. You don't need to try and make this more than what it is for my benefit."

"That's what I'm trying to tell you, Tiffany." His hands were warm on her lower back. "It wasn't like I was looking for a random hookup and you just happened to be there."

"What was it like, then?"

He exhaled. "It was the first time in my life when our families weren't locked in a bitter battle. After all that time, I had the opportunity to talk to you, and I took it. I'm sorry for all the trouble I've caused you as a result, but I'll never be sorry for what we shared that night."

Tiffany's mind whirled with the implications of his statement. "After...all that time?"

Preston nodded. "For the one year when we were in high school together, I was *very* aware of your existence. So aware that I even switched one of my electives so I could listen to your goofy laugh when you stopped at your locker between classes."

Tiffany gaped at him. She flashed back to that

crowded hallway. All the times she'd accidentally locked eyes with him through the crowd.

"But you always looked so angry," she said.

"I was." His hands skimmed beneath the hem of her sweater to the ticklish skin of her waist. "Mostly that every other boy in the whole damn school could talk to you, but I couldn't."

Not that her balance had been anything to brag about as of late, but at that moment, a stiff breeze would have knocked her straight off her feet.

"Forgive me," she said, extricating herself from his arms to sit down so she could think. "I'm going to need a minute."

"Take all the time you need. In the meantime, I'm going to finish bringing everything in from the car."

From her position on the box, she watched the room fill up with the evidence that Preston spoke the truth. In every store they'd visited, if she so much as glanced at an item, he would throw it in the cart. She'd had to playfully wrestle the last several from his grasp, reminding him that they didn't know the baby's sex and also wouldn't need a potty-training chair for a few years yet.

"That's the last of it, I think," he said, plunking the oversize llama stuffed animal next to the giant box containing the crib they'd picked out.

A crib she now envisioned them assembling together.

Tiffany came up behind him, admiring the wide-winged muscle of his back through his dress shirt. Hooking her thumbs through his belt loops, she rested her forehead in the indentation between his shoulder blades and wrapped her arms around his waist.

"Thank you."

"For what?"

"For helping me at Chocolate Fix. For ordering me a shower bench. For buying every llama-related baby item available in Royal County. For taking me to a movie."

His chuckle rumbled through his back. "I don't know that I can comfortably take credit for that last one seeing as we didn't actually watch the movie."

"The not-watching was my favorite part," she said.

He angled a grin at her over his shoulder. "Mine too."

Tiffany slipped her hand in the pocket of his jeans, surprised by his already growing erection.

He groaned as she stroked him through the thin fabric.

"Hold that thought," he said, placing his hand over hers.

He disappeared down the hallway and returned five minutes later. "Eyes closed," he insisted.

"This may be a good time to point out that I've actually seen my own house before, so..."

"Eyes closed or I'll blindfold you." He held out a hand to guide her.

Tiffany closed her eyes and took it. "Don't threaten me with a good time."

She shuffled down the hallway in Preston's wake, feeling along the wall despite the familiarity of her surroundings. The golden light dancing through the thin skin of her eyelids was a giveaway even before the first crackle.

"Open."

Preston had pulled off the couch cushions to make a pallet on the floor, adding the pillows from her bedroom in addition to several throw blankets. Their movie snacks were spread out on the coffee table he'd moved aside to make room for the makeshift fort.

The oxytocin train plowed into her head at the scene her mind constructed. Preston lying on his stomach, a small dark-haired boy or girl at his side in the exact same position. Cartoons flickering Technicolor across their faces.

Her eyes welled with tears yet again.

"Either you're going to have to stop doing nice things for me, or one of us needs to buy stock in Kleenex," she said, sitting down on the couch to take off her boots.

Preston followed suit, removing his shoes, socks and dress shirt.

"Sir?" Tiffany said, pretending to shield her eyes when he reached for his belt. "I was told this is a family-friendly establishment."

"I'm afraid you were misinformed." Preston slung the belt over the couch's arm and unzipped his pants. "This is Royal, Texas's first clothing-optional pillow fort."

"First?" She peeled her sweater off to reveal the soft undershirt she'd layered in case she had one of her hormonal sweat attacks.

Preston stepped out of his jeans and draped them next to the belt. "We're looking into franchising."

Tiffany peeled off her leggings and unhooked her bra, adding them to the pile. "I'm honored to be part of the grand opening."

She plopped down on the cushions and pulled one of the blankets over her bare legs. Clad in only his boxer briefs, Preston stretched out beside her.

They watched the fire in cozy silence.

"Did you ever want to do anything other than become the CEO of the Del Rio Group?" she asked.

Orange flames danced across Preston's eyes. "Nope."

"Not once?" she asked.

"Not ever," he replied. "I guess I always knew that running the Del Rio Group was never just a career path. It was my duty."

"And you never resented that?" she asked. "Having your whole life planned out for you?"

He ran his hand through his hair. "My father has always been the greatest man I know. Thinking that he believed I could be even half as great as he was meant more to me than the actual responsibilities."

She didn't miss his use of the past tense.

Tiffany leaned back against the pillows Preston had propped in front of the couch. "Do you know what I wish?"

Preston reached under her blanket to pull her legs across his lap.

"That you had Mandee Meriweather's uncanny ability to show up exactly where no one wants her to be?"

Tiffany grabbed a pillow and whapped his shoulder with it. "I wish our fathers understood how much harder it is for us to carry their grudge since we're even further removed from Eliza, Teddy and Fernando."

Preston's playful smirk softened into a sad smile. "I agree," he said.

He held her foot and began working his way up the tired muscles of her calf.

"This feel okay?" he asked.

"Amazing." She let her head fall back, determined to enjoy the decadence of a stolen midday fire with the wind blustering against the windowpanes.

"If anything is too intense, you'll tell me, right?"

"Too intense?" she asked.

"I read that's one of the changes that happens in early pregnancy with the influx of hormones."

"Preston Del Rio," she said, "have you been doing research?"

"Maybe."

"You're telling me you purchased actual books about pregnancy?" she asked.

"The kind with pictures and everything." His strong fingers migrated from her calf to her thigh. "I was... unprepared."

Tiffany knew this was putting it extremely mildly. Plenty of men, especially those of Preston's age and status, grew up largely ignorant of the intricacies of the female body. And even with a mother and sister in his household, she doubted if he'd had occasion to confront some of the brutal and beautiful aspects of the process.

She remembered her horror the first time her mom had sat her down and shown her actual pictures of childbirth. Tiffany had insisted that nothing would make her risk *ever* having that happen to her.

"You might just feel differently someday," Camille had said with a smile Tiffany now recognized as sly.

Lord, had she been right.

"And what else have you learned?" Tiffany asked.

"That the pregnancy hormones can turbocharge the libido and increase sensitivity toward the end of the third trimester." His fingertips brushed high enough on the inside of her thigh to make her pelvic floor clench.

"Looking forward to that, are you?" she asked breathlessly.

"I am." Preston pulled her in for a kiss that started sweet and soft but quickly became raw and real.

Tiffany filled her senses as a tonic against their uncertain future. Drinking him in now for all the times loneliness might yet visit her. Her hands splayed against the warm, bare skin of his pectoral muscles, before riding down his ridged abdominals and then shaping against his growing erection.

His attempt to hide it in the movie theater earlier had struck her as comical as it was adorable.

When he pulled back, he was panting. Looking at her with an expression of such disbelief and awe.

Tiffany felt it too.

Deeper than hunger. More primal and elemental than thirst.

He swung her legs off his lap and kneeled before her with the fire at his back. The look he gave her below his lowered lids kindled a pulse of heat straight in her core.

His eyes remained fixed on hers as he pushed her knees apart and anchored one of her legs over his shoulder.

She felt like a goddess on an altar. Unsure of how to be worshipped.

"Do you know what I regret most about that night?" Preston asked, his voice husky.

"What's that?" she asked.

He stroked her through her damp panties. "Feeling like I had to hurry. Like if I slowed down for even a second, I'd wake up from whatever dream I was in, and you'd be gone."

Tiffany understood the sentiment. Both their joinings shared a furtive air. While the danger of discovery amplified the passion, it also made them fast and careless. With each other's bodies as well as their own.

She wished their child's life had had a more careful and deliberate beginning. That it had been conceived out of love rather than abandon.

This regret, Tiffany kept sealed in her heart.

She slipped off her undershirt and sat bare breasted before him in the firelight. "I'm here now, Preston."

The log popped behind him, sending a shower of embers out through the fire screen. They winked out like dying stars as they fell.

Preston planted his hands on the cushions beside her ribs and leaned in to kiss her neck, her collarbone, her sternum, before kissing each nipple. They had darkened already, the areolae larger and more prominent than she'd ever seen them.

When he closed his lips over one, the sensation made her gasp.

"Are you okay?" Preston asked. "I'm not—"

"I'm fine," she panted. "That just feels so...so—" The word was lost to a moan as he shifted to the other side, lightly flicking his tongue over the taut flesh. He slipped a hand between her legs, growling against the swell of her breast at her slick heat.

A fine sheen of sweat broke out over the almost imperceptible swell of her belly. Preston planted kisses there before moving downward and dragging her panties down her thighs.

He tossed the sodden scrap aside, grinning a contented cat smile as he lowered his mouth to her sex.

Rumors of his talent in this arena had trickled back to her group of friends by way of the local ladies who'd been the beneficiaries of his attention when he came home on summer and winter breaks. In hushed circles with heads bent, she heard whispered many times that Preston Del Rio's mouth could make a fence post come. That he'd once made a woman come so hard, she passed out.

For once, the rumor mill got it right.

To experience him this way was to know why he'd been as successful in the business world as he had as the quarterback of their high school football team.

Animal instinct and ruthless precision combined to devastating effect.

On both the occasions of their previous encounters,

they'd not slowed down long enough to pleasure each other this way. A fact he obviously intended to change.

Tiffany was no stranger to good sex. She'd had plenty of it and felt incredibly lucky for that.

But words like *mind-blowing* had always seemed like deliberate hyperbole.

Until.

Until she knew what Preston Del Rio's shoulder felt like beneath her thigh. His hands on her breast and hip. His mouth on the most intimate part of her. His tongue dancing against the sizzling bundle of nerves he'd woken to throbbing, vibrant life.

She surrendered to it all.

Allowing him to coax her into a writhing frenzy, past all decorum or care.

"Oh, baby," he murmured against her heated flesh. "I love seeing you like this."

"Like what?" She struggled to find air to get the words out.

"Wild."

His dark eyes smoldered like banked coals. The hand that had been fastened to her hip trailed along her quivering stomach, then his fingers delved into her slippery sex.

Then his mouth was on her again and Tiffany felt the first tremors of the release he had meticulously built for her. She grabbed a fistful of his hair, anchoring him in a spot that sent electric shocks of sensation singing from her belly button to her toes.

Lightning struck in a release that seared through her like revelation.

When her shaking had ceased, he pushed himself up on his knees to gaze down at her.

"What is it?" she asked.

He trailed a hand down her sweat-kissed sternum to her belly, before drawing a circle around her navel with the tip of his finger.

"You're imagining about what it's going to look like six months from now, aren't you?"

A dark wing of hair fell into his eyes. "How'd you guess?"

"Extrapolating data from our earlier conversation." She pushed the hair away from his forehead. "I never would've figured you for a breeding kink."

"Breeding kink?" He laughed, the movement rippling the washboard of his abdominal muscles. "I don't have a breeding kink."

Tiffany sat up. "I hate to break it to you, sir, but if you're looking at a woman's body and enjoying the idea of how a pregnancy you caused is going to change it, you have a breeding kink."

His mouth quirked upward at the corners. "Then I guess I have a breeding kink."

Tiffany pushed herself up on her knees and tugged Preston onto the pallet beside her.

"I'll alert the media," she said, lightly running her fingers over his stomach. His muscles tensed as she dipped beneath the elastic waistband of his boxers and circled his silky head.

"Tiffany," he ground out. "You're driving me out of my mind."

She stretched her leg long and hooked it over his

hip. "This may be the unsexiest thing I've ever said, but my gag reflex is kind of off the charts these days. I'll have to take it slow."

Preston cupped her chin in his hand. "You don't have to do that at all."

"What if I want to?"

"You could always wait until the second trimester." Preston brushed his thumb over her lips. "According to what I read, the nausea starts to let up then."

Tiffany parted her lips and licked the pad of his thumb. "Do you have any idea how ridiculously sexy that is?"

"The nausea letting up?"

"You reading about it." Tiffany hooked her finger in the waistband of his boxers and pulled them down to free his erection.

He was stone and silk beneath her grip.

Preston sucked in a breath as her palm grazed his already weeping head, coating him with the pearl of moisture she found there.

"Oh, damn." His lips were on her forehead, his hand buried in her hair. "That feels so good."

"Then lose those shorts and make it easier for me to make you feel good."

He quickly complied.

Tiffany took a moment to admire the sight before her.

His lean hips and muscular thighs. His small, flat nipples, long-toed feet and thick, beautiful cock.

A guttural grunt escaped him when she wrapped her lips around his head and began to move. With slow and painstaking care, she began to move up and down his length, learning every inch of him through touch and taste alone. Each rise and ripple. Each vein and ridge. Each sigh and scowl of his seduction.

Hypnotized by his reactions, she'd fallen into a rhythm when he closed his fist over hers.

"Whoa. You've got to give me a minute."

A single bead of sweat trickled down his long, smooth neck. Tiffany straddled his hips and angled her head to capture it with her tongue.

Preston cupped her ass, lifting her as she positioned his cock between her thighs. "This okay?"

"More than okay." Tiffany rested her hands on his shoulders and impaled herself in torturously slow increments.

Watching the battle unfold on his face proved reward enough for her troubles. The tendons of his neck and elegant trenches forming a V over his hips stood out in sharp relief when he met with the delicious resistance at her core. A fine film of sweat formed on his forehead.

"It's all about the sink," she said, only to be rewarded with his fingertips digging into her hips.

Their breaths mingled as she began to move. Rolling her hips to introduce him to every part of her. Wanting to feel him in every curve and hollow. As deep as he could go.

Preston waited until she'd fallen into a rhythm before finding one of his own.

Meeting her fall with his rise.

He sat up, their torsos glued together by sweat, his hand buried in the hair at her nape.

Meeting him at eye level this way felt shockingly intimate. Like he could see straight into her soul. His forearms hooked beneath her armpits, and he gripped her shoulders to pull her even deeper.

She threw her head back and released the cry that had been building inside her like a storm. "You feel good, Preston."

He surged within her, drawing an answering clench. "I love that part of me is inside you."

"So do I," she said.

He bucked beneath her, driving her skyward. She contracted hard around him on a ragged cry and felt herself falling, pinned beneath him for his final, brutal strokes as they came apart together.

His weight on top of her felt like gravity, securing her to the world and everything within it. What they would do tonight, tomorrow, a month from now, she didn't know.

Only that what she felt in this precise moment, she wanted to feel forever.

Safe. Owned. Filled.

Found.

With these words on her mind and the father of her child on her body, she at last surrendered to sleep.

Eleven

Preston woke with a start. Knowing in some primal way by the light on the comforter covering their bodies what his phone screen confirmed seconds later.

He was late.

Due at the Texas Cattleman's Club in thirty minutes for the Diamond Gate negotiations. His father already called him twice and left voice mails both times.

He launched himself out of bed and quickly pulled on his rumpled clothing.

Tiffany rolled over, and stretched, her mouth opening in a sleepy yawn. "What time is it?" she asked.

"9:30," he said. After tucking in his shirt and buckling his belt, he turned to examine the full-length mirror. He looked like exactly what he was—a man who would soon be making a very public walk of shame into a vitally important meeting.

"Oh man." Tiffany pushed herself up in bed and ran a hand through her sex-rumpled hair. "I can't believe I slept so hard."

"I can." Preston bent to plant a kiss on her warm forehead. "I'm afraid I've got to run."

Her eyes were full of concern when he pulled away, her slim fingers resting on his forearm. "Is everything okay? This isn't because of what we...because of last night?"

"Not at all," he insisted, not entirely sure this was the truth. Between his sex-and-sleep-fogged brain and the metallic fear creeping up to the base of his throat, he hadn't really had a chance to process any of it. All he knew was that with every passing second, the odds of this turning out well for either of them drastically decreased. "I'm just late for the Diamond Gate mediation at the TCC."

He gently disengaged her hand and kissed her knuckles before setting it back on the snowy blanket. "I'll call you later?"

Tiffany did not look at all comforted by his explanation. She had yanked the sheet up over her breasts and crossed her arms. "Will you be coming by this evening?"

"Sure," he said. "I'll bring some dinner with me."

"Please, don't," she said. "I'm already going to end up freezing half of what my mom put in the fridge."

This felt like an olive branch, and he greedily grasped for it.

"Okay," he said. "I'll give you a shout when I'm on the way."

"All right," she said. The sadness in her voice brought on a powerful wave of self-loathing.

He hated running out like this.

He hated the worry he'd put in her eyes. He hated that he had no choice but to leave her there when he should be bringing her breakfast in bed. Reassuring her that opening up as she had wasn't a mistake.

He hated that assurance wasn't his to offer.

Thirty-one minutes later, he pushed into the foyer at the Cattleman's Club with a sheen of sweat on his forehead and an apologetic smile pasted onto his face. The apology he had rehearsed on his speed-limit-testing drive over died on his tongue when he saw his father waiting beneath the giant chandelier comprised of tiered layers of antlers.

He looked... *Happy* to see him.

"Well," he said. "Look what the cat dragged in." The brightness faltered, but only briefly, during the quick but obvious scan he conducted of Preston's distinctly unimpressive state. "I thought surely after yesterday, you'd have plenty of time to rest and get ready for this morning's proceedings."

Ah.

Now his father's uncharacteristic cheerfulness made sense.

He had assumed that *Sunny* was the reason Preston had left the reception early. By extension, he thought that Sunny was the reason Preston had bailed on work the day following.

Preston straightened his spine and stiffened his resolve. "I'm really sorry about that, Dad. About the announcement, the party, everything. I've been meaning to talk to you about it, but—"

"Are we ready to proceed?" Jack Chowdhry stood in the doorway to one of the club's private meeting rooms. Attired in an impeccably tailored dark gray suit complete with a pristine white shirt and navy blue silk tie, he made Preston feel like he'd just rolled out of a ditch.

"We'll be right in," his father answered, waiting until Jack was gone before shooting Preston a conspiratorial look. "Don't worry about it, son. We've all shown up to a meeting looking like the morning after the night before. Especially in the aftermath of an evening spent in such pleasant company. But I know you won't make a habit of it."

Fernando clapped him on the shoulder, not even waiting for an answer before turning on the sole of his loafer and proceeding toward the conference room.

The reception Preston received there was far less friendly.

Joseph Winters sat on the far side of the table, flanked by Marcus on one side and Alisha on the other. Face as grim and impenetrable as an Easter Island statue, the Winters patriarch shifted his eyes to Preston, who took a seat next to his father on what he perceived to be the Del Rio side of the table.

"Sorry to keep everyone waiting," he said, settling into his seat.

"Quite all right." Presiding at the head of the table,

Jack took a sip of his water and placed it back on its coaster next to the leather padfolio before him. He cleared his throat before proceeding. "As you know, the Del Rio necklace has been in the possession of the Department of Public Safety. I'm happy to report that both the necklace and Eliza Boudreaux's confession letter have been fully authenticated by a second source."

Fernando's chest puffed with a sound somewhere between a snort and a grunt.

Jack's neatly combed dark head turned to him. "Is there something you'd like to say regarding the authentication?"

"The necklace's authenticity was never in doubt. The letter, on the other hand..." He trailed off.

"Are you suggesting that the letter was a fake?" Joseph Winters's question crackled with barely concealed animosity.

"I'm sure that's not the case," Jack said evenly. "Especially not since I have here the documents confirming the letter's authenticity." He extracted two sheets of paper from his padfolio and held them up so both parties could see.

Preston's father remained silent for a beat longer than was comfortable. "I'm not saying the letter was a fake. Only that the timing of its discovery struck me as especially convenient."

"Convenient for who?" The gold bangle on Alisha's wrist winked in the morning light as she folded her arms. "Because I sure as hell would have preferred Marcus *not* to have discovered a stolen necklace on my property in the middle of a ridiculously expensive renovation."

"All the more reason why your decision not to disclose its existence immediately was somewhat confusing," Fernando said.

"Excuse us all to hell for trying to think of a way to resolve this without bringing about World War III," Marcus chimed in. His dark eyes were stormy. His mouth an unamused twist.

"The point is," Jack said, attempting to regain control of the room, "the necklace will be returned at your convenience, and we can move on and put this matter behind us once and for all."

He opened the folder and withdrew two multipage documents, sliding one down each side of the table. "I have here an agreement documenting the official terms of the necklace's return to the Del Rio family. Please feel free to look over them before we proceed."

Fernando captured the paper beneath his palm and pulled a pair of reading glasses out of his suit coat pocket to read the fine print.

A buzzing interrupted the tense silence as Alisha's phone lit up and began to vibrate on the table. She looked down at the glowing screen and frowned before glancing up at Jack. "Would you excuse me for just a moment?"

"Of course," Jack said.

Alisha power-walked for the door, returning a few minutes later with a scowl on her face and thunderheads in her eyes. Resuming her seat, she gave Preston such a withering look of contempt, he was tempted to slink under the table despite having no idea what he'd done to deserve it.

His feeling of unease swelled into worry when she lifted her phone again and quickly thumb-typed a text message.

It had to be something about Tiffany.

He checked his own phone and found it empty of notifications.

"I see no issues with the contract as it is currently proposed." Joseph Winters leaned back in his seat and pushed the papers out in front of him, his voice taking on a more emphatic version of its usual Texas twang. Preston had often wondered if he subconsciously—or consciously—played it up in circumstances like these.

"Of course you don't," Fernando muttered.

"And what is that supposed to mean?" Marcus placed his forearms on the table, his hulking shoulders rounding as he leaned in.

"It means there are no consequences whatsoever for the Winters family despite your being in possession of a very valuable stolen piece of property for a hundred years."

"Property that was stolen before anyone seated at this table was born," Jack pointed out.

"The fact remains that the necklace was stolen and the entire town of Royal now knows who was responsible." Fernando was clearly addressing his plea to Jack. "As public as Diamond Gate has been, I would be eager to make some sort of restitution, were the situations reversed."

Preston's irritation at his father grew stronger by

the second. This ridiculous pride, eating away at both families like a cancer over events so far removed from any of their immediate existences. All of it now making his life far more complicated than it needed to be.

"How about a donation?" Preston hadn't meant to give voice to the idea the same second it arrived in his head and was unprepared when all eyes in the room swiveled to him.

His father's bored into him like drill bits. "What sort of donation?"

"The sort relevant to the circumstances that contributed to the theft in the first place." He rocked back in his chair, balancing on the back legs as his mother had so often scolded him for.

"Such as?" Joseph Winters pinned him with his cold blue stare. Though Preston knew there was no way Tiffany's father had intuited how he'd spent the previous evening, he couldn't shake the feeling that Joseph suspected him of something.

"Like an organization that supports sustainable diamond mining," Preston answered. "Something that would make it clear to the people following these ridiculous proceedings that the most prominent families in Royal, Texas, aren't just playing an elaborate game of tug-o-war over a necklace that belonged to people who are little more than dust by this point."

The room fell silent as if in contemplation of his idea. It was Jack who spoke first.

"I think this sounds like an excellent solution."

Joseph Winters cleared his throat. "I suppose, if

this is what's required to put this matter to rest, we would be amenable."

His announcement failed to shift Marcus's glower, or Alisha's tight-mouthed irritation.

Jack turned to Fernando. "And you? Do you find this to be an acceptable resolution?"

His father looked at Preston before nodding. "Yes."

"Wonderful," Jack said. "I'll make the necessary updates to the agreement and have everything emailed by this afternoon." He stood and began to gather his things, giving everyone permission to do the same.

Grabbing her bag, Alisha then jerked it onto her shoulder and mumbled an apology to her father and brother before barreling out of the room. Preston was so taken aback by her hasty departure that he ended up nearly knocking over his chair as he stood to go after her.

He had to sprint to catch up with her in the parking lot. "Alisha! Wait."

She aimed her key fob at her car and made no sign of slowing.

"Alisha, *please*."

Her hand hovered above the door handle, her back stiff and her regal head of dark curls cocked at an irritated angle.

"Will you just talk to me for a minute?" Preston asked.

She whirled on him. "I have *nothing* to say to you."

"I know that this wasn't the friendliest of circumstances, but I'm not sure what I did to deserve this."

Her mouth dropped open. "Not sure what you—

you know what? Never mind. I am so over this dumb innocent oblivious man act."

"Oblivious about what?" he snapped, his irritation finally outpacing his concern.

Alisha folded her arms across her chest. "You're really going to stand there and look me in the eye and pretend like you don't know what I could *possibly* have to be upset about?"

Preston felt like a man drowning in broad daylight. "Seeing as I have absolutely no idea what you're upset about, I'm not sure how many other options I have."

Her eyes narrowed. "Really?"

"I'm not sure how many other ways I can say this. *Really.*"

Alisha dug into her purse and pulled out her phone. She stabbed at the screen and flipped it to face him.

Preston's stomach dropped into his shoes.

The picture had his face and Sunny's bent toward one another. Her hands pressed to his chest. His fingers hovering just above her elbows. Their lips meeting in a tender kiss.

That Sunny had initiated it, or that Preston had allowed it as a final gesture of closure between them, appeared nowhere in the frame.

A quick glance at the newspaper's caption confirmed his very worst fears. *Old flame sparks anew for Del Rio heir! Look out, ladies. One of Royal's most eligible bachelors may soon be off the market. At a celebration announcing his official ascension to CEO of Del Rio Group, Preston Del Rio locks lips with former fiancée, Sunny Rothschild...*

The words began blurring together as Preston's blood boiled.

Preston's hands bunched into bricks at his sides. His stomach felt tight and high. His head, light and floaty.

"Congratulations," Alisha said snidely. "You made the 'Hip Happenings' section."

Preston couldn't even bring himself to rise to her deliberate barb. His brain was spinning out. Careening wildly into scenarios like concrete barriers. "The call you took during the meeting. It was Tiffany?"

"What do you think?" she asked.

The image of Tiffany, still nude under the covers, opening her phone to be confronted with this picture, poured down on him like scalding tar.

The downturned rosebud of a mouth. The wounded, doe-in-the-headlights eyes, spilling quicksilver down her cheeks.

"I don't suppose it would do me any good to tell you this isn't what it looks like," he said.

Alisha's eyes narrowed into dangerous slits. "I get a call from my pregnant and very emotional sister, who's been bombed with a picture of her baby's father locking lips with his ex-fiancée, and that's the best you can do?"

"It's the truth. I had no idea Sunny was going to be at that party. In fact, I had no idea that this party was going to happen until that afternoon. I was completely blindsided."

Alisha had mastered the posture of an offended queen. Shoulders squared. Neck arched. Nose lifted.

"So blindsided that you stumbled tongue-first into your ex?"

Preston felt a stab of irritation at having to explain himself when he objected to being placed in this situation in the first place.

"In review, I had no idea my father was going to name a retirement date, no idea he'd arranged a cocktail reception to celebrate it and not the foggiest fucking clue that he'd invited my ex-fiancée." He ticked the facts off on his fingers as if this would somehow make them more solid.

"And you ended up kissing *how*?"

"I asked her to go for a walk to talk. She admitted that my father had invited her. When I explained that I'd moved on, she understood but wanted to kiss me goodbye. I let her. If you want to hate me for that, you can go right ahead."

"Moved on to my sister, you mean."

"Yes!" Preston threw up his hands in frustration. "That's exactly what I did. I left my own party to go check on her after I tried to call her, and she wasn't picking up. I was with her that night, all of yesterday and this morning until I walked through these doors."

Alisha's voice dropped low. "And after you walked back out of those doors, what was your intention then?"

"I'm sorry?"

"After the negotiations. After your workday. After doing whatever it is you do to rule the Del Rio oil kingdom. What then? Where does Tiffany fit in?"

"Tiffany has a say in that too, Alisha. It's not up for me to decide what her—"

"If it was?"

Preston's brain felt like a lump of meat between his ears. "If *what* was?"

Rattling flags from the big leaf maple on the side of the building danced in a sudden gust of wind.

Alisha released an exhale that seemed to take some of her fire with it. "If it was up to you. How would this story end?"

He read the entire volume in that one look. The fierceness of Alisha's love for her younger sister. The protective fury. The sliver of hope that he somehow, against incomprehensible odds, would figure out how to say or do the right thing.

"Preston?" His father's voice echoed across the parking lot. "Is everything all right?"

"Fine," he called back. "Be right there."

Alisha held her ground, waiting for an answer.

An answer Preston couldn't even give himself.

"I'm going to be there, Alisha. For Tiffany and for our baby. Whatever it takes."

Her nostrils flared as she stared down at the pavement. When she lifted her eyes again, they'd gone cold. "If this is what being there looks like, I'm not convinced that's the best for my sister or her child."

A bitter reply burned at the base of his throat. "Are you going over there now?"

After yanking her car door open, Alisha tossed her purse aside. "I'd be there already if it wasn't for you."

Preston placed his hand on the doorframe. "Please—"

"No. You made me regret helping you once before. I'm not doing it again." She elbowed him out of the way to push open the driver's-side door. "If I were you, I'd keep myself as far away as possible until you figure out what the hell you want. We have three brothers and I'm guessing they're not going to be big fans of yours once this shit properly hits the fan."

Alisha raised a hand to wave to Marcus, who stood on the curb outside the club watching them through obsidian-chip eyes; his massive arms crossed an equally massive chest.

"Now if you'll excuse me."

He stepped back so Alisha could close her door and watched as she screeched out of the parking lot in a cloud of blue smoke.

He had an answer to her question.

Had it been up to him, he knew exactly what he wanted.

He wanted to turn back the wheel of time.

To rewind the minutes that separated him from the warmth of Tiffany's warm silky back pressed against his chest. He wanted to put his hand on her stomach and know that the life they'd created was growing beneath it. He wanted to stay in that moment and forget everything else in the world.

What he wanted, was impossible.

"What was that about?" his father asked when Preston was in earshot.

Try as he might, Preston couldn't make the words fall from his mouth.

"Well?" his father prodded.

Preston drew in a deep breath and let it out slowly.

"It's about the picture of me and Sunny from the

Glass House. The one that's prominently featured in the newspaper's gossip section?" He took a step closer. "Any ideas who might have taken it?"

A small, sly smile tugged at the corners of his mouth. "How would I know that?"

"Because you orchestrated it. Announcing your retirement out of the blue. Arranging the party. Sunny showing up out of nowhere."

"You told me yourself the split was amicable. I just thought a reunion might give you the chance to work things out."

"You just thought you could shove us together and I'd fall in line like I always do?" Preston could feel the cold sweat gathering between his shoulder blades and beneath his armpits, but he couldn't stop.

"I don't appreciate your tone, Preston."

"And I don't appreciate being ambushed and manipulated."

Since he was a child, Preston had feared his father's uncanny ability to read him cold.

Fernando's icy expression thawed with a patronizing smile. "Forgive a father for noticing that his son has been pretty isolated as of late."

"Isolated because I've been pouring every single ounce of my effort into proving that I'm ready to take over as CEO!"

"Keep your voice down," his father whispered harshly.

Preston felt his pulse quicken and bit down hard on the quick rush of anger. "Sunny and I were engaged and the most time you'd ever spent with her was a dinner. A *dinner*, Dad. Did you honestly think you could choose a potential partner for me based on a shared meal? You didn't even know her."

His father cleared his throat and scuffed his loafers on the pavement. "You two certainly looked happy to me."

"Of course we did. She's an Instagram influencer. I can show you dozens of posts where we had a terrible fight exactly fifteen minutes before she's holding a mimosa and smiling in front of the neon sign at brunch. Looking happy is kind of the whole deal."

No, he thought, *not the whole deal.*

Looking beautiful. Stylish. Privileged.

That's when it hit him. The image had been part of why his father had selected Sunny. How they looked on paper. And now that he was about to step into the role of CEO, his father was expressing a sudden interest in his relationship optics.

"If you're so upset that I invited her, why did you leave with her?" Fernando asked.

"I didn't."

His father's dark brows drew together, creating a crease in the center of his forehead. "But this morning...your clothes—"

"You're right. I did spend the night with someone last night. But it wasn't Sunny Rothschild." He took a step closer to his father and held his iron gaze. "It was Tiffany Winters."

The November light dimmed as the sun dipped behind a cloud. A crow barked its harsh tidings as it flew overhead and perched on the club's pitched roof. Though he had never believed in omens, Preston couldn't help but feel his future had dimmed along with his admission.

"Tiffany Winters?" He saw the wheels of his father's mercilessly brilliant mind turning. "You told me those rumors about the engagement party were just gossip. I *defended* you, Preston."

The knowledge of his lie felt like a crack opening in the sidewalk between them.

"You've been seeing her ever since that night?"

"Yes." Preston knew this wasn't strictly the truth, but had neither the desire nor the energy to explain all that had unfolded between him and Tiffany since that first night together.

Another mournful cry shivered the early winter air.

"You deliberately disobeyed my wishes."

Preston squared his shoulders and met his father's eyes. In them, he saw his past and his future. The things that he'd wanted and had spent his entire life trying to achieve. "Yes."

The angular planes of his father's features turned stony. "How can I trust you with my legacy when I can't even trust you to tell me the truth?"

It wasn't an altogether unreasonable question, as much as Preston hated to admit it. Back in his office, his father had accused him of having a soft spot when it came to the Winterses. He'd been right. And for longer than he knew.

"Because this particular truth has nothing to do with my ability to effectively lead the Del Rio Group."

"Doesn't it though?"

A frigid wind howled around the corner of the building, biting Preston's cheeks.

"The night before last, some of the most important people associated with our family of companies were gathered to honor you. People that I've worked to maintain relationships with for decades. Had you stayed, you'd have had the opportunity to forge your own connections. Instead, you snuck off to spend the evening with Tiffany Winters. Your performance has been slipping lately and now I know the reason why."

Cold fury numbed Preston's heart. After all he had done, after all he had sacrificed, the hours, the minutes, the days he had given away all to be told by his father that it meant absolutely nothing compared to the couple weeks where his schedule had been hectic enough to be noticeable.

"The only thing slipping is my ability to keep my mouth shut and pretend to agree with you." Preston's entire body vibrated with adrenaline, making his words sound shaky. "This entire time, you've been obsessed with the idea that you've been wronged somehow. That you're owed some kind of restoration. You've been so blinded by your own selfish desires that you can't even see what's right in front of you."

His father's posture stiffened. "I see it. I see it wearing yesterday's clothes and a petulant expression. I see it making a mockery of the trust I publicly placed in you."

Acid ate at Preston's empty stomach.

"The only thing being mocked is your pride, Dad."

They stood on their opposing sidewalk squares as if they were desert islands. Each of them marooned by their individual circumstances.

"Nevertheless, I'm still the acting CEO of the Del Rio Group, and the head of this family. I have no intention of handing the company over to you while you're carrying on some ridiculous fling with Tiffany Winters."

Preston looked at the parking space Alisha had peeled rubber to exit. "It's not just a fling."

Fernando blew a hot breath from his nostrils. "Spare me the forbidden fruit melodramatics."

"She's pregnant, Dad. She's going to have my baby."

This was the first time he had spoken these words out loud.

The dimple in his father's chin deepened. The creases next to his eyes seemed to branch further toward his temples.

"Pregnant?"

"Yes," Preston said. "We're going to raise the baby together."

His father blanched. "I suggest you think very carefully about your options, Preston."

"I always have." He turned and left before he could say anything else he would regret. He barely even registered the feeling of the parking lot's asphalt under the soles of his shoes or the familiar scent of leather in his car. He only knew that he needed to get to Tiffany. His entire world seemed to reorganize itself around this one urgent point.

The glowing blue numbers displaying his rapidly

decreasing speed winked at him from the dashboard's display as he eased his car to the side of the road.

What would he even tell her?

What could he say to make her understand? His knuckles whitened as he gripped the steering wheel, resisting the urge to punch something.

His whole life, he'd worked to prove he was worthy of the Del Rio legacy. The one thing he'd thought he wanted. Until he saw Tiffany Winters across the crowded room at his sister's engagement party and understood what wanting truly was. For a brief and beautiful moment, he'd tasted what it would be like to have both.

If he didn't somehow find a way to salvage this, he was in danger of losing everything.

Twelve

"I promise you, you'll feel better." Alisha uncorked a small jar of bath salts and added them to the steaming tub in Tiffany's master bathroom.

Tiffany looked at the glass-green water with eyes stinging from hours of crying. "I appreciate the thought, but really I just want to get into bed and forget this day ever happened."

"Spoken like a deeply depressed woman."

Depressed? Yes. Deeply? Tiffany didn't have access to a mental health professional to confirm this diagnosis.

Whatever it was that made her heart sore and her brain blunted at the same time, she had that.

Tiffany chewed her ragged cuticle as she leaned against the counter. "I just don't understand. Their engagement broke up over a year ago. Why would he let her kiss him?"

Alisha's jaw flexed, hinting at her annoyance. They'd been over this already, but the answer she received hadn't quite quieted her mind.

"Honey, I don't know why he did what he did. All I know is he did it. You can sit here arguing, or you can just get in this bath that I have lovingly prepared for you. Personally, I recommend the latter."

Tiffany knew she was being tedious. Her sister's input wasn't necessary to inform her of this.

Despite Alisha's exceedingly logical explanations, nothing she said about Preston carried the ring of truth. She called him a bastard. A scoundrel. A rich boy wastrel. A sycophantic privileged suck-up.

None of it helped.

"All right. I'm getting in." Tiffany shucked off her fluffy bathrobe and slipped into the foamy tub while Alisha's back was turned.

The water lapped her neck and shoulders. The tension she'd felt since she woke up this morning dissolved into it.

Alisha handed her a washcloth, which Tiffany dipped into the steaming water and laid over her face only to yank it off again.

Anytime her eyes were closed, she saw the picture.

And every time she saw the picture, the cavernous ache in her chest deepened.

They hadn't spoken of fidelity. They'd made no commitments. She had no expectation of exclusivity. But it still stung.

"What exactly did he say?"

Alisha had already unpacked this several times before, but she indulged Tiffany anyway. Perching on the edge of the tub, she gave the same basic summary. Preston's father put her up to coming. Preston let her down easy. Sunny gave him a kiss goodbye. He drove straight over to Tiffany's house—

And told her that they needed to keep things platonic. He had even slept on the couch.

But then, everything that had happened between them the following day...

Something just wasn't adding up.

Had he been thinking about getting back together with Sunny? Trying to buy himself more time?

She had mined Alisha's brain again and again but hadn't come to any better conclusions.

"Look on the bright side," Alisha said. "At least all the buzz about him and Sunny overshadows that damn gossip reporter Mandee Meriweather telling everybody and their dog how she saw you two coming out of a movie theater in Coleman looking guilty as hell."

Tiffany's life would have been just fine without that particular indignity.

She took a small, mean satisfaction in thinking of this news getting out despite Preston's generous donation.

At least she had only agreed to donate a chocolate basket.

"I guess I should be grateful that so far you and Mom are the only ones who know about the pregnancy."

Alisha cleared her throat and reached for a packet of

pore-refining kelp face mask. "Is this stuff any good? I've been hearing all about it on those makeup blogs."

"Alisha."

"Because with the change in seasons, my skin has been dry as hell. I'm in the market for something that will stand up to the Texas winter."

Tiffany carefully rotated in the tub and plucked the mask out of her sister's hands. "Who knows about the pregnancy?"

"Just Tremaine. He overheard me talking to Mom on the phone. You know Preston is a good friend of his. I figured maybe we could talk some sense into him."

"So you, Mom and Tremaine."

"Right," Alisha agreed. Then, after a beat, "And Marcus."

Water splashed up on the edge as Tiffany sat forward. "Marcus knows?"

"He was in the parking lot when I almost bit Preston's head off," she explained. "He called as soon as I was driving here. I couldn't just *not* tell him after that. But don't worry," she said quickly. "He was sworn to secrecy."

"You know, Marcus knows, Tremaine knows and Mom knows," she recited. "Is there anyone else?"

Alisha's golden-brown eyes skated to the side. "It's possible that Marcus told Jericho."

"Are you serious?"

"I can't be sure, but Jericho called a few minutes after Marcus and was asking me some very leading questions."

"What kind of leading questions?"

Alisha's shoulders jerked upward. "Oh, you know. About how you are. If I'd heard from you lately. If I noticed that you and Preston looked awful cozy at his engagement party."

Tiffany grabbed the washrag and buried her face in it. If only she could stay in this gray, dark, warm place and never speak to another human again.

"Do you know if Preston told Maggie?" Alisha asked.

"Not as far as I know. We were trying to keep it under wraps until after the wedding."

"As much as I understand the sentiment, I think it might be time to have Mom bring Dad into the loop," Alisha said. "With the way Marcus, Jericho and Dad talk, it's only a matter of time."

Tiffany allowed her shoulders to slump forward. "I don't understand how this happened."

"I do." Alisha's voice suggested she was now leaning against the counter. "The scruff."

The world had a bluish cast when Tiffany pulled the rag away from her eyes. "The scruff?"

"The scruff," she repeated. "At the engagement party. Preston had that sexy three-day scruff thing you're such a sucker for. You shouldn't have gone within ten yards of that man."

Tiffany couldn't disagree.

She remembered the way he had looked that night. His dark hair, shaggy and tousled after a few songs on the dance floor. His sky blue dress shirt unbuttoned just enough to show the smile of an undershirt beneath. How that undershirt had looked against the smooth tawny skin of his neck. She remembered his scent best of all. Fabric softener, woodsy soap, clean skin. The sexy smirk. The dangerous bad boy edge.

Man-thrax, basically.

He had said hello to her at the bar and it was all over but the sonograms.

"I derailed my entire life because of facial hair," Tiffany said.

Alisha picked up a fluffy makeup brush from the vanity and dusted the underside of her palm. "I mean, I derailed mine because of the way Tremaine's butt looks in a pair of jeans, so I'm in no position to judge."

Tiffany hugged her knees. "Do you mean that?"

"And you oughta see him in coveralls. He looks even better. If he doesn't finish laying those tiles in the downstairs bathroom soon, Preston Jr. may have a cousin about the same age."

Her sister had meant to lighten the mood, but hearing that name was like a sucker punch to the heart.

"I meant the judging. Are you sure you're not even just a *little* disappointed?"

Alisha put the brush down and perched on the edge of the tub. "That you had unprotected sex with Preston Del Rio?"

Tiffany nodded.

"I might at least suggest a fertility-tracking app, so you have a vague idea of the best times to be reckless, but no, Tiff. I'm not disappointed."

"That's the thing! I already have one. I wasn't even supposed to be ovulating. I was on day twenty-five of my cycle. I was due to start any day."

Alisha's eyebrows drew together. "That's some crazy pheromones shit right there."

"Alisha, I seriously can't even explain it. It was like this—" she paused, searching for an appropriate metaphor "—like this magnet. Or like there were magnets in every single one of my cells. I don't normally have to work to resist somebody. Almost like our being together was the default setting or something."

Tiffany leaned back in the tub. "But maybe it was only like that for me. He hasn't even tried to call me since that picture came out."

Alisha dabbed at a water droplet that had landed on her beautiful cream-colored slacks. "To be fair, that could partially be my fault."

"Your fault? How?" Tiffany asked.

"I may have told him to stay the hell away from you until he knew what he wanted. Maybe he's still figuring it out."

Tiffany took a deep breath. It wasn't the easiest thing for her to hear, but she knew it needed to be said.

"I'm going to ask you a question," her sister said, studying her face. "You don't have to answer it now. But I feel like it might help for you to consider."

"Go ahead."

"What was the first thing you felt after you saw that picture of Sunny and Preston together?"

Tiffany answered without hesitation. "Devastated. Gutted. Completely and totally wrecked."

Alisha pushed a damp tendril back from Tiffany's forehead. "What I know is, whether or not Preston gets his act together and realizes what an idiot he would be to lose you, you are going to be an amazing mother."

"How can you be so sure?"

"Because I know you, Tiff. Everything you do, you do with heart. But it sounds like maybe you need to tell Preston what's in yours."

Tiffany's chin rested on her knees. "I just can't. I can't face him right now."

"So don't," she said. "Put it in a letter. You know, like Mom used to make us write anytime we were in an argument we couldn't settle?"

They had been so close for so long, Tiffany had forgotten how much bickering there had been growing up with her siblings. Over space, art supplies, video games, toys, the TV in the basement where everyone liked to hang out.

Somehow their tempers had always cooled in the time that it took them to elaborate about their grievances on paper.

"I'll think about it."

"Good girl." Her sister squeezed her shoulder and stood. "I'm just going to leave you here to relax for a bit. You want some more hot?"

"Sure."

Alisha lifted the kettle from the marble counter and poured in the steaming water as Camille had done for both of them whenever they were in need of comfort as kids. It had never occurred to them to question their mother's claim that water boiled by hand put extra love in the bathwater.

Her sister kissed her fingers and pressed them to the crown of Tiffany's head. "You've got this, little sister."

"Thanks, Lisha," she said, using a nickname she hadn't since they were children.

Tiffany sank down into the tub after she was gone, letting the bubbles kiss the underside of her chin. Her head fell back against the rolled towel Alisha had propped at the back of the tub.

Her hand found her belly beneath the water.

The life they had created was the size of a blueberry now, the cells that would become its heart just beginning to flutter. In that moment, she made a vow to her child and herself that she would do everything she could to protect that tiny heart from feeling the kind of pain hers did now.

Preston had gotten good at hiding from the daylight.

When he first moved into his upscale town house, he'd installed blackout curtains on every single window. With the odd hours he ended up working, he sometimes hit the sheets as dawn's gray fingers had begun to creep across the ceiling.

He lay in the inky darkness now with no idea what time it was and no desire to find out.

He knew he needed to get up and start his day, but he just couldn't summon the desire to peel himself out of bed.

He still hadn't heard a word from Tiffany, but he kept imagining her reaction to the photo, then switching to hear his father's parting words. These both ran a loop in his head accompanied by the memory of the scorching disappointment in his father's eyes.

Fernando had been right.

Preston had been irresponsible. He had let his feelings for Tiffany compromise his commitment to Del Rio Group. Maybe his father had been right to second-guess his decision to name Preston CEO.

His attempts to exercise his brain into exhausted oblivion had so far been unsuccessful.

Shifting his aching body beneath the covers, Preston rolled onto his side, determined to squeeze another half hour of sleep out of this strange timeless interval.

He was just drifting off when a banging popped his eyelids back open.

His front door.

Preston stayed inert. Even going so far as to hold his breath even though he knew no one could possibly hear him.

Maybe they would just go away. After about a minute, it stopped.

Preston heaved a sigh of relief and pulled the covers up to his chin.

When it resumed three feet from his head on the glass pane of the window, Preston sat straight up in bed and released a string of curses.

"I know you're in there! You always leave your kitchen light on when you've been up all night working." Maggie's muted voice sounded unreasonably sunny and amused. "I brought you coffee."

The magic words.

Preston threw back the covers, dragged himself

upright and pulled on sweatpants before padding over to the window and throwing back the curtain.

His sister stood outside it, looking chic and incredibly fresh.

Her mouth shaped into an O of shock when she saw him. Preston didn't even need to look at a mirror to guess how he looked.

He jerked his head toward the front door and made his way from the master bedroom down the hallway and through the kitchen to let her in. Crisp air scented of wet leaves gusted in as he stepped out of the way to grant her entrance.

Maggie set the cup holder and white paper bag down on his kitchen table and shrugged out of her rain-dampened coat.

"This one's yours." She set one of the white cardboard cups next to him. "I also brought a big cinnamon roll from Royal Diner to share."

"Thanks." Preston popped off the coffee's lid and inhaled the rich, roasty brew.

"Your usual," she said.

His usual tasted just a little bit more bitter by comparison.

"I'm giving you exactly ten sips for the caffeine to kick in before I ask you what the hell is going on with you. Just a heads-up."

"Much appreciated," he said. "Did Mom send you over, or is this a reconnaissance mission?"

"Neither," she said. "I have something for you."

After digging in her purse, she pulled out an envelope the size of a greeting card. His name was written across the front in an elegant cursive script.

"I already got a wedding invitation," he said, cutting a look toward the magnet on his refrigerator holding Maggie and Jericho's engagement photo aloft.

"This isn't wedding related."

"Then what?" Preston dug a thumb under the envelope flap and carefully peeled it open. A quick scan of the creamy paper made his heart leap into his throat.

Tiffany Winters.

He glanced up at Maggie. "Where did you get this?"

His sister removed the lid from her own cup and blew away curls of steam. "Jericho gave it to me to give to you."

Preston pressed a hand flat against the cool marble countertop. If Tiffany had given this to her brother, then...

"I can't believe you didn't tell me!"

"That was only five sips," Preston said. "Tell you about what?"

"Cut the crap, Pres. The whole town knows about you and Tiffany Winters."

All the blood drained from Preston's head in a dizzying rush. His cheeks prickled as if thousands of tiny pins were dancing over his skin.

"They know about the baby?"

Maggie's mouth dropped open. "Wait, what?"

Shit. "What were *you* talking about?" he asked.

"The engagement party," Maggie said. "What were *you* talking about?"

"I think I'm ready for this now." Preston reached toward the paper bag, but his sister slapped his hand away.

"Preston Oliver Del Rio, you better tell me everything and you better tell me now."

"You know the full name thing only works when Mom does it."

"How about this then? You tell me everything right now, or I'm leaving and taking the cinnamon roll with me."

His sister had always known how to drive a hard bargain. Sagging onto a bar stool, Preston scrubbed his sleep-creased skin.

"We hooked up the night of your engagement party and Tiffany got pregnant. She's keeping the baby and we've been together a couple more times since. Dad told me I can either be with Tiffany or be the CEO but not both. Tiffany saw the pictures of me and Sunny kissing in the newspaper."

He was surprised how easily his troubles summarized.

"Dad knows?"

Preston nodded. "I told him after the mediation."

"Who else knows?"

"Camille Winters, Alisha, Tremaine—if the text message I got is any indication, and I don't know who else."

"Wait." She sat down on the stool next to his.

Preston deflated, leaning forward until his forehead rested on the cool marble counter. As if the soothing sensation of it might help calm his hectic thoughts.

"The day you missed work, what the heck were you doing?" Maggie asked.

"Tiffany and I went shopping."

Her gasp made him jerk upright, expecting Sasquatch to be staring in the front window.

"You were shopping for baby things, weren't you?"

"Tiffany's been turning her guest bedroom into a nursery. I just wanted to help her out."

His sister's wide brown eyes gleamed, her fingers rising to hover by her heart.

"It's not a big deal, Maggie," he insisted.

"Not a big deal?" she repeated. "Not a big deal? Preston, you're going to be a father. A *father.*"

"Yeah," he said. "I got that part."

"Oh my God. I'm going to be an aunt!" She touched her flushing cheeks.

"You're just now realizing that?" he asked drolly.

"Forgive me if this comes as a bit of a shock. You've been an uptight, blindly ambitious workaholic for the past three years, then you go and randomly knock up Joseph Winters's daughter at my engagement party."

Preston winced. "First, it didn't happen at your engagement party. It was later that night. Second, can you not say it like that? It wasn't like it was some random thing."

Maggie brushed her dark hair away from her cheekbone. "You're not saying that you and Tiffany were a thing before that, are you?"

"No," Preston said. "The night of your engagement party was the first time. But it wasn't out of the blue."

She folded her arms across her chest. "All the time

I've known you, I've never once seen you so much as look sideways at Tiffany Winters."

"Then you weren't paying attention."

"I mean, I remember you guys were both part of the drama department for a minute," she said.

Preston ran a hand through his disheveled hair. He supposed there was no way around this. "I joined the drama department because of Tiffany. I thought maybe if I volunteered on sets, I might have a chance to talk without it being this huge thing."

"That's right," Maggie said, sipping her coffee. "I remember now. It was that semester that the school did the tribute to Shakespeare. You ended up getting cast as Romeo."

"Correct," he said. "Tiffany was student directing so I volunteered. It was only supposed to be a behind-the-scenes kind of thing. But when both the leads got mono, Mr. Overton had me and Tiffany stand in for Romeo and Juliet for the balcony scene during re-hearsals one day. He ended up casting me."

Realization rolled across his sister's face like the tide. "You mean, all this time?"

Preston didn't know exactly how to describe what it was Tiffany had meant to him. He had heard it described as carrying a torch. He supposed that was as close a metaphor as he could think of. In all the years he'd spent pouring every ounce of his effort into their family business, his attraction to her remained dormant but still very flammable. A place within himself ready to be ignited at a moment's notice.

"I can't believe I never saw anything." Maggie tore

open the white paper bag and pulled out the plastic container to reveal a gigantic cinnamon roll with a thick blanket of white icing and two forks.

The heavenly aroma of sticky, sweet cinnamon tickled his nostrils when she opened it. "Apparently Dad did."

"What do you mean?" she asked, handing him a fork.

"Just a couple days before he named me CEO, he accused me of having a soft spot for Tiffany Winters and brought up the engagement party. But it had been weeks since we'd spoken by that point."

Maggie forked up a giant bite. "I can't believe he gave you an ultimatum."

Preston snorted. "He's only been doing it for our entire lives."

"Not to me," Maggie said.

Preston swallowed, the mouthful of dough passing the ache in his throat.

"So what did you say to Dad?" his sister asked.

"I haven't given him an answer yet."

"And you and Tiffany?"

"We were actually in a pretty good place until that picture with Sunny was printed."

"Define 'good place.'" She collected a crumb of frosting with her fingertip and flicked it into the container's lid.

Preston reached for his coffee. "We'd talked about moving in together, actually."

Maggie stopped with the bite halfway to her mouth. "As a couple?"

"As co-parents."

"Co-parents with benefits?" she asked. "Because if you guys have still been hooking up—"

"Okay," he said, holding up a hand. "We really don't need to talk about that part of things."

"I'm just saying, the woman is having your child, but you didn't give her any kind of indication about what the relationship between the two of you would be independent of the baby?"

"Not really," he said, forking up more cinnamon roll.

Maggie set her fork aside and swiveled her knees to face him. "For someone so ridiculously brilliant, you are incredibly dense sometimes, Preston."

Preston arched an eyebrow at his sister, not quite following her line of logic. "Yes."

"Seeing as she's the one whose entire life and body will be changed by this no matter what else happens, you didn't think that maybe you ought to tell her how you're willing for your life to change for *her* specifically?"

"Not exactly."

Maggie shook her head ruefully. "Let's start here. How do you feel about Tiffany?"

"How do I feel about her?" He repeated the question to buy time, not because he wasn't already well aware of the answer to that question.

"Can you see yourself *with* her long term?"

Preston got up from his stool and began to pace. Seeing himself with her had never been the problem. That, he'd been able to imagine for years. It was the real-life implementation that always remained the problem. The families' rivalry. His job. Her dreams.

"Yes," he said. "But I have no idea if she feels the same."

Maggie cleared her throat and cut her eyes to the envelope sitting next to her purse. "That might help."

Preston stared at it like he might at a grenade whose pin had been pulled.

"I can leave if you want privacy while you read."

"Please don't," Preston said. "Whatever this says, I'd rather read it with you here."

Maggie reached over and squeezed his fingers with a hand warmed by her coffee cup. Preston drew in a deep breath and plunged in.

Preston,
You told me once that you wanted to know ev-
erything. Everything I'm going through. Every-
thing I'm feeling and thinking. So here goes. I'm
hot all the time, which is why I've been leaving
the windows open. I feel like the heat is coming
from inside me and the only thing that helps is
to have air moving over my skin. I'm terrible
at sleeping and when I do, my dreams are com-
pletely bizarre and beautiful. I'm equal parts
terrified and ecstatic about what is happening
to my body, and my brain, and my life. This is
the furthest thing from what I had imagined for
myself and yet I already can't think about any
future but this one. I'm scared. I'm scared of
not being a good mother. Of never achieving

what my siblings have. Of never knowing what I might have been if this hadn't happened. But I'm especially scared of the fact that if I had made even one decision differently, I wouldn't be sitting here writing this letter, growing a life we made by accident.

Whatever you decide about your role in things, I need you to know that I'm going to be okay. We are going to be okay. For once in your life, I just want you to make your decision not out of obligation or expectation, but because it's truly what you want. I'll be here when you're ready. —T

Preston looked up at his sister when he was finished.

Before he'd completely retreated to his work, Maggie was the person he was closest to in the whole world. He didn't have to say anything. She already knew.

"Finish the cinnamon roll and get in the shower," she said. "I have an idea."

Thirteen

"Did we decide on the pink one or the cream for the Boots and Bows Brunch?"

Alisha emerged from the giant walk-in closet, a blouse in either hand. All morning, they'd been sorting through Alisha's considerable wardrobe of designer labels, attempting to determine which to keep and which to donate. Not how Tiffany normally would have preferred to spend her Sunday, but it proved an effective distraction.

"We didn't decide," Tiffany said, cinching one of the bags in the donation pile. "Because I haven't agreed to go."

"But it's a good cause," Alisha said, full lips turned down in a pout.

"I know that, because I've already contributed."

KEEPING A LITTLE SECRET

Scooting the bag to the side, she sank down on the corner of the bed. "I gave Mandee Meriweather a deluxe chocolate basket and even threw in a private truffle-making class."

Alisha hung the blouses back on the rack. "Don't you at least want to be there to see who wins your donation?"

Tiffany pretended to think about it for all of half a second. "No."

Alisha flipped off the closet light and stepped into a pair of stilettos that made Tiffany sore just to look at them. "You know who might be there," she said in a singsongy voice.

"All the more reason *not* to go."

She hadn't received any reply since she sent the letter to Preston via Jericho.

"You know you're going to have to talk to him sometime." Alisha's gold charm bracelet flashed as she picked up a bottle of lotion from the vanity and squeezed a dollop into her upturned palm. Her beautiful golden-brown skin glowed in the morning light. "Letter or no letter, you are carrying his baby."

"Oh, believe me, I am more than aware of that fact." And she wasn't the only one. News of her pregnancy had traveled like wildfire. She'd completely lost track of who knew and who didn't know and had decided it was no longer any of her business.

Facing the people who knew this in person was an entirely different proposition.

"How about this." Her sister bent to smooth the last remnants of moisturizer on her shins and shapely calves. "You go with me for one hour, and I'll treat us both to a pedicure afterward."

"I actually polished them myself this morning." Tiffany slipped her foot out of her black ballet flat and held out her crimson toes for inspection. "I figured I ought to do that as often as possible while I can still reach my own feet."

"A massage instead?"

Tiffany crossed her arms over her chest. "Thirty minutes, and if I see Preston, I reserve the right to bounce immediately."

Alisha stuck out her hand to shake. "Deal."

The first wave of dread washed over Tiffany as she saw twice as many cars in the Cattleman's Club parking lot as she had expected. Mandee Meriweather had honed guilt-based persuasion to an art, but Tiffany had never seen this kind of turnout for any of her previous events.

A quick scan of the vehicles did not reveal Preston's car to be among them.

Small mercies.

They parked and walked to the entrance, where Tiffany paused to pull in a deep breath.

"You okay?" Alisha asked.

As Dr. Everett had predicted, the medicine he had prescribed made a huge difference where her nausea was concerned. It did nothing for her nerves.

"This half hour can't go fast enough."

"Maybe it won't be as bad as you think." Alisha's

enigmatic smile did little to comfort her. "It's for the animals."

"Let's just get this over with." She pulled open the heavy wood door and held it for her sister. "You go in first."

"If you insist."

The foyer was eerily quiet, absent the music and chatter Tiffany typically associated with these kinds of events. "Are you sure we're in the right place?"

"Unless there's another Cattleman's Club that I'm unaware of," Alisha said with a smirk.

They approached the doors to the main hall, and as requested, Alisha swung one wide and strode in.

Tiffany ducked in on her heels, keeping her head down and her eyes on the polished wood floor.

"Surprise!"

The thunderous swell of sound stopped Tiffany in her tracks.

Alisha was no longer in front of her, but beside her, facing a sea of faces flushed with excitement at her arrival.

Her mother. Her brothers and their significant others. Moira and Steph, along with a few favorite customers from Chocolate Fix. When the initial shock had worn off, she saw the large table laden with gifts. The llama-themed centerpieces. The table of food.

"What is this?" she asked, turning to Alisha.

Her sister beamed a pearly smile at her. "We're calling it a *sprinkle*. A baby shower with all the perks none of the cringey games."

lle glided over and wrapped Tiffany in a hug.

Tiffany breathed in her familiar floral scent and felt a measure of the tension drain out of her.

"Happy sprinkle, sweetie," her mother said, kissing her cheek.

"I can't believe you did this! I'm not even in my second trimester yet."

Her mother and Alisha exchanged a look.

"With all the wedding craziness and everything that's happened lately, we just wanted to do a little something to show you how excited we are." Camille squeezed Tiffany's elbows and released her before guiding her to a seat at a nearby table. "Your father so wished he could be here. But with this being so last-minute, he just couldn't get away."

Her eyes were full of apology and Tiffany knew it was more than just a missed baby shower.

She couldn't help but feel she'd taken the coward's way out in allowing her mother to be the bearer of her dramatic news following Alisha's suggestion that her father be let in on the secret. Somehow, it still didn't offset the ache of the awkward silence that had elapsed in the days since she'd received a call from Camille letting her know that Joseph had been told. She hadn't expected him to show up with a marching band or anything.

It was an unplanned pregnancy, not a long-anticipated addition to a stable, happy family unit. But just once, she'd wanted her father to look at her and see not a child in need of protection and guidance, but a woman blazing a trail all her own.

The ache in Tiffany's throat bloomed into a sheer

of tears when she spotted all three of her brothers and their respective partners making way toward her. Jericho came first with Maggie in tow.

"Congratulations, Tiff." Jericho bent to plant a kiss on her cheek.

Reaching up from her seat, Tiffany wrapped her arms around her brother's broad shoulders, clinging to him with a fierceness she couldn't quite explain.

He released her and Maggie surged forward.

"I can't believe I'm going to be an aunt!" Her future sister-in-law's effusive warmth was enough to dispel the lingering worry Tiffany felt about potentially upstaging their wedding with this shocking news.

She accepted hugs from Marcus and Jessica next, followed by Misha and Trey.

Alisha remained by her side as she helped Tiffany circulate the room, accepting hugs and congratulations from all the attendees. Despite her relief at the total lack of judgment she felt from her family or friends, a subtle but persistent ache had taken up residence in her chest.

She wished Preston was here.

This was far from the first time this thought had visited her since their contentious parting. The scent of him still lingered on the sheets she couldn't bring herself to wash. The items in the baby's room she had made herself organize and put away—each came ʷith a memory of exactly what he'd said and how he'd ˙d when he had sneaked them into the cart. He ˙ᵐly imprinted on her home as he was on her body. His absence in both arenas left her with a keen sense of longing.

Of groundlessness.

After they'd made their rounds, Alisha deposited Tiffany at a table and whistled around two fingers to get everyone's attention.

"Now I know on the invitation, I promised that there would be no cringey shower games, but I may have lied just a little." There was a spatter of polite laughter.

"You'll be relieved to know I only have one activity planned, and right after we play, we're going to get to that beautiful spread provided courtesy of Ms. Jessica Drummond."

Alisha nodded, and Trey picked up a chair and brought it out into the center of the floor.

"I'm going to need the guest of honor to come sit right here."

Tiffany's cheeks burned as she stood and walked to her sister, who pulled a scarf out of her sleeve with a magician's flourish.

"What are you doing?" Tiffany asked her from the side of her mouth.

"Just trust me," Alisha said, squeezing her shoulder reassuringly.

And of course, Tiffany did. She always had.

The scarf was silky, warm and perfumed with Alisha's signature scent. Her sister carefully tied it with the knot at the back of Tiffany's head and then tugged to secure it.

"Does that feel okay?"

"Nothing about this feels okay," Tiffany muttered.

Alisha's footfalls moved from behind her to out front. Tiffany turned her head to the sound.

"The object of this game is simple. I'm going to put something in your hand, and you have to tell me what it is, and what it has to do with having a baby."

A round of warm laughter echoed through the hall.

"Ready?" Alisha asked.

Tiffany's forehead began to sweat against the fabric as she held out her hand. "I guess."

The first three items, she guessed right off the bat. A pacifier. A baby bottle. A onesie.

The fourth made Tiffany wonder if Alisha had selected the others to lure her into a false sense of security.

The shape and material were easy enough to discern. Heavy and made of wood, the cube was the width of her hand and covered in strange grooves. She was running her finger along the fissure closest to the center when the entire thing came apart in her hands. The pieces clattered to the floor, startling her.

"No peeking," Alisha scolded when Tiffany scooted out of her chair and attempted to feel around for the contents.

"Is it a puzzle?" she asked, patting around on hands and knees.

"Guess again," Alisha said.

Tiffany's fingers moved among the angular shapes, pausing when she felt something round and smooth. She thought it might have fallen out of the object she was meant to be guessing until the crisscross pattern of laces informed her otherwise.

A shoe?

She yelped when the something within the shoe moved beneath her touch.

"What the—" Tiffany whipped off her blindfold and blinked to clear her blurry eyes.

A small shriek escaped her when the figure came into focus.

Preston Del Rio, down on one knee, a ring box held out to her on his palm.

Tiffany's heart raced, the muffled drumbeat in her ears drowning out every other sound in the room. She wanted to look to Alisha, to lean into her sister's comforting steadiness, but couldn't tear her eyes away from Preston's.

The fierce tenderness and naked longing in them swept over her like a wave, and she felt herself being drawn back to the engagement party. Then, as now, she'd been drowning in a sea of people and found an anchor in his eyes.

"What are you doing here?" she asked.

He glanced at the box in his hand, then back at her. "You dropped this," he said.

Tiffany reached for it with a trembling hand. The lid lifted with a tiny creak to reveal a diamond ring twinkling like a miniature star set against the midnight-blue velvet lining. Her hand flew to her mouth.

"Tiffany Winters," he said. "Confectionary genius, future mother of my child, I was wondering if you would do me the great honor of being my wife?"

* * *

Preston couldn't tell if his ability to effectively gauge time had deserted him, or if an eternity had elapsed between his question and Tiffany's answer.

He had bungled this entirely.

He was supposed to have handed her a note that told her to look out the window where a pair of llamas waited on the lawn. *After* she had been completely delighted and they'd had a chance to speak privately outside, he would kneel down by the longhorn statue where they had first kissed and propose.

That had been the plan, anyway.

Instead, his body had apparently decided he was doing this now. Right here in front of everyone without his having delivered the heartfelt apology he'd been rehearsing to himself over and over.

The sound of people shifting in their seats interrupted the pin-drop silence.

At least he wasn't alone in his growing discomfort.

His knee ached from kneeling on the hardwood floor. His clammy fist hung heavy at his side. He wasn't sure how long it had been since he last breathed.

Tiffany's eyes at last lifted from the diamond to find his.

Just as he had when she'd stood on the balcony in an impromptu moment of the role that had become his high school legacy, Preston willed her to see past the superficial circumstances surrounding their two families.

To see *him*.

The slow smile spreading across her lips broke

through his fear like the sun slicing through fog. Tiffany scrambled forward and threw her arms around his neck, the ring box still clutched in her hands. Into his ear, she whispered the one syllable that would change both their lives forever.

"Yes."

Preston breathed.

His arms wound around her waist and held him to her as the room erupted. The floor beneath them vibrated with the stomping of boots as whistles and shouts filled the air.

He got to his feet and lifted her with him, then he swung her around in a circle before he set her down. Chairs scraped as the party guests got to their feet and clapped.

"This belonged to my grandmother," Preston said, plucking the box from her hand and then sliding the ring onto her finger.

He caught his sister's shining eyes through the crowd, remembering what she'd said in his kitchen after they read the letter.

"Maybe what we really need is a diamond to fix what the Del Rio necklace broke."

Preston had objected when his sister pressed their grandmother's ring into his palm.

"I don't need it," she'd said, looking at the engagement ring Jericho Winters had placed there.

"There's something else I need to show you," Preston said to Tiffany between hugs of congratulations.

"Here?" she asked in a purr that shot straight to his groin.

"Outside, actually," he said.

Alisha gave him a conspiratorial wink and clapped her hands, herding everyone toward the buffet as they made their escape.

"Returning to the scene of the crime?" Tiffany teased when she saw where he was leading her.

"Maybe," he said.

But it was Preston who found himself shocked when, instead of the llamas he was expecting, he saw what waited on the other side of the longhorn statue.

His father.

And Joseph Winters.

Standing side by side.

Tiffany squeezed Preston's fingers. With her hand in his, Preston felt like he could kick down the very gates of hell. He and his father hadn't spoken since their confrontation in the parking lot. In proposing to Tiffany Winters, he had made a very public answer to his father's private ultimatum. Whatever the fallout, he had made his choice and was ready to defend it.

The dry grass crunched as they slowed to stand across from the two men whose legacies had cast a long shadow in both their lives as well as the town of Royal, Texas.

Fernando Del Rio stepped forward and Preston prepared himself for the inevitable dressing-down.

Instead, his father turned to Tiffany.

"Congratulations, my dear." The furrows beside his father's eyes deepened.

The hand he held out for her to shake was bypassed in favor of a hug.

Preston and his father locked eyes as he patted Tiffany's back. In that moment, all his fears washed away, and in their place, a warmth that fused with his very soul.

Fernando released her from his embrace and stepped to the side so Joseph could hug his daughter.

Preston watched the Winters patriarch fight to keep the emotion from his face, his jaw flexing as his eyes sheened. "I can't believe it," he murmured. "A grandfather again."

"Speaking of," Fernando said, stepping aside to reveal a large box wrapped in silver foil. "This is just a small gift to welcome you to the family."

Tiffany wiped a tear from her cheek, her eyes bright with excitement as she lifted the top off the box and gasped.

The beautiful old rocking horse glowed in the late autumn sun. Preston remembered having seen it in his father's collection, but it appeared to have been refinished. The wood sanded down and stained an amber brown, its carved mane repainted a deep, glossy black.

"This belonged to my grandfather," his father said. "Fernando the first."

"I don't remember this part," Preston said, rubbing a hand over the miniature saddle of gleaming leather on its back. "Is it new?"

"Very old, actually," Joseph said, stepping forward. "It belonged to Teddy Winters. Since this is the first grandchild for the Del Rio/Winters families, we thought you ought to have something that belonged to both ancestors."

We.

Preston and Tiffany snagged gazes at the same moment.

To imagine his father and Joseph having worked this out together was almost more than Preston could bear in his present state.

He suspected Maggie and Jericho might've had something to do with it.

"Are those stirrups adjustable?" Tiffany released Preston's hand to get a closer look, leaving Preston and his father standing opposite one another.

Fernando folded his arms across his chest and cleared his throat. "Son, I owe you an apology."

Rare words, in Preston's experience. He didn't add any of his own to compromise the moment.

"After you told me about Tiffany, I went to that bluff where we used to go when you were learning how to drive. I was so angry I didn't know what to do with myself. I just sat there looking at our family's land. Thinking about what I had pictured for your future. For the company's future. I realized that once I retire, we won't be building that future together anymore." He shook his head on a deep exhale. "I just haven't wanted to let that go."

Preston met his father's reddened eyes. "Then don't."

A furrow appeared between his father's dark brows.

"I may know a hell of a lot about being a CEO,"

Preston continued, "but I know next to nothing about being a father. I'm going to need your help."

Fernando looked down at his grass-flecked dress shoes. "I don't know that I'm the best example to learn from."

"I do," Preston said.

They looked at each other for a protracted moment.

"Should we go check out this spread I've been hearing so much about?"

"Let's," Joseph said, clapping Fernando on the back.

Fernando returned the brotherly gesture with a little extra oomph.

Preston and Tiffany watched them go, shaking their heads.

"How long do you think the truce will hold this time?" she asked.

The rocking horse bobbed forward as he stepped on the curved sleigh. "Hopefully long enough to try the brisket," he said.

"I wouldn't mind some of that myself," she said. "I'm starved."

Preston slipped an arm around Tiffany's waist and curled her against his chest. "Me too."

Their passionate kiss lit a fire in Preston's blood that found its way to his heart.

Hearing the clip-clopping of hooves on the sidewalk, Preston molded his hand to her chin to turn it toward the two special guests Trey and Dez were leading across the lawn.

At the sight of the llamas with their pink-and-blue

baskets full of party favors, Tiffany released a squeal that bordered on supersonic.

"Isn't that the sweetest thing you've ever seen?"

He drew back to gaze down at his fiancée, meeting her delighted grin with one of his own. "Almost."

* * * * *

COMING NEXT MONTH FROM

DESIRE

PATERNITY PAYBACK & THE TEXAN'S SECRETS
PATERNITY PAYBACK
Texas Cattleman's Club: Diamonds and Dating Apps
by Sophia Singh Sasson

Journalist Willa St. Germaine's interview with her ex, rancher Jack Chowdhry, is the perfect chance to settle the score. But their "professional" reunion reveals untamed desires—and Willa's secret daughter...

THE TEXAN'S SECRETS
Texas Cattleman's Club: Diamonds and Dating Apps
by Barbara Dunlop

Computer hacker Emilia Scott just scored her best hack yet—matching herself with handsome, enigmatic "Nick" on the K!smet dating app. She doesn't know he's successful CEO Nico Law, a man with secrets as complex as her own...

MIAMI MARRIAGE PACT & OVERNIGHT INHERITANCE
MIAMI MARRIAGE PACT
Miami Famous • by Nadine Gonzalez

Gigi Garcia will do anything to save her struggling film production—even marry to ensure her inheritance. Restaurateur Myles Paris is the perfect fictional fiancé, if she can seduce the sexy, stubborn chef into agreeing with her plan.

OVERNIGHT INHERITANCE
Marriages and Mergers • by Rachel Bailey

An unexpected inheritance thrusts Australian schoolteacher Mae Dunstan into the world of single father Sebastian Newport, her business rival...and now her secret lover. Will sharing his New York City office, and his bed, end in heartache?

FALLING FOR THE ENEMY &
STRANDED WITH THE RUNAWAY BRIDE
FALLING FOR THE ENEMY
The Gilbert Curse • by Katherine Garbera

After losing years to a coma, Rory Gilbert wants all life has to offer, including a steamy romp with Kitt Orr Palmer. Little does Rory know, she's the sister of Kitt's enemy—forcing him to choose between his desire for Rory and revenge.

STRANDED WITH THE RUNAWAY BRIDE
by Yvonne Lindsey

When wedding planner turned runaway bride Georgia O'Connor is stranded with loner Sawyer Roberts, they never expected attraction to turn into a heated affair. But when reality intrudes, can he let her go?

You can find more information on upcoming Harlequin titles, free excerpts and more at Harlequin.com.

Get 3 FREE REWARDS!

We'll send you 2 FREE Books <u>plus</u> a FREE Mystery Gift.

FREE Value Over **$20**

Both the **Harlequin® Desire** and **Harlequin Presents®** series feature compelling novels filled with passion, sensuality and intriguing scandals.

YES! Please send me 2 FREE novels from the Harlequin Desire or Harlequin Presents series and my FREE gift (gift is worth about $10 retail). After receiving them, if I don't wish to receive any more books, I can return the shipping statement marked "cancel." If I don't cancel, I will receive 6 brand-new Harlequin Presents Larger-Print books every month and be billed just $6.30 each in the U.S. or $6.49 each in Canada, a savings of at least 10% off the cover price, or 3 Harlequin Desire books (2-in-1 story editions) every month and be billed just $7.83 each in the U.S. or $8.43 each in Canada, a savings of at least 12% off the cover price. It's quite a bargain! Shipping and handling is just 50¢ per book in the U.S. and $1.25 per book in Canada.* I understand that accepting the 2 free books and gift places me under no obligation to buy anything. I can always return a shipment and cancel at any time by calling the number below. The free books and gift are mine to keep no matter what I decide.

Choose one: ☐ **Harlequin Desire**
(225/326 BPA GRNA)

☐ **Harlequin Presents Larger-Print**
(176/376 BPA GRNA)

☐ **Or Try Both!**
(225/326 & 176/376 BPA GRQP)

Name (please print)

Address   Apt. #

City   State/Province   Zip/Postal Code

Email: Please check this box ☐ if you would like to receive newsletters and promotional emails from Harlequin Enterprises ULC and its affiliates. You can unsubscribe anytime.

Mail to the Harlequin Reader Service:
IN U.S.A.: P.O. Box 1341, Buffalo, NY 14240-8531
IN CANADA: P.O. Box 603, Fort Erie, Ontario L2A 5X3

Want to try 2 free books from another series? Call 1-800-873-8635 or visit www.ReaderService.com.

---

*Terms and prices subject to change without notice. Prices do not include sales taxes, which will be charged (if applicable) based on your state or country of residence. Canadian residents will be charged applicable taxes. Offer not valid in Quebec. This offer is limited to one order per household. Books received may not be as shown. Not valid for current subscribers to the Harlequin Presents or Harlequin Desire series. All orders subject to approval. Credit or debit balances in a customer's account(s) may be offset by any other outstanding balance owed by or to the customer. Please allow 4 to 6 weeks for delivery. Offer available while quantities last.

Your Privacy—Your information is being collected by Harlequin Enterprises ULC, operating as Harlequin Reader Service. For a complete summary of the information we collect, how we use this information and to whom it is disclosed, please visit our privacy notice located at corporate.harlequin.com/privacy-notice. From time to time we may also exchange your personal information with reputable third parties. If you wish to opt out of this sharing of your personal information, please visit readerservice.com/consumerschoice or call 1-800-873-8635. **Notice to California Residents**—Under California law, you have specific rights to control and access your data. For more information on these rights and how to exercise them, visit corporate.harlequin.com/california-privacy.

HDHP23

HARLEQUIN
PLUS

Try the best multimedia subscription service for romance readers like you!

Read, Watch and Play.

Experience the easiest way to get the romance content you crave.

Start your **FREE TRIAL** at
<u>www.harlequinplus.com/freetrial</u>.

HARPLUS0123